The Speaking Stone of Caradoc

Book 2 in the

'Remember the Future'

Time Travel Adventures

by

Evadeen Brickwood

This book was the runner-up as Best Youth Fantasy Novel

in the 2018 Awards by Book Talk Radio Club in England

Katherine, Trevor and Chryseis embark on a ship and sail to remnants of the sunken continent of Atland. When a stolen speaking stone is found in their luggage everybody suspects the three friends. Will the time travelers be punished for the theft?
Suddenly everybody is after the mysterious stone from the fabled land of Lyonesse and some of the strange sea creatures are not as amusing as they seem.They escape only just a trap set by sorcerers in Prydhain and receive help from an unexpected source. Then the speaking stone has something to say...

Acknowledgements

To my family: I couldn't do it without you. Cobus Griesel for his technical advice. I also want to thank my editors and all of my dedicated test readers for their valuable contribution and finding those pesky typing errors. And all my loyal readers, who can't wait to read the next book in the series. Enjoy.

Map of the Atlantean Sea

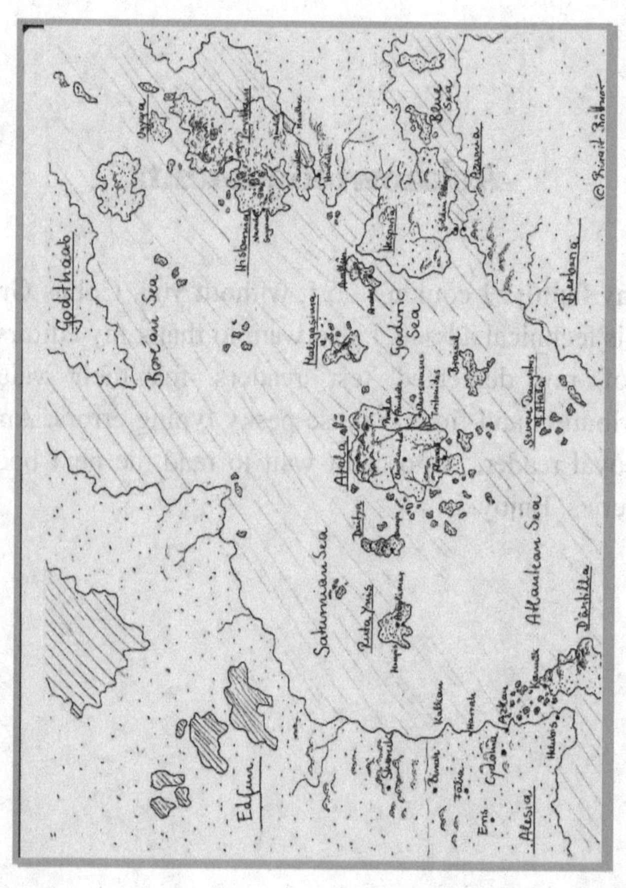

Map of Pryhdain

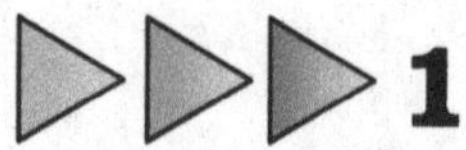 **1**   **A PREHISTORIC SEA**

In the early afternoon sunlight, the ocean resembled a blanket of shimmering scales. SPLASH! A school of dolphins accompanied the 'Navis Arion', diving effortlessly in and out of turquoise waters.

Trevor sat on a pile of coiled tackle, his hair tousled by the breeze. He steadied himself with his feet against the railing as he concentrated on drawing a colourful seabird perched close to him. Good thing he had brought his pad and pencil, but drawing the floppy thing over the bird's beak was a bit of a challenge.

It was still a complete mystery to them what swam around in these prehistoric oceans. They had only just left the country of Alesia and there were so many things they still had to learn about this ancient world.

"How clear the water is!" Katherine gazed longingly into the shallow sea. "I wish we could just stop the ship right here and go for a swim with the dolphins."

"You're kidding, right? It's not safe to swim."

"I guess so," Katherine said.

It hadn't even been a month since their trip through time began and Katherine sometimes still wondered, if this Alesian epoch was for real.

"Do you remember how it was in the beginning?" she asked Trevor. "How scared we were when we saw our first giant?"

"Túvar?"

"Yes!"

"Sometimes - and for your information, I wasn't scared."

"Hah, sure you were," Katherine teased him.

Her accent was still faintly British, unlike that of her two American friends Trevor and Chryséis . The people of Alesia spoke an Akkadian dialect, so nobody cared much about English accents, and the time travellers had learned to communicate in this ancient language. At first, Katherine had been so scared of taking the trip back in time. Even in the name of science. Now she couldn't wait to see more of the 'Known World' the Lady of Cydonia had told them so much about.

"I like it here. I'm glad we stayed."

"Yeah, I'm glad too," Trevor said and looked up briefly.

They had been exploring this long-forgotten time ever since the vortex had released them in Cydonia, the capital city of Alesia. The nature reserve of Carter Valley had been ideal for their time travel experiment. Not far from the school, but fairly remote and no major electromagnetic interference. They were smart, but not in their wildest dreams would they have expected a marvelous prehistoric city in the middle of Carter Valley! This civilisation was so terribly 'modern'.

It had all begun with a school project in quantum physics: an endless energy source that powered a time-portal-finder. Nobody had tried that before. Not even other gifted children at the Pemberton Academy. They were planning to present their project in class next week — well what meant 'next week' here in the past? They were almost 12,000 years in the past now. The other kids would fall off their chairs when they saw the pictures!

Imagine that: twelve millennia. Twelve! It didn't matter how long their sea voyage took. They would return at precisely the same moment they had left the future when they decided to go back. So they had decided to stay for as long as it took to travel to Atala and back. A few weeks more or less surely didn't make a difference.

"Are those merpeople under the boardwalk? There at

the tip of the peninsula?"

"Hard to tell, could be sea cows." Trevor squinted to get a better look. "No, definitely merpeople."

The 'Navis Arion' had left the seaport of Aztlan on the safe mainland over an hour ago. Safe, if one ignored the fact that giants had started a war against the country of Alesia there. An unsuccessful attempt at war. Before their time travel began, they had been afraid to bump into cavemen and dinosaurs or land in a volcano.

Who would have thought of mermaids and evil giants? Okay, there were actually cavemen and small dinosaurs and probably also volcanoes around, but nowhere near as scary. In fact some cavemen, known as Konks, were sailors on the ship. As they moved east in a gentle seesaw motion, the citadel of Aztlan became a tiny white speck against the dark hills and the Alesian coastline slowly merged with the sky.

The dolphins leapt into the air and splashed back into the water. "Ooh, careful you guys. I'm getting all wet," Katherine laughed.

Technically, their ship was on its way to D'ântilla, an island state in the Caribbean Sea. Only that D'ântilla no longer existed in the future and the Caribbean Sea did not yet exist. It didn't trouble the time travellers one bit. Even people with green skin and the hairy Konks with their human faces seemed normal after just two weeks. They would visit a few Atlantean islands and prehistoric England, then return to Alesia and travel back to the future through the time portal. It was a good plan.

"Trev, where's Chryséis ?"

Trevor shaded his eyes with his hand against the sun. "I think she's in the front with Kheton and Lelani."

Kheton and Lelani were a young Cydonian couple. Kheton was their guardian and some sort of junior citadel judge, and had agreed to take the children as far as the main island of Atala.

"I'll go and see what Chryséis is up to."

"Okay, I'll just keep drawing this bird here. Can't believe it hasn't moved."

"Maybe it's sleeping. Why don't you just take a picture?"

They had brought a small digital camera with them.

"I like to draw, and besides, I have nothing else to do."

Trevor gazed at the screeching seabirds sailing through the air. They had humped beaks and were featherless. Featherless?

"Could be flying therasaurus, the way they are gliding down from those rocks," Katherine said as if she knew what he was thinking.

"Or maybe they're just a strange, featherless species of birds," he answered.

"Yes, sure. Don't fall into the water while I'm gone," Katherine grinned and Trevor looked up crossly.

"Funny," he grumbled, feeling his ears go red. "Will I ever live that one down?"

He was still embarrassed by the incident in the harbour. A sharp push by someone on the landing had sent him into the murky waters just before they left.

"Oh come on, I'm just kidding." Katherine grinned.

"Whatever."

"Okay then, see you later."

Katherine staggered along the railing. She had to get past the colourful seabird with the parrot beak, Trevor had been drawing. The bird suddenly took to the air with a loud croak and gave Katherine a mighty fright.

"Hey!"

"Scared to fall into the water, Katie?" Trevor grinned and scrawled a few more lines on the paper.

"No, not at all." Katherine's voice trembled a little, but she walked on bravely to the front of the ship. Trevor put the drawing pad aside and studied the view. They were just leaving a small island behind that was all covered in tropical plants.

The ship was close enough for Trevor to see horseshoe crabs scurrying along the beach with hungry seabirds in pursuit. Soon they passed another island that looked rather less inviting. Stark rocks jutted out of the foaming surf that thundered against the steep shore. The rocks were covered in shrieking white dots, while large birds circled the shallow bay.

If they were birds at all.

Just as Katherine returned with Chryséis in tow, a deep growl rose in the distance and echoed off the rocks. The dolphins that had accompanied the ship until now were nowhere to be seen.

"Look over there! Is that — a whale?" Chryséis cried.

The hulking body of a large animal with a long neck and broad flippers dived just below the water surface and waves sent the ship wobbling.

"Looks just like the whale in Aztlan. Don't you think?"

"You mean that huge thing on the beach? I'm not so sure." Chryseis shrugged her shoulders.

"What else can it be?" Trevor asked.

"Oh, I don't know. But it was sad how the fishermen cut it up and stacked all that the blubber. It had to be a whale."

"Well, it's their job, isn't it?"

"It's still sad."

The sea animal with the long neck came up and stared at them with intelligent eyes while paddling on its back. The three friends stared back.

"That's so amazing. Get the camera, quick!" Chryséis leaned over the railing.

"Where did you put it?" Katherine asked.

But it was already too late. The 'whale' dived and was gone, just to reappear with a bigger companion in a cloud of water spray. They both darted off into the open sea. The ship wobbled again and seawater splashed up against the railing.

"Whoaaa!" Chryséis jumped back. "I'm getting all wet."

"Did you see that? If those are whales then I'm Mickey Mouse!"

The ship lifted ever so slightly off the water and the wobble stopped. They floated effortlessly on the water's surface due to a standard anti-gravity device, which impressed the time travellers even more than the strange animals. Trevor managed to take a picture and zoomed in to have a better look.

"Let me see that." Chryséis took the camera. All she could make out was water spray, a long thin neck and a triangular fin. "It's too fuzzy. Could be a big fish. We should have brought a better camera with sound and video function."

"Sure, let's quickly go back home and fetch another camera."

"Ha, ha — too bad we can't use a cell phone!"

"Maybe they're dinosaurs…Elasmosaurus…saurus," Trevor stuttered as he put down the camera, hardly daring to say the words.

"Yeah, just like the monster of Loch Ness?" Chryséis laughed and shoved him. "Get real Trev, Elasmosaurus?! They died out ages ago. I mean ages!"

"It's not impossible."

"Here we go again —" Chryséis teased, but she felt uneasy.

Trevor could be right, of course. After all, they had seen strange farm animals back in Cydonia. What if saurians still roamed the oceans?

"Do you think there are lots of 'Nessies' out there?"

"Who knows," Katherine said casually. "Nobody on the ship seems to mind them. They seem to be quite harmless. Probably just wanted to check out the ship close-up."

"What if they're not so harmless?"

"Oh get out of here. I'm sure the ships are prepared for that with rayguns and stuff like that. If there's trouble, they'll just zap them."

"Nicely put, Trevor."

Trevor shrugged his shoulders and sat back down on the heap of tackle next to Chryséis.

"Oh well, if we can't get a proper picture, I'll just make a drawing."

Chryséis stretched her neck to get a look at the bird Trevor had penciled earlier. As far as she could tell, it was quite life-like, right down to the feathers and eyes.

"Trev, that's very good! I didn't know you could draw like that."

"Oh it's nothing, just a dumb sketch." Trevor drew back, a little embarrassed, before turning over the page.

"That's more than a dumb sketch. You're good!"

A light splash announced that the cheerful dolphins were back. Katherine leaned over the railing and whistled just as the mermaids in Aztlan had taught her yesterday. Did the dolphins jump a bit higher?

"They understand you," Trevor said admiringly.

"You think?"

"Mhmm."

Trevor wiped water droplets off his page and carried on drawing the sea monsters from memory. Two of the dolphins 'danced' backwards on their tails and answered Katherine's whistling with excited chatter.

"Oh, they're so cute!" Katherine whistled some more.

"Those birds are making a heck of a noise," Trevor complained.

"They don't come with volume control. It's called nature," Katherine said.

While Katherine and Trevor were having a friendly squabble, Chryséis observed the birds fishing in the shallows. Black-rimmed wings tucked back at the last moment before the dive, then bobbing to the surface with wriggling fish. Just before the ship rounded a massive wave-beaten rock, a long snout with sharp teeth broke through the surf, snapping at the birds.

"Wow, what was that?" Chryséis caught another

glimpse of the jaws clamping one of the featherless birds. The ship rounded the rocks and the animal was gone. "Did you see that thing?"

"No, what thing?" Trevor looked up from his drawing pad then lost interest again.

"Oh, never mind, you won't believe me anyway."

"What?!" Katherine insisted.

"It looked like…a huge crocodile. In the surf and I think there were others underwater, catching birds. You know like the one in Aztlan."

"Yeah right. You're trying to scare me. Thanks." Katherine glowered at her.

"I'm not joking!" Chryséis cried.

"Okay, must be a saltwater crocodile then. They can get really big."

"Still feel like swimming?" Trevor was being sarcastic.

"Okay, I get it. It's too dangerous to swim in the sea." Katherine shrugged her shoulders.

"It was enormous – just like the one in Aztlan. Hey!" Chryséis yelled. A big blob of gray slime had spattered onto her head and sleeve.

"Yuck, that's bird poo, so gross!"

"Oh no," Katherine began to laugh. "Ghastly!"

"Oh you!" Chryséis waved her fist at the sky. There were so many birds that it was impossible to tell which one had dropped the bomb.

"At least it's not me this time," Trevor gloated and Chryséis glared at him.

"How on earth do I get this stuff off me?"

"A wild guess would be water and elbow grease," Trevor suggested.

Katherine asked one of the hairy Konk sailors for a bucket of water and a cloth. Then she vigorously wiped the muck out of Chryséis ' hair. Chryséis just stood there stiff with disgust.

"Oh, it's so gross. My hair's all sticky," she wailed.

"Excuse me, who is cleaning you up here?" Katherine washed her hands again in the bucket water. "You can wash your hair tonight."

The Konk sailor came and took his bucket and cloth away without saying a word. He needed them and they knew that Konks didn't like to speak. The long red hair on the sailor's arms and under his fleeing chin flattened in the breeze as he waggled his ape-like head and a coarse red ponytail peeked out from under his blue cap.

They tried not to stare as the Konk chucked the dirty water overboard and walked away.

"Gee thanks, I only still need it," Katherine moaned and hurried after him. Chryséis tied her sticky blonde strands into a ponytail with a disgusted grimace. Trevor suddenly had an idea how to distract her.

"You could send Alun in Cydonia a telepathic message," he suggested. Alun had been their first prehistoric friend and was Kheton's younger brother.

"Do you think it'll work?" Chryséis slowly unscrewed her face.

"Why not? You did it before."

They had all learned how to use telepathy in Cydonia, but only Chryséis had managed to use it properly.

"I must relax first." She sat down on the tackle next to Trevor.

Trevor squinted at his sketch. Not bad, not bad at all, he thought. The head of the sea monster was still a bit too big, though. He erased the lines and drew the head again.

Soon, Katherine reappeared with clean hands, just as Chryséis closed her eyes to visualize Alun's face.

"What is she doing?" she asked Trevor, but he just shook his head and put n index finger on his mouth.

Chryséis concentrated on a message to Alun and the answer came back promptly: Enjoy your voyage, friends. Remember to visit the observatory in Kamûk! You must tell me about the new raygun they have there. May the

Earthmother bless you.

Chryséis told the others excitedly about the thought transfer. "Oh, these boys! All he can think about is the ray gun."

"I wish I could do that," Trevor said. "This thought transfer."

"You just have to practice more."

"If you say so...," he felt a little jealousy creeping up on him.

"Let's go to the front," Katherine said. "They have proper seats there and we can watch where the ship's going."

"Okay, I'm done here anyway." Trevor stuffed his drawing pad into the daypack and followed the girls to the bow of the ship. Kheton stood by the front railing, his long tunic fluttering in the breeze, showing off his muscular chest. There was a rumbling and the ship rolled a little.

"What was that? Do you think we rammed something?"

Trevor scanned the water. "I can't see anything."

"Ho, Tian! Go see what's making the noise below," captain Thëlamôn bellowed from the captain's cubicle above the stairs. The cubicle contained the steering wheel and all sorts of interesting-looking instruments.

"Aye, aye, captain." One of the younger sailors sprinted down the stairs below deck to investigate.

"Did you see all those gadgets in the captain's cubicle?"

"You think they have radar?" Chryséis whispered.

"Not just radar, I wonder how he lifted the ship up earlier."

A minute later, the sailor called Tian reported back. "Two bales of cloth wrangled free and were knocking against the hull, captain. I fastened the bales." In Aztlan, the ship had taken fine Alesian silk cloth aboard, destined for the island of Daitya. The cloth would be exchanged for a cargo of Daityan woolens. Daityans were a funny bunch, only interested in wool and raising sheep, forever spinning and knitting all day long.

"No danger then, just some loose cargo in the hull," the captain announced to the passengers. Then he continued to survey the ocean ahead.

Katherine let out a deep breath. "Thank goodness!"

They sat down on low canvas chairs and soon Chryséis and Katherine were chatting about this and that, while Trevor took a nap. This morning, they had seen all sorts of weird and wonderful people at Aztlan harbour. Like the 'fairies' with their flowing hair and butterfly clothes and a woman with green skin, who had been carried in a sedan chair. The girls debated the likelihood for inheriting green skin for a while. But, there was something else they remembered. Two Gabari giants in dark cloaks near the cooking house where they had eaten seafood.

"Those guys were creepy," Chryséis said.

"Yes, creepy."

"I wonder what they were talking about. Always looking around like that, as if they had huge secrets to discuss. Totally dodgy."

"Maybe undercover agents. James Bond chasing after the prehistoric villains of the 'Known World'!"

"The name is Bondûr, Jamon Bondûr." They laughed.

"Then they are not very good at hiding it. What good are agents you can spot a mile away? Nah, there was something else going on."

"As long as we don't have to see them again…"

"Now that would be really creepy."

The girls didn't realize who it was they had seen. And it wasn't a joke.

"Wonder what Kheton's thinking about."

"Lelani of course."

Lelani had gone below deck, checking on her dowry, while Kheton enjoyed the warm breeze. He would soon begin his duty as 'Honourable Junior Delegate from Alesia' in Algiras. Algiras was the capital of Atala, the Atland archipelago's main island.

Kheton thought indeed whether he should go looking for Lelani, when she came up the stairs and came to stand quietly next to him. He looked at her proudly. Lelani was so beautiful with her auburn hair all wind-blown and her cheeks blushed by the fresh sea air.

The sun dipped lower in the sky and the rippling waters were turning the colour of charcoal glass.

"Steady on! Let's reach Kamûk, before darkness falls and the monsters of the deep come out to play with ya dawdling seafarers," Captain Thëlamôn bellowed.

"Aye, aye captain!" the crew answered and the ship gained speed.

Captain Thëlamôn wore the customary dark-blue shirt with the captain's compass rose on the chest. He had sailed the Atlantean Sea on his father's trading ships from the age of four. The sea was in his blood.

Soon one of the sailors called out "Terreis – land. Terreis D'ântilla!"

They were thrilled. This had to be a remnant of Atlantis. Would D'ântilla be very different from Alesia? Chryséis checked her watch. It was twenty seven past five. She pointed straight ahead. "That's just so cool."

A massive lighthouse slid by to their right. Round rooftops above the seawall shone like copper pearls in the setting sun. The domes were coated in precious orichalcum and belonged to the temple of the sun god Raïs, the patron god of Kamûk.

"And look at all those ships flying their flags," Trevor said. He was all awake now. They joined Kheton and Lelani at the railing, determined not to miss a thing. On a hill to the left, a series of white, egg-shaped buildings overlooked the bay.

"That must be the observatory with the new raygun."

"Yes, looks like it." Katherine nodded.

"Alun says the cosmic deflector raygun is powerful enough to vaporize meteors and asteroids."

"Can't wait to see it for myself."

They hadn't visited the observatories in Alesia, only heard about them, but the Observatory of Clymene in

Algiras had been extremely interesting. The roof pearls were soon the size of large coppery onions and the entire town was bathed in a darkening orange glow as the 'Navis Arion' sailed through the harbour entrance.

"That's like magic," Chryséis said in awe.

"Trev, did you take a picture? Hurry up the sun is sinking fast."

"Not yet."

"Hurry up!"

Ahead of them, two junks with sails like red fish fins and flying brightly-coloured flags were following the navigator's boat to the docks. They landed shortly before nightfall. Close to the temple of the sun with the familiar sitting statue of a large bronze sculpture. Here, the crew would give thanks to the sun god Raïs as was Alesian custom.

"Make ready to go on land, athenai," Kheton said. He called them athenai – friends.

"We'll be ready. Just getting our things," Chryséis said.

They walked to the back as the dark water reflected artificial lights lit up one by one along the shore. Large vimaans transported merchandise from all over the Known World along the illuminated streets. The scents of vanilla and sandalwood mixed with the less pleasant harbour odors. The sailors lined up, looking forward to merriment at the amphitheater tonight.

"After the harp concert, they show 'Sons of Turennis', about the theft of magical objects and retribution," one of the sailors said.

"Great play, Saw it in Algiras. Quite a spectacle."

The passengers disembarked and dock workers began to clear the ship's cargo onto the landing.

"Well, I never…," Katherine stared down at a group of maidens on the broad steps leading into the water.

A welcoming committee from the citadel of Kamûk serenaded the visitors while a young apprentice maiden put flowers in their hair.

"From snow-capped mountains to the deep blue sea, D'ântilla Island welcomes thee. We hope you will enjoy your stay before you must be on your way. Welcome, welcome to Kamûk, welcome, welcome to Kamûk…"

Good manners demanded that they listen politely. So the time travellers stood awkwardly on the landing with everybody else, until the maidens had finished their song.

Kheton, being the visiting diplomat, held a short speech, officially thanking the maidens for their musical effort and hospitality. Then a vimaan with the emblem of Kamûk's citadel carried them through cobblestone streets and up the citadel hill, before descending in the court yard next to an ornamental fountain.

They were treated to a lavish dinner in the great hall. Crab patties, the local specialty, were heaped on golden platters with fried octopus heads and other delicacies of the sea.

Later, the young travellers watched the harbour skyline from their balcony. Kheton and Lelani had gone to watch the play at the amphitheater as official guests of the Lady of the citadel.

"I'm so glad they have bathrooms here."

Chryséis had successfully washed the bird muck out and was wearing pajamas she had found on her bed. Her jade-coloured Alesian silk suit was hanging over chairs to dry.

"Yeah, but why do they always put us into the same room?" Trevor sighed.

The maidens had assumed that all three of them were siblings. Nothing new, then.

"I'll take this bed." Trevor drew back the blanket on a bed by the window. "I'm beat."

"So am I," Katherine murmured. She was already half-asleep in the soft covers.

Distant clapping and cajoling drifted up from the amphitheater. Despite the peaceful mood, Trevor couldn't shake a feeling of unease. Something about D'ântilla felt very different. But what?

He had another dream that night. Of giants in dark cloaks. Of fairies, who cleverly fought the giants with magic tricks and of a large featherless seabird that devoured a black spider to the faint and distant tune of '...Welcome, welcome to Kamûk, welcome, welcome to Kamûk...'

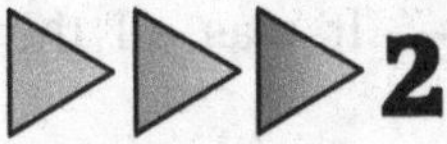 # 2   THE SPEAKING STONE

Their room was in a shambles. A citadel guard was busy searchingunder the table, bumped into Chryséis and she moved out of the way. "How much longer is this going to take?" she groaned and rolled her eyes. "What on earth do they want from us?"

The man apologised politely and began to rummage around on top of the carved cupboard. After the warm welcome yesterday, this was the last thing they had expected. Their morning outing had been rather pleasant, but when they returned a short while ago, guards were already searching their quarters.

Kheton was still in a conference with other dignitaries and could not be reached.

"A Speaking Stone went missing in Alesia and was taken to Kamûk." Lelani reported back after speaking to the captain of the guards. "The guards are searching for it. It is a grave offense to have such an object in one's possession." She was wringing her hands in despair. Lelani obviously knew what a speaking stone was. The time travellers did not.

"What has that got to do with us?" Katherine demanded to know from Trevor.

"Maybe they're searching everybody, who came from Alesia."

"Let's find out."

"Why do you search in our room, guardsman?" Trevor asked one of the men in halting Alesian, while the man rifled through the contents of a wooden chest. "Do you believe that a…speaking…stone is in our room?"

He watched annoyed as his drawing pad went flying onto the floor.

"So sorry, but the Lady gave orders." It was all the guard was willing to say.

"Careful with t h a t!" Chryséis took the palmtop computer from another guard and opened it so that he could see that there were no stones inside. "I knew something like this would happen. I knew it!" she said crossly.

"Relax, we haven't done anything wrong."

Katherine stood by the open balcony doors, wishing she could just make all this go away. "Why don't they just talk to the stone? If it can really talk, it will answer, right?"

"You mean like phoning your cell phone when you're looking for it?" Chryséis asked.

"As if. Who's ever heard of stones that can talk?" Trevor's patience wore thin. Another guard crawled around them on all fours. "Kindly move to the other side." He lifted the rose-coloured curtain hem, probing along the wall.

"Dear friends, guards. A 'Speaking Stone'! They are mere children…" Lelani finally gave up and sat numbly down on Katherine's bed.

At daybreak, she had looked forward to their tour around Kamûk, starting with the harbour district. Kheton had stayed behind to conduct official business.

Warehouse after warehouse lined the roofed-in docks and roads. After stopping at a cooking house, their guide had taken them to the observatory in the Iapetus Hills east of Kamûk. They flew past tropical plantations and farm stalls in a vimaan.

The observatory had been a real jaw-dropper. Not just because of the huge shark statue outside the entrance, but because of the sheer size of the five egg-shaped buildings. They had joined a group of tourists and listened rapt to what the astronomer had to say. He looked quite nerdy and introduced himself as Parnú of Lycia.

"Lycia is a small town close to the southern coast of D'ântilla, for those, who are foreign to our shores," Parnú clarified upfront. "The site of this observatory has a long history. Gabari natives erected stone circles before the great deluge, when D'ântilla was still part of Atland. These stone circles served as observatories to the ancients."

Parnú explained that the scientists of the modern observatory were trained to detect and destroy heavenly bodies posing a threat to the mother planet.

"You may have heard we possess an effective forewarning system. We now also have a powerful new raygun." He paused. "Effective against asteroids that can be dangerous to us. Ever since the planet Astra exploded eons ago, leaving behind rocks that now circle the heavenly realm, we deal with this danger. We will view the cosmic deflector raygun just now."

The time travellers nudged each other.

"Friend Parnú, please tell us about this planet 'Astra'," Chryséis asked shyly.

Parnú told them matter-of-factly that the planet had existed beyond the red planet, Xipe Xolotle for many cycles of arc. They already knew that a cycle of arc was thousands of years.

"A planet between Mars and Jupiter? No way!" Trevor had cried out in surprise.

The astronomer and other tourists seemed a little miffed at the impolite outburst in a language they didn't understand. An uncomfortable Lelani looked the other way and Trevor fell silent.

Parnú quickly changed the subject as he led the way through long passages with shining floors into another part of the observatory. The children from the future hung back and whispered to each other.

Katherine had a sudden brainwave.

"Listen, D'ântilla must be roughly to the southwest of

the Bermuda triangle…" She didn't get a chance to finish her sentence.

"We will now watch a mirage," the astronomer announced solemnly and led the visitors through metal doors that slid noiselessly open.

They had arrived at the planetarium. The tourists took their seats and a young thin man with a stubby nose, made ready to put the mirage roll into its wall slot. He had been in charge of 'Mirage Education' for only a few days and was proud of his new position.

It was a very good mirage and the visitors were usually quite impressed. The lights in the hall dimmed and the seats moved down into a horizontal position. The mirage showed scientists working frantically on control panels as a monotonous voice spoke.

"…the trajectory of an approaching asteroid, hurtling at high velocity towards the mother planet, was predicted through precise mathematical calculations. The asteroid moves in direct collision course with the mother planet. Engineers train a raygun on the approaching asteroid, emitting super-concentrated light rays."

Bang! The asteroid was destroyed just in time, with smaller pieces whizzing through space in a cloud of dust. They vaporised on impact with the earth's atmosphere in a spectacle of sparkling showers.

The mirage apparently depicted an actual incident not too far in the past.

"Our civilisation has nothing to fear when it comes to celestial hazards. We can now take on even larger planetoids."

The audience murmured approval. Next up was a tour of the new cosmic deflector raygun. The real thing! A large vimaan transported the visitors to the top of the hill where they were dwarfed by a huge apparatus inside an oval building. The domed roof was busy opening when they walked into the hall.

"Please keep sufficient distance, athenai, not beyond

this line," Parnú instructed and his voice echoed off the round wall and high roof. The awed visitors retreated behind a yellow line that was painted on the very shiny floor and stared up at the surprisingly plain looking raygun. There were no screws or wheels or levers. Just a telescope mounted on a dimly illuminated thick plate.

As Parnú led them around the apparatus, a control panel with different-coloured squares on the other side of the floor plate came into view. Two scientists seemed to evaluate lines and curves on the screen and spoke in muted tones.

"Why is it so flat and wide in front?" Katherine whispered.

"I don't know. Maybe because it's easier to program the angle they need. Did he just say they can use a pulse action from different angles?"

"I think so."

The flat, oval outlet looked like a giant mouth. The friends barely listened when Parnú told them about the other features. Trevor stayed behind and secretly took a picture of the raygun and the scientists in front of it. Then he took a photograph of the stone circles below through the great windows. In the background, the sky over the harbour looked hazy.

"We are coming to the end of your visit. Shukri athenai, thank you for your interest in our humble scientific establishment in the Iapetus Hills."

Parnú of Lycia concluded the tour and the visitors were transported down to the shark-guarded entrance of the observatory. Soon a flurry of vimaans rose into the air and descended on Kamûk. From here the palm-fringed beaches looked rather inviting.

"We will return to the citadel to freshen up. Then we will visit the famous aquarium on the other side of town," Lelani said. "Tomorrow we will spend time picnicking on the beach."

"That sounds really nice, Lelani," Chryséis said. "Tell us more about this aquarium…" That had been only half an hour ago.

Suddenly, one of the guardsmen held up a shimmering white object, that he had found in Chryséis' backpack.

"It is here, it is here," he shouted triumphantly. Lelani moved ever so slightly away from the children.

"Oh boy," Trevor said.

"What is this egg doing in your backpack?" Katherine asked Chryséis.

"I have absolutely no idea. Do they seriously think we would steal a silly stone egg like that? How ridiculous!" Chryséis was all flustered.

"This doesn't belong to us," Trevor tried to explain.

"No, it doesn't belong to you. You stole it." The guard was still holding up the egg and Trevor started to lose his temper.

"Now wait a minute, what do you mean? We have never seen this thing before. Why are you accusing us, guard?"

"Trevor, stay calm," Katherine warned him. "Don't make them angry – please. I'm sure they'll use telepathy to find out the truth. A lie detector test or something like that. Remember, they are civilised people and the Lady of Cydonia knows that we didn't do it."

Trevor unclenched his fists. "Yeah, and if not, we'll find out what a prehistoric dungeon is like."

Katherine had an unpleasant flashback of the caves at Shuruk with big tarantula guards and bundles of human bones wrapped in white fluffy stuff. She thought fiercely of running from the citadel and activating a time portal.

"Should we go invisible and make a run for it?" Chryséis whispered, having the same idea. "I don't want to go to prison."

Trevor felt braver, but then he hadn't been in Shuruk. "No, we can't do that now. Katie's right: they are too much like the Alesians to harm us. I have one of the time-portal-finders in my pocket and we are still wearing our VICs. If we need to run, we can do it anytime."

"Oh that's real comforting," Chryséis said sarcastically.

"Where is Kheton? He's our guardian, shouldn't he protect us?"

"I don't think Lelani can contact him. I'm scared. What'll they do to us?" Katherine sounded rattled.

"Come with us now," the captain of the guards interrupted.

The guards wedged the culprits in the middle, two on each side, front and back and the time travellers were led away like common criminals.

Suspicious eyes followed them as they trotted demurely through the citadel passages and up a flight of stairs. The citadel was a pretty building with wall paintings and statues everywhere, but the time travellers had no time for art. The guards stopped on the third floor in front of a massive wooden door.

"You wait here," the captain of the guards said roughly.

Had the dreaded moment arrived, were they taken to prison?

"Please tell us what you'll do to us," Katherine begged. "Citadel guards, athenai. We didn't do anything wrong."

No answer. The guards remained stone-faced. Chryséis panicked and lifted her hand to press the button on her aliceband.

"No Chryséis !"

She let her hand fall. The voice had sounded familiar.

Trevor and Katherine were studying the ironwork of the door and nobody was speaking or even looking at her.

So who had called out? Chryséis listened and understood.

"The Lady of Cydonia tells me not to do it," Chryséis said in a low voice.

"Do what?" Trevor and Katherine stared at her.

"Not to turn invisible and flee."

"How does she know you want to do that?"

"She read my thoughts," Chryséis answered.

"Seriously?"

The citadel guards gave Katherine reproachful looks and she lowered her voice.

"What else did she say, what are we supposed to do?"

"I don't know, I lost the connection. Maybe I'm too scared to keep the contact going."

"Great!" Trevor hissed. "What are we gonna do now?"

In an answer to his question, the door opened with a loud creak into the Lady of Kamûk's audience room. An elevated chair was mounted against the red wall opposite the door between two windows.

The Lady of Kamûk sat on the throne and looked sternly at them. It was clear that she sat in judgment of the three young travellers. Kheton had placed himself to her right, dressed in the formal tunic of a judge. At least their guardian was there. But his face was unsmiling and his arms folded across his chest over the embroidered red feather.

"Enter."

They waited. The Lady was a stocky woman and much younger than her Cydonian counterpart, but she wore the same robe of authority. Her eyes were large and slanted in a startling hazel brown and her thick blonde hair was pulled back from her face in a high bun. There was no trace of the friendliness she had displayed the day before at dinner time.

Katherine could feel her heart pounding in her throat, doo dum, doo dum. The guard carrying the translucent white egg stepped forward, cradling the precious object in his large Gabari hands as if it was a raw egg. He put the stone egg into a metal holder on a table next to Kheton and retreated. The children still didn't move.

"Enter," the Lady said again. Her tone was impatient now.

"Oh, I wish that the Lady of Cydonia were here," Katherine whispered before they were pushed through the door by their guards. The door closed behind them.

The three friends saw that the room was big enough to hold everybody, including some citadel officials in white robes, who had joined the proceedings. They waited with bated breath.

"Young visitors from Cydonia," the Lady of Kamûk addressed them formally without further ado. "You are accused of the crime of stealing and smuggling the 'Speaking Stone of Caradoc' to D'ântilla. Explain yourselves."

The Lady's words came flying at them like darts. They looked puzzled and Kheton repeated in simpler terms what the Lady of Kamûk had said.

"Oh, we don't know, honourable Lady, we don't know a...speaking stone," Trevor stammered and saw that Lelani's expression was anxious.

The Lady of Kamûk didn't mince her words.

"Let me be more specific, then. Are you spying for the Highpriest of Shuruk?"

They had heard much of the evil Edfunian leader, of course. Katherine and Chryséis had even seen him with Túvar in the dungeon of Shuruk, but being accused of spying for the giant sorcerer, who had also tried to abduct them at the Moti Market? Please!

"No, no of course not," Chryséis flared up. "We would never do such a thing. What has he got to do with this stone?"

"You should know that. Why did you smuggle this precious stone out of Alesia in your bag?" the Lady asked with pitiless urgency, pointing to the white egg.

Katherine suppressed a giggle. An egg made of stone, how comical! She concentrated hard on a carved flower in the window frame and luckily the urge to giggle vanished. This was not the time or place to break out laughing.

"We didn't, why would we do that?" she said.

"You tell me."

Kheton had been observing them closely the entire time, no doubt reading their minds. It was his job, wasn't it?

"Kheton, tell her that we didn't do it," Chryséis blurted out, but before Kheton could say anything, the Lady of Kamûk lifted her hand. She listened for a few moments.

Katherine thought she would surely faint if this went on for much longer. Chryséis slipped her hand into Katherine's and squeezed hard. Katherine started breathing again.

"I understand that you, young friend," she addressed Trevor, "…fell into the harbour basin in Aztlan before your departure. Just as the harbour guards had located the suspected Gabari thieves."

"Yes, Lady, I…fell into the…water," he answered the question with a sigh in broken Alesian. "I don't know about… those thieves."

"Explain."

Trevor was very pink in the face, feeling strangely guilty. What did his embarrassing accident have to do with all this?

But he didn't have a choice, so Trevor explained how he had felt a push and toppled into the water as they waited with Lelani on the pier. That he had seen something big and black fluttering past just before. That everybody had been very helpful and he was lifted out of the harbour basin by their Gabari guard.

Of course, Trevor felt embarrassed all over again.

Chryséis opened her mouth to try and help Trevor out, but Kheton lifted his hand and she closed her mouth without saying anything.

"So you tell us that someone in a black cape was nearby as this happened?"

Trevor thought about the question. "Yes, honourable Lady, I think so." What was she getting at?

"Did you see a black spider tattoo?"

Chryséis and Katherine looked at each other aghast. A spider tattoo like the one they had seen on the sorcerer's forehead before? Did that mean that the Highpriest of

Shuruk had been in Aztlan on the pier?

"No, I didn't see anything else, really. It happened so fast."

"The stone hasn't spoken yet," the Lady said randomly. Perhaps she was discussing the situation with someone telepathically. She closed her eyes. Had she gone to sleep?

Katherine felt like giggling again. The stone hadn't spoken yet? It was a STONE, hello!

Eventually the Lady opened her eyes again, but it was Kheton who spoke. "We have concluded that you did not steal the Speaking Stone. You were merely used as couriers. We have our suspicions as to who the culprits might be."

Katherine looked triumphantly at Trevor and mouthed, "See!" pointing to her eye. Lelani looked at her husband, then closed her eyes with relief.

"We believe that you, athenai, were used by the thieves to hide the 'Speaking Stone of Caradoc' from the harbour guards. And you, young friend Trevór, were pushed into the water as a distraction. We believe that the Highpriest of Shuruk is behind this plot."

The tension in the room lifted with a collective murmur. There was a perfectly good explanation for all this: it was the fault of the Edfunians. The children were innocent! The Lady of Kamûk spoke with the captain of the guards and he left briskly with some of his men to carry out her order.

Slowly the truth of the matter sank in.

"We won't go to prison. We're safe," Trevor said. "She must have spoken to the Lady of Cydonia. She came through for us!"

"That's amazing!" Katherine sighed.

Oh thank you! Trevor thought intensely of the Lady of Cydonia. He was not a klutz after all…or a thief. Could he hear the words 'It's a pleasure.' in his mind? He felt accomplished for communicating with the Lady.

"But what is a speaking stone and why did the Edfunians steal it?" Trevor couldn't hold back any longer, "Why is it so important? Stones cannot speak!"

The Lady's stern look softened. The foreign children were obviously ignorant. She gave orders to clear the room until only the children stood before her and Kheton. Then she nodded and Kheton enlightened his protegés at last.

"Young friends, this is no ordinary stone. The 'Speaking Stone of Caradoc' is one of three of its kind still remaining in the Known World. It is made from polished moonstone. The others are made from emerald and amethyst. They are the last of twelve such stones the gods left behind before they departed and the Dark Age began. They are very old and very precious. Every Speaking Stone contains the secrets of wisdom to help maintain civilised ways on our mother planet. The Edfunians and their evil Gabari brethren are greedy to possess these powers for their own benefit. To learn secrets."

"The 'Speaking Stone of Caradoc' was a loan by the Lady in Lyonesse to assist the Alesians with its counsel in our time of need. The stone's wisdom helped avoid an outright war with the Edfunians. Then it was stolen."

"That's incredible. Can the stone really speak?"

"Yes, it can, but it does so of its own will."

"Huh?"

"If one of the speaking stones ended up in the wrong hands, it would have disastrous consequences. That's why they must be safeguarded at all cost and cannot be forced to share their counsel."

"So we were caught in the middle. We would have been punished if found guilty?" Chryséis trembled at the thought.

"Yes, severely."

"But you could read our minds. You knew that we were innocent."

"I did indeed read your minds, but the procedures must be followed. Some try and conceal their real intentions...and thoughts."

"We don't know how to do that," Chryséis explained.

"The Edfunians know."

Soon the time travellers found themselves back in the long passageways of the citadel again. They were happy to be off the hook and on their way to their quarters and not to some gruesome dungeon.

"That could have easily gone pear-shaped," Trevor said when they were recovering from their scary experience in their room. The visit to the aquarium hasd been postponed until tomorrow.

"Easily," Katherine replied.

"I'm just glad the stone was found before the Edfunians could get to it."

"It would probably not even speak to them."

"Do they know that? They must have followed us to get the egg back. Maybe they're already here in the citadel."

"Hmm, I'm sure they're going to catch them if they try. I mean with all those guards around, where are they supposed to hide?"

"I'm exhausted," Chryséis complained. "A speaking stone with all the secrets of wisdom stored in it. You have a question and the stone tells you what to do. I mean, what's next?"

"Maybe they'll turn you into a frog. A speaking frog."

"Ha, ha, ha — really, a frog!"

"'Oh hi, Dr. Naidoo, I'm a speaking frog. I hope you don't mind.' Dr. Naidoo would have a heart attack in Natural Science class." Not that it was a particularly funny joke, but they laughed anyway.

"Not just Dr. Naidoo. Imagine Holly with a speaking frog in her bed."

"Oh my word! Stop." Katherine had tears in her eyes for laughing.

"'Be not afraid, it's just me Trevor. I'm a speaking frog today. You know, like a speaking stone…'"

They laughed and talked complete nonsense for a while, wild with relief. Their pact that if anything truly bad happened, they would immediately go back to the future, had not come into effect. This wasn't the end of their adventure. Not by a long shot!

*

A group of giants in dark attire bowed in greeting, as their stooped leader joined them in the dank room in a deserted part of the harbour. He dusted himself off and briefly studied two citadel guards, who lay stunned on the warehouse floor. They had walked in on the Edfunians just moments ago.

"I thought I told you to shield this building," the leader's voice rasped in rebuke. "Why is this area suddenly searched by guards?"

He glared at the Edfunian warriors before him. Their leader's eyes were compelling... compelling them to obey.

"Sire —" One of the men began and stepped forward, but was cut short with a hiss and an abrupt hand movement. The giant slunk back in a row with the others.

"Hush, I know none of you would dare to betray our cause, but we don't have much time." Their leader lifted his arms and a scintillating dome rose up around them, rendering the warehouse impassable. The guards moaned and moved a little.

"Today we have to act. It will be done as in Cydonia. Turn invisible and stun the citadel guards. Quick and unseen...no confrontation! We don't want any attention."

The Edfunians bowed their heads and asked no questions. There was menace in the Highpriest's voice and his bright eyes glanced at the two guards before glaring at his underlings.

"I will be awaiting you on the ship in the bay outside the harbour wall. The captain will take us back home...do not fail me!"

The Gabari skipper and his crew had been 'persuaded' by the sorcerer, unable to resist the hypnotizing eyes for long.

"The 'Speaking Stone' reached Kamûk on an Alesian cargo ship," the Highpriest continued. "Unfortunately the citadel guards discovered the moonstone before it could be recovered by us. Our Gabari spies report that the troublesome foreign children from Cydonia are among the travellers. Only a defenseless young woman keeps them company. Xipe Xolotle might be agreeable to fresh sacrifice... Ah, but the children might kick up a fuss."

He remembered how difficult they had been at the Cydonian market. "That's the last thing we need right now. The stone is what we want."

The warriors murmured consent. If all went according to plan, they would be on their way to Shuruk in no time – with the powerful stone.

"I must have this stone!" the Highpriest barked. "This is our chance. Power will be restored to Edfun and Alesia will be ours. And then Atland and then the Known World!"

The warriors couldn't wait to carry out the deed those bright eyes and the sign of the spider had ordered them to do! It would be easy enough to enter and leave the citadel unseen. No confrontation, the Highpriest had said.

They had to be careful when getting close to the 'Speaking Stone', lest it cried out and gave them away before it was dropped into the black velvet sack. They weren't sure what a speaking stone was capable of doing, but one couldn't take chances.

"Triumph will be Edfun's at last. Triumph over Alesia and the Known World! We will take back our rightful place among humankind. Go forth and claim your birthright. The Red One be with you! Ari-sūdana!"

"Ari-sūdana!" the warriors joined in the battle cry in a muffled tone.

One never knew if some busybodies were still around. But nobody heard the Edfunians chanting. The unconscious citadel guards were left behind as the giant warriors made their invisible way to the citadel hill at dusk.

The Highpriest of Shuruk could not have chosen a better time for his plan.

▶▶▶ **3** BERMUDA BREAKTHROUGH

"Miami, come in. Do you read me? Do you read me?"

Again, there was no answer from the airport tower, only static. Ever since his Cessna had unexpectedly hit a storm front over the Caribbean Captain Greg Pearson, an experienced pilot with the Transaviac Charter airline, had tried to contact Miami airport.

He hated not being in control of his aircraft. Dark clouds were swirling around them and not even the frequent lightening had made a difference. The sight had been absolutely zero. Captain Pearson ran his hand nervously through his short grey hair. He had never experienced anything like this before.

"This is your captain speaking. Please remain seated with your seatbelts on. I don't want to see anything else fly, except this plane."

He had made a few encouraging and even funny remarks over the intercom at first. By now he felt more like screaming at whatever it was that had taken over his plane. Six passengers had embarked on the chartered flight in Bermuda thinking it a stroke of luck.

The regular plane due to leave Hamilton for Miami at 7:25 am had been downed with a mechanical problem. The ocean had been calm and sparkling as the tiny, whining plane carried them across the blue sky morning. The passengers regretted their impatience sorely when a storm had hit them out of nowhere.

"Miami come in. Mayday!" The captain bellowed into the radio. "Mayday!"

Static answered. A hissing sound, which did not come from the equipment, had strangely risen and ebbed. None of the instruments worked from the onset of the turbulence, yet they hadn't plunged into the sea. The Cessna seemed to simply glide as high winds were pulling and tugging at the wings. Now the lightening and swirling dark clouds morphed into heavy fog. A thick dark fog. The tugging stopped. Well, they were still in the air, weren't they? But where?

"Betsy, keep them calm. Let them have champagne or whatever they want, just keep them calm," he had told Betsy Fuller the flight attendant in the beginning . Betsy had set her mouth in determination and went to work. She was a feisty woman with her black hair in a tight bun under the pert stewardess cap. This would not be her last flight, if she had anything to do with it. Jamal and Jerome, her three-year-old twins home in St. Petersburg needed their mother.

"Here is your Bloody Mary, sir." Betsy Fuller put the red cocktail down on the folding table.

Lafayette Thomas, a civil engineer from Ohio, seemed to be asleep with his head leaning against the window. She left him alone. A British historian, Dr. Peter Spencer, and his son Scott sat rigidly upright, their faces chalky white. The other passengers sat still staring ahead of them in anticipation of the inevitable crash. No need yet for oxygen masks, but the passengers were wearing their yellow life jackets. Betsy Fuller, efficient even in the face of danger, had made sure of that.

"Champagne, sir?"

"Champagne? Is there something wrong? How much longer do we have to endure this?" Dr. Spencer asked timidly.

"Sir, it will be over sooner than you think."

The plane lurched and Betsy had to steady herself against the seat.

"Have you ever been in weather like this?"

"Oh yes, sir, many times," the stewardess lied. "And I'm still here."

She poured a glass of champagne for the historian and a coke for his pop-eyed son. The strange hissing sound stopped abruptly.

"Ha, give me some champagne, too!" A half-drunk passenger roared at the back. "Why not go out on the good stuff?" He laughed hysterically.

"Mayday, Miami, do you read me?" Captain Pearson tried again to make contact with the airport, but the static had made way for dead quiet. "Great, that's really helping!"

The two engines sputtered back into action, but it was too dangerous to risk a blind emergency landing. All the captain could do was keeping the plane afloat. Then he saw lights on the ground. Could it be stars reflecting in the sea? But unbelievably, there was land that appeared through the thinning mist and the lights were on the land! Suddenly, his joy turned to dismay. There shouldn't be any land yet. Not in the Sargasso Sea, unless the force of the storm had driven them completely off-course. Then the fog lifted and Betsy entered the cockpit. "Captain what is going on?"

"Something very strange, that's for sure. There is land below, but I have no idea where we are."

"Why is it dark outside? It can't be that late. Darn, my watch stopped working."

A half-moon stood out brightly against the starry sky. It had been broad daylight just before the storm. They had left Bermuda at 9:15 am sharp. The captain checked his watch. It had stopped at 11:12 am, May 28th.

"Are you going to attempt an emergency landing?" Betsy's voice trembled a little.

"Without instruments? Too much of a risk. There is still enough fuel in the tank. We'll have to cruise, while I try and establish contact."

"What do I tell the passengers? They are asking questions."

"Tell them everything is fine. We're just a bit off course because of the storm, that's all." But before Captain Pearson could contact the nearest airport, the instruments came on again, blinking and beeping. The captain tried to operate them, but something seemed to have taken over from him.

The landing gear dropped and a few minutes later, the Cessna set down on an illuminated runway, narrowly missing two cone-shaped buildings. The passengers clapped. As soon as the plane touched down, people started to emerge from the buildings. Large people - in long white robes.

*

As if the theft of the 'Speaking Stone' had not been upsetting enough, the Lady of Kamûk had to deal with another unexpected problem on the same day.

A loud bang had ripped through the night air east of D'ântilla. Something had crashed in the sky, but there was neither a fire nor flying debris to be found and no heavenly body had been identified by the observatory.

Thermo detectors searched the area between Jamba, home to the largest ptarmigan farm on D'ântilla, and the eastern coastline of the island.

"The detectors then did pick up several individuals in a winged metal machine - presumably a vimaan – exuding smelly fumes," the scientist in charge reported. "The vimaan was safely teleported to Jamba's rarely used airstrip. On closer inspection we discovered that this noisy and smelly flying object is no ordinary vimaan. The five men, one woman and one child appear to be terrified of the rescue personnel. I can assure you, honourable Lady, that the Gabari on call are perfectly trained to handle such emergency situations." Thujan was a very serious man with longish grey hair, who spoke with authority.

"Interesting." The Lady of Kamûk listened to him

attentively. She walked next to the scientist toward the outlandish vimaan in one of the airport's hangars. "Very interesting." She had arrived in Jamba to inspect the flying object and its passengers and her suspicions were soon confirmed.

"Attempts to communicate with the passengers were futile. They don't seem to understand even one civilised language. Therefore, we decided to sedate them with sleeping gas in order to prevent panic."

"So it has happened again, Thujan." The Lady of Kamûk peered through the vehicle's big front window at the sleeping pilot. "What are we going to do now?"

"There is no doubt about it, honourable Lady. The vimaan is from another timeline. The cosmic raygun was tested yesterday and like before, objects from another dimension were attracted and most regrettably crossed through the barrier of space and time. The new raygun could be too strong. The sudden energy surge must be causing irregular fluctuations in the continuum. Just like before."

The scientist hinted at an incident two moon phases ago, when three fishing boats had suddenly appeared close to Kamûk, causing a sensation.

"The recent improvements did not help, then."

"My apologies, Lady, but it does not seem so. We will work harder."

Masters of harbours and airstrip commanders were required to report any unusual sightings and D'ântillans had witnessed only one such event before, a long time ago.

When the Lady had been a young maiden at the citadel of Lycia, the last member of a ship's crew of eleven died. Their vessel had broken through the space time barrier in the early hours of one fateful morning almost one sheaf of years ago.

The ship was found only two days later, which had made a reversal of the crossing impossible. The homesick seafarers had eventually come to believe that divine intervention had saved them from fighting a gruesome war in their own time. Thanks to a minimal adjustment of their memories at the 'House of Life'.

"We must keep this incident quiet."

"Yes, Lady. The last time some said that the hold of eternal ice on the continent of Annwynn at the pit of the globe may have lifted to release the poor, unliving souls of the dead. Ridiculous." The scientist was upset.

The Lady of Kamûk shook her head. "Superstition can become a problem. It is best to avoid such reactions this time."

"During the last moon we managed to send the fishing boats back to their own time. There is hope that this time, it didn't attract undue attention under the cover of night."

"Then let's do it the same way we did it then. There should be enough time for the reversal before daybreak." The Lady looked up at the starry sky. It was so peaceful out here.

"Honourable Lady, there is no reason why not. The random channel has not yet closed. We have the best prospect of success. The sooner after the crossing the objects are returned the better the chances. Otherwise, the channel will close again and the original point reference is lost."

"I'm aware of this Thujan. If the procedure fails, the object might be lost in time and space, so let's begin the procedure without delay."

They were both transported back to the observatory in the Iapetus Hills by teleporter beam, together with the flying object that had invaded their airspace and time. Thujan and his team of scientists went straight to work. He later found the Lady outside, watching the first sunlight appear on the eastern horizon.

"We were able to calculate the exact point of crossing. I am pleased to report that the reversal was instantaneous and successful, honourable Lady." He bowed a little and the Lady sighed with relief.

"The Earthmother be thanked. Let's get some rest

before the morning breaks."

The Lady walked to the waiting citadel vimaan and was soon on her way into town, where bad news awaited her.

Trevor, Chryséis and Katherine had been completely unaware of the nightly incident with the airplane. So were most of the D'ântillans. An event of a diferent nature, however, got everybody's attention when the port city awoke to another busy day.

News quickly spread that the 'Speaking Stone of Caradoc' had been stolen from the citadel.

Outrageous! A precious Speaking Stone stolen!

The tragic loss of two harbour guards was also reported as they had not been seen since the night before. And, to top it all, two of the Gabari citadel staff had gone missing as well.

The time travellers learnt about the theft during breakfast. At sunrise, as soon as the crime was discovered, the guards in the Lady's audience room had raised the alarm. They had neither seen nor heard or felt anything and Kheton confirmed this after a brief examination. But there was no doubt as to who had been behind the plot.

"These Edfunians mean business!" Katherine worked on a boiled harpee egg. "They seem really keen on that Speaking Stone."

"That's bad news. I wonder what the Lady's going to do now." Chryséis looked up from her mango compote.

"At least they can't suspect us this time."

"I thought we would hear the stone speak sometime soon."

"Oh Trevor, as if," Katherine was still skeptical.

"I'm sure there must be something to it."

"Sure there is. Why didn't it scream when it was stolen? That would have helped."

The 'Speaking Stone' was soon located thanks to a secret tracking device. The moonstone was moving north on an Alesian trading-navis, whose captain did not respond to thought transfer. The plan was obviously to reach Ruta Ynis before nightfall and then to cross the Saturnian Sea into Edfun. The D'ântillans had to act fast. If the priceless stone was taken to Shuruk, it would be near impossible to retrieve it. Soon captain Thëlamôn stood before the Lady of Kamûk.

"Thëlamôn, old friend, you have to change your plans."

The 'Navis Arion' was not simply a trading ship, but also a well-equipped fast ship that had been chosen to protect the important passengers from Cydonia.

Captain Thëlamôn was a former D'ântillian sealord. He had been among the allied counsel to advice the Lady of Cydonia during the recent conflict with Edfun.

"As you wish, honourable Lady. One is glad to be of service."

"The council of elders has decided. With your experience, you are the perfect choice to retrieve the 'Speaking Stone of Caradoc' from the Edfunians. The merchant crew will be exchanged for marine soldiers. More than one ship could attract too much attention. So you are on your own. The Cydonians will come with you, however."

"I will ready the ship. We can sail as soon as you say the word. But the children, honourable Lady..."

"I have my reasons, Thëlamôn. Just deliver them safe and sound in Atland, afterwards." The captain took a respectful bow and left the room.

The citadel proceeded to circulate misleading stories to throw possible spies off track, while the mission got underway. That the search had been abandoned, since there was no chance of finding the stone, that a delegation had been sent to Alesia, that an army were on its way to Shuruk to declare war, and the like.

The elders were also aware that Rutian elves could be quite moody. Elfinûr, queen of the elves, had to be won over gently with a worthy gift to lend her assistance. A small harp made of yellow songwood would be perfect, since it was a very special instrument to elves.

During all these quick preparations, the Lady of Kamûk

summoned the Cydonian visitors. "I admit that I do not fully understand the Lady of Cydonia's position in this, but she asked that the children accompany you throughout."

"So our good Lady has no doubts that we will retrieve the Speaking Stone," Lelani said.

The Lady of Kamûk sighed. "I do not approve of children being involved in a possible battle, myself. What is your opinion in the matter, Honourable Junior Delegate?"

As their guardian, Kheton needed to speak on behalf of the time travellers. "I bow to the wishes of my rulers," he said.

Before midday the Navis Arion had already reached the high seas to the north of D'ântilla, racing toward the island of Ruta Ynis.

And the time travellers were on board.

Kheton had asked the children to stay below deck, because the ship was virtually flying across the Atlantean Sea. It was lucky that neither Chryséis nor Trevor felt as seasick as before. Katherine didn't have a problem in any case. Her uncle Harold lived on the Isle of Man and sometimes invited the family to come and take a sailing trip on his yacht.

After her first sailing trip, Katherine had never been seasick again.

"This 'Speaking Stone' must be real special for them to race after it like that," Trevor said.

"I think we've already established that," Katherine relplied. "In any case, what's the big deal? Stones don't have brains - or lips."

"Why is everybody so keen to get their hands on this thing then?"

"Maybe the stone can actually speak," Chryséis gave her five cents. "I read in a history book about whispering stones and even moving stones. But they didn't mention any speaking stones."

"Moving stones? That must be some kind of trick," Trevor replied.

"What kind of trick transports a huge boulder tied down with metal straps from one island to another during the night?" Chryséis asked.

"I don't know. But it sounds impressive," Katherine answered.

"So you actually believe in this stuff?" Trevor mocked.

"Why not?"

"Cause it doesn't make sense."

"And an island where elves live. That makes sense?"

Trevor grinned. "Are you kidding? Of course it does."

"Oh, you're infuriating! So what are we doing chasing after some giants, who have nothing better to do than to steal an egg-shaped stone that can apparently speak?" Chryséis shook her head vehemently.

"I think they should just use the raygun to destroy Shuruk and be done with it."

"Yes Trevor, that sounds very civilised."

"What is it with boys and guns?" Chryséis rolled her eyes, but Trevor ignored her. "That reminds me… that we should tell Alun about the raygun and the stone and all that."

"Why don't you give telepathy a shot yourself for a change, Trev?" Chryséis asked him. "Then you can tell him about the nasty things you would do to save the world."

Trevor shrugged his shoulders and let it be. They sat on a narrow couch in the main cabin. One had an almost panoramic view of the sea through three large têrakhon windows. Another ship came from an easterly direction and quickly passed them on their right.

"Why didn't they protect this stone better if it's so important to them? I mean they have electromagnetic shields and all that stuff," Trevor said.

"Maybe the Lady of Kamûk was waiting for the stone to speak. And it can't do that with electromagnetic shields around," Chryséis suggested.

"Maybe that's why they managed to steal it in the first place."

"Or somebody helped them to steal it."

The sun dipped lower in the western sky.

"It's already afternoon. Seamen don't like to be out at sea after dark. I wonder if we'll reach this magical island in time."

"We'd better," Katherine grumbled.

Trevor was looking sideways at Chryséis , who dreamily observed dolphins diving in the distance. The 'Navis Arion' was going too fast for them to escort the ship like before.

"Let's see." Chryséis looked at her watch. It was almost 4 o'clock. "We have at least 3 - 4 hours before sunset. That gives us still some time."

"Is the time on your watch still correct? Or are we already too far in the East?" Trevor asked.

" Good question, but in order to work that out I'd need some time and a fixed location."

"Mhm. What are the Edfunians doing on this Ruta Ynis Island anyway?"

"They could've sailed straight past to Edfun," Katherine suggested.

"Or maybe the elf queen is involved in the theft," Trevor said and nibbled on a large white nut from a têrakhon bowl. Tasty travel food with the Lady of Kamûk's compliments.

"I don't think so, Sherlock and it's probably too dangerous to sail to Edfun after dark."

"Yes, right. The monsters of the sea," Trevor mocked and hummed the theme music of the film 'Jaws'.

"Funny."

"Must be a good reason. Nobody seems to like Ruta Ynis very much."

"Everything happened so quickly. Yesterday, we were still in Alesia and now we are chasing Edfunians to an elf kingdom because of some stone. Somebody keep up with that!" Katherine changed the subject.

"Yeah, somebody keep up with that," Chryséis mumbled then carried on admiring the golden sunlight reflecting on the ocean. "Think about that. Elves! Who knew?"

Katherine put headphones over her ears and hummed to the tunes of her favorite CD.

Five minutes later a repeated call announced land. "Terreis! Terreis!"

The thin green shoreline moved closer and closer and turned into a dense forest. They slowed down and before long, the 'Navis Arion' anchored in a secluded bay in full sight of the gravel-covered shore.

The Edfunian ship was moored on the western side of the bay and a rowing boat with armed men was sent over to investigate.

"Ship's deserted, Captain. Nobody aboard and no 'Speaking Stone' either," the four men reported back after a short while.

"They are on land then. We have no time to lose."

The captain ordered another boat to be readied. "We must tread with care. Elves can be an unpredictable and long-fingered lot. It's best if they see us long before we see them."

"Don't take the camera with," Chryséis warned Trevor, who sorted a few items into his moonbag.

"Why not? Don't you think it would be great to get pictures of elves?"

"We only have this one camera and captain Thëlamôn just said that the elves like to steal things."

"It's small enough to fit into my shirt pocket. I can cut a hole into the pocket. They won't see it."

Chryséis shrugged her shoulders. "Fine, take it with. Just look after it."

Minutes later, the three of them sat in a boat with Kheton, the captain, Lelani and two of the crewmen, heading for the beach.

Lelani was wearing a periwinkle-blue dress for the occasion of meeting with the elf queen. The two sailors rowed, while captain Thëlamôn gave them the lowdown on Ruta Ynis.

"Stick with the group and do as I say. We need to be careful."

"Because of the Edfunians?" Trevor wanted to know.

"Why no, because of the tricks of moody elves and fauns of the forest like to play on visitors. The satyrs in the western plains aren't much better. Wildmen with tails, a tribe more monkey than human, however sharp of mind and swift of foot. No love lost between them: the elves and the satyrs. We don't have to worry about the satyrs if we stay in the forest."

Trevor thought he knew everything there was to know about the people of the Known World. "They have tails?"

"Some say they are not human at all with their long tails," one of the sailors added, before he dug again into the water.

"The forest dwellers can appear and disappear at will and scare unwelcome visitors." The captain inhaled the smoke from a meerschaum pipe hanging from his mouth. Like the other sailors, he had tied his hair to the back.

"They don't sound very friendly." Trevor scanned the treed shoreline as the rowing boat dashed towards the beach in long pulls.

"Friendly? Moody's the word. Elves and sprites live in streams, trees and waterfalls. Beautiful Queen Elfinûr rules in the palace Arbộlimar, said to be wrought with spells. They say that her true love, the valiant sailor Talariêl sailed the seven seas and never returned. She is waiting for him still, to make him her rightful elf king - although he is not an elf at all. She's a bit mad because of it."

"Oh, that's so sad," Lelani sighed. "Love lost."

"Great. Not only an elf queen, but a crazy one," Trevor said.

"One must take care not to touch the crystalline wine served at her palace. Many a good sailor was lost to the world after drinking it. By the time he woke up, he found his ship long gone," the other sailor said and strained at his oar.

They soon reached the shore. The boat crunched onto the pebbles and the children jumped out, water splashing against their legs.

"Ah, there is the path just as I remember it," the captain said and pointed to an opening between the trees close to the beach. "Daimon and Fenrik. You two stay with the boat. The elves rarely venture out of the forest, but the Edfunians may still be around. We'll take these with us."

He picked up what looked like short hockey sticks and

gave one to Kheton, hooking another into his broad belt. Lelani carried the small harp made of yellow songwood, the special present for the elf queen.

"Let's go then," Chryséis said with determination and marched over the pebbles closely behind captain Thëlamôn.

They picked their way around smooth boulders until their feet touched the soft leaf-covered forest floor. The sound of trickling water led them to a mossy stone pool in the shade by the white stony path. Kheton sat down on the broad rim of the pool to dip his hand playfully into the sparkling water, but the captain held him back.

"I wouldn't touch the water if I was you. It might just put a spell on you."

Kheton pulled his hand back. Big red flowers grew between lush ferns and caught Katherine's eye.

"Look how beautiful these red flowers are," Lelani marveled.

They hung back a little to pick flowers for their hair.

"The palace is not far from here," captain Thëlamôn said, surveying the way ahead. "We will walk in pairs, never losing sight of the others. Be watchful of elf guards. Remember they will try and..."

"Captain, captain!" Kheton cried and everybody turned to look at him. "Lelani is gone!"

"And where is Katherine?" Chryséis looked around. "They are both gone!"

"The elves must have lured them away," Kheton cried and shook his head. The thought of any harm to his beloved Lelani was frightening.

"Such mischief! Courage athenai, courage." Captain Thëlamôn quickly considered their new situation. "Send a thought to Lelani and ask where they have been taken. We will have to negotiate with the sly elf guards for their release it seems."

"Will they still help us?" Kheton asked anxiously.

"The elves dislike uncivilised Gabari and surely know

why we are here. Speak to your wife now."

Kheton concentrated on a single silent question in his mind and the answer came promptly.

"They are in a clearing in the forest, at the end of this path," he announced.

"I'm scared. What did they do to Katie, those stupid elves? We must find her quickly." Chryséis quivered as they hurried after Kheton and captain Thëlamôn.

"Yes we must. Come on keep up."

"I wish I had my music with me then I wouldn't feel so scared."

"Listen Chris: we'll find Katie and get this stone back and be on our way."

"Yes we will," Chryséis said bravely.

She looked up and saw a large yellow snake curled into a tight coil, lying comfortably on an intertwined branch just above them.

The snake was curious and stuck its head out to get a better look. Chryséis gave a muffled cry and jumped back in surprise. The others were simply walking on. Nobody seemed to have noticed anything! She had no other choice but to pull herself together and gingerly passed underneath the branch to catch up with Trevor.

When she looked over her shoulder, the snake was still hanging there off the branch, head stretched out and stared after her. Chryséis felt a shiver run down her spine and walked faster.

"Come on, the others are far ahead of us. Katherine says we are getting closer." Trevor was proud that he could communicate with Katherine by thought.

"That's great, Trevor. Didn't you say you're not good at telepathy?"

"Oh I don't know. It just popped into my head."

The tree trunks around them were deeply furrowed and many of them as big as sequoias. Trevor brushed against a tree in the passing. It seemed to shrink away from his touch.

A small forest stream fringed by glistening ferns, gurgled softly to their right. They rushed on, climbing over buttress roots and jumping over puddles. A large root formed an arch over the path and thin mist wafted up between the spindly ferns fringing the stream. Large spider webs became visible with those tiny droplets.

"Uh, look at that." Chryséis felt another cold shudder.

"Must be enormous those spiders," Trevor said as they walked underneath the the tree-root arch.

"Gives me the absolute creeps."

"Such a strange forest. Do you think dinosaurs lurk around here somewhere?"

"Don't be silly, Trevor Huxley. There are no dinosaurs around here."

"But what about the farm animals and all…" Trevor began.

"Haven't you heard a word the Lady of Cydonia has said? They've banished the wild dinosaurs to remote areas and the farm animals are domesticated."

Trevor mumbled something like "How much more remote do you get?"

"There are no dinosaurs here, so drop it already."

Trevor stopped talking about dinosaurs. No need to make Chryséis nervous. She might just want to go back to the future as before. There was just a little sunlight that filtered through the vast canopy of trees. Chryséis checked her watch again. Only about an hour since the rowing boat had landed on the beach.

'Hurry up, guys, I can't move!' Katherine moaned. Trevor and Katherine stared at each other.

"Did you hear that?" Chryséis asked.

"Yes, Katherine's in danger. Why can't she move? Let's hurry up!" Trevor urged.

'We are coming, hang in there!' He transmitted to Katherine.

All of a sudden, ear-splitting screeches echoed between the trees. A horde of small monkeys, fluffy and white like ghosts, flew from branch to branch then scurried down a nearby tree trunk. They plunged through the undergrowth and were soon gone.

Alarmed tree frogs sailed down from lofty heights with outstretched webbed fingers and toes. A green frog with white rings on its back landed right next to Chryséis. She screamed in terror and flailed her arms around, nearly knocking Trevor off his feet.

"Be careful Chris, it's only a frog!"

"Only a frog?! It nearly jumped on me." Her eyes were wide from panic.

"Don't touch it or you might get warts," Trevor laughed.

"Thanks, just make fun of me."

The two men in front of them turned around to see what the commotion was all about. "Move along athenai," the captain called out. "No time to lose."

Just when it seemed that the forest couldn't get any darker, the path widened onto a forest glade. Dappled sunlight wove shady patterns onto the grass and the damp smell of the forest made way for the scent of wildflowers. Dragonflies stood still in the air above the little forest stream that now rippled gaily over rocks.

"Over there are Katherine and Lelani!" Chryséis cried and ran now.

One lilac and one periwinkle-blue shape stood stock still in postures of flight in the middle of the path. The little songwood harp lay at Lelani's feet.

"Who goes there?!" a whiny voice demanded.

The next moment, an elf in tattered brownish garb appeared seemingly out of nowhere. He was about Trevor's height and his shifty dark-green eyes observed them closely.

Chryséis wondered if he had pointed pixie ears under his green cap.

"Shelanti, good sir elf, you startled us," captain Thëlamôn greeted him in a friendly tone.

"You belong to these two, heh? Trying to steal my

beautiful ruby-red flowers?" he asked in a challenging tone and pointed to Katherine and Lelani, who still clutched red blooms, they had picked.

Before the surprised visitors could answer, they were unable to move a muscle. Only the elf's spell kept them from falling over. Luckily they could still speak.

"Katie, are you okay?" Chryséis called out to her friend.

Katherine answered with a faint "Yes".

The elf danced around the immobilised humans and gave Chryséis a grim look. "Welcome, visitors to Ruta Ynis," he said smoothly. "It seems we have many visitors today. Too many visitors! Did you come for free flowers?" He ended his lttle speech on a mischievous note.

"Oh, I'm forgetting my manners. May I introduce myself, Gump of Ruta Ynis. Gump the elf. Some people call me a faun, but actually on my mother's side ..." The forest guard rambled on until a much smaller elf next to him tucked on his sleeve. "...ehem, Her Majesty Queen Elfinûr's humble servant and guard in the royal forest. State your names and business."

"Sir Gump, greetings. My name is Thëlamôn of Kamûk. We are sorry about the…flowers. We are here on behalf of the Lady of Kamûk to retrieve an item that Edfunian thieves stole from her." The captain did have some experience with elves on Ruta Ynis.

Trevor was distracted. His eyes followed a troublesome fly that attempted to land on his nose.

"This good fellow's name is Kheton of Cydonia, the husband of the young woman over here by the name of Lelani. Then we have Trevór of Chicagó and Chryséis of Ethigevee…and Kathín of Oxfol," the captain introduced all of them politely. "Kindly release us from your spell, sir elf. We wish to convey the Lady's wishes to Queen Elfinûr of Arbôlimar and ask for her help."

"Not so fast, not so fast human. The Lady of Kamûk sent you, heh?"

The elfin guard's eyes narrowed and he scratched his upturned nose. Kheton wished he could do the same. The fly was still interested in him.

"Yes, that's true."

"You do not belong to these brazen Gabari, who trampled through my precious forest today?" Gump asked quite unnecessarily.

"No, they don't belong to us, sir elf."

He danced some down the forest path and cackled. "They are now lending their shade to our wonderful green home!"

Thëlamôn followed him with his eyes and understood. Gump pointed his chin at a group of young, sturdy trees, branches bent in all directions. The leaves seemed to rustle nervously.

"Is it possible that these trees are the giant Edfunians?"

"And their ship's crew. One can never have enough trees in a forest, don't you think, heh?" the elf guffawed. "Heh heh, not so forward now, are we?" He hobbled toward the young trees with challenging gestures.

A shudder went through the branches and the visitors felt a prickle of fear.

"Sir Gump, you surely have no reason to turn us into trees..." Captain Thëlamôn argued, suddenly afraid for their safety. "We are here to see the honourable queen..."

"Don't I have a reason? Some regret to ever having set foot on Ruta Ynis. Some get away and take with them birds in cages that are too small for them and worth a fortune in the 'Land of the Shaking Earth'. How do I know that you are not here to steal our birds and plants — or even our children?"

The time travellers already knew that the 'Land of the Shaking Earth' was Prydhain. The captain ignored the unreasonable outburst.

"We came to speak with your good queen and have brought a rare songwood harp as proof of our good will."

The elf guard danced over to the harp at Lelani's feet and gave it the once-over. With a wave of his hand, Gump made the young trees quiver. When he had had enough of his game, he cocked his head and listened. It was quiet. Even the fly had given up on Trevor's nose.

"Our revered queen will be ready to receive you in a little while. While we wait, let's play a little more. You won't mind answering a few harmless questions as is customary on our beautiful isle?"

Trevor tried to avoid his gaze.

"I see you want to go first young man…" Gump shook his gnarled finger at him.

"Emm, no, not really, I…"

Gump went right ahead and asked. "Perhaps you can tell us what flies in the air and has two legs?"

Oh no, not a quiz. Trevor was terrible at quizzes. What had two legs…?

"A bird, maybe?" Trevor tried cautiously.

"Yes, yes, yes, a bird, of course a bird. Unless you ever saw a flying Nepeshai, which I didn't mean in the first place…"

The elf babbled on about the Nepeshai people and how much they resembled giant butterflies, until the little elf pulled on his shirt sleeve again.

"Oh gosh," Chryséis sighed and rolled her eyes.

She was not exactly blessed with patience and wanted this annoying elf to get on with it. Her ear was itching and it was getting late.

"Oh gosh, oh gosh, what does that mean, oh gosh…heh?" The elf leapt in front of her, glaring at Chryséis through narrow eyes.

"Oh gosh means…means very clever, good sir elf. You are very clever!" Chryséis could smell his stale berry breath as he came closer.

Good save! Katherine praised her telepathically.

"Very clever, heh? Let's see how clever you are then?"

Chryséis tried to look not too frightened.

"What flies in the air and has four feet, heh?"

Chryséis thought for a second then took a deep breath.

"Two birds?"

"You are also clever youngsters, aren't you, heh? Gosh." He tried the word on his tongue. "Go s h, g o s h… I like it!"

Gump gazed from one child to the other. Kheton and the captain looked alarmed, but kept wisely quiet.

"Now you …, yes you. Pretty enough to be an elf yourself, heh?" He studied Katherine's face. "Round ears though, small and round. Ugly," he concluded with a snarl.

"If you say so, sir elf." Katherine tried to sound polite, despite her absurd situation.

What do I care, if the forest guard likes my ears or not. Bring it on, she thought, we need to get out of here.

I agree. Good luck, she heard Trevor think. Then Chryséis smiled. It's so easy to communicate by thought here. Must be something in the air.

"Sir elf, sir elf…" Gump mocked her, repeating the words like a parrot.

With a quick surprise move he took Katherine's bright blue hairclip in the shape of a butterfly and stuck it on his green cap. Then Gump continued as if it was nothing out of the ordinary. Katherine knew better than to protest.

"Let's see if you know the answer to this, young almost-elfin girl with ugly round ears… what flies in the air and has six legs?"

This guy is obsessed with legs, Chryséis thought.

Yes, some jerk! This time it was Katherine, who answered telepathically.

"Six legs? A fly?" she said aloud.

The faun was surprised, but composed himself quickly. "No, not a fly!" he jeered. "A butterfly, a butterfly of course. You see over there…heh?"

He pointed to a couple of white butterflies dancing around purple bell-shaped flowers then touched the blue hairclip which promptly fell to the ground. The little elf next to him scurried to pick it up and helped Gump fasten the clip to his cap.

"Of course - a butterfly, sir Gump. Forgive my ignorance." Katherine's voice sounded apologetic enough for the elf to take a softer line.

"You are forgiven, then. You are still young, little girl."

He tittered and danced in circles around the hapless visitors. The men still watched without speaking. Too many words could bring on the bad elfin temper. All they wanted was to find the 'Speaking Stone' and leave this forsaken island.

Patience, captain Thëlamôn thought and Kheton nodded. With the Edfunians turned into trees, things should be easier, he thought back.

Time was passing and the sun was sinking fast. Suddenly, the forest guard screwed up his face in a funny grimace and flicked his fingers, releasing the visitors from the spell.

"Ah, the good queen is ready for you now. I'm tired of playing anyway. The giants were more fun, didn't know a single answer."

Kheton stretched his stiff limbs and nearly lost his balance when Lelani sank into his arms. Katherine stomped her feet to get rid of unpleasant needles and pins.

"How could they know the answers? I made this up only yesterday," Gump mumbled, scratching his stubbly chin.

In a flash the forest glade came alive. An assortment of fairies slipped out of trees and ferns and even the gurgling stream. Some of them were as tiny as butterflies, see-through wings and all. They had all witnessed the quiz and laughed their sunny laughter at Gump's failure to trick the children.

The forest guard motioned grumpily for them to follow him down the path, while the fairies flew right above their heads twittering and singing and nudging them playfully.

At last they were headed for Arbôlimar, the palace of Queen Efinûr.

▷▷▷ 5 THE PALACE ARBÔLIMAR

"Hi," Katherine whispered into Chryséis' ear. She took care not to attract Gump's attention, given his fickle moods. But the elf was too busy striding out importantly in front of them to notice.

"Hi, right back at you. I'm glad we didn't end up as forest trees," her friend answered in a soft tone.

"So am I!"

"What happened by the pool?" Chryséis wanted to know.

"It was scary... we only tried to pick those red flowers and the next moment we were here." Her voice trembled a little. "I wanted to run - but then suddenly - we could no longer move."

"Good to have you back," Trevor said from behind, padding Katherine's shoulder. He had overheard what they were saying.

"I should never have touched those stupid red flowers. This elf..." she pointed her chin at Gump, "...scolded us like naughty children."

The forest guard stopped in front of a wall of clipped yew hedges.

"It's the entrance to fabled Arbôlimar," the captain murmured under his breath. The fairies fluttered around them giggling as the hedges moved apart to reveal a maze. Katherine planted herself on the white path.

"Can't you move? Did he do that spell thing again?" Trevor asked her.

Katherine's voice trembled. "No, no, that's not it. I'm just...I can't."

"What - go in there? Why not? It's the way to the palace. That's what we came here for." Chryséis looked confused.

"No way am I going into a maze and…get lost. If this elf feels like it, he'll just lock us in and close up the entrance. I've had enough of spells and moody elves," Katherine said stubbornly.

"But we've come this far. What else can we do? We must talk to the elf queen about the Speaking Stone," Trevor said.

"I can't explain it. But I just can't go in there," Katherine insisted.

"What's the holdup?" Gump asked impatiently and hobbled toward them. Captain Thëlamôn and Kheton stepped in front of the children and chatted to the forest guard to buy them some time. But no matter how much her friends tried to persuade her, Katherine would not move one step further.

"Katie, you can't just stay here. Remember, we must stay together." Chryséis could see that the forest elf looked increasingly impatient and even the little fairies had stopped giggling.

"Then come back to the beach with me," Katherine pleaded with them.

"We can't do that, the Lady of Cydonia is counting on us. The Speaking Stone is so important to everyone. We must try and get it back."

"Oh fiddlesticks! I don't care about a speaking stone or listening stone or whatever - and I don't like that crazy elf. I'll go back to the beach by myself and see you guys later."

Trevor and Chryséis looked helplessly at each other. Why did she have to be so damn stubborn?

"What's the holdup, little almost-elf person?" Gump repeated and pushed past the broad figure of the captain. "Come along, our queen must not be kept waiting."

Thëlamôn came to Katherine's defense. "Kathín is a mere child. Many an adult would feel queasy at such spells as yours."

When Gump glared at him, the captain added, "...which are very useful against evil giant intruders - to be sure. I'll best return to the beach with young Kathín and await your return. We have recutis in the boat."

"Well fine then," the elf snarled.

Turning to the others, Thëlamôn said in a low voice, "Just remember what I told you about the elf queen and her wine." They nodded imperceptibly.

"Can we get on with it then?" The forest guard jumped from one foot to the other. "Without the leader and the... girl if necessary."

Kheton looked worriedly at Lelani. She had closed her eyes and swayed a little.

"I can see that my wife is also weary. She should go with you, captain and rest awhile. We will manage on our own, won't we athenai?"

Chryséis and Trevor had no choice but to nod bravely.

"Kheton, I cannot leave you again," Lelani protested.

"My love, it is for the best. Just hand me the present for the elf queen. She will surely help us find the Speaking Stone and I will see you when we return from the audience."

Reluctantly, Lelani handed her husband the harp. It was only a tiny bit scratched from dropping to the ground earlier. Kheton now only had two children to his aid for their vital undertaking, but he decided not to show his disquiet.

"Yes your Highness, yes." Everyone looked at the elf, who seemed to be talking to himself.

"Queen Efinûr asks me to escort you back to the beach, captain," Gump announced with a theatrical sigh and bowed graciously in front of Kheton.

"I can't get away from him," Katherine mumbled unhappily.

"I will take you through the maze. Then you may enter Arbôlimar on your own," the forest guard told them. "Oh what a busy day I'm having."

"Shukri, sir Gump. For all your – effort." Kheton bowed

slightly back.

"You wait here with these ones until I'm back," the elf ordered the fairies and the small elf in a grumbling tone. "Let's move it then," he bristled and waved urgently.

Gump took his cap off that still had the bright-blue butterfly stuck to it, and the children could see that he indeed had pointy ears. Trevor winked encouragingly at Katherine, before she let go of Chryséis' hand.

"We will be seeing you later then, athenai. May Aïma and all the gods be with you,"Captain Thëlamôn said. Then Kheton and the children entered the leafy passageways of the maze. Gump accompanies them part of they way, so they would go in the right direction.

"Do you feel like playing a trick on the elf for a change?" Chryséis whispered after they had rounded a few corners. "For Katie?"

"Like what?" Trevor asked in a surprised tone.

"Like disappearing for a while." She winked and motioned to her VIC. Trevor just grinned and nodded.

"On my signal," Chryséis said and they pressed the VIC buttons. "Ooh Guhump, sir forest guard..." Chryséis coaxed.

Gump turned around and saw nothing, but he heard the children giggling.

"What, what is this, hey? Are you lost? Useless ragtag!"

He stormed past the two friends and they giggled even more. Gump turned a hedge corner and the children switched their VICs back on. Kheton might just turn around and be annoyed by their prank. Gump returned and they looked at him innocently. Kheton had not seen anything amiss.

"Where have you been you naughty children?"

"We were here all the time, sir Gump, you ran right past us. We wondered why."

"Oh, you! You are playing tricks on me!" The manikin thundered.

"Us? Never!" They tried to keep straight faces.

Gump stomped ahead of an astonished Kheton and they quickly reached the end of the labyrinth. A beautiful garden lay before them. Willows hung their branches into deep pools as clear as mirrors and brightly coloured peacocks strutted around the lawns, while parrots sat in the trees, croaking.

There were topiaries in the shapes of birds and deer and perfumed flowers lined the garden paths, where tiny hummingbirds circled plate-sized orange blooms. Trevor suddenly felt homesick, missing his quiet spot under the birch trees in the school garden at the Pemberton Academy.

"I'm leaving you now and will return promptly," Gump said abruptly and was gone in a flash behind the hedges of the maze.

Kheton was unmoved. "Oh, very well then. Let's go to the palace on our own." He began to walk on purposefully.

"Look at that!" Chryséis cried and pointed to the end of the path, where tall smooth trees formed the pillars of the palace, their branches bending over to form a roof with turrets and smaller domes. The sun's last golden glints reflected off the roof and translucent walls shone in bright colours, illuminated from within like an oversized lantern.

Kheton turned around to make sure that the children were still behind him. "When we stand before the elf queen, athenai, let me do the talking."

"Sure, no problem," Trevor said half to himself

Are you guys okay? Chryséis clearly heard Katherine's question in her mind. "Did you hear that?" she asked Trevor.

"Yes, it's Katherine." Trevor still couldn't believe his telepathic abilities.

Chryséis 'told' Katherine about their prank in the maze, the amazing garden, and that they were nearly at the palace.

Ha, perhaps I should have come with you after all. Just to see his face. Katherine had a good laugh. I'm already feeling better. We just got to the beach. The sailors caught some fish. They're looking at me funny.

Okay, stop laughing then. See you later alligator.

Kheton began to climb up the sweeping stairs.

In a while crocodile, Katherine answered in her thoughts.

Chryséis and Trevor had to snigger at Katherine's response and followed a puzzled Kheton through the dragonfly doors into a great hall with gleaming floors.

"Remember what the captain's said!" Trevor whispered urgently. "Better not touch anything. If something goes wrong, we get out of here."

"Ready when you are," Chryséis said.

Kheton cocked his head and listened to something.

"Maybe he's talking to Lelani and the captain," she whispered.

"Unless he's not under some kind of spell already."

"What are we gonna do, then?"

Trevor cleared his throat. When that didn't catch Kheton's attention, he nudged his elbow into the young man's side and at last, there was a reaction.

"Friend Trevór, it is rude to interrupt a thought transfer. Kindly be patient," he rebuked the boy.

"Good, he was not under a spell this time." Trevor winked at Chryséis. "I wonder what they're talking about."

Before the children could ask, palace elves ushered them to a low table in a bulging bay window. They sat down on chairs that were soft and yielding like large mushrooms.

The palace elves watched the visitors the entire time without speaking to them, but they didn't have to wait for long. A floral scent heralded the arrival of the petite queen.

She wore a yellow silky robe and a sparkling crown and was quite beautiful with her heart-shaped face and long black hair. Her dark eyes were large and slanted and she batted her eyelashes when she spoke.

"Welcome to Arbôlimar, valued visitors. Please feel at home in our humble forest abode," she greeted the guests in a captivating voice and batted her eyelashes.

"Greetings to you, Queen Elfinûr. I am Kheton of Cydonia."

Kheton bowed politely and introduced his companions. The elf queen nodded approvingly.

"The Lady of Kamûk sends her best regards. May we present your Highness with this humble gift?" He continued.

Kheton bowed again and held up the yellow songwood harp for the elf queen to examine. She gave a delighted cry and touched the instrument.

"So you haven't come to just take from us, but to bring me a lovely present? This is a very special gift indeed." She inclined her head in a childlike manner and clapped her hands before handing the harp to an attending elf.

"Yellow songwood, has the power to make those who listen weep and laugh." Queen Elfinûr spoke in a quivering voice and gave a quick jingling laugh. She touched Kheton's youthful chest with her dainty hand. He instinctively took a step back and put his hand on the hockey stick in his belt.

We have to be careful with this one, Chryséis transmitted to Trevor. She seems a bit crazy.

I'll say, he answered.

Kheton bowed carefully not to insult the queen. The queen took the harp again and strummed a little song. Then she handed the instrument back to the elf who took care not to drop the precious gift.

"I wish for the orchestra's harpist to use it in tonight's performance," she commanded. "Let's see how it makes the audience laugh and cry. " The palace elves all inclined their heads in agreement.

"We must speak to your Majesty," versuchte Kheton mit ihr zu reden.

"Soon, we'll have an opportunity for that," the elfin queen said and laughed. "Give my queenly thanks to the good Lady of Kamûk, Kheton of Cydonia. I shall much enjoy her gift. Now let's begin."

She clapped and waved toward a long table decked with crystal tableware and candlesticks and delicious-smelling food. Palace elves in long silken tunics hovered about, waiting for their whimsical queen's commands.

"Eat and drink and make merry with us tonight, visitors from far-off lands. Ah, I see that my other guests have arrived."

A number of fairies, fauns and elves approached. Queen Elfinûr took her seat at the head of the table and chatted and laughed with this one and that.

Kheton and the children were hungry and sat down on their chairs without protest. They passed on the crystalline wine offered in long-stemmed glasses. Instead, Trevor took out a can of peach-flavored iced tea he kept in his moonbag for emergencies and secretly shared the soft drink with Chryséis and a reluctant Kheton under the table.

It was the first time that they had used any of their precious rations they had brought from the future. Kheton awkwardly sipped the brown liquid from his glass and handed the can back to Chryséis .

"Shukri athenai. A drinkable liquid, but a rather foreign taste."

"We like it. It's better than drinking poisoned wine."

"Yes Chryséis, it is better indeed."

Trevor remembered to take photographs and moved his hand casually to his shirt pocket. The flash was hardly noticeable amid all the glitter of the banquet.

"Do you think it's safe to eat the food?"

Chryséis stared at the heaped plate in front of her. One of the palace elves served Kheton a glass with crystalline wine and Trevor put it immediately in front of the faun next to him, who chewed noisily on a crispy-fried bird leg.

"I don't know, but I'm really hungry and this looks really good."

"Kheton's already helping himself, so let's have some, too." Chryséis picked up a filled mushroom.

A wineglass was put in front of Kheton, who was distracted by the fairy next to him. He moved his hand to the glass, but Trevor saw it in time and took the wine glass away.

"If he's not careful, he'll make a mistake," Trevor said crossly. "He's supposed to take care of us not the other way around."

"I hope he doesn't forget why we're here."

"I'll remind him in a moment," Trevor said and ate some of the tasty stew.

Outside in the palace garden, a soft drizzle tapped against the domed roof and windows and moistened the plants. Soon the elf queen got up from the table and started the dancing with a round-bellied faun.

The children tried to concentrate on the sound of the rain, which helped against being lulled by the strangely moving music that had started playing. But the songwood harp worked its magic and a tear began to roll down Chryséis' cheek, then Trevor wiped away a tear as well.

Queen Elfinûr laughed and a pretty elf danced with Kheton. Soon he whirled around the hall with the forest creatures. Kheton seemed to enjoy himself a little too much. They had come here for a reason and it was not to dine and party.

We'd better do something now, Trevor thought and Chryséis nodded.

"Queen Elfinûr, Highness may we have word with you…please?"

Trevor's voice cut through the enchanting music. The guests looked up in surprise. This was very forward of the young stranger – to address the ruler of Ruta Ynis just like that, but the queen was in a good mood tonight.

"Soon child, soon. Enjoy the dance, amuse yourselves, then we will talk," she twittered.

The guests continued to spin dancing around the hall. Trevor saw that Chryséis began to sway to the melodious tunes and Kheton was holding hands with two enchanting elves.

Katie, what do I do? He communicated in thought with Katherine.

You have to do something. This has to stop right away, she communicated back. Again, Trevor's voice grated through the pleasant melody and the invisible orchestra stopped abruptly.

"We thank you…your Highness. Shukri, but we have to leave now."

Chryséis sobered at once, but it took Kheton a little longer. A trickle of sweat ran down the sides of his face and he breathed heavily. Maybe he felt hot in the hall with all those candles burning everywhere.

"Friend Trevór!" Kheton felt ashamed that the boy showed such bad manners, but the children weren't flustered.

"Kheton, the Speaking Stone," Chryséis prompted him. "We are here for the Speaking Stone…"

Kheton's eyes opened wide as he remembered why they had come to the palace of the elves. He straightened his tunic and took a deep breath as he remembered his duty.

"Forgive us, queen of Ruta Ynis," Kheton cleared his throat. "But we have come to ask a boon of your Highness."

The corner of the queen's mouth twitched and Kheton quickly continued. "Your Highness, we thank you for the excellent food and entertainment, but we must be on our way. We are merely servants of the Lady of Kamûk," he said slickly, gaining back his wits. "She commanded us to ask this from Lady to queen – and we must obey her."

His speech did the trick. Queen Elfinûr understood that servants had to obey orders. It wasn't any different in the elfin realm.

"What is it then that the Lady of Kamûk wishes of me?" she probed imperiously. The stranger was handsome and polite, but too serious and no fun at all.

"It is the 'Speaking Stone of Caradoc' we came for. One of the three true speaking stones still remaining in the Known World. It has been stolen."

An astonished murmur rose in the hall. A Speaking Stone!

"We came to Ruta Ynis, because the Lady of Kamûk has reason to believe that Edfunian thieves brought it here." There - it was out.

The queen looked annoyed. First the insolent boy, now this!

"And what makes you think that I know anything about this…this 'Speaking Stone', Cydonian?" the queen asked sharply.

Kheton was taken aback by her harsh tone, but he was a trained diplomat after all and kept his composure.

"We humbly ask for your help, so that the stone may be returned to its proper place in Caradoc — as we were ordered by the Lady of Kamûk." Kheton's voice was as smooth as silk. "Your Highness will agree that much evil may ensue, if a Speaking Stone falls into the wrong hands."

"Hmm, yes…" The royal mouth twitched.

"With the Edfunian giants turned into trees, we assumed that perhaps the Speaking Stone has been found on them…"

After a tense moment, Queen Elfinûr conceded. "The Lady of Kamûk and I seem to have the same goal," she said. "We must protect our realms from lawless creatures such as the Edfunians. I will help you where I can."

She felt kindly towards the handsome stranger, who now reminded her much of Talariêl, her true love. She smiled and clapped her hands.

"Truc, go and bring the moly flower to me this instant." There was a touch of madness in her tone. The attending elf shuffled away and returned in no time, carrying a small basket with the desired plant in it. It was a white flower amid long leaves.

"Ah, here it is. The precious moly flower with the power to protect against evil."

Truc delivered the basket to an astonished Kheton. The

moly flower was just closing its white petals for the night. The children looked confused and Kheton tried to hide his disappointment. A plant? How was he going to explain that he was bringing back a flower instead of the Speaking Stone of Caradoc?

"This may be what you are looking for…or not. But it is all I can do for you," the elf queen said offhand. She was growing bored with this serious business and decided to recite a riddle:

"The secret of the flower may be that
it whispers to you
    the truth that you desire."

The dinner guests applauded admiringly, which seemed to please her.

"Well done, your Highness." "Bravo." "Such elegant words."

"Ehem, shukri," Kheton stammered even more confused. "We thank you for your help and take now our leave, good queen."

There was nothing more the visitors could do or say. The audience was over.

"Yes, yes, it's nothing. If this is what makes you happy, go back to your ship and sail off to save the Known World. You won't forget to thank the Lady of Kamûk for her songwood harp, will you?" Queen Elfinûr sighed deeply. "This flower is very special. I trust you know its purpose…"

"Yes, yes I do and we thank you again."

Kheton knew of course about the moly flower's protective powers against 'obeah' or dark magic. But what did it have to do with the Speaking Stone? It was better not to ask her.

"Right, that's it then."

Trevor still stared at the plant and wondered how a flower, however special, might help them get the Speaking Stone back.

She clapped her hands one last time and graciously dismissed the disruptive visitors. Chryséis and Trevor bowed and followed Kheton to the dragonfly doors. Then the music resumed. The other dinner guests bowed to each other and continued to dance. Outside, night had fallen and Gump was waiting for them by the maze.

"There you are at last, there you are, heh?" Gump babbled grouchily. "What a nuisance those foreigners are. Don't I have better things to do? Like seeing to the wellbeing of the mushrooms by the river or the herbs in the meadow?"

Water drops that still sat atop the leaves showered on them from branches above as they negotiated the hedges of the maze and once outside, Gump carried on along the shining path through the dark forest without another word.

They passed the tormented Edfunians, and the leafy branches rustled sadly in the still air. In the bright moonlight, rhinestones dazzled inside the little stream and on the forest floor. The trees seemed to make space for them this time.

A faun, surrounded by a few fairies, sat on a rock by the pool close the beach and played his flute. He turned around and said, "ah, I see, you have received what you came asking for."

"What does a tootling faun know about that?" Gump muttered to himself and hurried on. The haunting tune followed them all the way to the beach.

Two little fairies, no larger than butterflies, fluttered unnoticed after them. Then suddenly, Gump was gone again.

Well, that was nothing new.

Soon they could see the 'Navis Arion' anchored in the small bay and a crackling fire was burning next to the boat on the pebbled beach. Fish were frying on sticks that were stuck into the ground.

When Kheton, Chryséis and Trevor reached the moonlit beach, Lelani jumped up and ran into Kheton's arms. Katherine and Lelani seemed quite recovered.

"You accomplished our mission then?" Lelani smiled

proudly at her husband then looked at the basket.

"I think so, I'm not sure."

Kheton held up the basket with the white flower and Lelani creased her forehead. "A flower?"

"A moly flower," Kheton explained and walked toward the fire place.

"Ah, there you are," captain Thëlamôn greeted them. "Come sit down, the fish are ready to eat. I'm sure that whatever you ate did not fill your tummies. Tell us all about the elf queen and her palace and what she had to say."

And so they told of the strange, gleaming palace and the garden full of colourful birds and flowers, and the slightly mad elf queen and the banquet. Soon they were all eating fried fish and drank from têrakhon water bottles.

"You took my advice and stayed off the crystalline wine, I see."

"But only just," Trevor said and blew on his steaming fish.

"And did she give you the Speaking Stone?" the captain wanted to know and pointed to the basket.

"She gave us a rare moly flower and said that this was what we were looking for," Kheton said haltingly and repeated the riddle.

"I see. Mad as she may be, the elf queen is surely as concerned about the Edfunians and their black magic as the rest of the Known World. Those foolish trees." The captain gave a guffaw. "Hah, she has a sense of humor - that queen. We'll leave at once for the ship and get some sleep. The riddle can wait until tomorrow." He said and extinguished the fire with some seawater.

Kheton helped Lelani climb into the boat and sat down next to her, carefully placing the basket between his feet. Three tired children and the captain followed them.

The two sailors pushed the boat into the water, jumped in and started pulling powerfully on the oars. The half-moon in the starry sky threw its bright rays on the rippling waves as they made their way back to the 'Navis Arion'.

In her palace Arbôlimar, Elfinûr sat alone in her enchanted garden long after the banquet. She watched the sun rise slowly in the east above the great tree tops. On a sudden whim she demanded Gump's, the forest elf's presence.

"Release the Edfunians from their tree spell." She clapped. "It is a bore to always entertain the same guests. I long for a different sort of entertainment today."

"But your Highness…"

"Gump!" Her voice left no room for backchat.

"Certainly, my queen. Your wish is my command."

The forest guard did not dare show his misgivings. The queen was in one of her moods again and it was better to do as she commanded.

"This should be interesting. Imagine the look on the Cydonian's face when the giants suddenly show up, hahahah." Her cruel laughter rang through the forest glades and Gump shrank into the foliage of the maze.

Elfinûr gleefully clapped her hands. "Oh just wait until the sea monster that roams the sea from Ruta Ynis to Daitya comes out to play a jolly game with their ships… Let's see who gets away and who doesn't. Evil giants or… maybe the Lady of Kamûk's servants?"

Spiteful fires glinted in her beautiful dark eyes. Then suddenly she changed to a more whistful tone. "Pity the nice-looking young man didn't linger. He resembled Talariêl so much, didn't he?"

But there was no answer. Gump had already gone to carry out the queen's command.

▶▶▶ 6 MONSTERS OF THE SEA

The moment the first sunrays appeared in the eastern sky, Captain Thëlamôn set sail for Atala. Katherine and Chryséis couldn't get away from Ruta Ynis fast enough. Moody elves weren't their cup of tea at all.

After breakfast, they settled on the couches below deck in the 'panorama room', looking out at the rising sun. The sea changed its shade slowly from dark grey to a dark turquoise colour as the ship slowly pulled out of the bay and settled on a steady course due east.

"Isn't it weird how we could all use telepathy on that island?" Trevor asked.

"I know, it's neat, but it probably won't last," Chryséis said.

"No, but we could practice it some more."

"Okay. We'll have time to do that in Algiras."

"I wish I could have seen the satyrs. Imagine monkey people with tails, who are smart and all," Trevor said. "There were none of them at the banquet."

"Hello, remember the captain told us that they don't like the elves? And they seem just as bad. So, please!" Katherine had no desire to meet any more inhabitants of this strange, magical island of Ruta Ynis.

"Think gorillas and chimpanzees. Okay, they don't have tails, but they are quite smart." Trevor just couldn't let it go.

"What's the fuss about anyway? Konks are far more interesting. Just like these sailors here." Chryséis pointed to one of the hairy crewmen, who tied some ropes outside on the deck.

"That's not the same," Trevor said stubbornly, but his friends had already lost interest in the subject.

Chryséis typed some notes on the palmtop and moved pictures from the elf palace around the screen. "Pity you took only 3 pics Trevor. Gump and the fairies would have been interesting."

"You didn't want me to take the camera at all, remember?"

Chryséis closed the palmtop computer and put it back in her daypack.

"Yeah, yeah."

"Do you think we'll get the Speaking Stone back now? I just don't quite understand what this white flower's has to do with it," Katherine said.

"Kheton and the captain are trying to figure it out."

"Why do elves have to be so difficult? The queen could have just given us the egg and be done with it. The Edfunians must have taken it with them when they got off their ship," Katherine surmised.

"Wonder why they went on land. That was a stupid thing to do. Now they are trees." Chryséis shrugged her shoulders and Katherine shook herself as she remembered the quivering trees.

"That's a good thing! Just thinking about that highpriest gives me the creeps."

"Hang on. She said that the moly flower protects against black magic - and she's basically on our side when it comes to the Edfunians. Why didn't I think about it before, it's so obvious!" Chryséis rolled her eyes.

"What's obvious?" Trevor didn't understand.

"Don't you get it? The basket!" Chryséis said excitedly.

"What about it?"

"I think she put the stone egg into the soil and planted the flower over it for protection."

"Get out of here," Trevor said.

"We talk to the captain. I mean, he and Kheton can't do more than laugh the idea off."

"Maybe they've already found it."

But they hadn't. The two men were still sitting in the top cabin, deep in conversation. Kheton looked up as they entered.

"Yes, young friends, do you want something?"

Captain Thëlamôn and Kheton listened attentively to what they had to say and then looked at each other. They had been guessing at some spell to be released, but it was worth a try. They carefully removed the soil from the basket, and soon Kheton wiped dirt off a shining white stone egg. The Speaking Stone!

"How very smart of you," the captain praised. "I shall let the Lady of Kamûk at once know how helpful you have been, athenai."

Not long after, Chryséis received a telepathic message from their old friend, the Lady of Cydonia. 'You have been of great help to us people of the Known World.'

'Yes Lady, thank you. Shukri. But Ruta Ynis was something else.' Chryséis communicated.

'I believe so. I'm pleased that all went well. The wise Speaking Stone will be back in Caradoc soon. I wish you a magnificent voyage to Atala, athenai.'

The Navis Arion made swift progress as wind conditions were favourable on this crisp morning. The crew was in high spirits, but little did the sailors know what was about to happen next.

A sea monster, a massive Tylosaurus, had as usual been dozing on his favorite smooth rock after the nightly meal. The sun warmed his long body with its notched fins all along the back right down to the pointed tail, while small seabirds picked clean his long sharp teeth. This part of the ocean was his undisputed territory.

No other Tylosaurus or any monster would come near this stretch of the sea, if he valued his health. The saurian flicked his scaly tail lazily, when out of the blue his single-minded reptilian brain was tickled by the elf queen's call. 'Attack, attack, attack.'

It soon felt too prickly for comfort. Stretching his back legs one last time, the fearsome Tylosaurus hurled himself into the waves and headed for another rock.

In the water, the monster sensed the Navis Arion's humming motion, the slight creaking of wood and hissing of the rigging. Then there was a faint noise that seemed to follow the first one at a distance, and the Tylosaurus changed direction.

"Course three knots south," Captain Thëlamôn ordered and the ship slowed down somewhat, while the crewmen took in one of the sails.

"Look at these rocks." Katherine pointed to a few smooth stone ledges jutting out of the water. The largest rock was the sea monster's preferred resting place.

"Dangerous, in the middle of nowhere like that," Trevor said.

"I'm sure the captain knows what he is doing and we're not on the Titanic."

The mighty dragon was still a good few lengths away from the schooner, when a rare giant squid decided to give the large wooden shell a try. The ever-hungry squid flung itself at the vessel and embraced it with 20-foot tentacles, suctioning onto the solid planks. The squid's beak was strong enough to crack open the toughest of shells and it tried to find the right spot to gnaw through the wood.

"Ho, what's that? Something is stuck to the hull. Activate ray-shield!" Thëlamôn ordered.

"Aye aye, Captain."

But before sailor Fenrik could do so, he found himself crouching against the cabin wall, the air knocked clear out of his lungs. The Navis Arion hung lopsided with the starboard rudder in the air and captain Thëlamôn clung to the cabin door for dear life, while trying to reach the instrument controls.

"Woaah, what's happening? Help!" Under deck, Chryséis flailed her arms, trying to sit and ended up on top of Katherine.

Trevor rolled along the floor under the seat by the opposite window.

"Chris, you are sitting on my back!" Katherine cried.

"I'm trying to get off." Chryséis struggled onto the floor that wasn't where it was supposed to be.

Then suddenly, the ship began to rock from side to side. The squid's weight pulled on the other side of the hull, dragging it dangerously low. One of the tentacles groped along the planks, then another. The men on deck tried to hold onto railing and tackle, seawater spattering all over them.

They murmured and shouted out prayers to the sea gods Tiamat and Nereus and all his daughters. Captain Thëlamôn crawled along the tilted floor in the captain's cabin, gasping for breath and still unable to activate the security shield that would emit electric shocks. he was worried that the vessel might catch water and capsize any moment now.

The children were helplessly piled on top of the panorama cabin's door, sobbing and moaning, while the cabin boy held onto a cupboard, beside himself with fear.

The sea dragon reached the ship. But what was this? A giant squid was hanging onto the vessel. Oh no, not in his territory! Forgotten was the niggling noise. It was monster against monster now.

With a mighty roar, the Tylosaurus dug his enormous jaws into the soft squid, pulling and tearing away at it. The fatally wounded squid let go of the ship and tried to wrap its tentacles around the dragon's body in one last desperate effort, then it died, tinting the seawater an ugly black colour.

The ship thudded promptly back into an upright position like a child's toy, throwing its occupants roughly around once again. Wing-like fins waved limply amid lifeless tentacles that began to drift slowly down to the bottom of the sea. The sea dragon fought to bite suction cups off his back and in a heart stopping moment, the crewmen saw the Tylosaurus rearing up and splash back into the sea. The ensuing waves sent the Navis Arion bobbing up and down.

"Aaaah!" One hapless sailor lost his grip and got himself knocked overboard by a thrashing notched tail. With his last bit of strength the man grabbed hold of knotted ropes by the hull's side.

"Hold on, hold on!" His mates stumbled to the railing and swiftly hauled the man out of the water. They were just in time.

Whipping up one last wave, the sea monster turned away and tried to make off back to his rock, a large piece of squid in his mouth. But it wasn't over yet. The terrified crew caught a glimpse of jaws with protruding teeth in a massive grey head.

A great shark wanted a share in the possible feeding frenzy.

"Holy Earthmother." The seasoned sailors watched the new danger weak at the knees.

The water seethed in red, foamy confusion, but the greedy shark was no contest for the furious Tylosaurus. He let go of the squid and ripped off the shark's head. Still frothing and snapping, it floated to the surface. A long row of pointed fins circled the gruesome object before taking off with the shark's writhing body.

Captain Thëlamôn was back on his feet in a flash, his ribs and left arm aching and a cut gaping on his square jaw. He reached for the hockey stick weapon in his belt, but another sailor was already pointing his weapon at the bloody melee. Death rays missed their target over and again. The captain ignored the pain he was in and acted quickly: there was only one thing to do.

His bruised hand touched the dials on the board and the ship's propulsion system sprang on with a shudder, carrying the Navis Arion above the water surface swiftly east.

This wasn't the worse sea monster attack he had ever witnessed, but a rather unexpected one. The experienced seaman heaved a sigh of relief. The damage was not too bad and he had not lost a single soul. The Earthmother be thanked.

"Wha...what was that?" Trevor was still stunned.

Frightened stiff, the time travellers struggled up and held white-knuckled unto the built-in furniture of the panorama cabin. The cabin boy stuck his head out from under one of the upholstered seat, promising the Earthmother and Nereus never ever to take food again from the kombuis when the cook wasn't looking.

"Ouch, my head hurts." Katherine felt a bump on her forehead.

"A sea...monster? Roaring..."

Chryséis still couldn't get a proper word out.

Thankfully, the three friends had only seen a glimpse of the shark's head, while they battled to find their bearings, but the roars, the splashing and creaking of wood had been enough to make their blood freeze.

Katherine's head hurt terribly and blood trickled down her forehead, her hand was probably broken although she couldn't feel much. Chryséis was holding her knee that had swollen to the size of a grapefruit. Only Trevor seemed unhurt thanks to the fact that had wrapped himself into a thick feather duvet he had found under one of the seats.

They stayed below deck only to be checked on by a pale and trembling Kheton until the ship pulled lopsided into the little seaport of Dweepa on Daitya Island. Their guardian dished out generous amounts of recutis from the ship's supply cupboard and took a large swig of the liquid himself, before taking the bottle to Lelani.

The Navis Arion steered past three ships along the pier, before it anchored. Soon crew and passengers sat quietly inside the harbour master's building, wrapped in woolen blankets, slurping hot fish broth and tucking into platters of wholesome fish dumplings. The dumplings were smothered in a sweet and salty brown sauce, an Atlandian specialty called 'garum'. Chryséis had picked at her garum-covered food at first, but too hungry to be picky, now ate her third dumpling greedily.

Katherine put her soup bowl down and wiped her mouth with the sleeve of her tunic. "Ah, that was good. I thought I'd never live to see food again."

The bump on her forehead was almost gone after the treatment and Chryséis' knee was just a bit bruised now.

"I think I've never heard anything so scary. What was that awful roaring? It couldn't have been a whale. The 'Nessie' with the long neck didn't make any sound at all. That thing out there was something else and definitely much larger."

"I think the captain wasn't lying when he told us about sea monsters."

"Right now, I don't want to know about it. I'm just glad we're alive." Chryséis padded her knee. "Unbelievable how quickly that's healing."

"Yes, my headache is also gone and my hand's fine." Katherine wriggled her wrist this way and that. "See?"

The harbour physician was busy treating the sailors with a handheld device and soon the harbour master's building resounded with lively discussions.

"I'm telling you it was a dragon. A monstrous dragon. If it wasn't for the shark, he would have eaten the whole ship with everyone in it." One wide-eyed sailor recalled the fearsome sight as he was clinging to the rigging.

"Yes, but the squid could have fed an entire city for a fortnight."

"Nay, those monsters don't taste nice. A friend of mine tried to fry a giant tentacle once. His crew found such a dead squid on the beach. Rotten taste, I can tell you."

"They forgot the lemon juice and spices, haha."

Everybody laughed.

"I have never heard of such attacks in broad daylight," captain Thëlamôn said quietly to the harbour master, worry in his voice. "Something's amiss here, for sure. Something's terribly amiss," the old man said in his broad Daityan twang. "I'll be damned. The samonster has never attacked like that and in broad daylight. Not in my lifetime have I heard of such thing."

"You think it might be obeah? Ouch!" The captain stretched out his arm to give the harbour physician a chance to heal his injuries. The physician moved the healing device slowly over the brawny arm.

"If I just knew. Nereus and Tiamat be thanked that you got away and the 'Speaking Stone' is safe." The harbour master drew smoke from his pipe.

"Yes, Nereus and Tiamat be thanked," Captain Thëlamôn said. "But what I want to know is, which enemy would set sea monsters on my ship. I'd give him a taste of his own witchcraft."

"Ah, Thëlamôn you want nothing to do with obeah, trust me. The attack may have just been coincidence. A mystery we cannot explain."

"We should give thanks to the gods, now. Our duty must not be neglected. Let's go and light incense at the Nereus temple, good men."

The harbour master grumbled his assent and the two of them strolled down the pier side by side, followed by some of the sailors. By the following morning the ship had been repaired and the wounds were healed. The precious Speaking Stone of Caradoc lay in a wooden box, cushioned with Daityan sheep's wool and soft velvet.

It was safely guarded by one of the sailors as the Navis Arion continued her voyage to Atala.

It didn't take long, before they approached the main island of Atland.

Around the same time, another ship, smaller than the Navis Arion, docked not far from the territory of the Little People on Atala's western coast.

Close to the rocky coast, half-sunken harbour buildings had been abandoned since before the Dark Age. It was a secret spot. Gigantic walls bordered on a small lagoon, home to a handful of merpeople. It was here that the bewitched crew and gloomy giant passengers of the ship disembarked and were welcomed into a colossal ruin, said to have once been inhabited by the 'Great Ones'.

Surrounded by bubbling hot mud pools and their sulphuric mists, the giants' abode would be fairly safe from detection.

"Why - by Xipe Xolotle - did the shark not smash their ship to smithereens? The spell has worked before!" the stooped leader of the Gabari thundered. He stomped up and down the long hall and his followers shrank back in fear.

"But sire, the Speaking Stone is aboard that ship…"

"Yes, yes, yes. It's for the best this way, I know. And we delayed them as planned."

The leader wiped back his untidy hair and sat his heavy bulk down on one of the stone seats. The other Gabari didn't dare move.

"Those elves and their rotten tree spell! But I showed the squealing little forest guard. Should have turned each and every one of them into frogs. Along with those troublesome foreign children! Damn nuisance!"

He banged his fist onto the stone table in the ruined hall.

"Sire… you need not concern yourself with children. We should not draw attention…," the bravest of the giants cautioned him haltingly.

"Ah, right you are. We will hide out here - nay - rest for a while. Then we'll return home victoriously with all the wisdom of a speaking stone on our side, to take our rightful place in the Known World once again. We'll show those wheedling worms who's still in charge!"

"And we shall, sire, we shall."

That day, a hapless deer that had been grazing too close to the hot mud pools found a swift end in the great fireplace in the hall. Farther south, the first thing the time travellers saw was a brilliant system of countless suspension bridges, connecting other remnants of the ancient continent of Atland with the nearby Atala.

Captain Thëlamôn navigated the Navis Arion through a narrow passage, before the ship passed under a number of bridges on its way to Algiras, the capital of Atala, and center of administration of the Known World. Due to a warm ocean current flowing, called 'The Wheel', around Atland's north, the climate was quite mild.

"That's so amazing!" Katherine stared at a red bridge suspended from great pillars raking the sky. "There are people up there and vimaans."

Moments later they passed under the bridge joining the island of Tamoanchan or the 'Place of Flowers' and Atala.

Perched against a steep cliff projecting from the rocky Atalian shore, was a village called Poseidonis.

Homes and roads on the upper levels could only be reached by stairs and stepladders. An interesting sight. Then as the ship rounded the southern Pandora peninsula, a massive seawall jutted up from the rocks and guided them all the way to the harbour entrance.

"Whoa!" Trevor was truly impressed. "Those are big stones."

"The seawall was built before the Dark Age by the 'Great Ones'." Lelani was giving the children a last minute lesson about Atala, based on what she had seen in mirages and read in books.

All the while the Navis Arion sailed toward the harbour entrance taking care not to get in the way of other ships.

"Atala is named after its white cliffs in the south. It means the 'Shining One'", Lelani told them eagerly. "Vast prairies are home to great beasts and cover much of the interior. The nomadic Leni Lepi and Nazhuatl tribes roam the countryside and hunt game. Purple heather and pink and white cosmos cover the plains for much of the year. It looked very beautiful in the mirage."

"What about the rest of the island?" Katherine asked and Chryséis shot her an impatient glance. Don't ask her so many questions or we'll be here tomorrow morning, she transmitted to Katherine vehemently, but couldn't be sure that her friend had actually heard her thought. It had been easier in Ruta Ynis.

"The cool rivers and lakes in the northwest teem with trout, eel and salmon."

Lelani had to think for a moment. "Thick pine forests grow into the Ourala Mountains to the far north. Highland mists often hide the tallest summits, the Smoking Woman and the Sleeping Giant." She tried to remember more details. "Tribes of wildmen and pygmies found a home in spacious caves in the mountains. Some say that large saurians still roam remote parts of the northern valleys of Fomor. It is not impossible. A few of the uninhabited islands are home to great lizards and feared by the local fisher folk."

"Oh, that's some place I will not go to then," Katherine said firmly.

"No, definitely not," Chryseis agreed.

"Sorry, what did she say?" Trevor asked. He hadn't been listening.

"There are dinosaurs in the northern mountains. Why don't you listen?"

Lelani could see the images of the instruction mirage in front of her inner eye. Years of training had sharpened her memory.

"Guanchis, who speak in a curious bird language, live in the valleys of the foothills by the vineyards of Gaswyn, the wineland. Most of Atala's fresh produce comes from this area with its central city of Challamdor and the river Triton. The Cercenes Peninsula and the mangrove forests of the Tritonides marshland are in the east."

The young Alesian woman was satisfied with her effort to educate the foreign children. She could have told them that beyond the Tritonides, the Gadiric Sea spread right up to the 'Passage of the Golden Pillars' and the warm Blue Sea and that along the western mainland, the Strait of Caldera connected the Gadiric Sea with the Gulf of Morbihan.

But she didn't want to bore them with too much detail and, in any case, it was time for her to find Kheton. Lelani had always imagined standing on deck with Kheton by her side, watching the statue of Atlas, while sailing into the harbour.

"Shukri, thank you friend Lelani. That was a very…ehem…precise description of Atala," Katherine said politely.

"It is my pleasure, athenai. You are making this voyage to learn more about our Known World after all."

"Just look at that over there! Is that a statue?"

Trevor pointed to a large bronze head that grew larger and larger. There was no answer. Lelani had already left the panorama room and was on her way to the deck. An outstretched arm with its bronze palm turned out appeared, but most of the statue was still hidden by the seawall.

"Impressive!" Katherine pushed her nose against the large window and the others laughed.

"What?! Let me stare, guys. I don't get to see Atlantis every day."

She wanted this so much to be Atlantis. Just imagine! "I wish Lelani had told us more about the city. I mean look at this." Every hill in sight was covered in streets and houses. Shining onion-shaped roofs and spires, stood out starkly against the grey sky above the seawall.

"Come on, let's watch this from the deck!" Trevor stood up abruptly and they all followed Lelani upstairs.

Kheton was proud of his young friends this morning. The mission to find the 'Speaking Stone of Caradoc' had been accomplished with the children's help. The sacred moly flower, famous for its protective powers against black magic, would keep thieving 'Evil Ones' at bay for a while.

"Shelanti, my husband." Lelani's voice woke Kheton from his daydream.

"Ah, my beautiful wife, come join me. Isn't this most beautiful?"

The young couple stood closely together, admiring the view of Algiras. The three time travellers tried to get a better look by standing closer to the railing. "Did you hear that growl?" Katherine pricked her ears and the others listened. A large ball became now visible that the statue carried on its shoulders. A globe.

"That's no growl, that's thunder," Trevor stated. They noticed how the grey sky had disappeared behind a heavy veil of dark clouds.

"Crikey!" Katherine cried when they heard another faint thunderclap.

"Have no fear, we are nearly there," Captain Thëlamôn called to them over his shoulder.

The Navis Arion would offload cargo and take water of life distilled from exotic fruits, aboard in Algiras. Ogygia was the next port of call before the ship took the 'The Wheel' ocean current back to Alesia. The captain was content with his achievements and his official duties would end here. The mission on behalf of the Lady of Kamûk had been brought to quite a successful end.

The massive bronze statue arched over the harbour entrance now. The captain had seen many times how the massive bronze legs were anchored firmly with each foot on a dressed ashlar. A viewing platform ran along the statue's metal hemline and perhaps he would be able to view the sea from up there this time around.

"Now that's what I call a statue!" Trevor stood gaping up at the bronze Atlas in wonder, while holding onto the ships railing.

"Does that remind you of something?" Chryséis' neck was beginning to hurt.

"What, the statue?" Katherine asked not moving one inch.

Their ship passed under the shadow of the statue and into the harbour. People on the viewing platform were still waving to the passing ships, but most of them got ready to leave. They didn't want to get caught in the rain the thunder was already announcing.

"Yes, of course the statue!" Chryséis couldn't believe that the penny hadn't dropped yet.

"Statue of Liberty?" Katherine tried.

"The 'Colossus of Rhodes'?!" Chryséis said impatiently.

Of course Katherine knew about the Greek statue that had fallen into the sea during a massive earthquake. "There were other statues like that before the Statue of Liberty in New York?" she joked.

"Yes, of course." Chryséis pulled a face and watched how garishly painted sculptures of animals were unloaded onto the docks from an odd-looking ship with sails like yellow fish fins.

"Was it as big as this one?" Trevor asked.

"How must I know?" Chryséis answered.

"I don't think so." Katherine still stared at the colossal statue, they were leaving behind. "Maybe it was in fashion for big harbours to have bronze statues at some stage."

"Sure, it's possible. Just that at Aztlan and Kamûk didn't have such statues at all," Trevor said.

"Mmhm, so much for my theory."

"Take a picture, Trev," Chryséis demanded excitedly.

"Just now. We're still too close".

Lightening cracked across the sky and the children jumped. The Navis Arion moved steadily toward the docks, when all of a sudden rain began to pelt the harbour, sending everybody running for cover.

"Where is the 'Wall of Three Ways'? I can't see it!" Lelani asked excitedly when they had settled again in the panorama room.

The 'Wall of Three Ways' was one of the oldest Algiran monuments. Made from crystal, copper and silver-plated stone, the walls met in the middle of the town.

"Not in this rain. We have much time to explore the metropolis…" Kheton gently squeezed Lelani's arm.

Through the wet curtain they could only see rows upon rows of storehouses. Under broad têrakhon roofs, transport vimaans were loaded and unloaded and the dockworkers hardly missed a beat. A broad promenade led away from the docks along the seawall and then into town. Double-storied shops were just behind the storehouses and pieces of washing were hanging on balconies to dry.

"Oh no, some housewives will be angry," Katherine sighed. "Maybe it rains here often. Just look at all those see-through roofs."

"And look at that bird!" Chryséis pointed to a group of children on the quay. Their pet, a tall heavyset bird like a giant ostrich, was tied to a pole next to a cooking house. Their parents were busy buying steamed dumplings inside. Two boys played with a large brown millipede poking it with sticks, while an older girl stroked the bird's plumage.

The insect was as large as a sausage and unrolled itself from a tight spiral whenever left alone for a while. The bird clucked and pecked at crumbs on the ground, shaking off occasional raindrops. The boys soon grew tired of their game and let the bird have its snack.

"Ho, move along shore. Lower anchor and fasten ship!" Captain Thëlamôn shouted and the ship came to a halt against the dock.

The usual delegation of officials was drenched and only now began to assemble under the dock roof to welcome the visitors from Alesia. Their welcome song was drowned out by the pouring rain and the dignified officials soon gave up.

"Welcome to Algiras honourable visitors. May I take this from you?"

A senior maiden called Jostia, officially received the basket with the sacred moly flower and the 'Speaking Stone of Caradoc'. The wooden box inside the basket was quickly secured in a protective transparent sphere.

Jostia decided that there was time for formalities later. They all hurried towards two citadel vimaans, while Lelani's heavy luggage was taken to a transport vehicle.

"Ah, it's clearing up quite properly," the maiden announced and the rain subsided gradually as the vimaans took the glistening wet promenade into town. They floated above deserted avenues and clean-swept squares usually teeming with people. The first square they passed through was decorated with a huge red coral mounted on a marble pedestal.

"Looks like a leafless red tree," Chryséis said.

Behind the coral was a terraced building covered in slabs of polished dark green stone and topped with a squat see-through tower. Small vimaans flew in an out of a high-lying platform by the tower.

"Dear maiden Jostia, may I ask what this building is?" the maiden explained proudly.

"I see, friend Lelani, you have an eye for the extraordinary. This building is the 'House of Etheric Science', the greatest research facility of science in the Known World. One of its recent achievements is the discovery of how to amplify thought power with crystals."

"I see." Lelani looked dumbfounded.

"Our most popular tourist attraction, the 'Wall of the Three Ways' can unfortunately not be seen from here. But I shall be happy to show you the monument on another occasion."

"Thank you dear maiden," Lelani said politely, hiding her excitement.

"Next to the green building is the city's main library or 'House of Knowledge'. As can be seen by the white statue with scrolls under his arm," Jostia continued.

"What's that other thing in front of the building?" Chryséis whispered.

"I can't see properly," Katherine whispered back.

As the citadel vimaans turned the corner, the broad frieze carved along the pink marble front continued on the side of the elegant building. Inlaid with copper and silver, it showed people in tunics studying books. Trevor turned in around in his seat to get a better look.

"We definitely have to see the library. Definitely."

Chryséis was especially intrigued by trees that were lining streets.

"They are pruned like giant broccoli," she said so that Jostia couldn't hear her.

"Yes, you're right," Katherine laughed. "Looks just like broccoli."

Next they passed a building with bulging green and blue balconies in the shape of waves. People started to populate the streets again and the vimaan floated uphill just as the sun broke through the thinning clouds.

"Oh, that's so pretty!" Lelani cried and gazed at the building as long as she could. The seawall marked by a white lighthouse became visible through a row of flowering frangipani trees.

"The eastern side of the harbour is reserved for artisans' workshops."

Jostia pointed to a row of colourful box houses atop an

embankment not far from the street. They looked down the embankment and saw sailing boats and fishing skiffs rocking gently in a see-saw motion in a smaller harbour basin. There were also artificial canals with houses and landings.

"Looks like Venice!" Katherine said.

"More like Palm Beach," Chryséis corrected her.

A screen of feathery bottlebrush flowers left and right of the street they were on, swayed softly in the breeze. Half-moon shaped 'apartment' buildings came next, with stairs curving along the outside were grouped around a small central square with water features and benches between palms and red hibiscus bushes.

"What a beautiful city," Lelani praised and wished that Kheton wasn't riding in the vimaan ahead of them. She sent a brief message to him and felt better. Kheton also admired the view.

"Once a freak tidal wave swept away such buildings closer to the water's edge. Tragic!" Jostia shuddered, while she told the story. "The gods of the sea sometimes demand more substantial offerings than incense and flowers."

"Does this happen often?" Trevor asked anxiously.

"No, not often. But what can be done against the will of the gods?" The maiden's story drifted to ancient times. "During the Dark Age, the bad time, people found shelter in high-lying caves," She said. "Despite the terrible loss of life, the ancient inhabitants of Atland clung to a civilised way of life. The few remaining 'Speaking Stones' have been invaluable in preserving celestial laws. But people suffered much in those times. Raw fish, roots and seaweed was their only diet — ugh!" Jostia stroked the transparent sphere protecting the 'Speaking Stone of Caradoc'.

The vimaan kept winding its way up the slope. Sprawling villas were surrounded by generous green gardens with red bougainvillea flowers spilling over garden walls. Just like in Cydonia, the capital city of Alesia, where their journey back in time had begun.

"Cydonia is so far away." Lelani sighed deeply.

"The city of Challamdor is very much like Cydonia," a cheerful Jostia assured her. "You can visit the interior soon, no doubt, and it will feel almost like home."

Lelani quietly wiped away a tear. "Yes, no doubt," she said politely, trying to ignore a pang of homesickness.

▶▶▶8 THE PYRAMID CLOCK

By the ruins on the western coast, an Edfunian warrior arrived back with bad news. "Sire, our spies in Algiras have been discovered." He stared at a scorpion making its way down the broken wall.

"Amah!" the stooped man, he had addressed as sire, bellowed angrily. "Useless lot! Did you make short shrift of them? They must not expose our plans."

"Yes sire, I did. We were not found out."

"The animal sacrifice did not please Xipe Xolotle then. He will desert us, his devoted servants, if we don't do better in future." He snorted contemptuously in the direction of a pile of skin and bones, leftovers from the deer they had recently roasted on a spit.

"Yes, sire."

"If we just had giant tarantulas, the messengers of the Red One, to aid us with the sacrifice — I heard they live in the mountains - you!" The Highpriest of Shuruk roughly yelled at one of the giant warriors. After a short exchange, the man left in a hurry.

"All is not lost, sire. The Speaking Stone has been delivered to the citadel. Alas, it is much better guarded now and will be on the move again soon. The Lady wants to send the stone back to Caradoc within a phase of the moon. That much, we still found out."

"We should enlist the help of our cruel friends from Hesperus, then. They are unbeatable at sea," the sorcerer mused before his fist came thundering down on the stone table. "First, Xipe Xolotle needs a better offering or our undertaking is doomed!" he bellowed. "We cannot wait until full moon this time around."

"Yes, sire. The lagoon is swarming with Ioannu. They have no inkling of their new neighbours." The messenger chuckled maliciously.

"No, no, no, far too dangerous, man. Those squeaking fish people may raise the alarm. A powerful beast from the prairies - or two - will surely please his godhood and bless our plans."

"Sire, the Leni Lepi are moving into their hunting grounds as we speak."

"Then we will give them a reason to move out again."

"Yes, sire. As you wish." The giant bowed.

"Ari-sūdana!"

*

"I look totally goofy!" Trevor pulled down the brim of his hat. Algirans wore sunhats made of straw and Kheton had given Trevor a hat to help him blend in. After the great rain that had greeted them in the harbour a few days ago, the blistering sun had not given rain clouds another chance.

"I think you look more like Huckleberry Finn. If you look goofy, then everybody else here does too," Katherine assured him.

"Like Huckleberry Finn?" He asked.

"Ja, wie Huckleberry Finn."

"That's not so bad then."

"Exactly," Chryséis said. "Can we go now?"

The thin veils the girls had bought in Aztlan came in handy now. Many Algiran women wore such veils as sun protection.

If not needed, they were simply tied up. The sunglasses, however useful, drew quite a bit of attention, and the children stopped wearing them after a while. As in Cydonia, people stayed indoors during the hot hours of the day. The city came back to life in the early afternoon when everyone who didn't have anything better do was trekking down to the beaches. They'd had only sunshine after the bad rainstorm and that's where they were probably headed again today.

Kheton and Lelani had moved into a two-story apartment in a complex together with the children in their care. Bamboo roofs gave their shade outdoors in the enclosed courtyard with its trees, flowers and colling fountains. The three time travellers were loafing around on sofas and had to remind themselves constantly that they were in the past, nearly12,000 years before their own time.

"This place is so damn cool! Feels like a modern city, just like Cydonia," sagte Trevor.

"Yes, without all the noise and exhaust fumes and stuff," Chryséis agreed with him.

"And no crime. It's so safe here."

"Who knows, maybe one day our cities back home will be like that too."

"Listen to you! Isn't the future supposed to be more modern?" Katherine scoffed.

"Come guys, let's go out." Chryséis loved to explore the city.

They had already taken a trip across the suspension bridge to the artificial island of Sveta to spend a few hours visiting the remnants of a historic sunken village and the Svetan aquarium. Together with other tourists they had fed a giant tarpon with small string herrings.

It would take weeks to see everything there was to see in Algiras, but they had to go and see the 'Garden of Civilisation', a large park, close to their apartment complex. Apparently a fascinating step pyramid stood right in the middle of the park. It was the major prytaneum of Algiras and some sort of a clock at the same time.

"Kheton said we shouldn't go out on our own," Katherine cautioned.

"But he's at the citadel today and Lelani has gone out."

"Oh, did I forget to tell you? He's sending somebody from the citadel again to show us the city," Trevor said and Chryséis sniggered.

"Oh, Trevor, you're getting old."

"I'm not!"

"Just kidding." She looked outside. "I think that must be him. When you speak of the devil...It's Gillead of Algiras again."

"He's nice, I like him," Katherine said and giggled a little.

"Shelanti athenai." A young man stepped under the bamboo roof and smiled broadly.

"Shelanti Gillead." Katherine giggled.

"Are you ready to go for a walk?"

"Yes, friend Gillead, we would like to see the 'Garden of Civilisation' first, please."

"The 'Garden of Civilisation' it is, athenai." Gillead quite enjoyed this temporary assignment as a guide to the foreign children. But he knew that the Lady of Algiras could summon him at any moment for a more serious task.

There were a few cobble-stone stairs to climb, past sun-bleached limestone walls and red tiled roofs. From here, one had a spectacular view. The farmland surrounding the great metropolis looked like a tapestry of colours above the glowing rooftops and as a backdrop, the turquoise Gadiric Sea shone in the distance.

Vimaans were whizzing around buildings and the gleaming bronze colossus Atlas with his outstretched arm looked so close.

"This is so great!" Chryséis sighed and paused a moment to admire the view. Click. Trevor had already taken a picture.

Gillead sauntered past a fountain in the shape of a charging bull before turning into the park entrance. Atalians seemed to adore anything to do with cattle and especially bulls. Herds of cattle grazed on fields inside the city walls and beef from the isle of Bovinia was praised for being especially tender. Even some wall mosaics in town bore the images of charging bulls.

"Nice park," Trevor marvelled. "Look at these plants. Maybe it's a botanical garden."

They hadn't seen bushes with big round red leaves yet or orange-flowering flame trees. On the way to the impressive pyramid, they strolled past people who were picnicking and playing games on the lawn.

Three girls were kicking a ball around. When it came flying at Katherine, she tried to kick the ball back and got caught up in her veil.

"Haha," Trevor laughed.

"Hey, I'm not David Beckham, am I?" Katherine said annoyed.

She stuffed the veil into a woven straw bag she was carrying.

"Yes, Huckleberry, don't be nasty," Chryséis came to her defense.

"Are you two ganging up on me now or what?"

"Come make haste, athenai," Gillead called over his shoulder.

He was ahead of them and had missed the whole thing. They hurried to join him at the foot of the pyramid.

"It looks a lot like a South American pyramid," Chryséis cried, forgetting that their guide didn't understand English. Some people looked around and laughed. Gillead graciously ignored the foreign gibberish.

"Come closer, athenai." He waved them toward him.

"Trevor where's the camera?" Chryséis whispered.

"Don't worry, already done." Trevor moved his hand from his shirt pocket.

The platform on top of the pyramid was enclosed in blue latticework and shaded by a Chinese-looking roof. Inside the lattice walls, the eternal fire of civilisation flickered in a large golden bowl. Two millstone-sized disks, one was golden and one silver, were mounted behind the golden bowl. At the foot of the monument, on each corner, stood one Gabari guard with a hockey stick in his broad fabric belt.

"It's almost like the prytaneum at the citadel in Cydonia!" Katherine said surprised.

"Yes almost." Trevor shook his head. "Apart from just

about everything but the metal disks. Did you see a pyramid anywhere in Cydonia?"

"You can be such a smart alec sometimes!"

"Why are there guards Gillead?" Chryséis asked their guide quickly to prevent a squabble.

"After the turbulent lawlessness of the Dark Age, it has become a tradition to protect this holy place."

Gillead also told them that this grand monument served as a giant calendar and pointed to the top.

"The 52 steps, leading up to the platform, stand for one sheaf of years and there are 366 yellow stone blocks for the days of the year. The current day and month are marked with a blue and red stone block on the current step."

"Hang on, 366 days of the year?" Katherine asked wide-eyed.

"Yes, of course. Every morning before sunrise, a Gabari guard moves the day block to its next position on the stairs and the month block if there is a change. At the beginning of each year, 4 yellow markers are moved on each corner of the new step. For every full sheaf of years, a smaller white block is placed on top."

Trevor counted. There were 13 of such white blocks.

"This month is called the 'Month of the Ripening Grain' and it is the 5th day of the month."

"Complicated system, but I guess it works."

"It works very well, friend Chryséis," Gillead assured her.

"But you cannot come here every day to check the position of the blocks if you want to know the date."

"No, of course not," Gillead laughed and Katherine giggled.

"We have miniature pyramids in public places all over town. But it is not necessary to know the passing time every day."

Chryséis looked at her watch. "Perhaps not, but it's helpful."

They hadn't noticed these mini-pyramid-calendars yet.

"Would you like to go to the beach now?" Gillead asked, tipping his straw hat into the nape of his neck. "We can take the stairs here down."

He walked up to the edge of the lawn and put his hand on a wooden railing. Being a true Algiran, Gillead enjoyed spending time by the waterside.

"Yes, that's a good idea," Trevor said.

They loved the warm tidal pools by the bridge. Katherine couldn't help but giggle again, which earned her a stern look from Chryséis. As they took the steps down to the rocks by the Basilea beach, they saw divers bring up pearls and sponges in baskets from underwater cultivation beds.

Divers, who waited their turn, sang about danger and friendship to pass the time. The time travellers were in high spirits and didn't notice the gloomy Gabari, sitting at the bottom of the stairs, watching them closely from under his wide-brimmed straw hat.

The pebbly beach was full of playing children and adults were walking along the gentle surf.

They strolled some way in the shallow water and then took a public vimaan up to the Urania quarter. Here they met with Kheton and Lelani at of one of the cooking houses above the western beach.

People liked to eat on the pavement in front of the eating establishments that was still warm from the sun, next to fragrant lemon and frangipani trees. They were seated by a fountain made of pale green stone with three seahorses spouting water into a round basin, and watched people leisurely walking past.

Kheton ordered a pitcher of lemonade and a dish of grilled meat covered in a spicy walnut paste and speared onto peeled rosemary sticks. The food was served in bowls shaped like eggshells with round crusty bread balls. A flask with 'garum' fish sauce and little bowls with pickled mangoes were on every table.

A Konk wearing a colourful, knitted cap trudged past.

"I wonder why he doesn't feel hot wearing that," Trevor said and took a piece of mango.

"The cap looks a bit funny on his domed head."

"Yeah, funny. Maybe they taught him in Daitya how to knit." Chryséis put another morsel of food into her mouth and sighed. It tasted really good.

Kheton and Lelani were chatting to Gillead about Atala's famous purple and pink pearls. Lelani had also seen the 'Wall of Three Ways' by now, so she had lots to tell. Katherine shot a glance at Gillead and giggled a little.

"What is it with you? Oh no, don't tell me you have a crush on our guide!" Chryséis looked openly at Gillead .

"Don't stare like that!" Katherine blushed deeply.

"Oh Katie, get a grip!"

Katherine swallowed angrily and nearly choked on a piece of pickled mango.

"Look at that one!" Trevor pointed with his chin at a woman with green skin like the 'princess' in Aztlan. Just that this woman's skin was all crinkled and nobody carried her in a sedan chair. They quickly looked away when she obviously sensed that the dining children seized her up and Chryséis forgot all about Katherine's predicament.

The following day, Kheton would teach sports at the citadel school. Citadel staff often coached sports and martial arts in their spare time and Kheton had already done so in Cydonia.

"May we join your class in the morning, friend Kheton?" Trevor asked the young Cydonian judge. The boys and girls had an archery lesson before Kheton was needed at the citadel.

"I don't see why not. If you can be ready by the time I leave."

"May I also watch the sport's lesson?" Lelani was bored with decorating her new home and never seeing her husband during the day.

Her only distraction was one of the neighbours, a chatty woman called Florini popping in daily to bring Lelani up to speed with the latest Algiran news. "It would be my pleasure to have you with me today." Kheton smiled charmingly at his wife.

At sunrise Florini's two green-spotted tortoises had escaped and wreaked havoc in the garden and she hadn't stopped talking about it. Lelani definitely needed to get away for a while.

Trevor, Katherine and Chryséis did not attend school in Algiras as they had in Cydonia and really missed it.

"Perhaps we could visit the library in the afternoon," Lelani suggested while they now spent the hottest time of the day with a pitcher of cucumber water in the shady courtyard in front of the apartment. Much to neighbour Florini's delight.

"Ah, friend Lelani, what a coincidence to meet you here," she pretended.

"Yes, isn't it just? Have you found you tortoises yet?"

"The gardener did. What a rude old man! My poor tortoises."

"He is just fond of his plants…any news?"

"I should tell you that the 'Day of Remembrance' is in two days. A big national festival. Horseraces are held at the at the Basilea race course all day. They say that even the Lady of the citadel will attend. I personally just adore the big black horses from Tregarn. They are powerful runners…"

She chatted on and from time to time cast an eye in the direction fo the foreign children. They had been sorting through curious objects from their bags, before sitting down on the thick lawn, dipping their feet into a water basin. The arrival of a citadel messenger momentarily stopped her flood of words.

"Shelanti, I am looking for the goodwife Lelani of Cydonia."

"That would be me." Lelani sat up.

"I bear a message for the children housed at this abode. Shelanti, goodwife."

He nodded politely at Florini, who barely managed to suppress a little gasp of surprise when she saw the citadel badge on his tunic. The messenger looked sideways at Trevor, Katherine and Chryséis and handed a handwritten note to Lelani.

Lelani welcomed the interruption and hurried to offer him a beaker with cucumber water. The children strolled over to receive the tiny scroll and Florini eyed the outlandish children suspiciously.

Why should they receive a message from the Honourable Lady of Algiras? Nobody she knew had ever received such a dispatch.

She couldn't wait to tell the other neighbours! Trevor broke the official seal and rolled the letter open. It was written in Alesian on papyrus paper. Katherine and Chryséis squinted at the text, but they couldn't read the handwriting and asked Lelani to help.

"Why, it is a message from my Gabari brother-in-law," she said in surprise. Florini gasped. A Gabari brother-in-law? What an odd family!

"Shelanti athenai," Lelani read aloud.

"I am here for the great Atland Cup Horserace
on the 'Day of Remembrance'.
Basilea Race Course. Have a surprise.
Will I see you there?
Greetings from Túvar, Son of the Moon."

A rough drawing of the moon was at the bottom of the paper. The children smiled at each other. So their friend Túvar was in town!

"What is a 'B a s i l e a Race Course'?" Katherine asked.

"Well, it is a place where people go to watch horses race," Lelani explained before her neighbour could launch into a lengthy lecture. "One of these places is in the Basilea district."

"Please tell Túvar that we accept the invitation," Chryséis formally told the messenger, who sipped his cool drink leaning against a bamboo pole.

"Very well, athenai. I shall convey your answer. Shukri, goodwife Lelani. Shelanti, the Earthmother be with you." He handed Lelani the empty beaker and left nodding at Florini and the children.

The nosy woman was speechless. The children had been officially invited to the Basilea Race Course by her new neighbour's Gabari brother-in-law, a competitor in the horse races!

"I..., I must go, friend Lelani. I have much to do. Shelanti," she stammered and was on her way.

"Shelanti. Thank you for stopping by..."

The next morning, Gillead arrived to take them into town. Kheton had to leave very early and was already at the citadel. Lelani, still unfamiliar with the roads, was afraid that she might get lost on the way there. As the young man walked toward the apartment, something in the flowerbeds caught his eye. Two rounded bodies moving through the flowers.

Gillead took a closer look, just as a long, hairy leg peeked through the pink dianthus flowers. Then another one. Gillead didn't think twice. He drew the short hockey stick from his belt and aimed. The giant spiders, however, went literally up in vapor, before anybody in the complex noticed anything. He noticed that the bloom of the Moly flower that was still in its basket on the window sill, had turned from white to a deep blood-red colour. A sign of obeah! Gillead kept mum about the incident and led the Alesians to the citadel vimaan.

"So this Basilea horserace is in two days on the 'Day of Remembrance'," Chryséis said as the vimaan moved swiftly past the sailing boat harbour into town.

"It seems to be an important festival," Trevor said. "I can't believe that Túvar is in Algiras. It's seems like an eternity since we left Cydonia."

"Yes, so it seems. It is an Atalian custom. There are races everywhere," Lelani explained.

"Did you watch a mirage about it?" Katherine asked her.

"Yes, I did."

"Why can't we meet Túvar before the race?"

"Why do you want to meet him before? He has things

to do with his horses and what not. And we don't know him all that well," Chryséis answered. "It's not long now and I'm sure he has news from Alun."

"You can talk by thought to Alun all the time," Katherine said.

"But it's different if we can ask Túvar."

"I wonder what surprise Túvar has for us," Trevor wondered.

"Another ride on his white horses maybe. I'm sure they will win the races. Oh, look at that enormous tower over there…"

The sports lesson in archery turned out to be quite interesting and Kheton allowed the three children to take a turn. After about one hour, they were on their way into town. As the vimaan set down noiselessly on 'Library Plaza', Gillead received an urgent thought transfer. Rumors that Gorgonas warships from Hisbernia had been sighted near Maligasima needed to be investigated.

Gillead was an advisor to the Lady of Algiras and as yet the youngest sealord in war times. He also needed to report something of importance. An unusual thing, very unusual in Algiras.

"I shall be back after the meeting, friend Lelani." He excused himself and walked the short distance to the 'House of Nations of the Known World' across the square.

"See, I knew there was something in front of the library," Trevor said meanwhile, and pointed to two stone lions stood guard on each side of a têrakhon dome before the 'House of Knowledge'.

"Impressive." Chryséis whistled.

Two school maidens herded a group of noisy nine-year-olds ahead of them. "Don't touch that Tiaan!" "No, this way, Rulani."

They patiently reprimanded the children and went straight up the stairs. Astonishingly, the group grew quiet inside the pink marble building.

"Let's explore then, athenai." Lelani led the way between the lions to the dome. Inside the dome was a large model of the solar system in motion. The planets of the solar system and their moons revolved around each other and the sun with regular precise movements. This showpiece was popular with visitors from all over and the visitors from Cydonia were no exception.

"Wonderful. Now let's see the famous library."

Lelani eagerly walked up the stairs and they entered a well-lit hall – the 'House of Knowledge'. It was the main library of Algiras. Bookshelves were arranged on three levels along the walls and a row of tinted windows let in much light. Here, one could sit in comfortable chairs and use viewing tables with crystal lenses. Scrolls with colourful drawings were unrolled and clipped onto the tables.

A squeaking sound came from one of the viewing tables, where a young woman studied the picture of a sea animal. The crystal lens she used had activated auditory information stored in the picture. Katherine tried to get a better look.

"How do they do that? Talking pictures?"

"Maybe they're like kiddies' books. Good idea really."

Another group of excited school children was ushered around the viewing tables by their teachers and disappeared out the entrance door.

"The mirage viewing section is upstairs and valuable knowledge is stored on thin metal foils hanging in vaults underground," Lelani told them, reading the signs. "They preserve valuable records here from all over the Known World."

"You know a lot about Atland, Lelani," Trevor marvelled.

The young woman smiled. "We also have a 'House of Knowledge' in Cydonia. It's one of my favorite places."

"Really? We didn't know that." Chryséis sounded disappointed. They had never been there. It was early afternoon by now and a golden sun shone through the big windows.

"There is still time to go through some mirage rolls, athenai."

Lelani asked for directions to the History and Geography sections on the second floor. There, they entered a viewing booth and watched a historical record about the first king of Atala by the name of Uranus, after the Dark Age. '…Uranus was the first king to rule in Atala after the great deluge." A recorded voice narrated. "He civilised the survivors, causing them to build cities and till the soil again. Skilled in astronomy, Uranus instituted the solar year and the lunar month. The people of Atland admired his skillful reign and paid him divine honours after his death. His most celebrated daughters were Basilea and Pandora…'

"Basilea? Like the race course?"

"Yes, intriguing, but there is nothing new here, really." Lelani took the roll out of its socket and reached for another one. This time a female voice began to speak:

'The 'Seven Daughters of Atlas' are a group of islands in the Atlantean Sea before the Puntian coast. Their names are Maia, Electra, Taygeta, Asterope, Halcyone, Celaeno and Europa. In the eighth year of King Busiris of Kem's reign, he unsuccessfully tried to 'rob the maidens' and occupied the islands for a few seasons…'

The mirage showed a number of green islands before the coast of Mauretania! A tall mountain called Mount Atlas was shown to the south of the Strait of Gibraltar.

"They call the islands 'Daughters of Atlas'? Kem must be in Egypt, but what happened to that mountain?" Trevor whispered and pointed toward the map. "The Strait of Gibraltar must be the 'Passage of the Golden Pillars' in the mirage and the Mediterranean Sea the 'Blue Sea'."

"Shhht!" Katherine hissed. She didn't want to miss anything.

'…A country called 'Azunia', Akkadian for 'abundance', lies east of the 'Golden Pillars'. It is the home to a nation we call the Ama-zûnas…'

Dramatic harp tunes were clanging.

'...After subduing many of the neighbouring Numidian tribes, the Ama-zûnas had one more enemy of equal fierceness: the Gorgonas of Hesperus...'

"That looks just like Portugal. They call it 'Hesperus' here," Chryséis said in a low voice.

Loud noise came from the viewing booth next-door. Some battle was fought in the mirage, and they had to listen more closely.

'...After the Dark Age, a savage tribe, the Gorgonas, fancied themselves descendants of giant lizards. A wild woman's face with snakes for hair adorns their shields to frighten the enemy...'

Katherine giggled a little and the voice in the mirage droned on. '...Atala wisely made peace with the fierce queen Mena of the seafaring Ama-zûnas tribe after she attacked the eastern peninsula with her hordes and destroyed the thriving city of Cercenes by the river Oceanus...'

The mirage showed armed people with long hair bound into high ponytails running and shouting while riding wild horses. '...shark teeth, threaded onto tendons, were the warriors' only jewellry and they wore thick armours fashioned from dragon hide ...'

Even in this mirage, some kind of war was being fought. The clanging of weapons and heart-stopping war-cries indicated that a battle was in progress. Shields were held up in defense.

"Can you pass the popcorn?" Chryséis asked and Katherine signaled for her to be quiet. She was too engrossed in the action.

The children ducked a couple of times when flaming arrows flew in their direction or a long-haired warrior ran toward them with a blood-thirsty expression, sword in hand.

The soundtrack informed the viewer that the battle had just been won by the Ama-zûnas. Then the picture of a great gathering with rejoicing people appeared.

"Ah, a happy end!" Katherine sighed.

'...the gentle Atalians wisely pacified Queen Mena and her troops. The Ama-zûnas founded a great city called Chersonesus, the 'City of the Peninsula' on Atland's soil and settled into a more peaceful lifestyle. The current chieftainess on the peninsula is Orellana. She cooperates peacefully with the Atalian administration and protects our eastern territory from the Gorgonas warriors to this day...'

"Phew they're ugly. Look at those teeth." Katherine was talking about the Gorgonas, who were now the focus of the story again.

'...At present, King Asol rules the land around the 'Passage of the Golden Pillars' on either side of the narrow strait that leads into the 'Blue Sea...' the virtual voice continued. 'No attacks on Atlandian territory have been recorded during his peaceful reign...'

When the mirage ended, Lelani told the children that the Gorgonas were the reason why Gillead had been summoned to the Lady of Algiras.

"Are they attacking Atala?" Trevor asked.

"They have amassed warships in a remote bay on Maligasima."

"Oh, what has that to do with Atala, then?"

"That's what the officials are trying to find out. Would you like to watch anything else, athenai?" Lelani seemed quite relaxed about the Gorgonas. Katherine nodded.

"Yes, actually, would it be possible to watch a mirage on Prydhain...my homeland?" She asked.

"Oh, but certainly, child, let me ask the librarian where such a mirage is to be found."

"Did you hear that?" Trevor said when Lelani left the booth. "They might start a war again. What's wrong with those people?"

Before his friends could say anything, Lelani returned with a roll titled 'Prydhain Today and Through the Ages'. She put the roll into the plug and said. "I will be right back." With that she quickly left the viewing booth.

"Maybe they'll tell us about tors and the standing stones at Stonehenge… and the huge images of a giant and a horse scratched into English hillsides…" Chryséis said.

Katherine held her breath and stared at the mirage. At first, much of Prydhain was surprisingly under an icecap that melted rapidly and created lakes. The land was bare without much life except for some plants and weird-looking animals they didn't recognised.

There were hills and a few forests, but the most amazing thing was that there were lakes and marshland between Hisbernia and Prydhain. In other words between Ireland and England!

'…Old legends tell us about 'Shadow People' as the first inhabitants before the long icy sleep of the Dark Age began. Then Gabari tribes settled in Prydhain. Many were skilled blacksmiths from Fomor in northern Atala…'

"But that's impossible!" Katherine protested.

"Shht!"

'…the largest lakes are called Mor Savadda, Mor Hrič and Mor Hylas. Mor Llyn Llion and Mor Maalbec are found in the country of 'Lyonesse'.'

Lyonesse was apparently a low-lying country that bridged the mountains of what would - in modern times - become Cornwall and Brittany. No English Channel anywhere!

The mirage took a swerve along the coastal Mohini cliffs and then swung over the major cities of Lyonesse: Meldoon, Maalbec and Caradoc.

'…Caradoc is situated on the banks of Mor Llyn Llion. Many merchant ships use the canals connecting the lakes with the Gulf of Morbihan. Haithabu is an important seaport south of Caradoc…'

"Isn't Caradoc, where the Speaking Stone is from?" Chryséis asked.

"I think so," Trevor said.

"But that's not Britain at all!" Katherine couldn't hide her disappointment.

"Katie, this is the 'Alesian Epoch'. Things are different now."

"I thought I would see something familiar. All this land where it shouldn't be and...lakes and cities," Katherine insisted.

"Well, the coast of Africa looks familiar and the Strait of Gibraltar as well..." Trevor tried to reason with her. "So what if some things are different now? I think it's totally the bomb."

"Scotland has still a lot of mountains," Chryséis threw in.

"But, there is no Irish Sea...and no English Channel...all that has nothing to do with Britain!" Katherine started then fell silent again. What was the use? This was a completely different epoch.

"I wonder why so much land has just disappeared," Trevor wondered.

"Well, earthquakes and floods and stuff had probably something to do with it," Chryséis said.

The mirage faded. Now they had missed the ending! Lelani came back and took the roll out of the socket.

"It's getting late, athenai, we should go."

"Lelani, who lives in Prydhain?" Katherine asked on the way to the first floor.

The young woman looked surprised. Shouldn't young Kathín know her own homeland? But she explained willingly all the same.

"There are the Alba and the Fenians. Dwendis and the ancient fairy folk still live inside the hills. The D'Ånu and the people of Lyonesse, who are your kinfolk and speak Dânvries, of course, don't see eye to eye with certain Gabari, who claim that ancient Lyonesse had once belonged to their ancestors —" Lelani interrupted herself. "you must have learned all of this at school, for sure. Dear friends, it is getting dark outside and our guide is waiting."

They left the now rather deserted library. A hulking figure lurked unnoticed in the shadows of the green terraced building next-door and began to follow them at a distance.

A few days later, they were spending time at the beach again.

"I can't believe we are really here - in Atlantis!" Chryséis marvelled. "It's just like a dream... until I touch things. Then it feels real."

She sat by their favourite swimming pool, stroking the mosaic border. There were mosaics even in the rock pools by the shore, where children learned to swim. Colourful dragonflies, dolphins and birds glistened through the clear pool water.

"We don't know that it's really Atlantis." Katherine sat in the shade and updated the travel journal, while Trevor dozed.

"Why, what else is it supposed to be?" Chryséis asked and Katherine shrugged her shoulders.

"Don't forget all that stuff about Prydhain," Trevor said lazily and Chryséis tickled his foot with a blade of sea grass.

"'vidya' – knowledge/ education, 'narina' - woman, 'kalah' - time, 'adih' - beginning, 'antah' - the end...," Katherine read aloud as she added new words to their glossary of the Akkadian language.

Gillead, who had been talking to a Gabari guard in a straw hat, came walking over. "Athenai, the Lady of Algiras is requesting your presence," he called out. That could only mean that they were going to travel to Prydhain soon.

"At last," Trevor said and yawned, scratching his foot.

Although they had enjoyed this Atlantis, some action was more than welcome by now. They were ready in no time and on their way to the citadel. Soon, Gillead lowered the vimaan in front of the citadel complex.

"Gillead, may I ask you a question?" Chryséis asked.

"It will be my pleasure to provide an answer if I can," their guide said charmingly.

"What does the name written on the corner of that building mean? 'Azurias Maya'. Is it the name of the square?"

"Well observed, young friend. Azurias Maya was a great explorer and astronomer from Algiras."

Trevor picked up the Akkadian past tense. "He was a great explorer?"

Gillead proceeded to explain that Azurias Maya of Algiras had unfortunately been lost at sea on a voyage to the country of Ta Neteru, which was on the continent of Punt. Most regrettable. "You see, the observatory of Mintaka in Ta Neteru was conducting a study of the third planet to the Dog Star Ninurta, which is revolving in opposite direction to the other planets. Azurias Maya decided to travel to Ta Neteru in person to compare the findings with his own calculations. Mintaka's chief astronomer informed the Lady of Algiras that Azurias Maya had not arrived as planned."

The children struggled to follow the story. There were still too many strange words they didn't know.

"The ship sunk in a storm in the Gadiric Sea not far off the 'Golden Pillars'. Invaluable notes and mirage rolls disappeared in the ocean together with the great Atalian astronomer. The square here was named after him in his honour."

"That's very tragic," Katherine said.

"Yes. A great loss to our nation. Here we are."

They were standing in front of an impressive building. A stern-looking marble statue held a sign that read:

"House of Nations of the Known World

Constant Vigilance is the Price of Freedom"

A citadel maiden led the way through an enclosed forecourt, which could have passed for a hotel lobby with its têrakhon dome and walls.

The area under the dome was practically an indoor garden

with three bubbling fountains in a mosaic-tiled basin. They passed a small pyramid-calendar with tiny blue and yellow blocks. A board next to it announced that it was the 8th day since the 'Opening of the Skies' in the Month of the 'Ripening Grain'. Apparently, every month and day had their own name.

The Akkadian year started in spring with the month of the 'First Moon'. Then there were days like 'Third Day since Sowing the Fields', the 'Day of Victory over King Busiris' and so on. Tomorrow it would be the turn of 'The Day of Remembrance'.

"The air is so fresh in here. This place must have some kind of air-conditioning system." Trevor touched a long feathery fern leaf that curled up and seemed to shy away from him.

Grand steps led up to a spacious foyer. Guards demanded to know the visitors' business and let them pass when they saw Gillead. Upstairs was another inner court with more plants and fountains. Here, delegates from civilised nations of the Known World often assembled in a large conference room around a table in the shape of an oval ring. Gillead walked past it all.

"Are we not there yet?" Chryséis asked.

"Patience, friend Chrysies," Gillead laughed. "We are taking just a little detour to show you this building. The Administration of the Known World."

They walked around the table and stepped onto a roofed-in bridge. Below was a large, paved square and just ahead they could see the citadel on a mound higher up. This was the seat of the Atalian government and residence of the Lady of Algiras.

"It's is so much bigger than the citadel in Cydonia," Trevor marvelled and Gillead smiled proudly.

They walked across the bridge and saw that two amphitheaters were let into the ground on opposite sides of the busy square below. Entertainment was always a splendid affair in the metropolis of Algiras and the children were duly impressed.

As they reached the end of the bridge, Gillead led the way

through a double-winged door into the Lady's reception room.

The walls were painted in hues of blue and white and it felt like being on clouds in the sky. The Lady stood by one of the large windows and welcomed them with a nod.

There was something in the way the Lady of Algiras moved and spoke that reminded them of their old friend, the Lady of Cydonia. It was clear that this woman commanded a great deal of authority.

The three friends knew that she had time-travelled via modern London with the Lady of Cydonia some time ago. She must understand what time travel was all about. The Lady of Cydonia had told them that they had found especially Egypt, which was now called 'Ta Mery', would change a lot in the future.

"Shukri, friend Gillead and Ashkiri, you may go now." The Lady of Algiras thanked Gillead and the maiden, who had showed them into the room and they excused themselves. When they were alone, Katherine asked a burning question.

"Honourable Lady, is this really the Atlantis of legends?"

The Lady laughed at her forwardness and answered in slightly antiquated English. "Dear children, you lose no time at all, do you now? Let me answer then as truthfully as I am capable of doing so. As you know, Atala is the largest remnant of the great continent of Atland, the old land. The motherland to many nations."

She motioned for them to sit down in upholstered chairs. "Make yourselves comfortable. Isn't that what you would say in your own time?" She smiled and the children nodded politely.

"Young friends, I believe that Atland may be compared with the distorted memories of what has become known as the sunken continent of Atlantis. Although only a small part of it."

"Wow, I was right," Chryséis said.

"Many of the Atlandian people of old perished in floods of fire and water and many more succumbed to diseases after the catastrophe that prompted the Dark Age. A number of

Atlandians, however, managed to save themselves onto other lands and our motherland lived only in legends for years."

"The Lady of Cydonia told us about that, but we weren't sure about Atlantis," Trevor said. "We weren't sure if this is really a part of Atlantis."

"Well, so to speak. You may have noticed that things are quite different here to what you expected. I understand that it is the purpose of your journey to give you knowledge about our time for the benefit of the future. I hear that our good Gillead has accompanied you to the observatory of Clymene, the Garden of Civilisation and such places. I hope you found your stay in Algiras... enlightening."

The children nodded. "Thank you very much, honourable Lady, we think this town rocks," Chryséis gushed and the Lady laughed again.

"I am glad to hear it," she said. "Unfortunately, even your stay here must come to an end."

"If you mean that we have to leave for Prydhain right away, that's okay. We are ready now," Trevor assured her.

"We saw a mirage about Prydhain and it's very different to the England I know." Katherine still sounded a little disappointed.

"Indeed, and yet you are still intent on pursuing this - adventure?"

"Oh yes, we can't wait to explore further. That's what we are here for, right?" Chryséis piped up.

"Yes of course," the Lady said with just a hint of hesitation. "I should tell you that our plans for you have changed somewhat."

"Oh, are we not going anymore? Do we have to go back to Alesia?"

"No, no, nothing of that sort. However, the 'Speaking Stone' has spoken and declared that 'the foreign children' are to join a mission to return it to Caradoc in Lyonesse."

They stared at her, speechless. No way!

"Are you pleased, athenai? It is quite an honour."

"Oh yes, Lady," Trevor said. "The stone told you that?

How does it even know about us? That sounds awfully exciting. Lyonesse is close to Prydhain anyway, isn't it?"

"What else does the stone know?" Katherine asked.

"A great deal, young friend. It is one of the mysteries that make Speaking Stones so very valuable to us. The Ancient Ones created the stones in this way."

"So what do we have to do?"

"Your eagerness is much appreciated. However, there is one problem. It has come to our attention that Edfunians are lurking here in Atala, no doubt vying for the Speaking Stone. We need to apprehend them and keep you safe at the same time."

"No problem," Trevor said a little too quickly.

"What? But we thought that the Edfunians were trees on Ruta Ynis." Katherine was not so sure anymore about this new plan.

"We are almost certain that the Highpriest of Shuruk is among them. The elves must have released the thieves again. For what reason we don't know."

"Do you think they will be caught soon?" Trevor asked her.

"We surely hope so, child."

"But who else will be going to Lyonesse?"

"You will meet them..." She stopped talking. A frown appeared on the Lady's face, she closed her eyes, then stood up abruptly, turned around and grabbed into the air. She pulled hard and a scruffy-looking Gabari appeared instantly. The Lady was holding an amulet on a torn leather string in her hand. The children couldn't believe it.

"Up to the same old tricks, are we?" she said, her voice booming. The Edfunian spy was stunned.

Gone was the gentle Lady they had been talking to. She was now a tough commander. The time travellers watched wide-eyed as citadel guards, Gabari themselves, stormed into the room and immobilised the giant within a second.

"Take him for interrogation," the Lady of Algiras said coolly. "Make sure this one talks, before they eliminate him as well."

The guards dragged the man roughly out of the room and the Lady stood leaning on her chair for a moment. She took a deep breath and smiled, before turning into the wise and gentle ruler of Atland once again.

The children were stunned.

"I must apologize, he should never have come this far! This is not the only Edfunian spy we've detected in Algiras. No doubt, they are here because of the 'Speaking Stone's' presence at the citadel. The stone is kept safely in a secret vault, but the sooner it is handed over to Caradoc, the better."

"Aha," Trevor stammered.

"How did you know the giant was standing there?"

"Oh, but didn't you see how the air was slightly distorted?"

"No."

"Ah well. So, where were we? Yes, the mission…"

"Are you sure, it is safe for us to go? I mean we are only children." Chryséis had found her voice again. "We can't see invisible Edfunians and things like that."

"Athenai, if the stone says it wants you to come on the mission, then it has its reasons. The wisdom of Speaking Stones is far-reaching."

"So, we must trust in whatever a dumb stone wants us to do?"

"Not a dumb stone, but a very wise stone."

"Oh, I'm not so sure I can trust a stone to look after me."

"It is your choice of course, but perhaps it is time to meet the 'team'." She stood up and opened the door. "Ashkiri, we are ready!"

The Lady of Algiras no longer spoke English.

"Well then, I would like you to meet Prince Artû of Avallûn, the leader of the mission." There were more people an indistinct group standing in the doorway.

The time travellers looked up at a tall young man, his broad shoulders covered by a blue cape. A gold-embroidered head band held the prince's blond curls back from his handsome, stern face.

"Prince Artû, please meet the foreign children from Cydonia."

He stepped forward. The use of titles such as Lady, king,

queen and prince was confusing. This prince came from a country they hadn't even heard of. Warlords and sealords were appointed in times of war by the Ladies, but every country seemed to have their own rules.

"Shelanti athenai." The prince gave a little bow, but his expression remained serious.

"Shelanti, Prince Artû of Avallûn." They made the required hand movements to heart and forehead.

"Our good prince comes from Avallûn, an island state in the Gadiric Sea. You will be going there first. Should you decide to come, of course." The Lady inclined her head graciously and the prince copied her gesture.

"Why?"

"The assemblage of Gorgonas ships nearby must be investigated. We will not use telepathic communication after leaving Algiras," Prince Artû explained curtly.

"The Edfunians will try to intercept our communication," the Lady added.

"But how will we communicate then?" Chryséis was beginning to panic.

"We have our own means."

"I'm not so sure that I still want to do this. Now it's just taking a stone back to Caradoc, then it's an army of nasty Gorgonas. What's next?"

"Let's not 'jump the gun', shall we?" the Lady said cheerfully in English and waved. "This, athenai, is Amadis of Anaá."

The dark-haired Amadis stepped forward and bowed lightly. He looked just as impressive as the prince, but his brown eyes held a friendly twinkle and he smiled. Amadis wore green clothes and was taller than Prince Artû, but was definitely not a Gabari. A bow was slung across his shoulder and feathered arrows peeked out of a quiver.

"He looks just like Robin Hood!" Katherine murmured.

"Amadis is D'Ånu and hails from Anaá, capital of his people's ancient realm in Prydhain. He too is an experienced warrior and has much knowledge of Gabari ways and the

Little People… the Dwendi."

"Amadis looks way too young to be an experienced warrior," Chryséis said somewhat rudely.

"Youth is a mark of the D'Ånu people. They worked closely with the 'Great Ones' of old," the Lady of Algiras explained and Amadis looked very proud. "His people are invaluable to the Known World. They carry the flame of civilisation into regions still in the grip of the Dark Age. To help advance humans often still living worse than animals."

"Worse than animals?"

"Worse than animals. They need to be taught all over again in the ways of civilisation…Lubbo, old friend," the Lady of Algiras called out.

"Here I am, honourable Lady." A rather short, burly man appeared, his voice deeper than expected. "Shelanti."

"This is Lubbo of Pindala, young friends." He came then from the Little People. The Dwendi had a wise, old and at the same time child-like face.

"Shelanti," the three time travellers greeted him.

"Lubbo is an elder of the 'Little People' of Atala. The Dwendis are long-standing allies of the D'Ånu people and…"

"Let me through!" a high voice demanded resolutely outside. Another small person pushed past the guards and into the audience room.

"What is this commotion all about?" the Lady of Algiras asked.

Lubbo of Pindala seemed embarrassed and said pointedly, "my apologies honourable Lady, it is my sister Gwendola. She was supposed to wait until…"

"I want to go with them. I am just as good as any of the men."

"Gwendola, I told you not to…"

"No Lubbo, let her speak." The Lady held up a placating hand.

"You need a woman around when travelling with children. Three warriors, by the Earthmother! I am a woman and I am also a warrior. I can be their guardian."

Her muscular arms crossed, Gwendola, a swarthy Dwendi

woman, grunted with determination. She had made her point. A very good point.

"Hmm yes, Gwendola, that seems reasonable. I will consult the Speaking Stone about this," the ruler of Atland mused. "This was quite enough excitement for one day and I'm afraid I must attend to other matters now."

"You will let me know what you decide, athenai. The 'team' is leaving very soon," she said in English.

"Shelanti." "Shelanti, honourable Lady." "Shelanti, athenai."

Everybody seemed ready to leave and the three friends soon found themselves outside the Lady's quarters.

Gillead was preoccupied with citadel business, and Kheton took them back to the apartment. Chryséis was now quite upset.

"No way am I going with some 'companions' to chase after nasty Gorgonas just to take a dumb stone back to its hometown!"

Kheton had chosen to take an evening-walk with Lelani and the children through the 'Garden of Civilisation'. The time travellers paid little attention to their surroundings as they discussed what to do.

"What's wrong with it? It's so much better than just travelling around."

"Hellooo - it's dangerous! That's what's wrong with it."

They took the last steps up the city wall and entered the familiar park.

"And what else is new? I mean this is prehistory. We knew it wouldn't be a cake walk and still we came here to explore."

"Yes, but..." Chryséis was running out of arguments.

"If this Speaking Stone is so important to everyone, I think it'll be cool that it wants us to come with."

Chryséis thought for a moment. "Oh, whatever. Let's do it then."

"Yes!" Trevor punched the air, which earned him amused stares from bystanders.

"Look, we still have our timeportal finder and we can turn invisible whenever we need to. It's not so bad," Katherine said bravely.

"Do you think the stone knows that we are from the future?"

"You talk as if this dumb stone knows everything," Chryséis grumbled.

"Obviously it knows quite a lot. That's what everyone thinks. Wish we could take it with us to the future," Trevor said. A woman in a blue tunic suit walked past. She carried a small dog in her arms.

"Oh, that's so cute! I really miss Tepi." They hadn't thought much about Cydonia or the yellow puppy that had taken a shine to Katherine.

"So what are we going to tell the Lady then?" Trevor asked.

"That we'll come with the 'team' of course," Katherine replied.

"Alright then, we go," Chryséis conceded.

"Okay, cool. Wait up Kheton, we want to tell you something," Trevor yelled and walked faster.

The matter was settled by the time they arrived back home for dinner.

"Please fetch a bowl with salted cucumber pieces from the cooling cupboard outside," Lelani asked Trevor. They ate dogfish steaks, while chatting about a play Lelani and Kheton had seen at an amphitheater the day before. Nobody paid the slightest attention to the red moly flower.

Outside the apartment, in the shadows of the large jacaranda tree, their Gabari guard was relieved by a colleague. So quietly that not even their nosy neighbour Florini noticed a thing.

That night, they were too excited to sleep much. Chryséis completed a series of yoga postures called 'salute to the sun' and talked to Katherine about the horserace they would attend the following day. Just Trevor was unusually quiet.

"Hey Trevor, what's up with you?" Chryséis blurted out.

"What? Oh, sorry did you ask me something?"

"I asked you what's up, you're so quiet."

Chryséis stood up and began to brush her teeth over the small bronze basin. "It's the 11th of June tomorrow," she said and gargled.

"Really?"

"Duh, it's the 'Day of Remembrance' and we are going to see Túvar,"

"Yes, it's also…well…it's my birthday," Trevor mumbled.

The girls were quiet for a moment. Chryséis stopped rinsing her mouth in the basin. Then they both began to speak simultaneously.

"Oh sorry Trev, I totally forgot…" Katherine apologised.

"We have to celebrate that…" Chryséis put away her tooth brush.

"It's only a birthday, no big deal. Really." Trevor was embarrassed by the sudden attention. "Even my mother sometimes forgets."

"What, how can your own mother forget? Having your birthday in prehistory. Does that count when we get back?" Katherine asked. "I had my birthday in January."

"Sorry pal, we have to celebrate at least a little. Just got to explain to Kheton and Lelani. I'm sure they understand."

Chryséis was adamant. She'd had her twelfth birthday just before school started and it had been a lot of fun. Now it was Trevor's turn.

"Okay, if you think so…" Trevor was rarely this shy.

"Absolutely. Let me think of something." Chryséis crawled into her sleeping bag. She suddenly felt terribly tired.

"Night. What are these moths doing in here?" Trevor shooed two little fairies out the window, unaware of what they really were. He closed the window and also went to bed.

"Chris, what do you want to do about the birthday tomorrow?" Katherine asked in a low voice, but Chryséis was already asleep. It had been a really long day.

In the morning, Trevor was treated to a cheerful 'Happy Birthday to You' serenade just as he was about to wake up. Katherine and Chryséis had quickly organised a candle and some flowers as well.

"Sorry, Trev, it was impossible to get a cake so quickly, but I'm sure there will be cakes for sale at the race course today," Katherine apologised.

Trevor was so moved that he didn't know what to say. He just blushed.

"But…" Chryséis continued, "…we decided that in honour of your birthday, we will open a granola bar."

"Let's not waste the emergency provisions," Trevor protested. "It's really not necessary, just because…"

"Yes it is!" Chryséis said firmly. "And you will get the biggest piece."

Kheton and Lelani had been fascinated to learn how their foreign friends celebrated birthdays with cakes. It was not the custom in Alesia, but serenading on a special occasion was something they understood. They contributed the Cydonian song about baking a cake as the children came downstairs.

The time travellers remembered the song well from their excursion to the Moti market that nearly ended in them being kidnapped by invisible Edfunians. Kheton promised that if it were necessary to complete the ritual, he would find some cakes at the racecourse today. How fitting to celebrate a birthday on the 'Day of Remembrance'!

Outside in the streets, turquoise Atalian flags with the typical yellow sun wheel were hoisted from roofs and poles. Special foods were cooked to bear in mind that proper cooked meals were something to be treasured after long, cold years of sheer survival. On the way to Basilea, they walked past rows of lanterns strung up between trees that would be lit after dark.

Traditional music was played on street corners and people were dancing everywhere.

"Look, they are even dancing on the bridge," Katherine cried. "That looks like a lot of fun." She waved at the laughing dancers and two of them waved back.

The Basilea racecourse was just beyond the last canal bridge. Today, such horse races were held all over Atala and it was rather busy. Large bronze statues of horses, frozen in motion, adorned the front of the half-moon shaped structure. Behind the building were a big oval racecourse and two long fields for shorter races. Horseraces were held on special occasions and the annual 'Great Atland Cup' was always a grand affair.

Horses were led around by their handlers. Many of them were centaurs from the territories of Hipparion and Garanhir in the far northwest of the island state. They curried the fur of tall, dark horses and small hay-coloured ones with bristly manes; they cleaned hooves and fastened saddles.

Atalians promenaded around admiring the horses and showing off their festive outfits. Meat was barbecued over open fires and têrakhon mugs filled with caipirinha, a traditional drink made from lemons, were emptied rapidly.

They looked for Túvar in the booth reserved for the Lady of Algiras' special guests, but he wasn't there. Kheton had disappeared in the crowd to find some cake, so they went downstairs with Lelani to see the horses.

"There are just so many people around. How are we

supposed to find Túvar?" Katherine sighed. "He has to be here somewhere."

Next to Trevor three boys were having a lively discussion. "Come on, Curunir, let's go. I brought a ball with me. We can play Pigsnout in a corner outside," a round-cheeked youngster with dark curls piped up.

"We can't play there properly. No holes in the wall outside," a blond boy with almost white eyebrows objected.

"It doesn't matter. We'll pretend. I'll find something to draw holes with," the dark-haired one replied and made batting movements with his paddle.

"Anything is better than looking at boring horses," the boy by the name of Curunir said and pulled a face and the others laughed.

"Oh, the grace, the shining fur… such a powerful runner, a winner for sure…" The very blond boy mocked in a grown-up voice. The boys laughed again.

"Come on then, athenai. We must be back before our horse race begins or mother will skin me alive."

They scampered off towards the entrance and no doubt, to the corner where they could play. Pigsnout had become Trevor's favorite ballgame in Cydonia and he was tempted to join the boys. It would be great to play a game of Pigsnout again for a change. But he couldn't just run off and leave the others behind.

Besides, Kheton had just returned with three mooncakes topped with berry filling in honour of Trevor's birthday celebration. Lelani smiled when Kheton handed them the palm-sized cakes over on large mulberry leaves.

"I had to walk right to the other end of the stadium to find those cakes. I hope they are to your liking, friend Trevór." Kheton seemed to enjoy the novel idea of celebrating one's birthday this way and was doing his part.

"Shukri, Kheton. They look delicious," Chryséis thanked him. "Now we have to sing Happy Birthday again."

"Oh no, please, not here."

But Kheton had already begun to sing. "Hepi birds dé…" in a loud voice, giving Trevor a heartening look. Lelani and the girls joined in. People around them began laughing, not recognising the strange song. Some of the spectators even clapped to the rhythm. Prehistoric folk were always happy to join in with this kind of musical rendition.

Kheton finished on a dramatic, drawn-out note and Lelani beamed. It was proper to respect their guests' customs.

"Thanks Kheton, that was, that was… really nice of you," Trevor said, but all this attention made him feel quite self-conscious.

"It is a very great pleasure, friend Trevór. I hope you will remember this day as most pleasurable."

"Yes, yes I will." Trevor took a deep bite out of his tasty mooncake and the berry filling dripped down onto his hands.

"I can see that," Kheton laughed. "You can wash yourselves at the fountain, when you have finished your celebration meal. We will now go over there to see the horses."

Kheton pointed out a really big black horse and the couple ambled over to have a closer look. The sunshine made way for a thin layer of clouds and many of the women took off the veils that protected them from sun exposure.

"This tastes really good," Chryséis said and didn't stop eating her cake. "I wonder where all those horses come from. They all look so different."

"Well, at least one of them is coming from Cydonia with Túvar," Trevor said with a full mouth and scanned the stadium for the beautiful white horses of Alesia, but there was still no sight of Túvar.

As they stood at the fountain washing their hands and faces, a family of Dwendis dressed in their best clothes walked past just as a breeze picked up. The Dwendi lady tried to pin her hat down with her hands, but it was too late.

"Oh, oh, oh. My hat!" Another gust of wind swept the great flowery straw hat off her head and for a brief moment it floated in front of the head of the great black horse.

The horse reared up in surprise and a centaur groom tried to calm it down by hanging onto the leash and speaking to the animal."Shertán, down, ho. Ho Shertán!" the four-legged groom shouted.

Shertán reared up again and other grooms came galloping to help. Eventually the black horse allowed the grooms to lead it away, but now, a steppe-horse with a short stiff mane nibbled at the flowers on the hat.

"Oh my! My new hat is done for."

The Dwendi woman's tiny son walked over to pick up her tattered hat. People smiled at the comical scene, but the Dwendi mother was close to tears.

"It's not so bad mother," the boy chirped. "The horserace will be just as nice without the hat."

"Give the hat to the horses, then. At least they seem to like it this way," the Dwendi-father told him.

Soon, Kheton and Lelani returned from their spin around the grounds.

"The races are about to start. There are many steppe-horses here today. They are strong and resilient runners."

Kheton tipped his straw hat up and spotted Túvar near a group of Gabari girls, who eyed the handsome giant from Cydonia. The centaur Gobän was busy currying a white horse with a broad brush, while Túvar watched the other horses, ignoring the girls..

"There is my adopted brother at last." Kheton waved to him.

The young Gabari noble towered above many of the visitors and Kheton tried to get his attention, waving wildly. Eventually Túvar saw him, grinned broadly and waved back while approaching them in great strides.

"Shelanti, athenai. brother, sister-in-law. There you are at last. It is a pleasure seeing you again," he roared while shaking Kheton's hand, as if he wanted to yank the arm from his older brother's shoulder.

"Shelanti, Túvar. How is the family in Cydonia?" Chryséis called out.

"They are all well. I have orders to bring presents to Kheton and Lelani and Alun says…" He couldn't finish his sentence. A golden ball of fur bounced towards the children and very nearly knocked Katherine over. An excited Tepi licked their feet and jumped up at Katherine.

"Oh Tepi, what are you doing here?" The girl laughed.

"Tepi, stop jumping, you are not a puppy anymore!" Túvar told her off sternly. The young dog stood still for a moment, leaning on Katherine, tail wagging and ears tilted to one side as she looked up at the giant. What a surprise! Tepi had grown quite a bit since they had last seen her in Cydonia, but she was still her boisterous self.

Túvar was fond of the foreign children, especially of Chryséis, the adorable blonde girl who had saved his life by telepathically calling for help in Shuruk.

"Oh Tepi, you still can't keep your ears straight!" Katherine looked beaming at the dog's intelligent face and everybody laughed.

Gobän came trotting over to greet them, leading the white mare he had been currying. Prïnda was full of nervous energy with so many strange horses and people to see and hear and smell.

The children, of course, knew that Gobän and Túvar communicated telepathically with horses and Trevor had to think of the movie 'The Horse Whisperer'.

"Shelanti, athenai. Isn't this place just wonderful? All these mokis and steppe-horses from Maligasima. A gathering of the best breeds." Gobän thumped Trevor on the back.

"How are you Gobän?" Lelani inquired.

"I am well when my horses are well," the centaur answered and lowered his head.

"Some of the horses here look quite – unusual." Katherine was searching for the correct word.

"Look that one over there." Trevor pointed to strange looking animals that wouldn't have passed for horses at all in modern times.

The three shaggy animals were taller than the others, except for the great black horses from Tregarn. They had three big toes instead of hooves, but the most interesting feature was their trunk. Quite short but still a trunk. The time travellers had seen such animals from afar on their way to the seaport city of Atztlan.

"Why they are mokis, young friend, from Punt, no doubt. Mokis often serve as beasts of burden on lengthy caravan treks, but these ones are specially bred to race." Prïnda seemed to listen to Gobän's speech with pricked ears. The white mare neighed and pushed the centaur softly with its muzzle. "Yes Prïnda, you are the most beautiful of all of them!"

An Ama-zûnas man with a high ponytail strolled past nose in the air, proudly leading his chestnut-coloured steed. His young son walked behind his father, pulling a little wooden horse on squeaky wheels.

"So, this is your surprise!" Katherine beamed at Túvar. "It's Tepi!" She knelt on the ground next to the dog and buried her face in the soft golden fur. Tepi tried mischievously to climb onto Katherine's thighs.

"Tepi you are getting too big to sit on my lap!" The dog jumped off and enjoyed a good scratch behind the ears.

"Yes, friend Kathín. This is my surprise. Tepi has been pining for you since your departure from Cydonia."

"Oh, really?"

"Yes, so father Harun agreed to let Tepi come with us to Algiras. Alun wanted to come as well, but examinations are held at the citadel school."

"We could hardly believe it when we saw your letter, brother-in-law," Lelani said. "I am glad to see you so cheerful and in good health."

They chatted animatedly about who was doing what in Cydonia. Túvar also brought news from Lelani's family.

"Your uncle is now working with Azaes, aunt Mellea's husband. He is soon leaving to manage a warehouse in Tollùn on the Southern Continent of Pushkara."

"Those are very good news," Lelani said.

"You will soon travel to visit Prydhain then athenai?" Túvar asked the children.

"Yes, we actually will…" Chryséis began.

"We will leave soon and visit my home there." Katherine cut her short. She was about to reveal their secret about the Speaking Stone. The Lady had asked them not to speak about their mission. Chryséis blushed.

"Be careful not to trust everyone in Prydhain," Túvar warned them. "Some Gabari folk do not have good intentions. It will be for the best if you take Tepi with you on your voyage. She'll look after you." Tepi heard her name and looked up expectantly, wagging her tail.

"Oh, that's wonderful," Katherine crowed. "We'll also look well after you, won't we?"

"But what if we have to go… you know…"

"Oh Trevor let's not talk about that now," Katherine pleaded and Trevor dropped the topic.

Túvar was satisfied with the effect of his surprise and went to join Gobän. "I must go now. The horseraces are about to begin."

The white mare muzzled his shoulder in greeting. The horse handlers were getting their charges ready for the races and plaited ribbons in different colours securely into the horses' manes. The ribbons were flying up prettily as the horses moved their heads. The white Alesian horses traditionally wore yellow and red ribbons in the national Alesian colours.

Gverlún, a pompous Atalian official briefly joined Kheton, Lelani and their guests. They wished each other a happy 'Day of Remembrance' with a formal hug and kiss on the forehead, as was customary.

The children tried not to show how grossed out they were by this kissing business. It would have been too impolite.

"Ah, there are the white horses from the Valley of Heaven. Good steeds. You must be very proud of them,"

Gverlún said in a flattering tone.

"Yes we are. Over there is Prïnda," Lelani replied proudly.

You know much about horses, then." Katherine tried to be polite to Gverlún.

"I have been riding horses, when you were not even a twinkle in your mother's eye, young friend." The citadel official didn't know how very right he was.

"Some twinkle," Trevor said and Gverlún looked puzzled.

"I do, however, favour our own horses from the plains of Garanhir. The Atalian centaur country," the man said, brushing some imaginary dust off his tunic. When nobody seemed to listen, Gverlún went off looking for other important people, nearly colliding with some giddy ponies.

"I wish my sister Cassie was here. She adores horses. Oops!"

Chryséis felt a nudge in her back and turned around. She caught a glimpse of a moki's face. Its trunk-like snout drooped sadly and its eyes held a sad expression. "Aaah! Get away from me!" Chryséis jumped sideways and the placid moki trotted past them to the oval race course, followed by its centaur groom. The mokis were competing in their own races and lined up at the start line.

Kheton explained that most horses raced without a rider on their backs.

"Horses are guided telepathically along the track. There is often no need to for a rider."

But even without jockeys, there was much excitement as soon as the races started. The spectators whistled and cajoled. Some shouted, waving their country's colours the whole time. One of the Mokis from Ta Méry came first. Runner-up was a half-breed from Hipparion. Prizes consisted of gilded laurel wreaths that crowned the winning horse.

"Well done, hail the winner!" Kheton shouted with the rest of the crowd.

"Hail the winner!"

During the races, Tepi rested on the ground between the children, not leaving Katherine out of sight. These large creatures were not to be trusted. In the second race of the day, Túvar's horse Prïnda won. The mood was exuberant and a laughing Túvar lifted the laurel wreath up in the air.

After that, the races were getting boring. Always the same thing: an exciting start and an exciting finish with a long haul in between.

Trevor kept checking Chryséis' watch, but it seemed to be stuck. The time just didn't want to pass. When he saw the boys with the têrakhon ball again by the entrance, he quietly left to play with them. After the races were over, the victorious horses were led around the racecourse to the din of drum rolls, timbrel and cymbals.

"Where is Trevor?" She sounded worried.

Chryséis looked around. "I've no idea," she said.

"Perhaps he just went to the loo."

"To whom?" Chryseis asked.

"No — I mean to the bathroom," Katherine explained. For a moment, she had forgotten that Americans didn't understand the expression.

"Oh, I see."

"Why does he just leave without saying anything? It's strange. That's not like him at all."

"Come we go look for Trevor. I hope he's alright."

When the girls sneaked away, Tepi bounded after them.

"Oh Tepi, we're looking for Trevor. Can you help us find him?" Tepi looked intensely at Katherine, then started threading her way between moving legs out of the stadium.

"Do you think she understands?"

"No way Tepi understands what you just said," Chryséis said annoyed. "She's trying to run away from us."

"Maybe she does understand. Anyway, we can't just let her run out of here. Come on, she's over there." Katherine pointed to one of the fountains.

A pair of Leni Lepi performers played music with an ivory double-flute and a chunga, a guitar made from a large tortoise shell. A dance troupe in costumes made of paper bark and feathers, danced to the music, swinging hoops on their arms and legs.

Tepi thirstily lapped up water from the fountain, then she bounded on. The girls made their way after her and out of the entrance. They spotted Trevor in the middle of a Pigsnout game, catching the bouncing ball with a spoon-like bat, aiming for the marked hole in the wall.

"Trevor Huxley. What are you doing there? You can't just leave like that to play ball," Chryséis scolded, hands on her hips.

"Yes, we were worried. Túvar said we should be careful."

Trevor was out of breath. "Túvar was…talking about…Prydhain."

"Oh, don't start nitpicking. We must be careful even here. Did you forget the invisible Gabari in the Lady's chamber?"

"Yes, but it's safe here." He smashed the ball against the wall and another boy played it with his short paddle.

"Okay, okay, enough already. We'll discuss that later. Let's go back now." Chryséis was serious.

"Partypoopers. Let me just finish the game."

"How about not?" The girls were adamant. Just now, Túvar or Kheton might come looking for them.

"Alright…" Trevor said in a bored voice.

He waved to the disappointed boys and ran back inside the stadium after Tepi and the girls. Luckily, the others hadn't noticed their absence.

Soon it was time to leave the horseraces - and also to leave Atala. Kheton had received a coded thought transfer from the Lady of Algiras just as they were leaving and Túvar insisted on coming with them to the apartment.

"I will make sure they get safely onto that ship, Gobän, I'll be back at sunrise," he said in his deep voice.

A citadel vimaan waited by the horse statue outside the stadium and took them home past the citadel plaza. There was much festive activity on the square, but they could not stop and join in.

"Look over there, isn't that Jostia?" Trevor said.

"Yes, she is enjoying herself doing a formation dance with some Leni Lepi."

The senior maiden they had first met during the rainstorm in the harbour, had hitched her long white dress up to below her knees and danced happily around.

"I wish we could do that."

"Next time, Katie. We're going to England now. That's more important."

It was already dark when Túvar embraced the three youngsters in a bear hug and told Tepi one last time to behave. A few lonely raindrops splattered onto the ground.

"Pula means rain and blessing in Atala. The gods are blessing your journey." Lelani smiled and let the water drip onto the palm of her hand.

"A good sign. Ah, the summer rain has already stopped." Kheton slapped Trevor's shoulder amicably.

Why do they always have to do that? Trevor thought annoyed. Lelani managed a few tearful words while she hugged the girls. She had grown quite fond of the strange children. It would be lonely in Algiras without them.

"Do you think that Gillead will come to say goodbye?" Katherine asked.

"Obviously he has stuff to do. He's a sealord, not a babysitter," Trevor said. He was getting irritated with her crush on their Algiran guide.

"Yes, alright, I get it. No need to be so rude."

As the sky blushed into a pink haze, the three time travellers, Tepi and their four new companions were on a ship headed for Avallûn. They settled themselves on benches along the windows below deck. Tepi rested her head on Katherine's thigh. Tired from all the excitement, children and dog soon fell asleep.

The following day, the gardener found a small soft basket with a white flower next to the cooling cupboard by Kheton and Lelani's apartment. The flower with its longish leaves soon blended in nicely with the white and lilac pansies next to the complex entrance.

*

"What - kinsman Túvar is in Atala?" the Highpriest of Shuruk hollered.

"Yes, sire, he is here in Algiras for the horseraces."

"Aaaah! He is of no use to us here."

"No mylord. He is not."

"Aahhh! Let him go, then. Let him go. We will get my kinsman, the prince, later as soon as we have restored order in the Known World. Any news of the ...stone?" The sorcerer's eyes sparkled viciously and the Edfunian warriors stayed at a safe distance.

"They have caught our man in the citadel. The Lady unmasked him in front of the foreign children, just as she was telling them about the Speaking Stone. That's all we've heard sire, before the link was broken."

"Get somebody else then! Those troublesome foreign children. Are they still here?"

"I'm afraid so, sire. We are keeping an eye on them."

"The stone is more important than their sacrifice right now!"

"Yes sire. The stone is heavily protected at the citadel. Kept in a sphere inside a secret vault and it's impossible to get close to it now. This Lady knows what she is doing."

"Cursed womenfolk! Nothing is impossible, but we'll wait. Is the distraction with our Gorgonas allies working?"

"It seems so mylord. But we have not been able to intercept thought transfers relating to the movements of the stone yet. All we know is that somebody will be sent to investigate the ships."

"To Maligasima?" The Highpriest asked.

"To Avallûn."

"Not bad. They don't trust anyone. Work harder, Creban."

"Yes mylord. We are doing the best we can."

"You can go. Don't waste my time with mewling balderdash!"

"Very well sire."

138

Creban, the loyal Edfunian warrior, stomped off to give instructions. Another spy was installed at the citadel - and detected just as quickly as the ones before him.

As the Highpriest of Shuruk received the news, the hiding place of the Edfunians was nearly discovered, when he exploded in anger. But what could the Edfunians do about it?

It took them a while to catch up with the events, but by then the 'Speaking Stone' was already on its way to Avallûn.

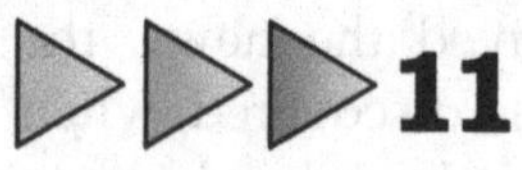 **11 THE ISLE OF GOLDEN ORCHARDS**

"Gee, is it daytime already?" "Chryséis yawned and stretched herself.

Sunrays tickled Trevor's face and he rubbed his eyes. The orange glow on the eastern horizon brightened. "That was a great birthday, thanks guys," he said.

"Yes it was." Chryséis was wide-awake now and shook Katherine's shoulder. "Come on sleepy head, wake up!"

"What, where am I?"

"You're on the ship to Avallûn, silly. Let's go upstairs and get some air."

"Ship? Sea monsters?" It took Katherine a while to cotton on.

"No, no sea monsters. At least I hope not!" Chryséis frowned and looked out on the ocean.. Everything seemed quiet and the ship was also completely steady. Tepi uncurled and began to lick Katherine's hand that was touching the floor.

"What's that?" Katherine quickly pulled back her hand.

"It's just Tepi. Hello... Tepi the dog... she's coming with us. What's wrong with you, have you forgotten everything that happened yesterday?"

"No. Just have to wake up." Katherine yawned broadly.

"Ooh, I can see what you had for supper," Chryséis joked.

"That's easy: we all had the same supper. I still don't understand why the stone wants us to come on this mission." Trevor also had to yawn and got up.

"Here we go again, the Speaking Stone that never speaks. Only in secret, perhaps," Chryséis said.

"But it sounds adventurous," Trevor said.

"Yeah, like we haven't had enough adventures already."

"Oh come on, Chris, we'll be home before you know it and then you guys will want to come back here and experience adventures all over again."

"I don't think so." Katherine got up and Tepi sat down, begging with her front paws. "Tepi seems to be hungry."

"I'm also starving. Let's see if there's any breakfast for us," Chryséis said.

Somebody came stomping down the stairs and the head of the Dwendi Lubbo appeared the doorway almost immediately.

He wore a green suit just like Amadis and a Robin-Hood-like hat on his unruly red hair. A jaunty young man, he had a carefree laugh with slightly protruding front teeth, a bushy red beard and a small paunch as neat and round as a melon. Kheton had told them that Lubbo was an artificer by profession, skilled in making fine tools.

"Athenai, I hope you had a good rest," he grunted. "The others are having their morning meal on deck now."

"With captain Thëlamôn?"

"No, this ship is skippered by captain Maclir." Lubbo wagged his head.

"Why? Where is captain Thëlamôn?" Trevor wanted to know.

"I would not know young friend. You are on the 'Navis Prydhwin', Prince Artû's ship. Aren't you lot hungry?"

"Yes, we are hungry. Shukri, friend Lubbo, we are coming with you." The children scampered up the stairs after the Dwendi.

"Another ship?" Katherine wondered.

"I wish I could brush my teeth," Trevor said.

"Oh please, how is that important now?" A breeze blew Katherine's hair into her face and she tied it back into a ponytail.

"A blessed morning to you all, athenai," Prince Artû greeted the children without as much as a smile. "Break the fast with us."

He waved at a long table decked with flatbread, sliced harpee roast with aioli, fruits and small cherry pies.

"Shelanti, Prince Artû. Shelanti Gwendola."

The dark-haired Dwendi woman nodded graciously and handed a cup with hot mint tea to each child. Tepi sniffed the harpee roast and Katherine hurried to feed the dog some of the slices, before she heaped a plate of food for herself. The famished time travellers watched the sunrise gather strength while tucking into their breakfast.

Amadis smiled charmingly at them. "I was told that your families come from Prydhain, athenai."

"Only my family," Katherine said between mouthfuls of cherry pie.

"Chryséis and I are from…Patala," Trevor clarified, but the D'Ånu warrior's curiosity was not quite satisfied.

"Where is your village then, what is it called?" He asked Katherine.

"Oh, it's called Oxford."

"Oxfól? I have never heard of a village by that name. Oxfól." He seemed quite surprised.

"It is a very small village."

"Stop asking all those questions, Amadis," Gwendola reproached the young man and whipped her crinkled black braids behind each ear.

Her swarthy round face looked friendlier now, but her manner was still stern. It was a matter of habit, since it was Gwendola's job to teach the younger generation 'ga i sced' meaning 'courage and valor', a form of Dwendi martial arts. The Lady of Algiras had handed over guardianship over the three children to her and a letter to prove it.

"Haha, dear Gwen. Don't put me in my place with your deadly kicks, please," Amadis laughed. "I do promise to be less inquisitive."

"Shukri Amadis," Gwendola said with some sarcasm. "If you hadn't grown up with my brother in the hills of Anáa, I should think you were a Firbolg."

Firbolgs werew nasty Little People, but Amadis obviously thought her remark hilarious, while the prince observed the strange children.

"Why so gloomy, friend Artû?" Amadis wanted to know.

"All this talk of Firbolgs might frighten the children."

Lubbo agreed. "The Prydhanian Gabari have caused us Dwendis much sorrow in the past, but the other Little People, the 'Firbolg of Prydhain' can be just as bothersome."

"What are the 'Firbolg'?" Trevor wanted to know.

"They are a tribe of ill-meaning goblins," Lubbo blurted out. "Mining metals and precious stones underground, often siding with evil giants against civilised folk. Amadis' grandfather lost his hand in a skirmish with the Firbolg in the Fûna Mountains back in his day. Giants cannot be trusted anywhere anymore, either."

"We have a very good Gabari friend. He lives in Alesia and helps the Lady of Cydonia…he was in Algiras to take part in the horseraces," Trevor began to defend the Alesian giants and Túvar, but Lubbo's expression was so grim that he fell quiet.

"When my grandfather was a young man, he had been assigned to a humanitarian mission in the foothills of the Fûna Mountains," Amadis explained. "The giants didn't appreciate the intrusion and told the Firbolg to attack their group. The D'Ånu medic replaced my grandfather's severed hand with an artificial limb made of bja metal…"

"…but the Dwendis and the Firbolg have been at loggerhead ever since. To attack the D'Ånu is unforgivable. And it wasn't the only time mind you," Lubbo finished the story, while eating with gusto from a plate of quartered green and pink figs.

"What is bja metal?"

"Ah, friend Chryséis , like têrakhon, it has many uses," said Lubbo.

"I'm not so sure I like this different England," Katherine

said softly. "These people don't seem to like each other."

"And what else is new?" Chryséis tried a piece of a small purple fruit that tasted a bit like guava. "We'll see what it's like. It can't be that bad."

"It's only a 'little' problem, right?! Get my drift?" Trevor chuckled.

"I think that sounded better in your head just now."

"Yeah, it did," Trevor said lightly, before attacking another piece of flatbread he had filled with harpee roast.

The ship passed what looked like some kind of factory in the distance, with black and sulphur-yellow smoke whirling from a huge chimney. A dark cone had orange lava streaming down its side. Clearly this wasn't a factory. The lava reached the seawater rumbling and spluttering. White steam rose high into the air and mingled with the dark smoke.

"What's this?" Katherine stammered, while Tepi was hiding behind her. "Not a volcano, is it?"

"New land," captain Maclir filled them in. He was just as burly as captain Thëlamôn, just with a lot less hair. "Has been spewing its innards out since after the feast of Hestia. Used to be a volcano before the earth shook and the waters came. This hasn't happened since I was old enough to remember."

The wart-covered backs of large sea creatures, swimming away from the volcano island, passed the ship and soon dived out of sight.

Chryséis pointed to the animals. "Are they makarah?" She was proud to be able to test a new word she had learned in Algiras. The prince paled visibly. These foreigners are so ignorant, he thought, they don't even know a walrus from a shark.

"No, no," he said aloud shaking his head. "No, friend Chryséis , these sea animals are not makarah. They are i v i k."

"Thank you for making this clear," Chryséis replied politely, sensing his irritation with her question. "He must think that we're stupid," she said to Trevor.

"At least they weren't sharks. Would have been rather big sharks. Wonder if the sea monsters that attacked us before were as big as that."

"Oh, don't even mention that." Chryséis shivered a little.

Prince Artû kept staring at the volcano and knitted his eyebrows in concern. "An 'Iti', a volcano child coming to life, is not a good sign," he said.

"Fiery upheaval has never been a good sign in the Atlantean Sea or anywhere else for that matter," captain Maclir agreed with him.

Soon the Avallûnian west coast came into sight. Hundreds of piked red-skinned lizards basked on the surf-washed rocks.

"Seamen often tell tall stories of huge red dragons guarding the precious apple orchards," Lubbo said. "The orchards are protected, but these little red lizards have nothing to do with it."

"But they are — small red dragons," Trevor said.

Avallûn was truly the 'Isle of Golden Orchards'. Blessed with a most agreeable climate, apple trees abounded in the valleys. Wheat and barley stood high and golden in the fields and flocks of sheep grazed on grassy slopes. Ancient windmills resembled giant spider webs and the sunhats of farmers harvesting wheat bobbed up and down in the fields.

"Come on, tell the children about Avallûn, Prince Artû!" Gwendola demanded, rousing him from his thoughts. "I'm sure they have never before been to your shores."

"Very well," the prince sighed. "Avallûn means 'apple trees', athenai. Avallûnians survived the devastating floods before the Dark Age in the highlands. The continent sank groaning below the mighty waves and Avallûn became an island." Artû sounded like a mirage commentator.

"Then Boreas, the god of winter, began to hold his reign in Avallûn. Stricken with frosty weather for sheaves of years, the survivors managed to save themselves and many a young apple tree in protected caves. After the harsh climate of the Dark Age had ended, apple orchards were once again planted and they thrived in Avallûn."

"Are apples that important?" Katherine asked.

"Yes of course, they are. The trees are returning the favour by giving the people of Avallûn many gifts. Food and drink and trade."

"That's rather interesting." Katherine gazed at the passing apple trees.

"What are those stone ships for?" Trevor asked pointing at strange boat-shaped stone heaps that were scattered along the coast.

"They are called 'navetas'. The seafaring peoples of old made them in honour of the gods. They are also said to protect the shore from flooding." The Navis Prydwhin sailed quickly along the coast. "We are now passing the grain fields of Edom. Hestia has truly blessed our people with fertile land," Artû said proudly.

"I thought the Earthmother was called Aïma." Chryséis frowned.

"Oh, the Earthmother goes by many names," Gwendola answered her. "Here, she is called Hestia."

Green pastures and apple orchards now took turns with fragrant lavender fields. A herd of auburn cows came into view. Two Gabari men with long staffs herded them inland and were followed by some odd-looking saurians. When Tepi saw the saurians, her curiosity got the better of her. The young dog ran up and down the deck, sniffing the air and whimpering.

"At times, dishonest sailors don't want to trade with the farmers and steal golden fruits in the dark," Prince Artû told them. "Our apples are precious and known to prevent the 'Nereus curse', a dreaded gum disease. Sometimes these sailors even try to take a sheep or cow, but our Gabari herdsmen often catch them with the help of these tame saurians. They are trained to protect the flock,"

"Pah, Gabari!" Lubbo snorted contemptuously. "Probably helping them to steal…"

Soon the white citadel of 'Caer Calvas' rose on a rocky cliff ahead. As they rounded the peninsula, the king's castle appeared leaning against the hillock. A sturdy apple tree of 'the first generation' overshadowed the front court. The quaint, east-facing harbour of Arvalos was nestled in the bay below. The castle was the home of Prince Artû, his parents King Avallach and Queen Nuada and his sister, Princess Harleia.

"To the right, beyond the 'Strait of Caldera', lies the coast of Hesperus," Prince Artû continued. "But too far from Arvalos to be seen even on clear days. Farther up the Avallûnian coast, warships of the Atalian fleet are moored at the naval base of Katú. The Lady of Algiras reacted quickly to the threat of Gorgonas warships in the area."

"Our Ama-zûnas allies oversee the shipyard of Katú and command the ships," Amadis completed Prince Artû's account. "They are admirable sailors."

He said this as the 'Navis Prydhwin' entered the mouth of the harbour. Captain Maclir dropped anchor in a reserved spot next to a D'ântillian freighter, ready to take a cargo of golden apples to Kamûk.

The exact time of the 'Navis Prydhwin''s arrival had been kept a secret, so there was no welcoming committee and for once, no singing.

"Look at all those flowers!" Katherine pointed in amazement at a myriad of blooms. Hibiscus bushes with red and pink and yellow flowers as big as dinner plates and fragrant citrus trees grew in every corner of the steep cobble-stone roads.

"How odd. What are those people doing?" Chryséis couldn't believe her eyes. "I can't say for sure, but I it looks as if they ride down the roads in huge baskets."

The people of Arvalos used an unusual method to

transport apples and their famous cider down to the harbour. And Chryséis had seen it quite correctly. Youngsters negotiated large willow baskets, called toboggans, down the slopes, sometimes racing against each other for fun. Strong Gabari youths pulled the baskets uphill again, laden with goods from the merchant ships or used by passengers.

Many an Avallûnian grandfather fondly remembered his own time as a toboggan driver and the occasional sport that went along with it. However, surprised visitors often managed to jump aside only in the nick of time.

"Wow, that's awesome." Trevor looked up at the imposing citadel and castle.

"Ho there, look out!" somebody called behind them, just before a large basket steered by a laughing youth came swooshing past, narrowly missing Trevor. Tepi began to bark and Katherine knelt down to calm the dog. The toboggan rattled onto the quay at a dangerous angle, headed for the freighter moored next to the Navis Prydhwin.

"Careful with that toboggan, lad!" Amadis cried. "Look out for pedestrians." But the basket was already out of earshot.

A handful of apples had fallen from the basket and Amadis picked up two of the golden fruits and gave one to Katherine. He rubbed the other apple on his velvety waistcoat and took a big bite. "A bit tart for last year's harvest," he said with a twinkle in his eye.

Prince Artû frowned at the insult, while Gwendola tried not to giggle. Clearly Amadis was trying to wind up the stern nobleman. Avallûnians were rather proud of the sweet fruits and easily took offense when criticised.

"I think the apple is delicious," Katherine assured Artû and ate the fruit Amadis had tossed her.

Prince Artû grunted and threw a corner of his sky-blue cloak over his right shoulder. Their transport baskets arrived and two Gabari boys in yellow court waistcoats pulled them up to the citadel on the hill.

"This place is so backwards, where are the vimaans?" Trevor whispered.

"There is one over there." Chryséis pointed to a red flying machine parked in front of one of the solid houses. "And one is right here."

Arvalos houses were built from rocks around an inner court. A roofed-in passage lead into the street and all the houses had large chimneys and tiled roofs.

"Hardly as busy as it was in Algiras."

"Looks more like a town in France," Katherine said. "I thought we were in back in the future. It feels more like being in St. Malo or even Marseille." A large greenish vimaan was headed down the hill and swished past them.

"Come on, when do you ever see vimaans and Gabari in France?"

"Okay, that's also true," Katherine conceded.

The royal family welcomed them in the citadel yard under the big old apple tree. The king looked like an older, bearded version of his son Artû, but had nothing of his son's petulant mood.

"Shelanti athenai, Shelanti. My son, we have been awaiting you," he greeted them cheerfully. "The Lady of Arvalos has already summoned the council to listen to the missive by the Lady of Algiras you brought with you."

Because the island was so close to enemy lands in Hesperus across the 'Strait of Caldera', there was a permanent need for a sea king on Avallûn. King Avallach was an outstanding sea king and much loved by his subjects.

"Shelanti, father, mother, Harleia. It is good to be back home," Artû said gravely.

"Oh, come on big brother, give us a hug." The pretty princess embraced him with a grin. "Don't be quite so solemn."

"The Earthmother be thanked, my son. You are back home in one piece," his mother said tearfully. "And so soon you will be off again to…"

"Mother!" the prince warned her and the queen fell silent.

Prince Artû looked around. One never knew if spies were present, but everything seemed normal. The staff in the yard were trusted Avallûnians.

"The Lady has requested the presence of your companions at the citadel after our conference. Dinner will be served on the veranda. Please follow me; I'm sure you will want to freshen up…" Queen Nuada led the way into the castle, while the king, Artû, Amadis and Lubbo were taken to the citadel by vimaan.

Gwendola stayed behind and made sure she was never far from the children. As the sun set in a spectacular sky, they sat down to dinner on the top veranda of the citadel. Needless to say that nearly all the excellent dishes were made with apples.

"How far you can see from here!" Katherine said dreamily. The sun had coloured the sea a dark orange colour and the light was now fading.

"Harvest time is very important in Avallûn," the queen told them during the second course of succulent roast pig with a lavender honey crust and roasted apples. "It is a pity that you young folk cannot stay until harvest time. Our youngsters sing and dance during the Festival of Manzán and marriages are arranged to be celebrated in the spring."

The Lady lifted her goblet with apple cider. The guests did the same, just that the children drank apple juice. "To the blessed harvest time."

"To the blessed harvest time," everyone answered in chorus.

"I'm far too young to get married," Chryséis said in a low voice and drank her juice.

Trevor helped himself to another piece of griddle cake and Tepi chewed on a juicy bone by his feet. He eavesdropped on King Avallach and Artû, who were discussing local affairs, while dancers and musicians entertained the guests.

"I saw that Tiamat, our mother sea, has claimed coastal land to the south, father." Prince Artû sounded worried.

"Good farmland was washed away in violent thunderstorms and high tides this last season," the king said. "There is talk that the farmers have reverted to the practice of human sacrifice on the navetas."

Trevor gagged on a piece of cake, but the two men didn't seem to notice.

"Father, this abominable tradition must not ever be allowed again."

"Fear is creeping into their hearts, my son. The fear that our wonderful island might disappear under the sea, like Atland, if the gods don't intervene."

The musicians did their best to entertain the party with fiddle-like instruments and flutes. There was not much singing, but the maidens performed studied dances. No one noticed how two little fairies broke off pieces of cake only to disappear again atop a marble statue of Tiamat.

"Did you hear that?" Trevor whispered to Chryséis .

She pricked her ears. "What?"

Katherine leaned over. "Did you say something?"

"I said… Did you hear that?" Trevor repeated softly. "The king and the prince are talking about human sacrifice."

Katherine looked surprised. "I didn't listen. I watched the dancers the whole time. Are you sure he said human sacrifice?"

Chryséis felt uneasy. "Maybe you didn't hear them right. The dialect is a bit heavy, and they are such nice people."

"You're right, I probably didn't understand them correctly." But Trevor still felt uneasy about the whole thing. What if he had understood them properly? Were these Avallûnians cannibals or something like that?

"The Ioannu report that a number caf Gorgonas warships were sailing along the Maligasima coast yesterday. Those pig-headed Gorgonas refuse to have telepathic talks with representatives of the 'House of Nations of the Known World'." King Avallach seemed frustrated.

"How very uncivilised of them. I will go to Katú tomorrow and speak with the commander of the Amazûnas," Prince Artû answered.

"We will send a messenger with a sealed letter to inform the Lady of Algiras as soon as we know more. Not even telepathy is safe under the circumstances."

During the last Gorgonas insurgence, still vividly remembered in local songs and plays, coastal villages in the Edom region had been cruelly pillaged. Although the attack was refuted, good men had been put to the sword and slaves were taken to Hesperus. This time Avallûn would be prepared.

"Have some more of the roasted pig," the king invited his guests with a generous gesture.

At the same hour, the shipyard of Katú was still brimming with activity by torchlight. One shipwright's apprentice, whose teeth were filed in the Gorgonas fashion, managed to slip away unnoticed from his place among the carpenters.

The man cautiously sneaked along a narrow path through a small wood down to the waterfront. He tripped over a misplaced tool in the dark, which alerted the Amazûnas guards. They investigated, but the man managed to hide behind stacked wooden planks just in time.

Down on the rocky shore, he hastily loosened a rope and climbed into a dinghy. He rowed the boat against the tide and struggled up the coast. He soon made out a schooner, hidden in a small creek. All the apprentice had to do now was to get his message right. Just as he had been told to do. An important message he had received from a page at the citadel palace before nightfall.

An hour later the shipwright's apprentice was back in his assigned place, hammering wooden nails into drilled holes, smiling to himself.

Making a wide berth around Maligasima, the schooner sailed straight for northern Prydhain under the cover of night, taking a chance with the monsters of the sea.

On a stretch of wild coast, a fierce-looking group of Edfunians went on land. The leaks the giants had driven into the hull soon sunk the schooner together with its captain and crew. They had served their purpose.

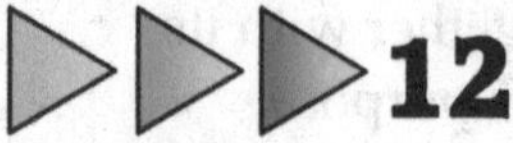 **12**   THE WATER WITCH

As soon as the sealed message had been sent from Arvalos to Algiras, the Navis Prydhwin covertly set out with its motley crew and the Speaking Stone aboard. The passage was uneventful at first and they moved swiftly toward the coast of Maligasima.

"Gorgonas warships, Gorgonas warships!" The frantic warning call tore through the peaceful mood. Two massive warships appeared out of nowhere on the horizon. At first, there were only faint shadows then the ships drew steadily closer.

"What is this? Maligasima is too far east for them to attack so quickly!" captain Maclir roared angrily. "They must have been laying in wait nearer to Avallûn."

"I will sound the alarm. The supervisor in Katú will act quickly."

"Make haste Artû, they are approaching!" Maclir yelled.

"How did they know about us leaving? The departure has been kept secret until this morning," Lubbo thundered.

"There is only one way: spies!" Gwendola piped up.

"Oh that's just splendid. We are being chased by warships and there are spies among us." Katherine watched the leading ship taking course for them. And the Gorgonas gained in speed. The Navis Prydhwin itself seemed to fly across the water, but captain Maclir's maneuvers had little effect.

"Why can't we just have a normal trip for once?" Chryseis rolled her eyes and Tepi looked up at her worried.

"I think it's so cool, a real sea battle." Trevor was beaming.

"Oh yes? You can get hurt or even killed in a real sea battle, you know - because it's not a computer game!"

"Okay, okay…but it's still cool."

"So much for this whole thing being over before we know it."

"The Gorgonas are in a great hurry to reach us." Amadis watched from the ship's bow, mockingly raising one eyebrow.

Prince Artû's face was rather serious, his lips pressed together. He had to take the chance and communicate with the commander at Katú . "They are coming to aid us," he announced after a brief telepathic discussion.

"Good. I hope they are not too late," was Lubbo's dry comment. "The Gorgonas are closing in fast. Only ten lengths away now."

"Ready the weapons, captain!" Prince Artû commanded.

Like the Navis Arion, the Navis Prydhwin was no trading vessel and fully equipped to defend its mission and crew.

"Shouldn't we try and reach the mainland, instead of preparing for battle?" Amadis didn't smile anymore. "Let's leave the fighting to our warships when they arrive."

"We won't have much of a choice, friend," Artû replied.

The warships were coming ever closer. Powerful Gorgonas men and women in their sturdy lizard hide armors and helmets were already in position on deck, their braided hair flying in the breeze.

"It's a good thing we can't see their faces yet," Lubbo said dryly.

Then out of nowhere, a sleek ship emerged in the south, swiftly also making good on the Navis Prydhwin. Then another one and yet another.

The Ama-zûnas caught up quickly with the bulky Gorgonas warships, causing them to split into two groups. But the confederates didn't fall for the ruse and a heated battle began between the trailing Gorgonas ships and the equally fierce Ama-zûnas. The first two ships held their course for the Navis Prydhwin – but not quickly enough. One of the enemy ships sidled up to them.

"What are you still doing up here?" Captain Maclir and Artû screamed at the same time. "Children below deck. Now!"

Twack! Enter hooks crashed into wooden planks just as the time travelers scuttled down the stairs with Tepi in tow. Ghastly-looking Gorgonas warriors pulled on the ropes and drew their ship closer.

"Get the backpacks, quick! We might have to get a vortex going. Where is the stone?" Chryseis yelled.

"Amadis had it in his shoulder bag just now."

"How can we be sure?"

"I don't care!" Katherine yelled back.

The ship shuddered and the Gorgonas made ready to jump with drawn weapons. The Navis Prydhwin received a mighty knock that hurtled two of the armed sailors overboard. Another knock shivered through the hull and the young passengers were in panic.

"Give me the TPF. Give me the TPF!" Trevor demanded.

"Aaah, they're going to sink us!" Katherine screamed, holding Tepi. The Navis Prydhwin shivered as one of the confederate vessels wedged itself nimbly between the two ships, prying them apart. The Ama-zûnas didn't jump a moment too soon and surprised the Gorgonas with blood-curdling cries. Then more help arrived. A number of Ioannu had set out to reach the battle scene on dolphinback.

"Look outside." Trevor pointed through a porthole to a merman busy rescuing the two dripping wet sailors, who had been flung overboard.

"Come quickly! Down the ropes - quick!" The Ioannu called up, waving.

Gwendola went down the side of the hull first, hanging from a rope in front of the porthole. The children didn't have to think twice, they pounded up the stairs and were immediately abseiled onto the backs of waiting porpoises and dolphins. Soon, Chryséis and Trevor held unto each other behind a Ioannu riding a large porpoise. Katherine and Tepi shared a dolphin with one of the mermaids.

"Hold on tight!" The Ioannu woman commanded and they swiftly rode the waves toward the coast.

"Quick, the lagoon of Narada!" Prince Artû yelled from the back of a dolphin that overtook them.

The Ioannu obliged quickly and instead of sailing into a glamorous prehistoric seaport in a ship, they entered a hidden lagoon, riding on the backs of sea mammals. None of the warships followed them as the warriors were still engaged in slashing and buzzing each other. The Amazûnas lost no time in destroying the two enemy ships and made short shrift of the despised Gorgonas. The damaged Navis Prydhwin was towed back to Katú together with the crew - but the battle was won.

The remaining Gorgonas fled back east. Atland would deal with them later. Meanwhile, the merpeople rode their flippered mounts through the lagoon toward a primitive landing. A stairwell led a short ways up to the ruined citadel of Narada. The Ioannu of the Gadiric Sea were no strangers to this place and the porpoises and dolphins lined up along the landing.

Prince Artû was already standing on the weathered planks, when a seal came waddling down the stairs to inspect the wet newcomers. Tepi leapt unto the landing before everyone else and shook herself generously that the water droplets flying. Dog and seal sniffed each other and decided that it wouldn't hurt to be friends. Hu, the seal, happily followed his new friend along the landing with a throaty bark.

"Shelanti, Ioannu friends," a woman in the attire of a Lady greeted them. "You bring me visitors? Welcome."

Her face was tanned and wrinkled, but her long blonde hair was that of a young girl. The contrast couldn't have been greater. Tepi sniffed at the woman. "Ah, Hu has found a new friend." She smiled and her face looked young.

"Hu?" Prince Artû asked.

"Oh, this is Hu, young man." She pointed to the tame seal.

"Shukri, Ioannu friends, you saved us from the battle," Amadis thanked the merpeople.

"It is our pleasure. We are glad to be of service."

The Ioannu had offloaded their passengers and now rode the porpoises and dolphins back to the ships to see if any of the warriors needed saving.

"Good health. We will see you later, athenai!" Their leader shouted over his shoulder before they disappeared from view.

Artû remembered his good manners. "Shelanti, honorable Lady of Narada. Please forgive our sudden invasion, but we carry an object of importance to Caradoc and…"

"…and tried to avoid meeting the Gorgonas at sea and have it taken from you. I know, son of King Avallach of Avallûn. I have been expecting you and your companions. Fierce warriors the Ama-zûnas, there is nothing to worry about."

Artû seemed surprised. "How do you know my name, Lady, and our purpose?"

"I am not the Lady of Narada, young man, just a maiden, who happened to survive the good Lady and everybody else in the citadel. And I saw your arrival in a dream."

"You have the second sight then, maiden?" Amadis asked.

"My name is Zeruana and – yes, I do," she said curtly.

"May we ask you for shelter, good maiden?"

"You are welcome to join me in my modest home, until you are ready to leave," Zeruana welcomed them formally.

She led the way up the path lined with flowering plants, round pebbles, driftwood and giant shells. Weathered wooden tablets, proclaiming the 'Laws of Loyalty', were part of the low border.

The visitors settled themselves on smooth stone blocks around a sheltered fireplace behind the citadel ruin. A stone slab served as a makeshift table and still bore the inscription '…the Path of Truth is often…' the other text had broken off. A small cauldron with roselle tea simmered over a bristling fire. Soon everybody was drying in the sunlight, holding cups with steaming red tea.

"Did you find the TPF?" Chryseis whispered.

"Yes, it's in my backpack. Where's yours?"

"Also here." Trevor pulled the timetravel device a little out of his backpack, to show them.

"Mine's in my pocket." Katherine felt it through the fabric. "Good thing that we wrapped them into sandwich bags."

"And a good thing we didn't have to activate a vortex," Trevor said.

Zeruana talked about this and that, while the visitors drank their 'welcome tea'. She told the story of how the quaint citadel and village of Narada had collapsed during an earthquake more than three decades ago. Zeruana had been sixteen and an apprentice maiden at the time.

"The Lady of Narada herself escaped unharmed and found me holding onto a rafter. I was bruised and my leg was broken. Everybody else had perished. Trained at the 'House of Life', the good Lady was able to heal my leg. The citadel was not rebuilt and we continued to live in the ruins here, until the Lady died of old age."

"You live here all by yourself, maiden?" Gwendola asked flabbergasted. Dwendis were a sociable people and living alone was unimaginable.

"Yes, I have been living by myself ever since. The good folk of Sogamosa call me the 'waterwitch'. I suppose I earned the name because I prefer the company of the Ioannu. We sometimes share meals of glasswort salad and sea urchin roe on the beach of the lagoon. And then there are my animals of course. They are superstitious, the people of Narada and Sogamosa, but they still come here for medical help."

"Why are they this superstitious?"

"Oh, they believe that the site brings ill luck and that

the ghosts of the dead roam the ruins. Perhaps they think that I possess special powers to keep the ghosts at bay." The waterwitch laughed resoundingly.

"Perhaps they think you are a ghost yourself," Gwendola added, creasing her forehead.

The 'waterwitch almost doubled over with laughter. "Yes, a healing ghost. That is very funny. I suppose it doesn't help that I have the 'second sight', seeing into the future and the past. Although I keep the 'dreams' to myself these days."

Katherine glanced at the ruined citadel. Two pillars held up a portion of the upper floor, forming a shaded porch. Zeruana had closed the open side of her dwelling with large pieces of strong cloth. An arched window that had once belonged to the 'Hall of Audience', overlooked the pale blue Mohini Cliffs in the distance and the Gadiric Sea.

"It is sad that everyone else died in the earthquake," Katherine said.

"Death is always a great loss, but I've come to terms with it. Nobody wanted to live here afterwards. It gets lonely sometimes, which is why I like having visitors the seagods send my way once in a while."

"Just like us?" Trevor asked.

"Yes, just like you."

The 'waterwitch' had mentioned that she kept her few belongings in a giant clam shell. When Lubbo learned that the clam chest did not close properly, he offered his skills to repair the broken latch.

"Thank you good Dwendi friend, shukri," Zeruana thanked him.

"Shukri, shukri good Dwendi..." a fiery-red parakeet on the low citadel wall squawked, bowing again and again on his perch. The visitors stared.

"This is Haapi. He was a present by a trader from Sogamosa. I safely delivered the man's twin boys and they are both married now." Zeruana told them.

"Haapi, Haapi, my sweet little friend…" The bird coaxed.

"Why doesn't the parakeet fly away?" Lubbo wanted to know.

"His wings were clipped, but he just decided to stay after a while. Haapi often rides on my shoulder and he speaks acceptable Akkadian."

As if on command, Haapi performed a little song in his croaking voice:

'Under foaming towers
Where the Ocean powers
Sit on their pearled thrones…'

Everyone roared with laughter. This prompted the parakeet to bow again and again, which was even more comical. The visit turned out to be more funny than expected. Zeruana stood up and walked over to the singing bird. She fed him a morsel of fruit from a têrakhon dish and Haapi responded with fluttering wings and jerky movements. "Krah, krah…ocean powers… pearled thrones… krah… krah…" he sang then gnawed at the fruit.

"Come Hu, come come come," Zeruana called her seal.

"Why is Hu so tame?" Trevor asked curiously.

Zeruana had to be a prehistoric cat lady, if he ever saw one.

"We understand each other. A seal colony is nearby and Hu is free to rejoin his kind whenever he chooses to."

Hu waddled gregariously up to her and received a few small fish from a wooden pail. Tepi sniffed at the pail, but decided that the moving fish were not for her. Then, to everyone's surprise, Zeruana began to speak in a monotonous voice.

"Sat athenai, seven friends…humans are ruled by the number seven. The life of man is divided into seven ages. With the child it is the teeth that appear in the seventh month and are shed at seven years. At twice seven, adolescence begins, at three times seven all our mental and vital powers are developed at four times seven we are at full strength, at five times seven,…" she recited the text she had learned as a young apprentice, then Zeruana shook herself slightly as if waking from a dream. She didn't seem to remember what had just happened and nobody said anything.

Odd or not, a maiden was worthy of respect after all.

"Would you like more tea? Drink good people, it'll give you strength. We will eat soon. You have a strenuous journey ahead of you..." She flicked back a strand of blonde hair.

"Speaking of...may I help with the cooking in any way?" Gwendola asked, feeling hunger gripping her stomach. They hadn't eaten since this morning and it was past lunchtime now.

"Oh, I am not cooking today. Have patience, visitors. We will eat on the beach," Zeruana said.

"Glasswort salad and sushi are not really my thing," Trevor said quietly to Chryseis and Katherine. "We can eat some beef jerky."

Gwendola settled back on her stone seat and sipped roselle tea. Zeruana told stories about the olden days, while Hu and Tepi didn't grow tired of racing each other up and down the stairs to the landing. Waiting for each other sniffing, only to race again. Except for the time travelers, everyone else had heard these stories before.

"High up in the north, the country of 'Mount Meru' had flourished for sheaves of years. Then the sky fell and the year became as one day and one night. The Dark Age began, but Mount Meru was spared by the god Boreas the grip of eternal winter. After a long time Boreas loosened his frosty grip and the ice began to melt in the world. But the god claimed Mount Meru as a sacrifice for returning the land to the Earthmother. Within moments the good land that had been spared, froze over and became milk-white. Those who managed to flee south to the country of Airyana Vaëgo settled in the fertile land around the great inland sea Thetys. Although Thetys is no more, the people of Airyana Vaëgo enjoy a blessed existence."

"Yes, the Earthmother be blessed for her bountiful gifts," the Dwendis said in response out of habit, hoping that this was the end of the story.

They were ready to eat raw fish just as the survivors of the Dark Age had and they weren't the only ones thinking about food.

"Sounds like this happened a long time ago." Chryseis checked a yawn. "I don't think she gets a lot of visitors here. Gee, I'm starving. Let's have the beef jerky."

"Shall we proceed to dinner?" Amadis asked. "We could catch fish for us all."

"Oh, no need for that, D'Ånu, but we can go down to the beach. I am used to fasting and sometimes forget how hungry my visitors get," the waterwitch said.

"I'll say." Chryséis dropped her backpack.

They would eat the beef jerky they had brought with them another day. A number of Ioannu had assembled on the nearby beach with a large catch of mackerels. A young Ioannu male introduced himself.

"Shelanti, I am Umantua, the leader of the Ioannu tribe in the Gadiric Sea. Honorable Zeruana, we have brought dinner, just as you asked."

Zeruana nodded graciously. Soon the fragrant aroma of fresh green herbs she had stuffed the fish with, rose with the smoke of the fire. The mackerels were so fatty that no oil was needed to fry them.

Katherine counted the Ioannu. There were eight of them and they had brought many more fish that Zeruana would hang up to dry later. While they waited, Tepi had curled herself up at Katherine's feet and snored peacefully, while Hu took a bath in the clear lagoon.

After the meal, the Ioannu visitors lingered awhile on the warm beach. Trevor tossed a pebble into the air and caught it a few times before he let it skip lazily across the water surface. After a while the conversation turned to serious matters.

"We would like to warn you not to go by boat to Caradoc, Prince Artû," Umantua squeaked. "It is better to take the land route through Tregarn. Gorgonas have attacked two trading ships in revenge for your escape."

"What else can be expected of stinking Gorgonas?" Lubbo grunted. The Ioannu squeaked in agreement. They've had much gripe with the wild Gorgonas tribe over the years.

"One of the trading ships came from Maligasima, the other one was on its way back to D'ântilla..."

"Not the Navis Arion I hope," Katherine threw in. "Not captain Thëlamôn!"

Umantua held his head askew for a moment. Then he smiled and said,

"No, it was not the Navis Arion from D'ântilla. The good captain Thëlamôn is still delayed in Ogygia, waiting for a load of smoked salmon. One ship got away, alas, the other one slumbers at the bottom of the Gadiric Sea with its load of jade and silver from Dilmùn. We were able to save many a seaman with the help of our valued friends with long snouts."

"The dolphins?"

"Yes, friends, the dolphins."

Zeruana said in a dreamy voice, "There will be no Ioannu to help you so far away from the sea. But our friends of small stature..." she nodded in the direction of Gwendola, "...will guide you on your journey."

Artû and Amadis gawked at the Dwendi woman. The little fairies from Ruta Ynis, hiding in Gwendola's braids, sat very still and nobody except Zeruana could see them.

"Plan your journey wisely. Take the longer road if need be. Never again must a 'Speaking Stone' fall into the hands of the selfish and cruel."

"The shortest route is not always the best," said Lubbo with a slight bow to the maiden and Umantua. "Be assured that we will use good sense to make our choices."

Prince Artû made a little bow just like Lubbo had. Manners were important even under dire circumstances.

The evening was mild and another deep orange sunset announced itself on the horizon. It was time for the merpeople to return to their home. They shared an island just outside of the lagoon most comfortably with a colony of walrus. As they made their way to the island, they greeted a herd of Zeuglodons.

They were strange-looking whales with longish bodies and small pointed heads. Soon, Zeruana and her guests headed back to the ruins then wild flutter in the haoma tree near the beach made everyone look up. The flutter died down.

"Are those birds in the tree?" Katherine asked.

"No, they are bats," the waterwitch said. "Very odd… the bats usually have their sleeping trees further up towards the hills. They never come this close to the coast." Zeruana shook her head and walked ahead on the rocky path. "The poor things may be lost. I'll give them some fruit in the morning."

But in the morning the bats had already gone and the visitors took their leave after breakfast. "Chudafis, goodbye, goodbye…krah, krah," the red parakeet croaked.

"Don't tell me we have to walk all the way, now!" Chryséis hated too much exercise.

"Don't be so lazy. It's just a little walk," Katherine sighed.

"Why couldn't they give us a lift on one of the ships or we could ride on dolphins…"

"Yeah well, apparently it's not safe on the water and do you want to get wet all over again?" Trevor rolled his eyes.

Prince Artû prepared to leave for Sogamosa when the 'waterwitch' demanded to speak to the three children alone. He didn't seem too pleased about the delay, but a maiden was still pretty important. The discussion was brief.

"All I want to tell you, children, is that our invisibility capes are not enough to protect you from harm."

"How do you know about that?" The children had surprise written all over their faces.

"Oh, I know things." Zeruana lowered her voice, "here is what you can do…"

Hu grunted sadly when he watched his newfound canine friend bound after the visitors and Tepi whined a little. They took a path the locals used between the town of Sogamosa and Narada. Artû and Amadis strode ahead, followed by the children and the two Dwendis.

"That was the most amazing witch I have ever met."

"Chris, she is the only witch you've ever met," Trevor grinned. "And she is not even a proper witch. Just a maiden, who happens to be a bit strange," he added. "Remember how she told us about the number seven? What was that all about?"

"I don't know. I think she was cool," Chryseis insisted. "Just the stuff she told us before we left…'I am putting myself in an armor of light'. Funny way to protect yourself. Maybe it works like a spell."

"It's probably a maiden's way of doing things. Cool."

They passed a knoll with a circle of standing stones. The fishing town of Sogamosa snuggled against the foothills of the blue Mohini range. A few dolphins dived close to the shore as if in greeting and Chryseis saw that one of them carried a mermaid, who waved to her.

"I cannot wait to see the prairies of Prydhain again. Grassland as far as the eye can see. Tregarn is very pretty," Lubbo said with longing in his voice. He had grown up in Prydhain with the D'Ånu and moved to Pindala only later.

"What are the standing stones used for?" Katherine asked innocently.

Gwendola looked surprised. Tthe young girl was supposed to come from Prydhain. Why didn't she know about the tors?

"Kathín you must have left the country of your birth very young, not to know this. The ancestors of the giants used it for fohar, of course!" She said eyebrows soaring. It seemed to be a Dwendi thing, these soaring eyebrows.

"Ah yes, right." Katherine had absolutely no clue what Gwendola was talking about. What was fohar? "Are there many of them in Prydhain?"

"There are more in the dragon country, close to the northern plains. Not my favourite place," Lubbo answered and his eyebrows twitched. "Nothing but dragons and bats, and cursed Firbolg. Dangerous."

Katherine had hoped that Prydhain would be like Alesia, and Atala perhaps. What she considered civilised. The Lady of Cydonia had assured them that giant lizards were kept in remote places far away from humans. The Dragon Country sounded very much like such a place.

"Where is this 'Dragon Country', friend Lubbo?" Trevor asked.

"Oh, way up north, lad. Nowhere we are going. The Fûna Mountains are beyond the marshes. And that's where they should stay in my humble opinion. Who needs dragons and evil Firbolg anyways?"

"Yes, who needs dragons?" Katherine said under her breath and a slow shiver went down her spine.

▷▷▷ **13** FIVE DANGEROUS BATS

Deep in the wooded Fûna Mountains, a flock of bats returned to their cave. Five bats to be exact.

The cave was warm and dark, and as soon as the bats had settled themselves, torches snapped alight all along the cave walls. The light revealed a round table made of dark gleaming wood inlaid with white magical symbols, and six massive chairs.

A bowl of beaten silver, filled to the rim with clear water, stood in the middle of the table and beakers with red wine.

There was no trace of bats in the underground chamber now. Instead, five dark-cloaked men, three of them pure-blood Gabari sat on the chairs around the table. The sorcerers were displeased. Very displeased.

One of them had a scarred face and sticky reddish hair. He came from Ta Mery and spoke with a strong Puntian accent. "How could they possibly escape the Gorgonas warships?" he growled.

"Perhaps the waterwitch helped them." The Gabari half-blood sorcerer of Dilmun spat out the words.

"No, we've been watching the broad. She doesn't use black magic. Although I wouldn't mind teaching her a lesson for all her meddling."

They began to down the strong wine from the wooden beakers.

"We have no time to waste with silly maidens. I have a better idea." The Highpriest of Hisbernia turned abruptly in his chair. "What are you hovering around here? Leave us until I call you!" He barked at a cowering Firbolg with crooked teeth.

The Firbolg nearly dropped his crock of wine to top up the beakers. He bowed over and over and crept past a tame saurian dozing in a corner.

The Highpriest of Hisbernia, with his hawk-like features and grubby black ponytail, banged on the table that the empty beakers danced around. "The Speaking Stone is leading them away from us. I want to get my hands on it!" He growled and squished the air with his fist.

"That's impossible! The stone is sealed and it's not even speaking to them," the sorcerer from Ta Mery shouted. The saurian opened one eye and yawned then carried on dozing.

"Perhaps they keep the children with them because they have the second face. Why else would the stone request their company?" the Highpriest of Shuruk scowled.

"You mean they possess the Power of Three? That would explain why everyone makes such a fuss of them. If we could get our hands on just one of them and…"

"Let's find out first what went wrong with the Gorgonas, shall we?" The other half-blood Gabari, the sorcerer of Maligasima, had been quiet and spoke now with a thundering voice. Five chairs scraped on the stone floor. The sorcerers closed their eyes and held their hands outstretched over the silver waterbowl.

"Bhavisyatâm!"

The water came to life with the image of a hulking warship anchored alongside other such ships on a rugged-looking coast. The sorcerers murmured more strange words in unison.

"Vikaran asaktih Goleón."

The captain of the Gorgonas ship appeared with a loud pop darkly tanned and in full armour next to the table. Just like that.

The Firbolg, who had been called, nearly dropped the crock of wine he was carrying. Lucky for him he didn't.

The masters were not in a good mood today. The scaly saurian opened its eyes, startled by the popping noise, only to close them again.

The image of the warships in the waterbowl faltered then disappeared. The wild-looking captain by the name of Goleón had fancied himself standing at the prow of his ship a moment ago, beholding the horizon over the Gadiric Sea. He wore golden earrings and an armband in the shape of a snake that seemed too tight for his muscles. Goleón looked startled when he realised that he was no longer in Maligasima .

He bowed awkwardly when he saw the sorcerers sitting around the table. "Masters!" the seasoned warrior uttered in a voice, hoarse with fear.

Nobody asked him to sit. Nobody spoke. Goleón was rattled. He took off his helmet and squinted nervously at the Fûna saurian behind him.

Without the comfort of a welcoming gesture, the Gorgonas captain bowed again, throwing back his leather-bound braids as he righted himself.

The saurian opened one eye halfway, fixing it on the newcomer, perpetually flicking its long forked tongue. It found a more comfortable position and knew that it wouldn't be long now to feeding time.

"At your service, Lord Masters," the strapping warrior said.

"Goleón, my man," the Highpriest of Shuruk coaxed in his hissing voice.

The Gorgonas warrior was unsure whether the tone had been friendly or threatening. Not a good sign, not good at all. Sorcerers could be devious at the best of times. He tried to hide his fear, but his trembling hands gave him away.

"We see…that the companions from Arvalos have managed to reach Prydhain with the stone still in their possession. How is this possible? Wasn't it your task – one little simple task – to stop the stone from being taken back to Caradoc?"

The voice seemed to mock Goleón.

His already thin lips clamped together even tighter. Goleón tried to think, but his plain, brutal mind was no match for the cunning magicians. When he spoke, rows of filed teeth showed.

"Our spies were at fault, Lord masters. They supplied the wrong information. We did our best, I assure you. Our rayguns were in place, but they started out sooner than we expected..."

The hissing voice exploded with rage. "Your best, you say. Your best? Let me see...you were not prepared for an earlier than expected departure? Not prepared?"

The captain's braids quivered as the stooped giant stuck his finger in his face. "We followed Prince Artû's ship. We were so close..." The Gorgonas warrior cringed at the memory of the encounter. "Then the loathsome Ama-zûnas got wind of our attack and chased us down. They destroyed two of our vessels at once and pried our ship from their's just as we were ready to board them."

"Are you telling me that the Ama-zûnas have outwitted you? Maybe they would make better allies for us? Tell me would they?"

The seasoned Gorgonas warrior clenched his fists. "I...I can't say, but if you say so, master..." He added, his left eye twitching uncontrollably.

"You are useless, unworthy of the trust we placed in you. Useless!" the Highpriest said full of contempt.

"But master, you promised. We are allies..." Goleón was close to panicking. His eyes darted around the cave searching for an escape route. Although he knew it would be no use.

"Allies? We don't suffer failure from allies. And you Goleón my friend have failed," was the merciless answer from the Magi of Maligasima.

"Perhaps we should have made a better choice. The Ama-zûnas..."

"Master you promised..." The Gorgonas captain said weakly.

"You talk of promise?" the sorcerer from Ta Mery hissed angrily. "All you had to do was play your part…and you failed! Thanks to you, the 'Speaking Stone' may be returned, before we can use it for the 'Cause'. I presume you know what that means? This may have been our best chance!"

The Gorgonas warrior knew that somehow these allegations were unfair, but his mind had grown dim with fear. He tried to speak, but his voice failed him.

"Thanks to you Goleón, we are not in possession of the 'Speaking Stone'. We expected more of you…"

"But lord masters…have mercy! I will do better next time."

Goleón fell on his knees and covered his face with big callused hands that had killed many a worthy enemy. Then in an unexpected move he clutched at a black robe. The sorcerer snapped his fingers and a group of Edfunian warriors entered the chamber from an adjoining room.

"There will be no next time." The Highpriest of Fûna shook off the man's hand in disgust as if he was dealing with an insect.

The Edfunians placed themselves between the Gorgonas captain and the sorcerers. Goblins sniggered spitefully at the back of the cave. Their long pointy noses pink with mirth. It was somebody else's turn for a change! Five glowering sorcerers stuck their heads together and whispered, ignoring the hapless man on his knees.

The sorcerers downed many a goblet, before they were satisfied with their new plan. It was ingenious. No allies were needed. Goleón still crouched on the cave floor, his spirit broken and the ugly little dwarves were sniggering.

At last, the Highpriest of Fûna snapped his fingers again. The saurian in the corner, recognising the signal, heaved itself up stretching stiff limbs, exposing an impressive set of curved fangs as it yawned broadly. Gently scratching the back of its head with one clawed hindleg, the reptile looked askance at its master.

Outside the cave, dusk had turned to starry night. A bright half-moon rose fast on its journey toward dawn and night owls hooted. Shiny eyes watched in the darkness.

A gloating roar coming from a cave in this black wilderness told of a successful hunt. Even insects were silenced for a brief moment only to immediately resume their buzzing more vigorously.

*

It had taken just over an hour to walk from Narada to Sogamosa. White flags fluttered on the beach and rows of silvery fish were drying on strings between rickety poles. Fishermen mended their nets torn by mighty tuna fish they had caught just hours before.

Brown-skinned women with bright laughing eyes scaled and gutted the hefty catch. Colourful fabrics billowed around their slender figures and their long black hair was bound with strings of seashells.

"Look how pretty they are. They look like Polynesians," Chryséis cried.

"Are they supposed to be English?" Katherine was unconvinced. "It's more like a part of western Ireland. Things will still change quite a bit of course. So they are strictly speaking — Irish."

"They don't look Irish to me."

"Oh, but they do." Chryséis winked at Trevor. "Just look, the guy over there is wearing a bowler hat and monocle."

"Very funny Chris. That wouldn't have anything to do with Ireland."

"Come on, what do you expect from Prydhain, Piccadilly Circus?"

"I don't know. Something a bit more...more familiar, I guess. All those aloes and palm trees... they are a far cry from the Britain I know. We could be somewhere in the South Sea."

"It's been like that since we came here. Cydonia is also not exactly Carter Valley. Get used to it already."

The strange drifters were eyed suspiciously as they

approached the town, but nobody spoke to them.

"Unfriendly bunch," Lubbo grumbled. "Does nobody ever come here?"

"Probably not from ghost-infested Narada," Amadis answered.

Nobody seemed to make the connection between the group of strangers and the sea battle that some of the fishermen had witnessed the day before.

And it was for the best. They wanted to remain anonymous, after all.

Tepi had discovered a heap of discarded fishbones and busied herself with a fishhead as big as her own. The fishtail also smelled really good.

"Come Tepi, Prince Artû isn't going to wait for us," Katherine cajoled her dog into following them. Fishhead between teeth, Tepi left the delicious heap reluctantly behind.

Smoke rose from another burning pile of fish offal they passed. "Uh, that really stinks. Can't they just chuck their rubbish into the sea?" Katherine asked.

"Can you imagine what that would be like? Disgusting."

"And if you want sea monsters all over the place, then sure…" Trevor rolled his eyes.

"Okay, it's probably better to burn the rubbish, then."

Unforeseen storms were enough for the fisherfolk to worry about. They sacrificed a part of their catch each day to appease fickle deities like Tiamat and Bel, the god of thunder and fire, and burned the rest. The sacrifice was given to a rugged people n the hills, the ancient Guanchi. They had mastered a curious bird language and kept mostly to themselves.

"We will go this way," Artû urged them on.

He led them past a few houses on stilts and then along proper streets and houses made from stone right down to the town square. If any of the people here were curious at all, they didn't show it.

The plan was to find an Avallûnian tribesman called Dantû. He would give them a message from the Lady of

Caradoc, telling them what to do next. They still had to be careful that thought transfers could not be detected.

"Zeruana said we should ask for directions in the town square."

"Then this is where we go."

Outside a ramshackle pottery shed, two young girls in rough brown tunics played a jolly tune on clay flutes. The glazed flutes looked much like little fat birds.

A man came out of the shed between a jumble of earthenware and chased the girls off a pile of stacked wood. He grumpily carried more wooden logs inside with the help of an apprentice to fire up the kiln.

"What are these people doing?" Katherine asked Amadis pointing to a row of women hammering away at seashells with tools of bone.

"Why, they are making disks for tender, friend Kathín," Amadis answered.

"They make money just like that?"

"Yes, of course. Mother of pearl is especially suitable for tender."

"What about valuable metals like gold or silver? Are they not used for tender?"

"No, too heavy," Amadis said. "Rare feathers and shells are more valuable and better to carry."

The time travellers already knew that prehistoric people had no use for money in the modern sense, and that much was still going to change.

"Here is somebody we could ask about the way."

Prince Artû's attention moved to a group of wizened old men leisurely smoking through long tubes from a glazed clay vase. They sat under the broad canopy of a haoma tree in what had to be the town square.

"Shelanti, athenai." Artû made the proper gestures and the men lifted their hands in greeting. Prince Artû opened his mouth to ask for directions, but one of the old men suddenly had a coughing fit. His face crumpled and he grew very red. His friends slapped him feebly on the back and the old man recovered. He bravely carried on sucking smoke from his mouthpiece before answering "Shelanti." in a hoarse voice.

They walked on with friendly gestures. "We'll ask somebody else, then."

A gust of wind carried tumbleweed across the dusty road and a few dark-feathered birds with long beaks pecked at crumbs on the square. A curious dull roar rose from behind a hill outside of town, before it died down again.

"Did you hear that?" For a moment, Katherine looked scared. There had clearly been shouting and booing.

"What do you think is going on there?"

"I don't know. A game of Pigsnout maybe?" Trevor said.

"That's not what it sounded like. More like an attacking mob."

"Then I don't know. And why should a mob attack? The people here don't seem to worry about it. You always have such strange ideas."

"Oh give me a break Trev. It's not like that," Katherine sulked.

Prince Artû walked on unperturbed.

Three old women in dark clothes sat on grass mats in the shade of a dried-up fountain, chatting and twirling spindles of flax. They followed the strangers with their rheumy eyes and carried on chatting.

"Shelanti, mothers," the prince approached the women

They looked up as if they had been unaware of the strangers until now.

Artû introduced them as Avallûnian visitors, who had just arrived in Sogamosa. The women stared in awe. He was a prince. A real prince!

"We are in search of the house of Dantû of Arvalos. Could you kindly show us the way?" he asked charmingly.

The women's wrinkled faces creased into toothless grins. It was shocking to see people in such a state of physical neglect.

Don't they have medics at a 'House of Life', who can fix teeth and slow down the aging process? Chryséis wondered.

"The merchant from Arvalos is who you are looking for?" one of them repeated.

"That's right, mother. He is awaiting our arrival."

"Ah, he's waiting. Dantû is waiting for them." The women sounded relieved. Knotted fingers pointed up the road. Every one of them wanted to feel important and they talked over each other.

"To the left by the pink statue of the Earthmother there," one of them said. "You will see the Gabari's smithy is right on the corner."

"It is up the road, then the third house to the right," another woman said.

"No, it is the fourth house to the left," the others contradicted her.

"No, Clovilda, the fourth house on the right."

"No, you don't know what you're talking about. It isn't. It's the third one…" the first woman insisted.

"You'd better ask the Gabari smith then."

"Yes the Gabari smith. He's in the smithy by the statue…"

Eventually, Prince Artû lifted his hand to hush the confused chatter. A foreign prince commanded enough respect to make the old women fall silent. He thanked the crones ever so politely and said goodbye.

"Did she just wink at Artû?" Chryséis asked.

"I think she did." Katherine shrugged her shoulders.

The pink statue turned out to be a rather dusty effigy of the Earthmother, standing with outstretched arms over a trough of running water. Hammering noises gave away the smithy across the road. A statue of Bel, the horned god of fire and thunder, and a wave of hot air greeted them in the blackened doorway.

"A Gabari smith of all people," Lubbo moaned. "It's getting worse."

Hot fires glowed in brick hearths at the back of the

smithy. A towering man lifted a mighty hammer in the air. He forced glowing metal with mighty blows into shape that sparks were flying.

His apprentices looked just as dirty and fearsome as their master. One of them took an orange scythe blade out of the fire and plunged it into a water bucket, while the other one kept the bellows going.

"Shelanti, good smith. We are strangers to this place and are looking for someone. The old women told us to inquire here."

The blacksmith turned around and squinted against the light. To the Dwendis' great surprise the giant smith turned out to be well mannered and helpful. "Who is it you are looking for athenai?"

"Dantû of Arvalos," Amadis answered.

"The merchant Dantû you lookin' for? Let's see. He lives in the fourth house this side up the road."

"Shukri, friend smith. The Earthmother be with you."

"Go well, athenai. Bel be with you."

The hammering sound accompanied them as they walked up the cobblestone street between daub and wattle houses. Only one single vimaan passed them.

"Not much traffic here," Gwendola said with contempt.

"What do you expect from such a backwater?" Her brother used the same tone.

A young woman was busy weaving cloth with zigzag designs on a simple loom that was strapped to strong hooks in a house wall. She didn't pay the slightest attention to them and they walked past her.

At last, Prince Artû stopped in front of the carved wooden door of the fourth house on the right hand side and knocked. They saw somebody behind the latticework window on the first floor.

"Open up. 'Avallûn's apples are the best'," Prince Artû said in a low, urgent voice.

"Must be a kind of password." Katherine's voice

dropped to a whisper.

"Mhm."

A boy of about six years opened the door and peeped curiously at the strangers. "Chachi, Chachi, come quick! Chachi!" he yelled for his aunt to come. An elderly woman in Avallûnian dress shuffled to the door.

"Shelanti, goodwife. I am Prince Artû of Arvalos and these are my companions. May we come in? Dantû is awaiting us. 'Avallûn's apples are the best'."

The woman was much impressed with the prince and bowed them into the house. Tepi sniffed along the tiled floor all the way to the back veranda where she found a fishhead on the stone floor.

"Dantû is my niece's husband. They are at the arena today, watching the 'Lizard Fight' finals. T'is the annual grand tournament of the Mohini region, honourable Prince Artû."

The aunt spoke shyly, bowing after each sentence, looking alternately at the prince and at her blue-striped linen shoes.

"So that's where everybody is. Watching a game called the 'Lizard Fight'," the prince said.

"I was right then. It must be a game of Pigsnout."

"Yeah, yeah, we know you love Pigsnout, Trev. But why is it called Lizard Fight? What do lizards have to do with Pigsnout?" Chryséis said.

"Maybe it's rugby or cricket."

"Sure, Katherine. We're in England after all." Trevor grinned.

"Ireland."

"Whatever."

Artû decided to meet Dantû at the sports arena. He couldn't wait until after the tournament.

"Can we come with you? We would like to watch the game," Trevor begged. "Please Gwendola."

Their current guardian agreed. Amadis, Gwendola and Lubbo stayed behind with Tepi and the 'Speaking Stone'.

"I cannot look after you, so don't be a nuisance," Artû

said testily.

"Gee, how can he always be in such a bad mood?" Chryséis complained when they walked the distance to the nearby hill.

"Never mind that. He's taking us to this sports game and I can't wait to see that," Trevor said.

"Oh right, boys and sports or what?" Chryséis rolled her eyes.

One of the house servants was showing them the way and they soon arrived. The front stands, eight tiers high, were hewn into the rock and wooden stands made up the three other sides. On the oval sand-covered pitch, two towering figures were engaged in some sort of dance.

Trevor glanced curiously at large wooden cages with open doors between the wooden stands on the opposite side.

"It is the last contest of the tournament," the servant shouted as he pushed through the crowd to the stands on the hillside. They were reserved for important citizens of Sogamosa.

Everybody jumped to their feet and cheered loudly, just as a screeching sound came from the middle of the pitch. The crowd settled down again. Nothing exciting had happened.

"So much for a game of Pigsnout. I've never heard the players screech like that," Katherine said.

"What exactly are they playing here?" Trevor asked.

"We'll see in a minute."

Dantû of Arvalos, his wife and their eldest son were sitting on the second tier, shouting and punching the air like all the other spectators. The Avallûnian merchant was as blond and strapping as the prince. He sported a long dignified moustache and an embroidered suit made from Cydonian silk.

"Yeah, go Eumolus, go go go! Go Eumolus, go go go!"

The jumping spectators made it difficult to move forward along the benches. They reached Dantû and the servant screamed something into the ear of his displeased master.

Dantû didn't appreciate being disturbed during such an important game. But he quickly saw who demanded his attention and performed a short version of the Avallûnian greeting. Space on the bench was quickly made for the son of King Avallach of Avallûn, his noble guest. Dantû signaled for his servant to leave. He ignored the three children who had come with the prince and they sat quietly down on the bench.

The merchant wasn't unfriendly, just that his prince was more important.

"We have been expecting you ever since the knotted string message announced your visit, prince," Dantû yelled.

"We are here now and you need to give me the message from…"

The crowd jumped up, booing, jeering and stomping.

"I cannot hear you prince."

"I said…," Artû repeated what he came to say.

From where they were sitting, the time travellers had an excellent view of the arena, but they couldn't hear what the two men were saying. They stared at the two opponents on the pitch. Unbelievable! There weren't two men slugging it out in the flying sand, but a Gabari and a…dinosaur!

"What kind of a sport is this?" Katherine was shocked.

There was no point in asking Prince Artû questions as he was in deep conversation with Dantû.

"They are fighting – like gladiators or something!" Chryséis shouted.

"Just that the one is a dinosaur. Cool." Trevor was excited.

The giant man, half Gabari half Ama-zûnas, wore a fitted lizard hide armour. His reddish hair was tied into a kinky ponytail on top of his head. His face and bare arms were tattooed with snake-like dragons.

"Eumolus, Eumolus, go go go-o-o-o-o-o !" the crowd roared.

The gladiator's face was distorted in a menacing grimace as he swung a short lance in one hand and a ball and chain dangled in the other. The scaly dinosaur was not much larger than the man with a long neck and beaked snout. The beast's stubby forelimbs were boxing in the giant's direction.

The time travellers hadn't seen anything like it. "Do you think that's a dragon from the Fûna Mountains?"

"What, here?!"

The crowd booed. They wanted to see action. The fighting raptor had not been fed in preparation for the contest, to ensure its ferocity. It bellowed and lunged at the giant.

Three sharp talons on each powerful foot slashed. Eumolus, the lizard slayer, ducked and aimed his lance carefully, only to change the angle again. The dinosaur bounced nimbly from side to side. Eumolus knew that was important to lodge the weapon into the soft parts. He had done this many times before.

"Aaaah!"

The lance hissed through the air and…narrowly missed its goal. There was more booing. The broken lance was stuck in the saurian's back whipping up and down. Only deep enough to make the raptor even more furious. The beast was spitting and screeching angrily.

The crowd was delighted.

The human contestant was one fight away from being hailed the champion of the entire Mohini region. A title worth holding out for.

"Eumolus, vah! Eumolus, vah Eumolus, vah, vah, vah!"

The resounding shouts grew louder, urging him on. But the raptor was clever. And fast. It ducked and jumped out of the way as the ball and chain came crashing down.

The crowd roared in anticipation of a bloody kick as Eumolus scrambled for his weapon. Katherine's face grew white with horror. This was no sport at all. This was cruel.

"I'm not going to watch this!" she yelled and jumped to her feet.

"What?" Trevor could barely tear himself away from

the game.

"I'm leaving!"

That was not so easy, because the arena was boiling with excitement. Katherine had to push her way past spectators jumping up and down on their seats, and nearly knocked her to the ground. Rough, burly men in leather armours sat inside the entrance playing a board game of owaré.

Unfazed by all the noise and goings on, they dropped stones into holes in the wooden board. Clack, clack, clack. They barely paid attention to the upset girl. Outside, Katherine slumped down under a tree, shaking. She started nervously every time the spectators screamed in a crazed choir.

There was a loud squeal and the angry howl of the giant roared over the clamour. "Oh no, they have killed each other!" Katherine cried.

She couldn't help herself and ran back inside to see what had happened. There she bumped into her two friends.

"Where have you been? You can't just run away like this!"

"I couldn't just… watch!"

"Oh Katie." Chryséis gave her a hug.

"That sounded dreadful. Are they both dead?"

"No, just flesh wounds, I guess. They're still at it," Trevor said with glowing eyes.

"How can you enjoy something like that? It's so, so awful!"

"It's prehistory, what do you expect?"

They got a glimpse of the fight. The lizard slayer had managed to pull out the lance from the raptor's back and as the furious saurian attacked again. The ball and chain flew around its feet. Before the dinosaur could struggle loose, the lance penetrated through the soft side deep into its heart.

"Kreeeeh!" A blood-curdling scream and one last shiver went through the body of the dinosaur, then the battle was over. Eumolus collapsed with slash and bite wounds on his arms and legs and helpers ran onto the pitch. His hard-fought victory was announced and the 'Lizard Slayer' champion of the Mohini region was led away with his armour in bloodied shreds. But he smiled and lifted his good arm in triumph into the air.

"Eumolus, param! Eumolus, param! Eumolus Eumolus Eumolus, hey!"

Victorious chanting rose and ebbed. The tournament was finished and bets were paid out. It had been a good day, full of entertainment, and soon the crowd headed for the beverage stalls outside the arena for pints of tesgüin, the local sorghum beer and sweets for the children.

"That was great. A football game is nothing compared to a gladiator fight!" Trevor was exhilarated.

"Glad you liked it," Chryséis said with sarcasm and decided that she would never understand boys.

Prince Artû appeared at the entrance together with Dantû and his family.

"We shall eat at the house," Dantû announced. "A celebration is in order! What a triumphant end to the season." The two men still had much to talk about. After briefly checking that the children were behind them, the adults walked ahead of them back to the house.

Barbarians!" Katherine said hotly. "Triumphant end to the season. My foot!"

"People do things differently here, Katie," Chryséis said. "This would have happened even without us being there. We just watched it."

"I know that. But it's still barbaric. And I don't want to watch anything like that ever again."

"That was a real dinosaur in there…A trained fighting machine." Trevor was still excited. "Would rather watch a game of Badminton?"

"Nonsense! I just think it was cruel," Katherine said stubbornly.

"Oh come on, what about Spanish bull fights or wrestling…"

Katherine glared at Trevor. "I don't like that either. Do you watch wrestling on TV? Gross!"

Trevor shrugged and said nothing. He caught up with Dantû's son and walked next to him. "Girls can be so boring!"

"I know," the boy sighed.

At the house with the latticework windows, arrangements for an early dinner were hastily made. Two of Dantû's servants scurried to the beach to purchase seafood for the guests. They returned with a gigantic clam and a basket full of rock lobsters and crabs.

"That thing must weigh a ton," Trevor estimated.

"At least 15 pounds," Chryséis said.

The meal was cooked over hot coals and served in the clamshell with dips and flatbread. Flasks of Avallûnian cider were brought up from the cellar and poured into trumpet-shaped têrakhon glasses ending in spiral bases. Tepi had fun licking the bowls on the floor clean of leftovers.

"Just look at that view," Katherine yawned. Slender palm trees stood out against the pinkish horizon as the sun set over the roofs of Sogamosa, and clouds drifted into the darkening summer sky above the Gadiric Sea.

"Fantastic. Let me take a picture."

"You do that. I'm going to sleep." Katherine yawned again and climbed the stairs to the sleeping quarters.

At sunrise, Dantû's vimaan ferried them north to the swamps, following the Lady of Caradoc's apparent advice. The merchant had given the message to his prince during dinner.

"One is glad to be of service. Your message will also be at once delivered to Arvalos," he said.

"Thank you Dantû. Chudafis."

"Chudafis, Lord… athenai."

Prince Artû knew he was one step closer to completing the mission.

For sure, by tomorrow morning they'd be in Tregarn and then in Caradoc by evening.

Inside Amadis's satchel, the 'Speaking Stone of Caradoc' lay safely in its protective see-through sphere under a dark velvet cloth.

Nobody noticed the warning glow that emanated from the stone and somebody else left Sogamosa that morning. Riding a powerful black horse hard into the foothills of the Fûna Mountains.

Another mission had been successfully completed. He had delivered the false message and the giant brethren would be pleased!

▷▷▷ 14 CROSSING THE SWAMPS

The message read: *'Go to the Fenians and cross the swamps. It is safer than travelling directly through Tregarn. A citadel vimaan will be waiting for you on the other side. It will take you to Tregarn and on to Caradoc.'*

The scroll bore the seal of the Lady of Caradoc.

Native to the swamps was a Gabari tribe called the Fenians. They knew the ever-shifting maze of bogs like the back of their hands. The marsh was also the territory of slimy newts, salamanders and roaming wildcats.

The Fenians were often hired by travellers to carry them across the swamps and into Prydhain. They would apparently take Prince Artû and his party of travellers through the swamps today.

'This is not the message we expected,' Amadis had said at first. 'It would be better for a vimaan to take us from Sogamosa straight to Caradoc. Why do we have to go through the swamps first?'

'The Lady of Caradoc knows best,' Prince Artû had answered. 'She is the custodian of the stone after all.'

They had had no way of confirming the message, so they followed the Lady's instructions. The swamps were not far from the coast after all. To the north lay the Fûna Mountains and in the east the prairies of Tregarn, the home of the famous black horses. But Lubbo was not happy about the course of events.

Dantû's vimaan had left over an hour ago and they were still waiting. A small pond was just outside a reed grass shack, scummed with algae and smelling of swamp mud.

"Something's not right. Something's not right," he mumbled to himself. Of course he couldn't openly question the Lady of Caradoc's wishes.

"No wonder there're so many flies here," Chryséis complained and swatted another one from her face. "I wish we could leave now and get it over and done with."

A fat Gabari woman with bobbing braids sat lazily in a huge chair in front of the shack. Totally incurious about the travellers, she sipped her tesgüin ale from an earthen mug.

"Not long now. Not long." She burped and slapped at the troublesome flies with a long horsehair whisk. Next to the chair was the food and beer Dantû's driver had left as arranged for payment.

"Why don't they have lavender and pennyroyal to keep the flies away like everywhere else?" Trevor asked annoyed and rubbed herbal balm from small têrakhon jars on his face that Dantû's wife had given them.

Finally, two truly giant Gabari in long boots stomped up the narrow path. They were the biggest giants the children had ever seen. The Fenians didn't say much to each other, because there was nothing to say.

"Listen up travellers," the taller and older one of them said boorishly. "You'll ride on our shoulders and must hold on tight. We will have a break halfway through the fens and nobody can leave the group. Nobody."

"Alright, we will abide by your rules, Fenian," Amadis said.

Before they started out, the giants asked the swamp fairies for permission to cross their land. The little Rutian fairies, who now accompanied them behind the turned-up rim of Lubbo's hat, started to giggle and nearly had themselves detected.

They knew that there were no fairies here anymore. The swamp guides bent down so that the travellers could climb onto their massive shoulders. The shorter, younger giant turned around and bellowed in his Fenian brogue. "Be back for lunch, Ma!"

The giant woman nodded and carried on swatting the flies lazily with her whisk. The giants walked in long strides along the pathway slamming their tree poles that served as staffs into the ground as they marched. It was a wobbly ride.

"I don't like this. I don't like this at all. Who's ever heard of going through the swamps to reach Caradoc?" Lubbo grumbled.

"Oh brother, what can we do?" Gwendola said. "It is the Lady's wish."

"Feels like riding on an elephant's back," Katherine said to Chryséis next to her. She held onto the fringes of the giant's leather waistcoat with one hand and cradled Tepi on her lap with the other.

"Never been on an elephant before."

She had to concentrate on balancing and not falling off the giant's shoulder.

"I have, actually."

"Good for you, Katie," her friend said. "My, these guys're in a hurry."

"It's a good thing isn't it," Katherine said and tried to make herself comfortable. "We want to get to Caradoc as quickly as possible."

*

Meanwhile, in a cave in the Fûna Mountains, a group of sorcerers gazed at the image in a shining water bowl. The reflection in the water showed a cloaked rider.

"They took the bait. They are on their way."

"Has the vimaan been conjured up yet?"

"A small vimaan for the humans just as you said, brother. The Firbolg are still painting on the emblem of the citadel of Caradoc," the Magi of Maligasima reported. "It looks believable enough."

The picture in the silver water bowl changed and the Highpriest of Shuruk fixed his gaze closely on every movement. "They should make haste. The Fenians are in a hurry to reach the other side of the swamp. Which one of them carries the 'Speaking Stone'?"

"It seems that the D'Anu warrior has the stone in his bag, but we cannot be sure. It could also be with the boy," the Magi of Maligasima said.

"Take them both."

"The children are inseparable, brother."

"It won't help them much, will it now?" The hissing voice broke into a hacking cough.

"We should take them all together. Xipe Xolotle has been waiting for a worthy sacrifice long enough. Ha, ha, ha." The Highpriest of Dilmun found the idea of sacrificing the children rather amusing.

"Where are the Fenians now?" the Highpriest of Shuruk croaked. The Gabari had veered off the beaten path and could no longer be seen.

"We will lose them. They cannot just disappear." The Highpriest of Shuruk lost his temper. He was easily displeased.

The Firbolg in the cave had learned that lesson fast and scattered fast. The water in the silver bowl trembled then the picture vanished completely. The black spider on the sorcerer's forehead seemed to move with his deepening frown.

"Patience, brother. Probably just the usual halfway-stop. No fear, we'll get the pipsqueaks and the Speaking Stone this time for sure."

"I've waited long enough! This better go according to plan. Wine!"

*

The rushed stop in the swamps had been plagued by an onslaught of flying insects, despite the herbal balm they applied. Only the giants remained unbothered. After a few sips from their water flasks, the Fenians were ready to continue. They waited impatiently for Lubbo to return from behind a clump of shrubs, when all of a sudden Trevor cried out and disappeared into the ground.

He had lost his balance on the edge of a bog of

quicksand when a flock of small swamp birds flew up in front of him. The giants were annoyed that the boy would make them late for lunch.

They stood sulking and watched howTrevor slowly disappeared in the dirty liquid.

"Friend Trevór!" Prince Artû reacted quickly and fired a series of instructions at Amadis. The D'Ånu warrior reached for his staff, miniscule compared to the ones the giants carried.

"Stop struggling. Hold onto the staff, boy!" he commanded.

Chryséis and Katherine were fighting back tears. Seeing their friend sink into the quicksand was so unexpected. Gwendola had to hold the girls back, so they wouldn't fall into the bog themselves, while Amadis spoke to Trevor. "Pull yourself up onto the staff and lie on it on your stomach."

Trevor grabbed the long pole Amadis had thrown across the bog hole and began to pull himself up. Artû held the staff down on one side and Amadis on the other side. Trevor slipped off just as he managed to get one leg over the pole. There was panic in his eyes and Tepi whined.

"Try again, boy. Take a deep breath. Now lie on your stomach. No, lengthwise. That's good, that's good," Artû repeated patiently.

"Trevor, crawl along the staff to the edge of the bog," Katherine piped up. Trevor lay on top of the pole for a moment then moved slowly along the staff to the safety of firm ground.

"You are nearly there," Amadis encouraged him. "That's it. Nearly there."

Gwendola and Lubbo bent the swamp grass aside. Trevor grabbed hold of Lubbo's strong hand and let the Dwendi pull him out of the quicksand.

He lay there with his clothes all covered in mud, drawing in air in big gulps as if he'd been close to drowning. His thoughts chased each other madly until they came to a grinding halt. Tears streamed down Trevor's face. He didn't care. He could have died.

Prince Artû was berating the giants angrily for their reluctance to help the boy. "You could have just grabbed him out of there…"

The two Fenians stood around sheepishly, hanging their heads and Trevor looked up at the blurry giants. He felt strange.

"Trevor, Trevor…look at me. Are you okay?" He heard Chryséis speak through white mist. Tepi licked his dirty face and the mist cleared.

"Breathe slowly, Trev. It's alright. Don't cry."

"What? I'm not crying." He wiped his face with a muddy hand and stammered. "It's just the mud. This… damn… Speaking Stone!"

"What about the Speaking Stone?" Katherine asked surprised.

Trevor falling into the quicksand bog had nothing to do with the Speaking Stone, did it?

"What about the stone? Nothing but trouble, that's what!" Trevor stammered.

"But Trevor, we have to make sure that it is kept safe…"

"Make sure? All we have to do is make sure that we stay alive and return home."

"What if we are supposed to do this and if we don't, history changes for the worse?" Chryséis pleaded with him.

"Since when don't you want to go back home?" He was groping for words. "I'm only thirteen. These stupid …stupid…stupid…"

"Edfunians? I don't like them either, but I think we must try and…do the right thing," Chryséis argued.

They didn't seem to notice everybody standing around them staring.

"We can't let the bad guys win," Katherine said firmly. "And that's that."

Gwendola tapped on Trevor's shoulder. "It is time to

go. You need to clean yourself." She tried to speak gently.

Lubbo helped Trevor up and walked him to the little brook running alongside the path. The girls watched him clean the dirt off his face and arms, while Tepi lapped up some water.

"Do you mind, I've got some washing up to do…"

Tepi looked up then continued. Although Trevor still looked pale under the layer of mud, his moment of weakness had passed.

"Alright then!" he cried.

"Alright? What do you mean alright?" Katherine asked him.

"Alright. I'm not a quitter," he said. "and don't you ever mention that my eyes were watering from the mud."

"Sure thing," Chryséis gave him the thumbs up.

"Okay then, can I finish washing myself now?" Trevor started to take his shirt off and motioned for the girls to go away. He needed some time to himself. Lubbo sat down to watch Trevor. Just to make sure that the boy didn't fall into the water.

Prince Artû and the others nodded good-naturedly when the girls told them that Trevor needed a moment to get ready. Chryséis shouldered her daypack and walked over to Katherine and Gwendola.

"What an unfortunate incident," Gwendola sighed. "The poor boy."

Soon, Trevor appeared with Lubbo in tow. He had put on new clothes and looked a lot cleaner than just now.

With the help of the giants, they made it to the other side of the swamp long before sunset and didn't waste their time with long good-byes.

"Good riddance, I say." Lubbo was glad to see the giants leave. "Scurvy, thick-headed Gabari."

They walked to a small wooden hut that was nearby. It was used by travellers as shelter from the elements and the every-present insects. Flocks of guinea fowl in white-dotted plumage were pecking the ground between clumps of grass. The scene could have been picturesque, but the Dwendis felt uneasy as the sun dipped lower in the sky.

"Where is the vimaan from Caradoc? It should be here already," Lubbo grumbled.

"The driver might be looking for us," Gwendola said.

"We have no choice then but to wait."

They ate the rest of the provisions Dantû had given them in Sogamosa and after a while a vimaan came floating towards the hut. It was clearly a citadel vimaan from Caradoc. Or so they thought.

Tepi growled and backed gingerly away from the vehicle as it set down, hiding behind Katherine and Trevor. The têrakhon cover of the driver's cabin was tinted, so they couldn't see inside.

Amadis knocked on the cover, but there was no reaction. The large oval bowl over the passenger section opened with a sucking sound.

"The driver seems eager to leave again. He will take us to Tregarn and then on to Caradoc. That's what the message said," Gwendola reassured them. Despite a faint feeling of unease, Artû urged them to board the vehicle. "We should not spend any more time in this wilderness. The children go first and then the dog."

Tepi needed some coaxing though. "Come on, Tepi, Tepi," Katherine crooned. The dog jumped into the cabin and went to lie whimpering on Katherine's feet.

"It's okay, Tepi." She tried to calm the dog.

"Now, Gwendola and Lubbo...and Amadis."

The bag with the speaking stone slipped off Amadis' shoulder and he adjusted the strap across his chest. Artû was the last one to sit down in a comfortable seat.

Without further ado, the têrakhon cover closed and the vimaan lifted off the soggy ground. It was bliss to just ride above the landscape with its lengthening shadows, safe from insects, mud and dangerous quicksand.

The air inside the cabin was pleasantly cool, but the

time travellers felt sweaty and dirty and looked forward to a proper bath. As the road forked before them, the vimaan followed the sign to Tregarn to the north. Tregarn however lay in the east, but nobody noticed it.

The road seemed to skirt the foothills and carry on through green prairie. None of them had ever come this way before.

"Ah, Tregarn is a nice place," Lubbo grunted. "Civilised and clean and hardly any Gabari. I'm in dire need of some soap and warm water in a proper bathroom."

For a fleeting moment he thought of the fermented mare's milk called koumiss, a Tregarni specialty. He couldn't wait to taste it again.

"It won't be long now, brother," Gwendola said.

The vimaan left the sign and the fork in the road behind and the sign changed immediately, pointing once again quite properly to the east. There was no northward bound road here, only a small path into the foothills of the Fûna Mountains.

The vimaan took the seven unsuspecting travellers deeper into the wooded highlands and closer to the cave that resounded with shouts of triumph. From inside the vimaan, the landscape soon looked like Tregarni grassland with grazing black horses and long grass swaying in the afternoon wind.

What they didn't see was that outside the hills grew higher into dark forbidding mountains. The spell was perfect.

Amadis checked on the Speaking Stone. It was still resting securely inside its protective sphere. Convinced that everything was going well, he put the object back into his bag and allowed himself to nod off like the others.

When he awoke, the landscape was unchanged, and while he still thought about this, a strange thing happened. The vimaan began to jerk up and down and left and right. Their vehicle stuttered and came to a full halt just before another bend in the path that looked somehow familiar.

"We have been here before. Are we going around in

circles?" Lubbo now also wondered and yawned.

"We've stopped." Amadis reacted fast and opened the hatch.

Tepi jumped out first, eager to get away from the eerie vehicle, and started barking. Lubbo had been right all along: something was wrong here. The others followed quickly, lugging their bags out of the vimaan just in time. At once, the vimaan shook, creaked and disappeared into thin air with a hollow puff.

"Crikey!" Katherine gasped and stared at the empty spot. "Well I never!"

It was morning, but they were not in Tregarn at all. They stood next to a mountain lake lined with trees.

"By the Earthmother, the vimaan was a trap!" Lubbo cried.

"What just happened?" Gwendola asked still half asleep. "Why are we in these mountains?"

"It was a trap!" Her brother cried angrily. "The message must have been forged."

"To goad me into believing that the Lady of Caradoc would send us into the swamps. I can't believe that I was so stupid to believe it," Prince Artû reproached himself.

"The message appeared to be genuine. We had no reason to doubt its content," Amadis protested.

"The vimaan. It looked so real," Lubbo said flabbergasted. "Obeah of course. I suppose we are in Gabari and Firbolg territory. In the Fûna Mountains."

"It cannot be." Gwendola still couldn't believe it. "That just cannot be."

"Look around you. Do you see the grasslands of Tregarn?"

"Where is Trevor?" Katherine almost yelled the words. "Trevor, Trevor!"

They searched in the underbrush and on the slope right down to the lake shore. Nothing. Trevor was not there anymore.

"I have his bag." Katherine felt cold fear grip her. "Was he…is he still in the vimaan? That bogus vimaan? He was asleep when I last saw him. He must have been still sleeping inside the vimaan when we got out!"

"Oh, by the Earthmother!" Gwendola cried. "They have taken the child! I should have kept an eye on him. How could I just fall asleep myself?" Gwendola felt responsible.

"No doubt the Edfunians planned to take all of us. And the Speaking Stone as well," the prince complained. "Something must have gone awry with the vimaan."

"How could they have known about our plans? That we would go to Sogamosa." Amadis sat down on a rock. "That we would stay with Dantû?"

"The bats. It had to be the bats. Sorcerers are known to turn into bats."

"Why are you not doing something to find Trevor?"

"What would you have me do, Chris?" Katherine stammered.

"I don't know, please find him!" Chryséis felt tears welling up. "Please find him," Amadis said.

"First we must leave this spot. If those behind this trickery find out that there is only the boy on board, they will come looking for us."

They staggered along the path skirting the lake. Still in shock, Chryséis was crying a little, but then she decided to be brave and wiped her tears away. "We will find Trevor, Katie. We will," she whispered.

Lubbo shooed a flock of wild harpees out of the way. They hissed in protest and inflated their collars only to waddle down the sloping lakeshore, where deer were drinking the murky water.

This place felt hostile somehow, but just how hostile they were about to find out. Grunting and roaring noises came from the far end of the lake.

A herd of fat saurians with long necks and large flippers wagged their snake-like heads up in the air. They were basking in the sun, their young feeding on slimy deer meat.

On the rocks above the beach, flying saurians flapped their featherless wings, hoping for some scraps later.

"We are in Jurassic Park!" Chryséis said to Katherine as

they hurried after Amadis and Artû with the two Dwendis trailing behind them. Luckily, thick foliage gave them cover between the jagged rocks along the footpath.

"Look at that. They are fighting."

The girls stared in fascination as two of the males started bawling. They squared up to each other, grunting rhythmically, moving back and forth baring their teeth. After a moment, they flopped onto the warm sand and the younger bull moved away with loud grunts.

"They only mock-attacked," Chryséis said in a low voice. "I just hope those creatures can't see us."

The growling grew fainter as the group moved away from the lake. They didn't notice a female saurian that was busy tearing chunks from a deer on the shore just below.

She picked up a strange scent above and decided to investigate. A large snake-like head slowly emerged from behind the rocks and an awful lipless grin exposed a mouthful of needle-sharp teeth. She roared a heart-stopping warning.

"Aaaaaah!" Gwendola screamed.

Birds nesting in the rocks alighted in a flurry. Amadis and Artû drew their weapons, but the dragon was simply too big and too close. There was no time for a challenge. Suddenly, the long neck shot forward with a loud hiss.

"Run this way. Run!" Artû yelled.

Without thinking, Katherine and Chryséis ran as quickly as they could. Behind them a frantic commotion urged them on, but they didn't look back. The saurian herd below splashed into the water, taking the young to the caves under the surface of the lake.

Out of breath, they reached an enclosed valley and hid behind trees. Luckily, the saurian did not pursue them.

Here, a number of small waterfalls rushed down the stark rock faces to meet a foaming stream below. The others were right behind them and reached the trees.

"We are in… dragon country. Oh those damn… Edfunians!"

Artû sat down and breathed hard. It wasn't until Amadis suggested that they made camp on the other side of the valley that they saw a long sharp tooth still stuck in Lubbo's arm.

"The dragon has bitten Lubbo! We have to pull the tooth out!"

"No, wait! There are hooks on it. We'd hurt him even more. We have no medic with us, no device," Amadis warned.

"Then what do we do?" The prince asked.

"I think this dragon species has no fire bite, no poison." Amadis inspected the wound. "But we need to find a medic and fast."

"It's getting dark and there is no 'House of Life' anywhere near this place," Artû replied.

"Then we must ask for help by thought," Gwendola urged. "It's an emergency."

"What about the Edfunians? We cannot risk drawing attention to us."

"They already know where we are."

"I don't think so. No thought transfer." Lubbo's face was all creased with pain.

"My brother, you must have treatment. We'll set out immediately."

"It will be dark soon and we cannot walk in dragon country at night." Lubbo held up his good hand. "No, Gwen, no more talk of this. We will rest here and walk in the morning."

They camped under the broad canopy of araucaria trees. The noise of the rushing water was only a murmur here and the ground was soft and fragrant with pine needles.

Butterflies fluttered between wildflowers, not bloodsucking little vampires as in the swamps. A green chameleon sat motionless on a tree branch, rolling its eyes at the butterflies. A narrow, overgrown path wound upward to some ancient ruins half-hidden among the rocks.

"It was thoughtless not to bring medical supplies," Artû said as he scooped up water with a wooden cup.

"We could have been in Tregarn by now without delay, if it wasn't for those cursed Edfunians," Gwendola answered.

The girls kept quiet.

"It is my fault. I should have made sure that everything was in order," Prince Artû said.

"None of us could have known," Amadis countered. "We cannot be too far from the plains. We will find help."

Amadis had speared fish for dinner in no time and soon they were frying on peeled sticks over a small fire. The girls said nothing for quite a while, still in shock, because they had seen a huge dinosaur in the wild and that the vimaan had disappeared with Trevor in it.

"That…thing…was big!" Katherine began eventually.

"Yes."

"They keep saying that we're in dragon country."

"They mean dinosaurs," Chryséis corrected her.

"I know that."

They fell silent again and listened to the gurgling stream.

"What do you think the magicians did with Trevor?"

"I don't know. I hope nothing bad. Trevor is smart and he has his VIC with him." Chryséis touched her aliceband.

"Yes, he must just keep it together, until we find him."

"But Lubbo is hurt and they are talking about finding a medic. How are we supposed to search for Trevor with all of that also going on?"

"Artû will make a plan. Trevor could be anywhere," Katherine answered.

"I'm not so sure Artû cares that much."

"Oh, don't say that. He's just worried. He'll make a plan."

They looked over to where the injured Lubbo was leaning against a tree trunk with his eyes closed. He looked rather pale. Gwendola sat next to her brother offering him tea in a folded leave cup. She cut the fabric around the saurian tooth open and Lubbo winced with pain.

"We need more fire. What if dragons attack us tonight?" They heard him say through clenched teeth. "Not to speak of the Firbolg. We're in dragon country after all."

"I wish he would stop saying things like that. Dragon country. I'll never sleep now," Chryséis grumbled. She had gooseflesh all over her arms.

"Look brother, Amadis is already making a fire circle around the trees," Gwendola said and pointed at small fires that Amadis was feeding with dry branches.

"That's good, the dragons are scared of fire."

Lubbo sat still under the tree while Gwendola fed him tea of wild chamomile flowers. Everyone was holding their own leaf cup of tea.

After a simple meal of freshwater fish and honey from a bee hive in one of the pine trees, Chryséis and Katherine crawled into their sleeping bags. Lubbo groaned in his sleep, his skin turning red all around the bite despite the poultice Gwendola had applied.

*

The vimaan, supposedly from Caradoc, floated outside the hidden mountain cave between gnarled trees and underbrush. Inside the vehicle, Trevor had a bad dream. Of something slithering up his leg, while he was standing in a bog of shifting mud, unable to move. He wanted to scream, to climb out. But he couldn't.

Suddenly he felt so light. Nothing was holding him back. The quicksand became like water between his toes and he could simply fly out of the bog. The feeling of freedom was unbelievable.

Just the black bat, staring at him from a thornbush across the pit, was weird but Trevor didn't linger. He flew over the swamp. It was so easy.

A flash of light bothered him. Trevor woke up. Ah, it's over now. We are there, he thought contentedly and stretched himself.

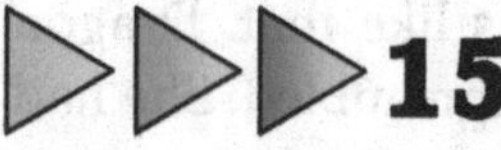 **15**   # THE ESCAPE

Chryséis and Katherine woke up at daybreak to grumbling noises and far-off roars. The others were already busy preparing breakfast.

"Oh no, it wasn't a nightmare," Katherine moaned. "We are still here in this - place." She looked around.

"Yep." Chryséis sat up. "Dragons everywhere."

Katherine shuddered. "Do you have to say it like that?"

"Why? Come on, let's get up."

Gwendola and Amadis were pouring water on the remains of the protective fires.

"It is time to leave this place. Just in which direction do we go?" Prince Artû gazed at the winding path into the hills and the ruins on the slope. It was obvious that nobody lived there.

"We could always send a thought transfer to Caradoc requesting a teleporter beam," Gwendola suggested.

Artû didn't agree. "There are too many of us and the boy is still missing. And it is not safe."

"I say we make our way east. What else can we do?" Amadis reasoned and carried on gutting fish they would eat for breakfast. He caught a glimpse of movement from the corner of his eye. "Friend Lubbo, how are you this morning?"

"Oh Amadis, friend. I don't want to complain, but it hurts. I wish we could find a 'House of Life' or at least some human dwelling soon." The Dwendi's crumbled face looked flushed. "Did you see the butterflies? They are so - big."

Artû and Amadis looked at each other with a worried expression. Was the fever muddling his brains? After a breakfast of more fresh fish, Prince Artû was in a hurry to leave. The water bottles were quickly re-filled.

"All packed?" He asked and pointed to the hills. "We will take this path over here."

"Let's go then." Lubbo stomped to the front of the line ready to lead the group.

He swayed a little and Gwendola planted herself in front of him, arms akimbo. "You will be sensible brother. Amadis can carry you for a few hours, not so?" Amadis nodded and knelt down.

"I won't be carried like a child," Lubbo protested.

"I am sorry old friend, but you shouldn't walk in your condition. I will be your vimaan for today."

Amadis picked the flustered Dwendi up and placed him on his shoulders. "Careful, Amadis. Don't you dare stumble and drop me on my head."

They were ready to start walking when out of nowhere, a swarm of butterflies descended on the valley.

"Just see how colourful they are!"

"Yes and big." Katherine had a closer look.

"Everything is big here. Maybe they are dinosaur butterflies."

"Just listen to yourself, Chris. What are dinosaur butterflies supposed to be?" Katherine frowned.

"It's a joke. Don't take everything so seriously."

"That's a bit difficult with Trevor missing and we are stuck in a dragon country. I have no time for jokes."

"Alright, alright. Keep your hair on."

But the butterflies turned out not to be butterflies at all. The little fairies who had come with them all the way from Ruta Ynis knew that at once.

"Shelanti," they eagerly greeted their Prydhanian cousins with tinkling voices. "Shelanti," came the answer.

They started a lively conversation and the fairies circled the group. Prince Artû was so astonished that he nearly fell into the cold ash of the main fireplace. One of the fairies landed on Amadis's sleeve and spoke first.

"Greetings, Amadis of Anaá. I am Brigas of Fûna and these are my cousins from Ruta Ynis."

If he was taken by surprise, Amadis didn't show it. "Greetings, friends," he answered. Gwendola and the children came closer to see what was going on. "Where did these fairies come from? Are they here to play tricks on us?" She asked.

"They better not!" Her borther replied gruffly.

"Amadis, you and your friends are welcome in our land," the fairy spokesman said formally and pointed at the two little Rutian fairies. "Our cousins here have come with you all the way from Ruta Ynis to keep a watchful eye on the Speaking Stone."

"Your cousins? They followed us all the way to Prydhain, but how?" The astonished prince demanded to know.

"We have our ways, athenai. They tell us that you narrowly escaped a trap by evil Gabari. Is everybody well? Apart from this brave Dwendi, of course." Brigas looked up at Lubbo. "Dragons can be rather unpredictable."

"Our friend Lubbo is in urgent need of a medic's attention." Amadis turned away so that the fairies could see the Dwendi's arm with the large tooth still sticking out. The bite wound was red and inflamed.

"Ah yes, not a nice sight, but it is not a fire bite or the Dwendi would be dead by now."

"Oh lucky I am," Lubbo tried to speak in a jovial voice, but he didn't feel lucky at all.

"The rest of us are well, Brigas," Prince . But a boy called Trevór was taken. He was asleep in the fake vimaan when it disappeared. We must find him soon. Can you help us?"

Brigas listened to a fairy, who whispered in his ear at the same time.

"We hear that the boy is in a cave in the Fûna Mountains. Not far from this valley." He pointed east.

"Oh thank goodness," Katherine began to sob with relief. "Then let's go there."

"Do not cry young one," Brigas said kindly. "The boy is unharmed. For now. We will devise a rescue plan. We have to avoid the giant sorcerers and Firbolg."

"Giant sorcerers and Firbolg?" Chryséis asked.

"Yes, you surely know about 'the Cause'?" He saw that she clearly didn't know anything about 'the Cause'. "To steal the Speaking Stone of Caradoc and to bring the power of the Known World back into the hands of the evil Gabari? There are a few of those in our neck of the woods."

"No, we didn't know that." Prince Artû felt disheartened. "Is the boy in the hands of these evil sorcerers?"

"Yes. They have been using the cave for a while now. We'll have to look out for bats. They turn themselves into bats when it suits their purpose."

"I knew it!" Lubbo jumped a little on Amadis's neck.

"That is bad news, friend Brigas. What do we do?" Amadis asked him.

"First you must go to Rusálka, a solitary maiden in the woods. She is a medic and will help your Dwendi friend."

"So are we leaving now?" Katherine asked impatiently.

"Yes, indeed we should go. We can ill-afford yet another delay," the prince said.

"Rusálka lives in a nuraghi tower, a ways through dragon country. Some of us offer to guide you, big fellows. You need a tiny little bit of help around here."

The fairies sniggered at Brigas' joke and the Dwendis didn't even seem insulted. "Shukri, good fairies. Lead us then."

They took the path east and walked past the ruins with a handful of small fairies still around them. Soon they were out and above the valley. The group passed something looking like a thin white veil crumpled against thorny bushes. Chryséis froze, remembering the gruesome white parcels in the cave of Shuruk. "Nothing to worry about, athenai. It is only skin that a large snake shed not too long ago," Brigas explained.

"Oh that makes me feel so much better." Chryséis

looked anxiously over her shoulder. "What if that snake is hungry?"

"We'll just have to be watchful," Prince Artû ended the discussion.

There was no giant snake to be seen anywhere, only large iguanas with broad snouts. They stood on strong hindlegs and made a meal of green araucaria leaves and were nothing like the small pet in the Lady of Cydonia's rooms. Chryséis made sure that Amadis, who still carried Lubbo and Artû were between her and the iguanas. But the reptiles didn't pay any attention at all to the hikers.

A couple of hours later, the northern plains lay before them in all their glory. From the lofty height of the mountain path, they saw stone circles and giant dwellings amid ripening grain fields. One of the buildings was oval and made entirely of glittering white crystals.

"Civilisation at last!" Lubbo cried.

"Yes, but still far away. We'll go to Rusálka's tower now," Brigas said with determination.

The foothills looked like scruffy buffalo fur, all covered in brownish grass. Gabari shepherds went about their business in the low-lying fields. Here and there, gingko and oak trees spread from higher-lying ground into the plains.

The sun was already past its zenith when the fairies guided the travellers through a cheerless highland valley. All grey rocks and gravel.

Had it not been for some giant lobelias, patches of spongy moss and orange lichen for colour, the travellers might as well have been on the moon. And the cloudy sky didn't help much, either.

"Prince Artû, may I suggest that we walk faster, Firbolgs could be skulking around here," Brigas warned.

To be safe from detection, they threaded their way along the rocky edge. If they wanted to reach the tower soon enough, they had to cross the grey moonscape, like it or not.

A true son of the sea, Prince Artû used his 'solaris ring'

with a dolphin crowned by a rainbow-coloured stone, to find the direction of the rising sun. The colour of the stone changed to a light blue whenever pointed directly at the sun.

"No need for this around here prince," Brigas insisted. "We'll guide you safely to your destination."

"I should have done more sports at Pemberton to build stamina." Katherine wiped sweat from her forehead.

"Too late for that. I hope we'll find this Rusálka soon."

"I wonder if Trevor is alright."

"We could ask Brigas what's going on in that cave."

"No, let's just keep up with Artû and Amadis. The fairies promised to take care of Trevor and I'm sure they will keep their promise." Katherine wanted to believe it so badly.

*

"I told you, I don't know where they are. I was asleep in the vimaan, and then I found myself here. Amadis and the others were gone." Trevor wished he knew where his friends were.

Why had they not been in the vimaan with him?

He was tired of giving the same answer to all the questions he had to endure. The Gabari had been rough on him and his bound wrists and ankles were sore by now. He felt more miserable by the minute. Actually ever since he'd been pulled from the vimaan and thrown onto the cold cave floor.

"Aaah!" the Highpriest of Shuruk hollered and banged his tankard on the table. Trevor winced. It was not the first such tantrum. This guy had been so angry that none of the companions were with him. Especially, Amadis. Apparently, something had gone wrong with the vimaan.

Trevor's mind was struggling to comprehend what had happened. One moment, they were floating along the road to Tregarn, the next, he was alone in a mountain cave with those ill-mannered giants.

"How long is this boy going to last? Did you give him the potion?"

"Yes, lord. Twice. But he doesn't know. He just seems to think that…" The servant was at a loss.

"What?" The sorcerer hollered.

"That you are…ugly, sire. That's all I could get from him."

"Oh really, how would he like being all ugly himself?" The Highpriest spoke in Edfunian and glanced at the pet saurian in its corner for a moment. Nestum, the saurian, belched and continued to pick a thighbone clean. Trevor desperately wished that he could open his moonbag and get the Swiss army knife out, but the sorcerer watched his every move. Better not risk having the moonbag taken away from him…

"Lord, there is no time for sport. When they get to Tregarn or Caradoc soon, it will be too late." One of the Edfunian guards bowed his head in front of the sorcerer. Trevor had only seen Gabari in the cave so far and some ugly goblins.

"Don't you lecture me, underling. I know that very well myself." The Highpriest of Shuruk belched and pulled roughly on the bowing Gabari's hair.

"Yes lord, my apologies," the warrior stammered. "I spoke out of turn."

"Pah!" The Highpriest let go of the man's hair, stood up in a huff and left the chamber, followed by a number of other giants. The two Edfunian guards remained in the chamber with Trevor.

"Are you letting me go now?" Trevor thought it was worth a try.

"Did the pipsqueak say something?" the one guard mocked and rubbed his smarting scalp.

"I don't understand flea language, hahaha," the other one guffawed.

"Yes, he's a flea. Haha."

"Hilarious," Trevor said to himself and rolled his eyes.

The giants turned around and poured wine from a jug into tankards on the table. They didn't have to keep watching the boy. He wasn't going anywhere. After a few minutes their noisy conversation grew more muffled. Trevor had dozed off.

"Psst."

Trevor looked around. What was that?

"Psst over here." A fairy stood on a protruding stone in the wall, waving.

"Am I going crazy or dreaming or something?"

"No, friend Trevór. I am here to help you get out of the cave."

"Oh yes? How do you know my name? Playing tricks like Gump did on Ruta Ynis - why should I trust you?"

"No, no tricks. I am from Ruta Ynis that's true, but I'm here to help. Our cousins in the Fûna Mountains are with your friends. They are safe, well except for the Dwendi, who was bitten by a..."

Trevor sat up with a jolt. "You know my friends? How can you be from Ruta Ynis? That's all the way across the ocean."

"I came with you when you left our island and were attacked by sea dragons and stayed in Algiras and..."

"Okay, okay I'm getting the picture. You followed us." Trevor began to relax. "Who was bitten?"

"Sssht, not so loud. These guys must not know that I'm here."

"What is your name?" Trevor lowered his voice.

"My name is Parmini of Ruta Ynis."

"Shelanti, Parmini of Ruta Ynis. I am Trevor of Chicago."

"I know. No need for formalities. I will help you now."

"Oh really...how are you going to do that? They are all giants."

Trevor glanced over at the table where the guards were drinking wine.

"Never underestimate a daring fairy," Parmini said.

"Alright, so what did you have in mind?" Trevor said softly.

"Turn with your hands to the wall."

"What? Why?"

"No time for chitchat. Turn around."

Trevor moved just enough so that his back faced the wall. Parmini fluttered down to the ground and began to loosen the ties that cut into Trevor's wrists. It wasn't easy for the fairy and Trevor giggled a little at the ticklish feeling. The Gabari guards turned around and eyed him contemptuously.

"Hey, what's your problem boy? Crying for your mommy?" the bigger one of the two asked him.

"Yes, I'm sad," Trevor said sarcastically.

"Oh, mommy's boy, mommy's boy," they mocked him and Trevor rolled his eyes. In the meantime, the fairy had made progress. So Trevor thought it best to play along. But the giants soon grew tired of their bullying.

"Almost there," Parmini announced and then Trevor's hands were free.

"I will tuck the string under and now I'll free your feet."

The fairy began to work on the string around Trevor's ankles and he smiled stiffly at one of the Gabari guards, who had turned around to check on him. Luckily, the fairy was hidden by a keg.

Two Firbolg stumbled past, carrying a wooden board and a small sack with white pebbles. They put everything on the massive table and bowed their way out of the chamber.

The guards played a board game to pass the time, but soon the giant whose hair had been pulled said, "I need to go somewhere," and scrambled to his feet. "Can you keep an eye on the flea so that Nestum doesn't eat our mommy's boy? The lords have plans with him."

"Go and relieve yourself. I'll keep an eye on our flea boy." The other guard threw pebbles into the round depressions on the wooden board. Clack, clack, clack. "When you come back, we'll play another game." Clack, clack. He poked in his teeth with a twig and turned his back to the prisoner.

"Listen carefully," the fairy whispered into Trevor's ear. "You also have to go. You know...outside. Tell them...now." Trevor nodded.

"Hey guard...I must relieve myself also. I don't want to

sully your clean cave." That was something of a joke, of course, that was lost on the giants.

"Did the flea say something?" The shorter one asked.

"Haha, yes, he needs to pee. Haha. The flea needs to pee."

A Firbolg carrying a bowl with food stared at the guard.

"Get out of here!" the Gabari snarled at the dwarf.

"Yes, I need to pee." Trevor tried to sound calm and manly. "So what about taking me outside with you?"

"I don't know about that..." The guard at the table seemed unsure.

"What is he going to do? Run away? I'll take care of him," the other one, who also had to take a leak said. "Better than having a stench in the cave for the rest of the day. I'll take the dragon along. It's also due for an outing."

"Fine, but don't take too long. Get up you disgusting lizard." The guard whistled.Nestum dropped the bone and heaved itself up. The Gabari guard led the tame saurian to the cave mouth.

"Come on, flea, hurry up, let's go," he bellowed.

Trevor stood up awkwardly and hobbled after the Gabari and the plodding dinosaur through the tunnel entrance. His hands and feet were loosely tied, just so that the guards had the impression that he was still helpless. They didn't consider for a moment how he was going to do his business outside.

"When you are outside, stand behind the Gabari. Look out for the dragon - then activate your VIC," Parmini whispered in Trevor's ear.

"You know about that?"

"No time to explain. Then you turn to your right. You'll see a hollow tree. Climb in and close it with the bark door."

"Got it. Close bark door."

The sunlight was blinding him andTrevor held his hand up to shield his eyes. As soon as the guard had stepped behind a bush, Trevor pressed the button on the VIC. He turned invisible at once and Trevor shook off his ties. They dropped noiselessly onto the mossy ground. The guard didn't notice a thing.

The dragon had found itself a tree not far from the guard and relieved itself.

"Ooh, that smell is disgusting," Trevor whispered back.

"Dragon excrement is not very nice. Don't pay attention to it. We are invisible now. Turn to the right." Parmini sat still on his shoulder as invisible as Trevor himself. He turned right as she had told him and walked around the cave as quietly as he could. Some dry branches under the leaf cover cracked. Trevor stopped and held his breath. But the dragon didn't do as much as lift its head and flick its tongue.

"That's the tree over there. No, the next one. Yes that one, go inside."

The hollow tree was big enough for at least three people. Trevor squeezed through the opening, found the bark door and closed it. "What do I do now?" he asked.

"We'll stay in here for a while and wait."

"Will they not find us? We are so close to the cave."

"They can try all they want, but this tree is...protected."

That was not much of a surprise, but Trevor thought a little extra protection couldn't hurt. "I'm putting myself into an armour of light," he said to himself.

Soon he heard stomping and calling outside and sat perfectly still.

*

In the moonscape, the fairies flew tirelessly ahead. Prince Artû was eager to leave the highlands and didn't want to stop. The sooner Lubbo's arm was taken care of, the sooner they could start looking for the boy. From the tower, it would be a breeze to get to Lyonesse and Caradoc.

The girls were slowing down. Katherine's sandals chafed and she had two blisters on the soles of her feet. Artû glanced back, obviously displeased at their slow pace. He still couldn't understand why the wise Speaking Stone had insisted on the children joining the quest.

"Friend Artû, we need to take a rest," Amadis said and lowered the injured Lubbo from his shoulders.

"Have we some water left?" the Dwendi asked feebly. "I am very thirsty."

Gwendola gave her brother water to drink, while Amadis stretched himself and turned his head from side to side. Even the weight of a Dwendi could become cumbersome after a while. Katherine sat down and took care of her blisters. Thank goodness they had packed a box with band-aid.

"Do you have the antiseptic?" she asked Chryséis .

"No, but maybe it's in here." She rifled through Trevor's daypack that she had been carrying on top of her own. Katherine applied the cream and band-aids. Gwendola looked on in fascination and Tepi rolled around in the moss.

Amadis picked up his bow. He had discovered a flock of wild ptarmigan. It was a good idea not to come empty-handed when they got to the tower. He stalked the clucking flock up the rocky slope and a well-aimed arrow struck down a fat hen in no time.

Amadis went to fetch the bird and had barely reached the spot when Brigas fluttered up and down in front of him. "Hide friend Amadis. There is danger about."

Amadis picked the bird up and hid in a crevice in the rock. All was quiet. Had the fairy played a prank on him?

Then he heard the crunch of footsteps, saw a couple of small shapes approach. Two Firbolg!

There was no telling how many more of them were crawling around. Amadis flattened himself against the rock, trying to control his breathing. He pushed the ptarmigan with his foot to the back, cocked an arrow in his bow and waited.

He saw from the corner of his eye that Katherine and Gwendola had ventured up the slope. Katherine glanced up and looked straight at Amadis – ready to shoot his arrow. He gave her an urgent look. The next moment she saw the Firbolg and ducked quickly behind some shrubs, pulling hard on Gwendola's tunic. She mouthed the word F I R B O L G noiselessly and Gwendola understood. Amadis peered out from his hiding place and saw one of the Firbolg lift his spear.

Fearing the worst, he threw himself around and in position. But before Amadis could aim and shoot his arrow, he heard a triumphant cry. The two Firbolg had speared a ptarmigan rooster. They slunk away with their prey without noticing the D'Ånu warrior or the other companions. There might have been some fairy dust involved, dulling their senses.

"A close shave. We must be careful, athenai. Firbolg are a wily bunch," Brigas said as he reappeared.

"Best for your people to keep a look out then." Amadis took a deep breath.

"Right you are D'Ånu. We will place sentries at vantage points along our route."

"It's best to move along. The place is swarming with goblins," Gwendola said when they returned.

"You saw them?" Artû's gaze fell on the bird tied to Amadis' belt.

"Yes, two of them. They were hunting ptarmigan. Didn't see us, but it's best to get out of here fast."

They didn't come across any more of the dreaded Firbolg, just Komodo dragons lying motionless on the still-warm rocks, basking in the moonlight.

At times, the companions felt observed. But when they turned around, fully expecting man or animal to stare at them from behind a rock or through waving branches, there was nothing.

The fairies had been right: the moonscape made soon way for greener surroundings and jst after midday, they arrived at the nuraghi tower. It was a round tower made of rough stone. Nuraghis had been part of ancient citadels in

Prydhain and there had also been such a tower in Zeruana's ruins.

"We are here," Brigas announced and flew ahead with his posse of fairies. Broad stone steps led up to a platform that was enclosed by a low wall.

"Maiden Rusálka, shelanti, we come as friends!" Prince Artû called and entered the tower. But Rusálka was not at home.

Two barn owls sat on perches in a corner under the ceiling and hooted. One of the birds swooped through an open window to catch a fat lizard sunning itself on a pippala branch outside.

The fairies took care to keep well out of the owls' way, not to be taken for mice or such. A hungry Tepi had caught a large rat behind the tower without delay and was eating it ravenously, much to Katherine's disgust.

Amadis and Gwendola placed the feverish Lubbo on a bedstead and covered him with blankets. He mumbled and moaned.

Gwendola fetched water with an earthen crock from the deep well in front and wiped her brother's face with a moistened cloth, while Amadis used dried wood that was stored against the outside wall to feed the fire in the hearth. Chryséis and Katherine watched them from the edge of the well.

"Who are you?" a gruff voice asked surprisingly firm behind Artû. He turned around and faced a cloaked woman. She looked as wrinkled and dry as an autumn leaf, ready to crumble at the slightest touch. A few of the fairies had found the maiden picking mushrooms and had called her to the nuraghi. Rusálka stood waiting for an answer compelling Prince Artû with her eyes.

"My apologies for intruding in your home...we are friends and in dire need of your healing skill. Shelanti, Rusálka, I am Prince Artû of Avallûn..." He went on to introduce them and the old woman's expression softened.

"You say you are in need of my skill, Artû of Avallûn?"

"Good woman of the woods, our Dwendi friend Lubbo was injured when we were attacked by a dragon yesterday. He suffers from a fever, and the dragon tooth needs to be removed."

"Why did you not announce your arrival by thought?" Rusálka scolded. "Or better yet, why not call for help from one of the citadels. A vimaan or teleporter beam could take you quickly to the nearest 'House of Life'."

"We dare not draw attention to our presence, maidenRusálka. There is an item in our possession, to be returned to Caradoc. We just escaped a foul trap, set by evil sorcerers."

"Who is this?" She pointed rudely with her chin at Gwendola and the girls behind Amadis' tall shape.

"A Dwendi, Gwendola of Penda. It is her brother, who has the dragon tooth in his arm. And two children."

"No Firbolg vermin?" The maiden asked.

"No, no Firbolg."

"You say that sorcerers are after you? A good thing you didn't draw attention to my nuraghi then. What is this item in your possession?"

Artû was astounded at her forwardness, but he had to remain respectful to the maiden many years his senior.

"I may not say, maidenRusálka, but please trust us. We must keep the item safe from the sorcerers."

"Yeah, yeah yeah…" Rusálka waved off his answer with the abruptness of old age, but she seemed somewhat mollified. "Where is this sick friend of yours?"

"He lies on a bedstead in the tower."

The old woman went inside and examined Lubbo carefully. "There is no poison. I will prepare medicine and take out the tooth. Your friend might recover or not. Who is to say? Tststs. Taking children on such a dangerous journey…" She spoke to herself while plucking dried herbs off bundles hanging from the low kitchen ceiling.

The basement of the tower looked like an alchemist's

laboratory. Between candles dripping beeswax into little mounds on the tables along the rough stone wall, there was an array of distillation equipment, pots and pans.

"Ah I see, water has been boiled. That's a good start."

Gwendola scrambled to her feet as Rusálka bent over the steaming pot.

"Five-finger-grass, an inch of fevertree bark and 'herb-of-grace'," the maiden mumbled to herself, as she crushed the dried herbs into a bowl and poured hot water over the concoction. Rusálka motioned for Gwendola to help her strain the brownish liquid into a cup. Then she took it to Lubbo.

"Here drink this slowly, Dwendi," the crone said.

Lubbo was half-awake and stared at the strange woman with feverish eyes. "Och, leave me sleep," he said in a cranky voice.

"Don't give me trouble Dwendi. You do as I say or you could die."

She handed the cup to Gwendola, who managed to give Lubbo half a cup of the bitter brew.

The maiden worked fast on a painkilling willow bark infusion before she removed the dragon tooth effortlessly from Lubbo's arm and dressed the wound. The other travellers were ordered to sit on grass mats and drink recutis to calm their spirit.

Later, the musty smell of the tower mingled with delicious aromas of mushrooms and roasting ptarmigan that ended up feeding all of them. Tepi was still hungry and chewed greedily on scraps and bones, while the fairies preferred to drink nectar from large lobelia flowers nearby.

"I wonder how she did it. The tooth was so large and had all those barbs on it. She only has her herbs and no devices at all." Chryséis was obviously impressed.

"Lucky the bite wasn't poisonous, just infected."

"The dragon by the lake was so scary. I never want to go a dragon country again, thank you very much." Chryséis shook herself. "All that because of a fake vimaan..."

"I wish we could just go and get Trevor now." Katherine stared out of the window. They are working on it, right? To get him out of that cave."

"Brigas would have told us if he wasn't okay, and yes, I'm sure they are."

Katherine stole a look at Amadis, who sat on the low wall outside. He had protected her from the Firbolg in the moonscape valley. Mighty grand of him. By nightfall, Amadis kept watch outside the nuraghi. They had to remain vigilant. Rusálka had given him a quilt for warmth and an incredible night sky with sparkling stars kept him company.

Amadis searched for the Archer star sign and found it high above. The D'Ånu people attributed protective powers to special stars and the Archer was his own star sign.

Soon, a fat, yellow moon hoisted itself over the mountain peaks. Father Moon. An owl hooted, shaking him from his dreamy thoughts. Amadis groped for his bow and arrows. They were still next to him.

He pulled the quilt tighter around his shoulders and listened to the fading sounds of the forest.

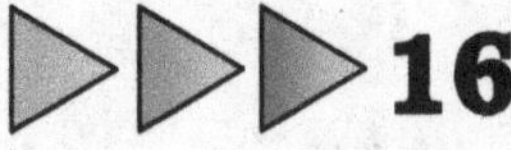 **16**   **IN THE WOODS**

Trevor opened his eyes. Just a little. Dappled light filtered through the cracks in the flimsy bark-door. It was almost dark inside the tree and smelled strongly of resin. He yawned and stretched himself. Good, he was not in the cave anymore. How long had he been asleep in this hollow tree? "Parmini, are you there?"

"Yes," a small voice answered from a ledge above Trevor's head.

Thanks to the protection charm around the tree, the tame saurian hadn't picked up his scent. Trevor had been safe from detection in here all day. Maybe the 'armour of light' had also helped a little.

"We must have been here a long time."

"It is afternoon," Parmini said.

"What do we do now? I'm hungry. These disgusting giants didn't give me anything to eat," Trevor complained.

His stomach was grumbling. All he'd had was water from an earthen vase inside the tree trunk.

"We must wait for nighfall."

When the light outside became dimmer, Trevor had watched a spider weave her net and ants carry off crumbled wood through the cracks, but other than that there had not been much entertainment. All he could do now was sleep again.

"It should be safe enough to go outside and find your friends - and some food," the fairy said and stopped cleaning her wings. "I'm told that the Firbolg and the Gabari are far from here still searching. Those guarding the cave won't notice us. You will become invisible again and if we leave soon, we might even get to the nuraghi tonight. You can pick berries and nuts to eat on the way."

"What's a nuraghi?"

"You will see. Your friends are there."

"Then what are we waiting for? Let's go." Trevor stood up and grabbed the bark door with both hands.

"No, stay!"

Parmini whistled and a faint whistle echo answered. "It is safe outside, you may open the door now," she said.

Two other forest fairies joined them and Trevor walked where they led him. When they were a good ways farther east, Parmini pointed out hazelnut shrubs and edible berries that Trevor stuffed into his pockets and ate while he walked.

"Are we getting any closer?" he muttered while peeling the soft hazelnut shells off with his teeth.

"Yes, but it will be very dark soon and we must be watchful of wild animals and Firbolg, despite the moonlight. Stop here for a moment." They couldn't take any chances.

Faint whistling came from a pine branch overhead and they knew that it was safe to proceed.

*

During the night Chryséis woke up and saw dancing lights in the low brush outside. She wondered what they were. Then tiredness overcame her curiosity. She fell asleep again, snuggling up against Tepi's warm fur. The dancing lights were soon forgotten.

The following day, grey mist hung heavily over the hills, veiling everything into a gloomy light.

"It will be difficult to walk in the mist. I cannot use my ring in these conditions and the evil ones might just creep up on us."

"Yes, it is better to wait until the mist has cleared, with your permission maiden." Amadis smiled charmingly. "Lubbo will hopefully feel better. We are also awaiting word from the fairies."

"No skin off my nose," Rusálka said. "You'd better eat something."

"Shukri good maiden, how may we be of help? Will Lubbo be able to walk?"

"Ahh, you'll just be in the way. Here, sit by the fireplace, while I see to your Dwendi friend."

Gwendola had slept next to her brother and now sat by his side. A mountain lizard darted across the floor and hid under a grass mat. Gwendola shrank away from the mat in surprise.

"How are you today, Dwendi?" Rusálka asked. She could tell that he was no longer feverish.

"I am feeling much better. I believe the arm is healing fast. Shukri, thank you for all your help, maiden," Lubbo said.

"Good. I'll change the dressing before you leave. You should also eat something," Rusálka said in a tone that left no room for objections. She went back to the fireplace preparing breakfast and medicine.

"You can leave your dog here if you want to, girl," the maiden offered Katherine casually as she stirred the porridge. "She'll be good company for an old woman."

Rusálka had only owls for pets apart from lizards and rats. A smart cuddly dog would be nice to have around.

"I am very fond of Tepi. I'd like to keep her with me," Katherine declined the offer politely and put her arms around the young dog. Tepi snuggled a little closer to her. The old maiden shrugged her shoulders. "Keep her then. No skin off my nose."

The girl blushed when Amadis leaned over and brushed her shoulder to put down firewood. He seemed not to notice and a tear made its way down Katherine's cheek. She caught it with her tongue. The maiden saw the young girl's mood change.

Matters of the heart were never easy and the last thing this child needed. Rusálka brewed a tea with some tiny leaves in a small pot and poured the contents into an earthen cup.

She plunked the cup on the wooden board next to Katherine.

"Here drink this, girl," she ordered gruffly.

Katherine looked doubtful, but she didn't dare disobey. The maiden nodded to herself and smiled, busying herself again with the food preparations. After a simple meal of fried mushrooms and millet porridge, they heard noises outside the nuraghi. The landscape wavered in the fading morning mist and something emerged from the trees. A dragon or a Firbolg? Amadis trained an arrow on the approaching figure.

Then up the hill walked – Trevor.

"Trevor!" Chryséis and Katherine ran down the slope and greeted their friend.

"Hi," he said tiredly. "I've been walking all night. What does one have to do to get something to drink around here?"

"What's wrong with your arm, why is there blood on your sleeve?"

"Oh, it's nothing," he said. "Only some brambles I walked into," he added on a lower note and shuddered,"…and wild harpees."

"What? Didn't you switch on your VIC? How could they see you?" Chryséis scolded.

"I'd switched it off so I could see myself."

"Not very smart."

"No, I know that now."

They reached the platform by the tower, where the others were waiting.

"We can't thank you enough, friend Brigas, for freeing the boy," Prince Artû said to the fairy spokesman. "You saved our lives in this dangerous territory."

"Our clever Parmini here deserves much of the glory. She helped the Trevór escape from the sorcerers' cave." The little fairy smiled.

"You were in a cave with the sorcerers?" Katherine stood with her mouth open.

"Yes and a tame dragon, they call Nestum…"

And Trevor told the whole story how he woke up in the vimaan not knowing where he was. How he was bound and interrogated for hours, how Parmini had freed him from his ties and taken him invisibly to the hollow tree protected by a spell and how he'd walked through the forest in the dark.

"We haven't seen any Gabari at all." Chryséis said.

"Lucky. Trust me, you don't want to have anything to do with these guys." Trevor trembled a little.

"I faintly remember what that feels like."

"Oh yes, of course, the caves of Shuruk. I almost forgot. I'm thirsty," Trevor repeated and Katherine rushed to bring him some water. Trevor drank thirstily.

"We ran into Firbolg," Katherine said. "But they didn't see us..."

"There is leftover millet mush and mushrooms, young man," the maiden interrupted. She stood right behind them with a wooden bowl and a cup of tea. They had completely forgotten about Rusálka.

"How did you end up here with this old lady?" Trevor asked the girls while eating breakfast.

'We had to find a medic, because Lubbo was bitten by a dragon and a dragon tooth was stuck in his arm. So the fairies took us to the maiden Rusálka and she took the tooth out and Lubbo is much better now."

"Is that why you didn't come looking for me?" Trevor sounded reproachful.

"Yes, Lubbo could have died. And we needed shelter. We were going to look for you today."

"Well, the Highpriest of Shuruk had plans for me with this tame dinosaur. It might have been too late today."

"Oh crikey." Katherine went pale.

"We must leave, athenai," Prince Artû interrupted. "The maiden doesn't want trouble with the giants and Firbolg. We'll walk a ways and find a good spot to rest. From there I'll call for a vimaan."

"More walking?" Trevor was tired from being on foot

all night.

"It cannot be helped, athenai. We must leave. The sun is a little stronger now." He held his hand with the ring up. "We are headed this way."

They said quickly goodbye and thanked the maiden, then they were off.

Hours later, they rested on the mossy ground still moist from the morning dew. Lubbo was healing fast, but still couldn't walk much. Artû had decided that this was a good place to summon the vimaan from Caradoc.

He had checked on the 'Speaking Stone' and was about to put the têrakhon sphere back into Amadis's bag, when a sudden earth tremor travelled through the ground.

"Earthquake! Save yourselves," Amadis yelled. The sphere dropped from his hand and rolled down the rocky ledge of the cliff. A screaming Chryséis was unable to hold unto anything. She tumbled over the edge after the têrakhon sphere. As soon as the trembling stopped, the companions rushed over to the cliff and stared down.

Chryséis sat dazed on a broad ledge about five feet down. Her fall had been cushioned by her backpack and some dense thicket growing horizontally away from the rock. Something white and shiny lay not far from her left foot in a tuft of dried pine needles. One more aftershock and the 'Speaking Stone' would surely fall straight down.

"Are you alright down there?" Trevor called.

Chryséis sat stunned, leaning against the rock and watched two large iguanas clawing their way up the rock.

"Ooh, no I'm not alright. What if I fall, what if I fall?"

A shower of small stones rained on the ledge when one of the reptiles lost its footing. Chryséis cried out and stared at the green iguanas in terror, trying to move away from the sliding reptile.

"Get away from me. Get away from me." She held onto the shaky thicket. The iguana found its footing again and continued its climb.

"Don't move, friend Chryséis ," Amadis warned her. Nothing would have stopped another fall down the sheer cliff.

"Chryséis , are you injured, child?" Gwendola yelled, trying to control her voice, not to alarm the girl into dangerous movement.

Chryséis looked up as if in a dream. "I don't think so, my backside... hurts," she said, feeling her bruises.

"Can you move your toes?" It was all Katherine could think of.

"Yes... it's just my backside. And I have some cuts." She looked at her arms. Katherine breathed a sigh of relief. The iguanas clambered over the rock ledge and disappeared into the cover of underbrush.

"That's good — I mean under the circumstances," Katherine called down.

Amadis pointed to the white egg in its têrakhon sphere. "Look to your left, friend Chryséis ," he said as steadily as he could manage. Chryséis stretched her neck and looked to her left.

"Do you see the white egg in the sphere? Try and stop it from rolling down. Perhaps you could put it in your pocket."

"I can see it." Chryséis nodded. Her mind slotted painfully into gear. Egg. Speaking Stone. It seemed so far away. She began to crawl off the bouncy thicket. Her foot touched the sphere slightly. The companions held their breaths, but the object lay unwavering on its cushion of dry pine needles. "I...I don't know if I can..." Chryséis bent forward.

"Please Chryséis , you must try," Katherine pleaded.

Chryséis knelt and blocked the sphere from rolling off the ledge with her right hand. Then she nudged it closer.

"Excellent. Now try and pick it up. Don't look down," Prince Artû said quickly when he saw Chryséis glancing down over the extended shrub.

She grabbed the sphere with both hands, trying not to lose her balance and sat down again.

"You've got it?"

"It's in my pocket," she called up.

"Hold tight, friend Chryséis ," Amadis instructed her. "We will bring you up now." He extended both his arms down, while Prince Artû held onto his legs. Gwendola grabbed Chryséis as she appeared over the ledge, pulled her up and led her away. Dwendis for all their small stature were quite strong. Chryséis collapsed onto the soft moss.

"Darn, it's not my lucky day…" she said to Katherine. "I could totally have fallen…"

"I think you've been very lucky Chris! What… on earth?"

Something else came crawling over the rocky ledge and it wasn't another iguana. Gwendola caught sight of the three Dwendis first. A second look confirmed that they were goblins.

"Haaaa!" She dealt the Firbolg closest to her a powerful kick. He lost his balance and tumbled all the way down the cliff.

Another kick sent the next one flying. Amadis and Artû drew their weapons, but Gwendola had already made short shrift of the third Firbolg. He fell with a long, bloodcurdling scream. Tepi, still shaking from the frightening earthquake was barking wildly. Gwendola eased out of her 'praying mantis' posture and took a deep breath.

"Friend Gwendola. I must say…that was very…powerful," Artû praised. Who would have thought that the feisty but also quiet Gwendola could spring into action with such deadly speed?

"Courage and valor!'" The Dwendi woman delivered the requisite battle cry and bowed with her right hand on her heart.

"It's okay Tepi, shush now. It's okay," Katherine said soothingly to the dog.

Lubbo smiled proudly. "That was simply splendid, sister!"

"Thank you friend Gwendola. They were after the 'Speaking Stone' for sure," Prince Artû said.

Katherine screamed as another goblin jumped out from behind a tree, wielding a bone knife above his head. Tepi went for the Firbolg's feet and bit him. Amadis threw himself around and fired off two arrows that hit their mark instantly. The Firbolg knife thrown haphazardly in his direction, dropped to the ground and the evil creature lay gasping and spurted blood from mortal wounds

"Come here Tepi. Don't sniff at that."

Lubbo kicked the body of the Firbolg over the cliff and the children watched in shock. "Are there more of those hiding in the woods? We must find out," he said.

"Lie down and don't move. We will investigate. The dog comes with us."

Artû motioned for Lubbo and the children to lie low. Then he searched the surroundings with Amadis, Gwendola and Tepi.

They came back soon. Amadis had finished off another Firbolg, who had been hiding behind a hazelnut bush. "If the Firbolg know where we are, we must depart immediately. This forest is not the right place to call a vimaan for us." Prince Artu nodded.

They had no choice but to continue their descent from the hills into the lowlands, D'Ånu country, by foot.

"Do you thinkRusálka's a witch like Zeruana?" Katherine asked Trevor.

His eyes were red from lack of sleep, but he tried not to show how tired he was.

"She looked like one to me. Like from a Brothers Grimm storybook."

"Yeah, she was odd and grouchy. And she wanted me to give her Tepi. That was odd. But she healed Lubbo so quickly. I mena look at him now."

The sturdy Dwendi man was walking on his own steam, shoulders back and head high. Amadis helped Chryséis over some stones in a trickling brook when two Konks passed them in the opposite direction.

"Shelanti." Being shy country people, they didn't stop to chat.

"Shelanti athenai," the companions answered.

One of thethe Konks had his arm in a sling. They were on their way to ask the old maiden in the hills to treat a broken arm.

They nodded and were gone.

Katherine was deep in thought. She had decided that Amadis didn't really like her. He had just done his duty back in the moonscape valley. Strangely it didn't bother her. The butterflies in her stomach had disappeared.

"Careful over there. Mind the hole." Amadis probed the ground with his staff. "The spongy ground might hide bogs."

They made it to the edge of the forest dry of foot. The thick forest was thinning out into stands of pippala and ginkgo trees down the slope.

"We must leave you now, Prince Artû. We are creatures of the wooded mountains." Brigas and his fairies fluttered in front of them. "You are not far from friendly folk down there."

He pointed towards grain fields and houses. The fairies hung back under the shady trees and their shiny wings fluttered incessantly.

"Of course you must remain here, then. We thank you for your help and guidance, friend Brigas," Prince Artû said.

"Our cousins from Ruta Ynis will accompany you a while longer. Bring the Speaking Stone safely home, athenai. Farewell, may the Earthmother be with you."

"Farewell, good fairies. Chudafis."

"Only cursed giants to worry about now," Lubbo grumbled and stomped down the hill.

After a while the mossy ground gave way to patchy grass and the footpath became so stony that they had to take care not to stumble.

"Civilisation at last," Lubbo sighed and kicked a stone out of the way.

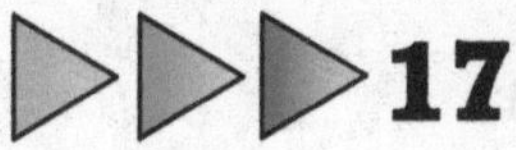 **17**   SUMMER SOLSTICE

Village children ran across the field, skimming through tall, dry grass to greet the strangers. They ogled the travellers curiously, chattering and giggling. Tepi jumped happily around them, wagging her tail and made them laugh at her antics.

Sheep with white corkscrew locks and brown horses grazed between the grain fields. Not the big, black Tregarni horses but smaller hay-coloured steppe horses. It was a pity that they had to give country of Tregarn a miss. A few shepherds lay sleeping under a hedge lost to the world.

"Not exactly vigilant," Trevor said to Chryséis and she nodded.

They had just escaped from the Firbolg by the skin of their teeth and here people were without a care.

"Anaá is yonder those hills!" Amadis called out, delight swinging in his voice. "This is my homeland."

"I'll say, Amadis. You have been out of the country and in Algiras far too long it seems," Lubbo said.

"So it seems, friend Lubbo." Amadis pointed to a broad hill covered in short grass and shrubs." The entrance to Anaá lies inside this hill behind the village."

"Then this is where we will go now," Prince Artû announced. "You'll rest with the children in the village for the day. It's Midsummer and not the time to travel any farther." The holiday of the summer solstice was the shortest night and longest day of the year.

"You stay at the 'House of Life' and I will leave for Anaá with Amadis. We come for you later," the prince said. "It is better not to send thoughts just yet."

"Make sure to come back in a vimaan, then. Lubbo and the children have done enough walking for today," Gwendola instructed.

"I can walk to Anaá," Lubbo bridled.

"I have no doubt you could, brother, but you must regain your strength. You are no good to anyone in that sorry state." Lubbo grumbled a little, but gave in under Gwendola's stern gaze.

"We shall announce us to the Lady of Anaá and return by vimaan. You will be safe here, athenai. We will take the stone to be secured at the citadel," Amadis added with confidence. "Let's hope we have seen the last of the sorcerers and Firbolg of the Fûna Mountains. This area is under the protection of the D'Ånu people."

They walked on and soon reached the village. The modest buildings were suitably decorated for the important festival of 'Midsummer', the festival of the life-giving sun, the vehicle of the Earthmother.

The first house they reached was the 'House of Life' with its 'flame of civilisation' lamp flickering outside. A couple of snuffling pigs rooted in a smelly puddle next to the entrance. The community was far too small for a proper citadel.

"Shelanti good people. Come in, come in," the only resident medic welcomed them. He was short and red-haired and had a friendly face. They sat down in the reception room, where the floor was covered in a round mosaic and there was a small water feature that bubbled merrily.

"If this is not Amadis of Anaá. What an honour, athenai. The most valiant D'Ånu warrior of all times." It was astonishing that the medic recognised Amadis, but it was his homeland after all.

"I doubt that very much, good medic, but thank you for your hospitality. A few days ago, our Dwendi friend here was injured by a dragon. Kindly see to his wound. I will take my leave with Prince Artû for Anaá at once. Our friends will remain in your valued care until we return."

"We will look after your friends honourable Amadis. The guesthouse is spacious."

The medic seemed to be a doctor and innkeeper rolled into one. The word guesthouse was music to Trevor's ears. He was terribly tired by now.

After Amadis and the prince had left, food and drink was brought in for Lubbo, Gwendola and the children. Chryséis filled a bread pocket with vegetables and aioli and looked around, while she ate her fill. The place was remarkably empty.

"Where are all the other people? There is nobody else in the 'House of Life'," Trevor asked.

"Young friend, the village folk of Catrev are sadly convinced that medical treatment is 'magic'. And 'magic' makes them suspicious."

"Suspicious?" asked Katherine.

"Yes, they are a hardy breed of pioneers in the land of the 'Shaking Earth'," the medic told them while he removed Lubbo's bandage. "I am from Tregarn myself and sometimes wish I was back home and not in this backward place."

He cleaned the healing wound and moved a device over it.

"That looks not too bad, friend Dwendi. Whoever tended to this wound knew what he was doing."

"It was seen to by the maiden Rusálka. She lives in a nuraghi in the forest and took care of our friend Lubbo's injury," Chryséis said.

"Rusálka? You must be mistaken. She has been a legend for no less than three sheaves of years. Only the D'Ånu still reach such old age in Prydhain."

"Really? She seemed old, but alive and well."

"Astounding."

"Astounding indeed," Gwendola said and reached for the food on the table.

"Ah, I've heard of her legendary skill. Here, medics are good enough for setting bones and stitching up wounds. For everything else the locals go to their witches. And…" he sniggered, "…vimaans make them feel nauseous."

"That explains why there are all the sickly people we have seen since landing in Prydhain," Katherine said. "They don't seek medical help."

"Yes, that's probably why." The medic moved a healing device over the wound.

"Where do the villagers come from? I thought they were all D'Ånu." Chryséis took another bite of her bread pocket. Trevor had eaten up and was already fast asleep on the sofa next to her.

"No, the D'Ånu live only inside the hills. The ancestors of the villagers in this province arrived from Airyana Vaëgo sheaves of years ago, after the Dark Age. Like so many other early settlers in Prydhain. This village is named Catrev. It means 'one hundred'. Founded by one hundred settlers. It was a large number of people in those days."

"They must have forgotten civilised ways," Lubbo said.

"Yes, yes. We have a long stretch ahead of us," the medic sighed and shook his bald head. "Gabari and Dwendi settled here as well, but not many."

"Our young friend Kathín is from Prydhain herself." Lubbo flinched as the new bandage came on.

"Oh, but then you must know all of this. Why am I lecturing you? You can tell your friends by yourself."

"Oh no, my family settled here much later. I don't know much about the history of Prydhain at all," Katherine said and stroked Tepi. The dog lapped thirstily water from a bowl and sniffed at the food Katherine had put on the floor for her.

"I see, I see. Enough talk. You may rest in the guesthouse. Friend Dwendi, and you should be as good as new by tomorrow. The children might want to join the Midsummer celebrations. They fires will be lit at nightfall."

Gwendola left Trevor on the sofa and put a blanket over him. "You run along girls. I will stay here. It should be safe enough in the village."

So Katherine and Chryséis went for a walk on their own.

A group of children sat on the ground in front of the 'House of Life' by a tall flowering cactus. Two small pots of white paint stood in front of them.

One of the girls beckoned Katherine to sit down. "Shelanti, visitor. Join us for Midsummer face painting."

Another girl was busy painting a traditional white disk on a boy's forehead. When she was done, she dipped her finger into the white paint again. The girl painted a line of white dots above Katherine's left brow over the bridge of her nose and under her right eye. Katherine held still for the girl to finish.

"Now it's my turn," Chryséis said. "Looks cool!"

"Let me paint your face as well, friend," the girl offered.

The girl pulled on Chryséis' trouser leg and motioned for her to look down. "You are pretty."

"Oh, I don't know…thanks. Maybe we should walk around a bit more."

"Come on, don't be a party pooper. It's for the celebrations tonight," Katherine replied.

"For pretty face," the girl said and smiled.

Chryséis could hardly say no and ended up with a white sundisk on her forehead and a dotted line on her chin.

"Trevor is sleeping like a log. He'll miss the festival," she said.

"Poor guy. I told Tepi to stay with him and she actually did. What a thing he went through in that cave, and then he walked through the night to find us." Katherine shook her head.

"I'd be dead-tired too. I'm glad he's back with us, but I'm sure he'd also enjoy the party. You know that we've been here for so long. Soon we'll be back home. Can't wait to see my family again. I really miss them," Chryséis said longingly.

"It's going to take me longer to see my family," Katherine sighed.

"Actually, you are at home already. Just not at the right time."

"Feels weird."

"I bet."

When the village girl had finished painting Chryséis' face, she said,

"shukri, dear friend, we will take a walk now and have a look at your village."

"I will come with you," the girl offered. They still didn't know her name, but it didn't seem to matter in Catrev. She took them along the dirt roads right to the center square. Polished brass discs and wreaths of sunflowers were pinned over doorways and the people wore festive clothes in shades of orange with flowers and ribbons.

"I feel out of place in my Alesian suit," Katherine said.

"Only for a day. I'm sure they change again into normal clothes tomorrow." Chryséis made a beeline for the food tables on the square.

Everybody could help themselves to the food to their heart's delight on these tables that were covered in orange cloths.

The village women had laid out saffron bread disks, a symbol of the sun, on large platters. The sun disks had laughing faces made of nuts and seeds and in green bowls boiled eggs cut in half were piled high. They were eaten with a sauce, all green with chopped herbs.

"Eggs are… sacred food," the girl explained. "Egg yolk like orange ball of the sun and green sauce for the sun makes plants grow."

"Ah, that makes sense," Chryséis admitted.

"Here for you, take!" The girl took some bread from one of the tables, dipped the pieces into the green sauce and handed them to Chryséis and Katherine.

"Shukri. It looks delicious."

"This is not for children." The girl pointed to traditional tesgüin beer in tightly woven grasspots that was prepared from fermented sorghum. Wooden ladles were hanging from the rims of the covered pots.

"Woven pots?" Katherine was astonished.

"Haven't you seen this before? The moist fibers swell and make them watertight," Chryséis lectured her.

"Actually no, I haven't." Katherine touched the outer bottom of the pot, but nothing was flowing out. "Hm, look at that."

They chewed on their bread and walked around the village square. Bread ovens, shaped like huge white pears, were arranged in a half-circle in the middle of the square. The ovens had been fired with wood since dawn.

Women balanced flat baskets with rounds of yellow dough on their heads. Older village folk sat on benches, watching the goings-on for entertainment. The girl, who was showing Katherine and Chryséis around, greeted them respectfully and answered curious questions about the strangers.

"Everyone looks forward to…the feast. To pir-oggies and small oggies filled with savory…ragout," one of the women said and pointed proudly to a tray of pastries that looked much like pies.

"Yummy," Chryséis said politely. 'I can't wait to try them."

Seeing all the cheerful orange decorations, Katherine had an idea. She rummaged in her backpack and soon found what she had been looking for. "Here catch!"

Chryséis caught the orange Frisbee with ease. The villagers stood open-mouthed. Who'd ever seen a sun disk game? Who had ever heard of anybody throwing a sun disk around? But it seemed appropriate for today's festivities.

The village folk began to laugh, shaking their heads and soon, children joined the strange young visitors in their game, after inspecting the orange disk. Standing in a circle on the central village square, throwing and catching the flying sun disk, they carried on until the sun readied itself to set behind the hills, spelling an end to the exciting game.

"We'd better get back to the 'House of Life'." Katherine put the Frisbee back into her daypack.

"Yes, I'm sure Gwendola won't be happy if we are out that long."

"Where is our guide?" Katherine asked suddenly.

"I don't see the girl anymore, so I guess we must just find our own way back," Chryséis moaned. "Don't tell me we are lost".

"I think we came from over there." Katherine pointed to a road behind the bread ovens. "The village can't be that big. We'll just ask someone." They started walking.

Nobody on the square noticed how a band of Edfunians manhandled a local Gabari in a dark, narrow street nearby. The music was too loud.

"Where are Prince Artû and his band?" yelled one of the giants.

"I don't know who they are."

Another punch sent the Gabari tumbling to the ground.

"Stop!" a gravelly voice commanded. "We will retreat now, before the village folk see us. You better be quiet, if you know what's good for you!"

They let the trembling man lying where he was. Not all Gabari were supportive of the 'Cause', but killing him would have quickly alarmed the entire area.

"We were too hasty. The prince is a cunning man," the Highpriest of Shuruk grunted. "They will have gone to Anaá. Too late now." With that, they melted back into the darkness.

Katherine and Chryséis found the 'House of Life' after asking a friendly Gabari woman for directions at the end of a road that was illumined by torchlights.

Chryséis had been right. Gwendola wasn't happy at their late arrival. Amadis and Artû had come back to Catrev by vimaan as promised.

"It is not safe to walk around after dark," she scolded. "We are ready to depart for Anaá."

"Sorry." Katherine and Chryséis held their earlobes in

the gesture of apology they had learned. "But what about the celebrations?" Chryséis asked.

"There'll be plenty of that at Anaá," Lubbo laughed.

Trevor was ready with their daypacks. "Where have you been? I thought Gwendola was going to have a fit."

"Tell you later," Chryséis said and climbed after Katherine into the vimaan. It was big with a bench of upholstered seats all along the windows.

As they flew out of Catrev, village youths began to stuff straw between the spokes of large wooden wheels, symbolising the sunwheel.

The straw was set alight at small fires that were glowing atop two hills outside the village. All over Prydhain, burning wheels were rolled down slopes tonight to much laughter and singing.

Gwendola noticed the children's amazement at the goings-on. "It's called 'Dipta'. The Blazing. In commemoration of the time when the sky fell and the sun disappeared. 'Dipta' is the final triumph over the 'Dark Age' when sun and warmth returned," she explained. "The village elders make sure that burning wheels are quickly put out and at dawn the wheels are thrown onto bonfires."

When the vimaan set down at the hillside that enclosed the town of Anaá, no official welcome committee waited for them. Instead, there was merry confusion inside the hill.

Fuelled by sorghum beer, everyone burst out in song, while dancing with rehearsed steps to cheerful music. They pushed through the tipsy dancers and followed Amadis deeper into the hill. The D'Ånu were tall and good-looking, just like Amadis and moved around with graceful ease.

"We will stay at my family home," he yelled over the noise. "Follow me this way."

The time travellers looked around. The entire hillside seemed to be hollowed out and the yellowish walls of the big hall were covered in moss up to a man's height. One side of the hall was cut into a terraced amphitheater and long narrow windows at the top let in light by day. During the night, lanterns illuminated the passages and halls and the windows were covered with heavy drapes.

"Wow, that's an awesome place." Trevor whistled and Tepi pricked her ears and sniffed the air.

Three goats were roasting on spits at the bottom of the amphitheater. Before soon they'd meet with the same fate as all the oggies and sircroûte sour cabbage and disappear into hungry bellies.

Two passages along the side of a narrow waterway led away from the hall. The water tumbled down shallow steps under wooden bridges. Chambers were built into the rock on either side of the brook.

"Everybody is out and about celebrating, but make yourselves at home," Amadis said and showed them into two rooms with a proper bathroom. " Lubbo you might want to rest awhile."

"What and miss all the fun? Not in another Dark Age I won't."

After they dressed into fresh clothes, the travellers joined the festivities. Many stood outside on hidden terraces watching the Dipta wheels glowing like giant fireflies.

"Look at that one!" Trevor took a big bite out of a stew-filled oggie and pointed to a fast-rolling fire wheel bumping down a hill in the distance.

"Do you think that's Catrev over there?" Katherine asked.

"Could be." Chryséis ate roasted goat meat from a bowl made of leaves.

"Awesome." Trevor finished his oggie and eyed a plate with roasted goat's meat.

They went inside and sat down on a bench by the little stream. Tepi lay under the bench, busy with a large bone, while Prince Artû and the others were amusing themselves elsewhere in Anaá. It was safe enough to leave the children to their own devices.

"Tepi! Stop shedding your hair on me please."

Katherine pulled golden fluff off her pants. The dog's fur had started to fall out by the handfuls in the summer heat.

Tepi heard her name and wagged her tail. She looked at Katherine with big innocent eyes. Time for play? But her friend didn't show any sign of a playful mood and just kept eating her food. Tepi flopped on the ground with a grunt and attacked her bone again.

The children were too excited to think about sleep. Two magicians showed off tricks that could have fooled any modern audience. At the end of the performance, two colourful silk cloths danced in the air to the top of the dome. The cloths twisted around each other before jumping back down to roaring applause. Then the dancing started again.

Tepi barked when a dancer pulled the girls off their seats and made them do dance steps with the crowd.

"That's fun!" Katherine cried and concentrated on the dancing feet.

"Watch out!" Trevor warned them, but it was too late.

A pair of Konks with drink-soured breath bumped into them and sent a whole row of dancer to the ground. Everybody laughed and got back on their feet. The Konks were led away by two D'Ånu men to sleep off their hangover in a quiet corner.

Then, Midsummer was over with the first light of morning. The children slept in soft beds and woke up only when Gwendola came into the room.

"Come, athenai, or you'll miss breakfast."

"Oh, is it time to get up already?" Chryséis yawned.

"I don't want to. I'm too tired," Katherine objected. Tepi happily licked her face.

"You're also coming," Chryséis insisted.

"Okay, enough." Katherine pushed Tepi aside and lugged herself out of bed.

They followed Gwendola to the amphitheater where breakfast bowls were handed out. The Dwendi woman showed them proper D'Ånu table manners. She expertly picked the solid pieces from the stew with chopsticks, then the soup was slurped noisily and bread dipped into the remaining liquid.

"What is this stew, Gwendola?" Trevor asked.

"Good, isn't it, friend Trevór? It is made with frog legs," she answered.

Frogs! The children stared at their bowls, then at each other. "Is frog stew a D'Ånu specialty?" Trevor's face crumpled.

But before Gwendola could answer, Katherine started retching and Chryséis had to thump her hard between the shoulders until she got herself under control.

"Know what? We'll survive. It's not so bad. Aren't frogs a specialty in Italy?" Trevor frowned at a piece of light-coloured meat.

"I think it's in France." Chryséis stopped hitting Katherine's back. "And don't Chinese people eat frogs and rotten eggs and stuff like that?"

Katherine's eyes grew big again and she took a deep breath.

Gwendola was staring at her. "Are you well, friend Kathín?"

"Yes, shukri, I'm well." Katherine felt embarrassed. "Will you stop talking about that already?" she hissed at her friends.

Worried that she had offended their hosts, she carried on eating bravely. We are scientists after all, she thought, and scientists aren't squeamish, right?! It's just a source of protein. What difference does a little frog stew make?

"Here." She fed Tepi a few morsels.

"And people in deserts often eat fat flying termites… and crickets," Trevor added.

"Thanks guys. Is that supposed to make me feel better?" Katherine glared at her friends, but her cheeks were rosy again.

"Just rub it in, as if you've been eating frogs and termites and rotten eggs all your lives," Trevor said and winked at her.

A woman next to Gwendola still seemed concerned.

"Here, young friend. Have some of mine. That's better breakfast food." She enjoyed a bowl of crunchy fried cockroaches and offered some to Katherine as if they were cereal. Katherine declined politely and took care not to look at the fried insects too closely as they crunched between the woman's teeth.

"I'm actually not that hungry. Shukri, athenai," she refused.

They heard growling thunder in the distance and a strange stomping rhythm. "Another storm?" The D'Ånu woman wondered.

But then they realised that the earth had begun shaking below their feet.

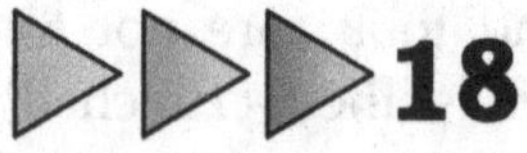 **18**   THE EARTH QUAKE

The morning activities in Anáa came to an abrupt halt, but the shudders were too regular for an earthquake, so something else had to be responsible for the shaking ground.

"It's an army of Gabari!" The harried call spread like wildfire around the town inside the hill.

Powerful Gabari troops stomping toward them were enough to make the ground tremble. What's more, Prydhanian Gabari held the belief that the sound of war drums would fire up their warriors before battle. It was no more than a near-forgotten memory and the stomping feet of a Gabari army hadn't been felt in Prydhain for a long time.

Fearful voices sounded through the hill.

"Why, what do the giants want of us?'

"The Gabari are turning on the D'Ånu?"

"They are breaking the peace!"

"They will not succeed!"

The D'Ånu knew that they were fairly safe inside the hills, it was, however, best to establish what was happening outside. Those in possession of arms moved quickly to the disguised terraces and the time travellers were carried along by the crowd.

The terraces on the hills were soon filled with D'Ånu warriors, holding hockey sticks outward and arrows cocked against large bows. What they saw were rows upon rows of tattooed giants in red battle gear marching down from the northern plains.

"They go to war over that stupid stone?" Chryséis

couldn't believe it.

"Looks like it. The Edfunians must have egged them on, somehow," Katherine said.

Stealth and sly planning had failed to bring the Speaking Stone of Caradoc into their possession. Now the sorcerers were taking the stone by force. The troops came to a halt, close to the inhabited hills. There was still movement in the valley to the south.

"What are they doing?" Trevor asked and was immediately drowned out by D'Ånu-voices.

"What is this? There are more Gabari coming from the other side."

"These are loyal to the D'Ånu!"

This time, giants in green garb, devoted to the cause of civilisation, marched from the east and south to meet their wild brethren in battle. Gabari were set against stomping Gabari.

The leaders up front had frightful tattoos all over their faces and held their weapons high above their heads. Strange, ancient weapons made from hardened wood set with sharpened flint stone triangles like teeth.

The heavy booming of drums and stomping of feet was taking on a frenzied rhythm now. Katherine lost her nerve at the sight.

"They look so scary. What if they break into the hill? We better get out of here," she wailed.

Trevor agreed with them. "Maybe we should get out around the back. Where is Tepi?"

"I don't know, I don't know..." Katherine cried, clasping her face. "I can't think with all that noise!"

"Katherine MacDougal, pull yourself together!" Chryséis scolded her.

"We are all going to die, I don't want to die!"

"You are not going to die! Let's quickly switch on the VICs."

"We can't do that. Not just yet," Trevor shouted.

"I'm putting myself in an armour of light. I'm putting myself in an armour of light..." Katherine kept repeating under her breath, as Zeruana had taught her..

"Where is Amadis?" Chryséis looked around.

"He's over there on the other terrace with Prince Artû and…"

The stomping and drumming stopped abruptly, and after a few seconds, the clanging of massive war harps tore through the sudden quiet.

Bloodcurdling war cries rose from the plain as great bodies clashed and threw each other off balance. Katherine sat down, leaning against the grassy balustrade, covering her face with her hands.

"I can't watch it," she cried. "I want it to stop!"

The noise rose and ebbed as the giants battled on.

"Come up here and watch this." Trevor was fascinated. "They are swinging their swords at each other. They are massive."

"No, I can't watch!"

"You'll never be good at computer games."

"I don't care about computer games and I don't want to see it!"

The gigantic combat was well underway, when the ground of the battlefield began to heave and cracks appeared on the paddocks. The earth shuddered and groaned before the quake travelled to the hills.

The battle cries stopped, but it took the opponents a few moments to understand what was happening. In living history the earth had never shaken during a battle. Never. The gods were angry!

"An ill omen!"

"Xipe Xolotle is displeased!"

"The Earthmother help us!"

"Retreat!"

The fearsome warriors in red and green untangled and staggered in opposite directions, dragging injured comrades with them. Another lighter tremor shook the ground. The walls of the cave town seemed to move.

"What's happening?" Katherine stood up. "What is that?"

She peered into the valley. There, weapons were lying

around and rocks. Inside the hill, people scrambled to hurry outside.

"I don't know. I think an earthquake... a real one." Trevor felt dazed. "Wow." Another aftershock trembled through Anáa.

"I hate this place!" Katherine began to cry again.

"Don't get all hysterical on me," Chryséis said impatiently and then on an urgent note. "We have to get out of here. What if the hill caves in?"

"The earthquake came so damn sudden."

"Earthquakes are always sudden. Come on, get up." Chryséis pulled Katherine to her feet.

"We can't leave the TPFs here!" Trevor declared.

That was true, so Trevor, Chryséis and Katherine scampered along the path by the little river back to the chamber to get their things. Then they somehow found their way to the back entrance next to the amphitheatre in a confusion of aftershocks.

Outside, panic-stricken animals were breaking through fences of their enclosures and needed to be rounded up. Children cried. The D'Ånu were beginning to clear rocks away, despite the panic. The three friends followed a frantic crowd through the back entrance where they ran into the arms of Prince Artû. Amadis and the two Dwendis stood glowering next to a vimaan.

"Look they are waiting for us!" Katherine shouted.

"But I saw Gwendola inside just now." The time travellers' relief turned to suspicion. Something was fishy about this.

"Climb into the vimaan!" the prince commanded.

He seemed to be in a rush.

"Why? Why now?" Chryséis asked him, taken aback.

"Because of the earthquake and…because the Speaking Stone has spoken… and said that it doesn't need you anymore. We'll take you to the ship that will set sail for Aztlan tomorrow. It's for your own good," Prince Artû insisted.

There was something strange about his voice, though. It quivered. Artû could be grumpy at times, but he was always confident. Something didn't quite add up.

"Where is this ship?" Trevor asked in a suspicious tone.

"You're asking too many questions, boy." Amadis was getting tetchy.

"No, it's alright," Gwendola answered. "In Sogamosa. The ship is in Sogamosa."

"In Sogamosa? Why? Where is the Stone, then?"

"We have it.," Amadis answered.

"Wait a minute. The Stone is supposed to be with the Lady of Anaá. Why doesn't she tell us about this herself and why the hurry?" Trevor grew more suspicious by the second.

"Get into the vimaan now!" Amadis sounded unusually grouchy and moved toward Trevor. Trevor moved aside.

"There's something wrong. What's going on? Who are you guys?" Chryséis backed away from the group and the vimaan.

"We are exactly who we think you are. Now get into the vimaan!"

People were still scrambling all over the place, trying to round up animals, carrying rocks and a few injured people.

A kid goat stood next to the vimaan, bleating. It was picked up by a young man and carried away.

"Where is Tepi?" Katherine asked.

"What?" Prince Artû gave her an impatient look.

"Tepi, my dog." Katherine looked around anxiously. "Maybe she's hurt."

"Forget about your dog. You have to come with us now. The Stone…said so."

"I want to hear it from the Lady herself – or from the stone," Trevor demanded and stood with his arms akimbo.

"You are children and you will do as you are told!" Amadis shouted.

"No, we will not!" Katherine's face was flushed with anger.

"You dare gainsay your elders?"

"I do dare… you… you… oh, there's something wrong

with you!"

"Run back inside!" Trevor suddenly yelled. "They're phony."

"You come here!" Lubbo grabbed Katherine roughly and carried her kicking and screaming to the vimaan.

"Let go of me, let go!"

"Leave her alone!" Trevor switched his VIC on and disappeared in an instant. Then Chryséis did the same. Trevor kicked the phony Amadis on the shin and stormed past him to the vimaan, while the D'Ånu warrior held his leg in astonishment.

"Give me your hand." Trevor pulled Katherine out of the vimaan and she disappeared as soon as he pressed the button on her aliceband. Lubbo let go. "Chris, where are you?" No answer. "Run inside and hide."

Prince Artû snatched in the direction of Trevor's voice, but the two children were already behind him, darting back through the opening and into the hill.

"Who…was that?" Katherine was invisibly catching her breath as they sat down in the amphitheater.

"I wish I knew. But they're phonies for sure."

"How? They looked so real."

Chryséis appeared and sat down next to them. "Oh come on. They're sorcerers!"

"Wouldn't be surprised," Trevor said and turned himself visible again. Then Katherine also appeared, but nobody gave them the slightest attention.

A young D'Ånu woman tried to soothe her sobbing children on the step below. A little girl turned around and stared at the foreigners with round, teary eyes. The mother gave the girl something to eat and she calmed down. Katherine was still confused. "How did they manage to look like that?"

"Duh!"

"Athenai, where have you been?" A familiar voice called out.

The three friends spun around. Amadis and Lubbo

were standing there with concerned faces.

"How did you find us so quickly? Stay away!" The children jumped to their feet and sprinted up the steps and down the passage toward the sleeping quarters.

Amadis and Lubbo stared at each other. "What is the matter with them?"

"Shock maybe. They are children after all," Lubbo said in surprise.

Gwendola was in the room they had shared. And Tepi. The dog jumped up Katherine's legs and whined with delight.

"Oh, you found Tepi!" Katherine sat down and hugged her.

"Athenai, she found me and has been following me around."

"Then you are the real Gwendola?"

"Whatever do you mean?" The Dwendi woman asked.

Trevor, Katherine and Chryséis looked at each other. "I think she's okay," Chryséis decided.

So they told Gwendola the story of seeing Prince Artû and the others outside or who they thought Prince Artû was. How he told them to come with them, of Lubbo bundling Katherine into the vimaan and how they had run away. They left out the part where they had turned invisible.

Gwendola listened with a serious face, shaking her head now and again. "We must report this to the Lady of Anaá. At once." She resolutely put down a garment she had been folding.

"It's okay, you go, I'll take Tepi and look for the others," Trevor offered.

"How can you be sure they are the real men?"

"I can't, but Tepi will know." The yellow dog barked once as if she had understood.

"Fair enough. Well, see you later alligator."

"In a while crocodile." Trevor grinned and smoothed his tousled hair.

"Tepi, stay!" Katherine ordered her dog to stay behind with Trevor. Tepi already understood a few commands she had taught her. The young dog slumped down next to

Trevor and looked suitably snubbed.

The girls went with Gwendola to find the citadel. The only way get there was through a sequence of passageways to the top of the middle hill. Caer Anaá, as the citadel was called, was cleverly disguised by the high sides of the bowl-shaped hill, complete with hanging gardens and a central amphitheater. Above the broad archway entrance into Caer Anaá was the likeness of a carved wooden swan bending its head backwards to a smaller swan.

Interesting, Katherine thought as they climbed a last flight of stairs, walked through the archway and stood in a flower garden.

Meanwhile, Trevor walked with Tepi back to the amphitheater. If the real Amadis, Lubbo or Prince Artû were looking for them, they would find them here. Somebody handed him a mug with tea and Tepi decided to take a nap. For a passing moment, Trevor felt a stab of homesickness.

However fascinating their adventure into prehistory had been so far, it would be great to go home – even just for a while.

Katherine had left the Discman in his moonbag. Trevor listened to music, humming a little to the catchy tunes of Katherine's favourite band Bliss 5. He sighed and closed his eyes. Just for a moment.

"Shelanti, friend visitor!" a guttural male voice cut through his dream.

Trevor sat bolt upright. Had he been asleep? A middle-aged man dressed in a cream-coloured chamois shirt smiled winningly and took a bard's harp off his back. He sat down and put the instrument in his lap.

"Shelanti athenai, I am Trevor of Chicago," Trevor said.

"I am told that you come from Atala, young friend Trevór." The man spoke with a slight accent, because the language of his northern home was Danvries.

Trevor should have never allowed himself to doze off. "Who are you?"

"My apologies, may I introduce myself? Venûtiu of Amelút, currently bard and storyteller to the honourable Lady of Anaá." He saw Trevor's confusion. "Ah, you don't know Prydhain yet? Amelút is our northern-most seaport on Lake Maalbec, gateway to the northern oceans."

Trevor could have sworn that Venûtiu resembled Dr. Broadbent, the principal of Pemberton Academy. Just a younger version of him.

"I see you have been left behind by the lovely maidens."

"Ah yes, they are actually my friends from school..." Trevor could have kicked himself. "It's hard to explain."

The bard didn't miss a beat. "Do you mind if I keep you company for a while?" He didn't seem to be a sorcerer or a spy, so Trevor nodded. Soon the two of them were chatting about this and that. Trevor let the surprised Venûtiu listen to the CD through earplugs. Although mirages were a common thing, the bard had never heard music from a box through buttons before.

"Small buttons are making that music?" He asked.

"It's normal to do that – at home." Trevor shrugged . It was too complicated to explain this to the man.

"Indeed. Would you like to listen to music we make at home in Amelút?" Venûtiu strummed the harp and people were forming a half-circle around him to listen.

"Tell us a story, bard!" one of the boys demanded, when the soothing melody ended. Everyone chimed in. "Oh yes, a story, tell us a story."

"Well, well, let me see what I can do." He thought for a moment. "Do you know the river Brigadhu, meandering like a silvery snake between the hills?" Venûtiu asked his listeners.

Of course everybody but Trevor knew the beginning of this story. Tepi pricked her ears and let out a brief whimper. Was Katherine coming back anytime soon? But when nothing happened, she closed her eyes again with a grunt. The bard continued with his story.

"Beyond the hills, at the mountain source of the river

Brigadhu, a lake monster dwelled. In the olden days, before the 'Dark Age' had cast its shadow on the land of Ereint.

Beautiful homes covered much of the land not used for grazing or planting. A temple, dedicated to 'Na Tri Dee', or 'the three gods', overlooked the green valleys of Ereint. This temple was on a man-made hill housing the shrine.

One spring time, the lake monster threatened on a whim to send an avalanche of water that would carry away the holy shrine and much of the village below. The price the monster demanded to spare the villagers was cruel. Two unblemished youths were to be sacrificed every spring to guarantee relief from the flood. An unthinkable feat. "

The crowd murmured.

"The good village folk refused. But after the temple and village had been rebuilt too many times, the villagers finally relented. Instead of consulting with the deities, it was decided to give in to the monster's demand. The sorrow was great when the youths were led to the hill. A hundred voices joined in a plaintive chorus:

'Where is the house of crystal
Where is the house of precious shells?
In Atland, our Atland...'

For the people of Ereint believed that the youngsters, the treasure of the village, would be carried to Atland, the old land. That to Atland in the west, all the departed souls went for their final rest."

"Ooh." The audience was spellbound.

"This went on for some time," Venûtiu continued his tale."Until a noble young Gabari by the name of Fantû, happened to pass the village on his way north. He encountered the sad procession to the top of the mountain. After learning the meaning of it, he persuaded the villagers to return.

'I shall slay the monster and free your village from the yoke of cruel sacrifice.' Thus Fantû told them. And indeed, he took two men from the village as guides with him to the mountain lake and slew the monster with his great obsidian-toothed sword..."

Venûtiu finished the tale and his audience applauded. He had managed to distract them sufficiently. A slight aftershock rattled the walls around them, but nobody seemed too concerned about it now.

Trevor looked up and saw Artû and Amadis walking toward him. The Avallûnian prince pushed through the crowd and sat down next to him. But was this the real Artû?

"Here you are, athenai. We have been looking for you children," Prince Artû grumbled. "Where are the girls?"

"They went to see the Lady of Anaá." Trevor didn't say too much - just in case he was talking to the impostors.

"Why?"

"Gwendola didn't tell you?" Trevor was referring to telepathic thought transfer, but drew a blank with the prince.

"No, we haven't seen her," Artû said just as Amadis joined them.

"Another story, another story!" the crowd clamoured around them. "The legend of the sunken city of Ker-is."

In these stories, there is a lot of water for sure, Trevor thought, while he still tried to figure out if these two men were really his companions. He was still on his guard.

"Shukri, good people, shukri," Venûtiu held up his hands. "Another time. I have business to attend to."

The audience was disappointed, but dispersed quickly without complaining. The bard picked up his harp and introduced himself to Amadis and Artû.

"We have an artful bard in our midst. My name is Prince Artû of Avallûn and this is Amadis of Anaá. We will be on our way to the Lady's hill."

"Ah, good friends. May I join you? No offense, but the good Lady has sent me to keep an eye on this young man here. I will return to the citadel now that you have arrived."

A nanny? Trevor didn't like that thought very much.

Amadis and Artû looked guilty. It had been their duty

to look after the young foreigners.

"The earthquake…" Amadis said apologetically.

"Yes, the earthquake and other things. Shall we go?"

And so they went to the citadel together with the bard. On the way, Venûtiu told a shocked Artû and Amadis what had happened to the children earlier. So somebody must have told him.

They had just walked through the entrance with the wooden swan, when they already saw the Lady of Anaá. She looked graceful in her flowing silk gown, dark hair streaming down her shoulders. Her only jewellry was a golden circlet with a great aquamarine on her forehead. Was she an elf queen? But when she began to speak, there was nothing elfin about her.

"Shelanti, athenai and my thanks to you friend Venûtiu. I see you have brought with you just the men I wanted to see," she greeted Trevor, Artû and Amadis with a nod and bent down to pat Tepi. "The battle noise in the valley must have been frightening to you, my girl. And then the earthquake," she spoke kindly to the dog. A Lady without airs and graces.

"Shelanti, honourable Lady. May we join you there?"

He meant a round garden pavilion where the Lady was now headed.

"But certainly Prince Artû. It is high time that we met," she said. "Here, wer are not standing in the sun."

"Ahem, yes." Artû still felt guilty for leaving the children to their own devices. "My apologies if we neglected our duties during the earthquake. We are prepared to protect the children from charlatans."

"I'm just glad it's really you and Amadis and not some impostors."

They chatted for a while, until the Lady said, "let's eat now and be merry." She seemed to have forgiven them. The Lady of Anaá turned around and walked out into the open garden, followed by maidens carrying platters with food.

Gwendola and the girls were already seated on red cushions by a gurgling water feature. On a low table in front of them stood crystal glasses with pomegranate juice. The platters were deposited on tables and the lady waved the maidens away. A frame with linen cloth above the table protected them from the hot sun.

Tepi flopped herself on the lawn behind Katherine with a grunt and Amadis occupied the seat next to the Lady. She knew him well, as Amadis was her brother's eldest son. The meal began. There was hazelnut loaf with berry sauce and grilled grouse and dishes the children didn't recognize. Everything was delicious.

"I hope it's not full of insects or frogs," Katherine said.

"Nope, doesn't look like it. I think you are eating a fried mushroom." Trevor grinned and put a mushroom into his mouth.

"I'm glad. It tastes so delicious," Katherine sighed.

"So, I hear that evil Edfunians came close to Anaá yesterday and tried to abduct our precious children here." The Lady began with just a hint of reproach. "In the village of Catrev?"

"I… we didn't know that," Prince Artû stammered. "Those sorcerers…"

"I understand. Valiant warriors like you had their hands full celebrating." Amadis and Artû didn't quite know what to say. "Venûtiu, my priceless bard here was friendly enough to offer much needed guard to our young friend, while he waited for you to find him today."

She looked kindly at Trevor and Venûtiu bowed slightly. The Lady's voice lacked sarcasm, but the remark was clearly meant as reproof. "There was dire need for protection, considering that the evil Edfunians were impersonating you today."

"We will do better from now on, Lady aunt, we promise," Amadis apologised an she gave him a smile.

"That you should do. The Highpriest of Shuruk is a powerful sorcerer and changing shapes is child's play for him and his conspirators. We must be more vigilant at such a time as this. I was glad to learn that the sorcerers fled from Anaá as soon as their plan had failed."

Soon, they chatted about this and that. and Lubbo carried on as usual about how much he disliked giants. "Only the Earthmother herself could have stopped the skirmish in the plain with an earthquake...those Gabari cowards! Ran like a herd of goats. Haha."

"We have taken measures to better protect the hills of Anaá and our land, but the Speaking Stone told me that it is time for you to go on to Caradoc."

"At last!" Lubbo said. "Oh, I didn't mean...thank you for your hospitality, Lady, it's just that..." He stopped talking.

"No offense taken, my blunt friend. The mission must be brought to a favourable end." The Lady smiled graciously.

Afterwards, the bard Venûtiu performed on his harp. Of course, the time travellers didn't understand a word he sang in the ancient Sha-kari bard language, but it didn't matter - the beauty of the music created a magical atmosphere all of its own. Chryséis secretly snapped a picture of him, because he reminded her a little of Dr. Broadbent.

When the sun dipped below the hills, two maidens accompanied them back to the great hall, where a group of Dwendi and D'Ånu women were working on a large wallhanging of interlocking autumn leaves on the terraced seats of the amphitheater.

Guided by nimble fingers, bone needles flew in and out of the fabric, while the women sang.

"So it's finally over." Katherine sat down and watchen the women in fascination.

"If you say so," Trevor said.

"Why, didn't you hear what the Lady told us about what the Stone said?"

"I heard that. I just wonder what they have up their sleeve next. I mean if the sorcerers can shape-shift and all that. I'm not keen running into them ever again."

"Surely they won't try again. They've been caught out," Katherine said.

"Do you really think they stopped the battle because of the earthquake?"

"Isn't that what everyone says?" Chryséis answered with a question.

"Weird. Why didn't they just storm these hills? Gabari are so big and powerful." Trevor shrugged.

"Who knows? I'm tired. We're delivering the stone tomorrow and then we'll go back to America. I can't wait."

"Alesia, actually," Katherine corrected her friend.

"Whatever." Chryséis got up and Tepi ran ahead to their sleeping quarters. That night everyone in the hill slept uneasily, half-expecting another earthquake to shake them out of bed.

Trevor had a strange dream of Amadis changing into a laughing bat. Trevor was afraid of the bat.Then he held a slingshot in his hand, bent down to pick up a stone and downed the bat on the tree branch. Trevor tossed and turned. He was suddenly back in Carter Valley and flew all the way to Pemberton - only to land on the bench in the rosegarden.

At the citadel of Caer Anaá, the Lady consulted a glowing egg until the wee hours of the morning. There were a great many things to discuss.

The earth, however, slept tightly that night — and for some time to come.

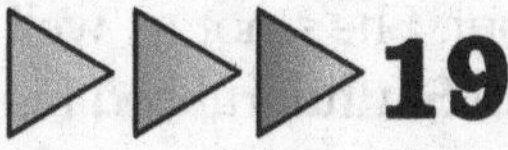 **19** **LURKING EVIL**

The mood in the mountain cave was tense. The sorcerers were angry. Two Firbolg lay in a heap against the opposite wall. "Xipe Xolotle has forsaken us, brother."

"Nonsense," the sorcerer addressed as 'brother' barked. "They have more luck than wits. That's what it is. If it wasn't for the earthquake we would have brought the stone into our possession by now. No doubt it is helping the meddlesome Lady of the D'Ånu. By Xipe Xolotle's bones!" He kept folding and unfolding his hands.

"The stone seems unwilling to come into our possession," the Magi of Maligasima said impatiently and stared at the water in the silver bowl. "But why are they not using their powers to destroy us?"

"What a thing to say, brother. Don't give them any ideas, they might hear you."

The water's reflection showed maidens dressed in white keeping a watch over the 'Speaking Stone of Caradoc' in the garden of Caer Anaá. The whole Anaá region was now under a protective shield. Apparently, the D'Ånu weren't taking any chances.

"The 'Speaking Stone' will give advice to whoever is his keeper!" the Highpriest of Shuruk croaked.

"It's their pigheaded ideas. Doing only good for all," the Highpriest of Hisbernia sneered. "There are the foreign children again." The other sorcerers moved closer around the water bowl. "Mark my words, the children are the key to our misfortune. Something about them…"

"They are not like other children. They must have

something with them… powers stronger than our spells. We must find out their secret."

"What secret?"

"We could torture the Lady to find out. She's not as well protected as she thinks." The Highpriest of Shuruk rubbed his hands together.

"No, we cannot take the risk. We must bide our time. Prydhain is not Atala, but the long arm of the civilised law reaches far. Even as far as Anaá. Brute force will achieve nothing now. We must be patient like a snake, striking at the right time." The Magi made a snapping gesture with his hands.

"You let them slip through your fingers. We could have known by now," the Highpriest of Shuruk croaked.

"The Speaking Stone will have to tell us, then. If we have both the Speaking Stone and the children's powers, we'll be unbeatable. All we have to do is wait for the D'Ånu to move the stone."

"Wait… I am tired of waiting. I am all for action." The Magi growled.

"We could send Firbolg on their heels."

"The Prydhanian Gabari are swaying the other way. Some say 'the cause' brings ill luck. We must act."

"A murrain on them. We have sacrificed too much. There won't be another chance. Not anytime soon. We must succeed this time with or without the Prydhanians!"

"The 'Speaking Stone' and the children will fall into our lap like ripe apples from Avallûn." The Highpriest of Hisbernia cackled. The other sorcerers joined in. Their ghastly laughter echoed back and forth between the cave walls. Even the pet saurian trembled in his corner.

"I have a proposal to make." The Magi of Maligasima tore his gaze from the reflection in the silver bowl. The other sorcerers fell quiet. "How would you like to practice your Avallûnian accent some more, brother?"

"By Xipe Xolotle. You're not saying…"

"Only better this time. They won't suspect a thing," The

Magi smacked his lips. "The Red One will get his sacrifice and we'll get the stone... and power."

He told them of his plan and the other sorcerers bellowed with delight.

"Not bad, brother. Not bad at all. It might just work."

"It has to - Ukur!" The Kemnite sorcerer threw back his hood. He yelled rudely at a waiting Firbolg and cuffed him behind the ear. "Serve dinner, we are starving."

Soon they were all guzzling mugsful of strong beer and tucked into the haunches of a giant deer still dripping with blood.

*

The following day, a formal message arrived in Anaá for the Honourable Prince Artû of Avallûn. Curiously, the Dwendi messenger waited outside the hill for an answer. He refused any refreshments and took care to stay out of the guards' way.

"I have been summoned by the Lady of Caer Sidi nearby," the prince told them. "She has an urgent message from my father, the sea king. Amadis will accompany me."

"Why don't we all come with you?" Chryséis asked.

"It will be safer here in Anaá. The talks may take some time. You will stay behind with the children," Prince Artû said to Lubbo and Gwendola. "Make sure you keep an eye on them at all times."

"Another delay! Will we ever get to Caradoc and complete our mission?"

"Friend Lubbo, I must heed a call by my father. It might influence our mission," the prince replied and Lubbo just nodded.

Before he left, Prince Artû handed the 'Speaking Stone' to Chryséis in the Lady's audience room. "I give you the stone for safekeeping until you all come to join us."

"But..." Chryséis began to protest.

"I know what I'm doing," he said in a low voice. "Don't tell anybody. I trust you."

When they were summoned a couple of hours later, the

children could hardly wait to get into the vimaan.

"Ah, nearly there now. Prince Artû is finished with his talks. Now it's off to Caradoc." Lubbo rubbed his hands together.

They left the village and hills of Anaá and floated over the foothills of the Gogmagog mountain s. The citadel of Caer Sidi lay in rough terrain compared with the rolling landscape they had just left. Caer Sidi meant the 'citadel on the man-made mountain'. and the time travellers should soon find out, why it had that name. The mountains were the last barrier before the fertile plain of Lyonesse.

"Are there supposed to be mountains here?" Trevor asked Katherine.

"No, not in the future they aren't." She frowned. "Only cliffs."

The vimaan approached the citadel from a mountain pass, then a suspended bridge spanned over a thrashing river. Drawbridges made the mountain citadel near invincible and roaring stone lions stood guard at the western gate, but there was no sign of human guards.

"Lions still roam the mountains. They can no longer be found in the lowlands of Lyonesse," Gwendola told them just before the vimaan was welcomed by one of the maidens. No welcoming committee or serenade greeted them here. The maiden was a short and unsmiling woman and seemed to look right through them. She bade them curtly to wait on the large east-facing terrace, where one had a view of the plains below.

"That can only mean that Prince Artû and Amadis are already on their way. But what a glum folk they are around here."

"What a view!" Katherine sighed as she stood at the stone balustrade..

"Yes, Lyonesse is a unique country. The lakes of Mor Maalbec and Mor Llyn Llion are the blue jewels in the crown of Lyonesse. Caradoc to is to the far right and the capital with its citadel of Caer Llion." Lubbo waved with his hand to the right. "And on the other side to the northeast are the lands of Twiskland and Danesbode."

Weeping willows on the shore hung their long branches into Mor Maalbec right in front of them.

There were sailing boats and ducks on the rippling water. Stands of araucaria trees covered much of the western lakeshore right up to the foot of the mountain. A canal connected Mor Maalbec with the larger Mor Llyn Llion. Trade ships and smaller boats were sailing this route in both directions.

"There are lots of good fish in the lakes and giant mushrooms grow along the shores. One of those mushrooms can feed an entire family for days," Gwendola said. "Speaking of which, where is Prince Artû. Isn't it near time for lunch?"

"Patience my sister, he is surely on his way," Lubbo said. The children couldn't think of food now. This magnificent land had cast a spell on them. "What is that over there? Are those roofs?" Trevor asked.

"Why, it's the city of Maalbec," Gwendola answered.

Katherine pointed to some wooden dwellings on stilts. "Is that a village in the shallows?"

"Why yes, the Mor-zaaten or lake dwellers have been living in these lakes for generations," Gwendola explained. "They believe that they have a special relationship with Ruhnu, the 'God of the Lake'."

"Well I never…" Katherine couldn't help staring in fascination at the dark-skinned women in their colourful saris down by the lake. They were quite distant, but easy to make out. "What are they doing?"

"The women are picking waterlily roots in the mud. They are boiled, dried and pounded into flour. The usual thing."

"Of course."

"Only a question of time until this whole plain down there, this Lyonesse will sink under the sea," Trevor said a little harshly. "And becomes the British Channel."

"Oh Trevor, it won't be until thousands of years into the future before all this sinks into the sea," Katherine said.

"Whatever gave you that idea young friend?" Gwendola

was flabbergasted. "The city of Ker-is was submerged a long time ago."

"Hmm yes, that's what I meant."

"The boats look just like butterflies," Katherine said dreamily.

"Where in Prydhain is your home Kathín?" Gwendola asked unexpectedly. Had the Dwendi-woman become suspicious?

"Oh, it's a place called Oxford." Katherine felt embarrassed that she had to lie, because Oxford didn't exist yet, of course.

"Oxfól?" Gwendola looked puzzled. She'd never heard of such a place. "Don't you want to see your family, child?"

"I would love to, but …that's not possible. They are no longer there."

"Oh you poor thing! You lost your family in an earthquake then?" Gwendola gave her a compassionate look

"Well, something like that."

"They are not there yet," Trevor mumbled and said aloud. "This is perfect for abseiling. I wish we could climb down." He leaned forward to admire the steep rock face.

"Yeah well, I don't." Chryséis could imagine a million things she'd rather do. The sheer drop from the mountainside looked intimidating.

"What's keeping Artû and Amadis?" It was Lubbo's turn to fidget.

"Can you see the coast of France?" Chryséis strained her eyes.

"Could be that dark line, oh I don't know," Trevor said.

Crowned cranes flew into the air with a rustle as a boat came too close. Tepi barked. She couldn't wait to get down there and chase birds.

"At last," Lubbo blurted when the two men came walking toward them.

Tepi wagged her tail and sniffed prince Artû's robe. Then she snarled and moved away from him. A feeling of foreboding crept into the pit of Katherine's stomach, but it didn't make sense. It had to be the real prince.

"Shelanti athenai," Prince Artû greeted them.

Tepi didn't seem to share his friendly sentiment. She stood protectively between the men and the other companions and growled.

"Ho, Ho, Ho. What's this doggy?" The prince laughed. "Don't you recognize us anymore?"

"Enough now Tepi," Katherine commanded her and the dog slunk back, tail between legs. "What is wrong with you?"

"That's better. Did he see a ghost?" Prince Artû was in an unusually good mood. Amadis waved for them to follow. "It is time to go, athenai!"

Prince Artû didn't ask for the stone back, so Chryséis just left it for now.

"But how are we getting down from here?" Trevor asked frowning. "Aren't we taking the vimaan?"

"No friend Trevór, we will take the stairs inside the mountain down to the shore of the lake. We will then take a boat and proceed to Caradoc," Amadis explained.

"Stairs – inside the mountain?"

"Yes, this is a tin mine and the Dwendi miners use the stairs all the time." From the terrace, a door led into the mountain and then down some steep stairs. Nobody came to see them off, which was unusual.

"Where is everybody?" Katherine wondered. "Where are the maidens?"

"Maybe the Lady doesn't want to hold us up," Chryséis tried to convince herself.

"Come on you two." Gwendola and Lubbo looked back in irritation. Amadis didn't seem as polite as usual with the two Dwendis. None of them noticed that the eyes of their companion weren't dark anymore.

"Were the news bad?" Lubbo asked grumpily, but Artû and Amadis weren't willing to discuss their meeting with the Lady of Caer Sidi at all.

Slowly the children got used to the dim light inside. A clever system of airshafts helped to circulate fresh air and narrow windows in the outer wall let in some daylight. Round and round they groped their way along the banister. Every now and again they reached a platform.

From those platforms doors led into various mineshafts.

"The Dwendis must be working really hard deep inside the mountain." Trevor frowned at the lack of activity.

"The tin is transported down and loaded onto boats bound for Maalbec," Lubbo explained curtly and pointed to a broad ditch below the bannister.

"Oh, that's clever, they just push it down," Katherine marvelled.

Halfway down, one of the doors was not completely shut. Was there a murmur behind the door? Amadis ushered them on. Katherine slipped and nearly fell, but Artû caught her in time. "There, there young friend. Be careful with those little legs."

"That was weird!" Trevor whispered into Katherine's ear.

They had become used to Artû's gruff manner during the journey and showing a sense of humour wasn't like him at all. Lubbo and Gwendola were particularly uneasy around the two men.

"Why is there nobody else around, Gwen? Where are all the miners?" Lubbo asked his sister. She shrugged her shoulders. "I wish the helpful fairy guides were still around." But the last of the fairies had said goodbye in Anaá. Chryséis checked her watch as they walked through a concealed doorway. It had taken about half an hour to the bottom of the mountain.

Trevor looked back and saw Amadis push a stone cube with a carved lion on it back into a groove. The stone door creaked shut on strong ball bearings and became one with the rockface again.

Trevor surveyed the area outside. A large stone arch towered to their right over a paved road lined with wych-elms. The road led straight into the city of Maalbec on the other side of the lake. The arch was tall enough for two Gabari - one standing on the other one's shoulders - to march comfortably through. Singing birds had made their nests in the chiseled relief running along the top lintel of the massive monument. Why were they taking a boat then, when there was a perfectly good road?

Left and right of the arch, big round cacti formed a natural barrier. This must be the long bright green line they had seen from the lofty height of the terrace. A dense emerald forest stretched to their left.

They walked the short distance to the lakeshore through a gap between the prickly cacti. The boat was moored against a twisted tree branch leaning over the muddy beach into the water.

"Quick now, climb into the boat. We can still make it to Caradoc today," Amadis said confidently.

Trevor took one look at the muddy beach and the wobbling boat. "I don't understand why we can't go by vimaan or take the road," he said obstinately.

Lubbo was just as reluctant to leave dry ground and lingered next to Trevor. The smile disappeared from Prince Artû's face, who was sitting down in the boat next to four Dwendis, who were just as unsmiling, short square oars ready in hand. "We'll go by boat and that's it!" he said.

As Amadis extended his hand to help Katherine through the mud, Tepi began to growl again. "Shush, Tepi… " Katherine began then she saw Amadis' reflection in the water and understood why Tepi was so hostile. His hair was turning a mousy blond and his features had changed. Then she saw Prince Artû's reflection.

She backed off, holding tightly onto her backpack.

Katherine held Gwendola back as she stepped toward the boat and pointed to the image. Instead of the Avallûnian prince, it showed the sorcerer Chryséis had seen in the awful prison caves of Shuruk. There was a spider tattoo on the forehead. Tepi growled louder.

"Don't look into his eyes, he hypnotizes people," Katherine said in a calm voice so that he couldn't hear. She could have said, 'Oh look at the beautiful lake' in the same tone.

"Athenai, make haste!" the Highpriest tried one last time.

Gwendola kicked at Amadis' hand with lightening speed. The tall man stepped back in surprise and slid into the mud.

"Run!" she yelled. Without giving it another thought, Chryséis turned around and began to run.

"What's going on? Why are we running away?" Trevor demanded to know as he was catching up with Chryséis.

"Shuruk - Trev - Shuruk!" she cried out of breath.

The Highpriest of Shuruk was fuming with anger. He jumped up and grabbed one of the oars, hitting the water. So close again! So close!

One of the cursed companions had to have the 'Speaking Stone'. They had not found it on the real Prince Artû and Amadis, whose lifeless bodies were up there in Caer Sidi. The altar on the small island in the lake had been prepared last night and now, there wouldn't be a sacrifice. Again.

Tepi barked and mounted a mock attack. The sorcerer stumbled on the hem of his cloak and fell back into the boat.

"This damn dog!" He pointed at Tepi and a lightning bolt shot at the dog. But the bolt missed its aim and sizzled a black mark into the ground.

"Tepi, come here!" Katherine called and the dog bounded after her.

The boat was drifting into the lake. The false Artû turned around slowly and saw that he was alone in the vessel. The Dwendis, who weren't Dwendis at all, but disguised Firbolg, were on their way to the bottom of the lake. The sorcerers had not reckoned with the noiseless merpeople in their watery element.

Another man appeared out of thin air next to the twisted tree branch where a bat had hung upside down. A black cloak hung loosely over powerful shoulders. He moved surprisingly fast toward tall araucaria trees for cover. While he ran, he changed fully back into the sorcerer of Dilmun.

As he was about to enter the forest, something invisible threw him to the ground. Lying on his back he saw the apparition of a woman in a golden silk robe, hems lined with two purple stripes. She floated in the air between the trees. A larger-than-life hologram of the Lady of Cydonia! Then another Lady appeared. And another. The Ladies of Anaá and Algiras.

"Aah, you weak, detestable women!" the sorcerer rasped.

The Ladies laughed lightly, which infuriated the sorcerer even more. He tried to throw an energy bolt at the wavering hologram of the Lady of Cydonia, but found himself bound by an invisible force field.

Virtually paralysed, the sorcerer of Dilmun saw from the corner of his eye that his two evil brethren, the Highpriest of Shuruk and the Hisbernian Highpriest in the mud, didn't fare much better.

The dark magician in the boat tried to turn himself into a bat and flee. But his spell remained incomplete. Head and arms had already hideously shrunk, his cloak turned to dark wings, while the rest of his body remained that of a giant. So he stood in the boat as if turned to stone. The Lady of Algiras waved and merpeople pulled the boat to the shore.

"You will be detained for your ill deeds," the Lady of Anaá's voice boomed. "Right here in the mountain. Stripped of your powers, stuck inside the cold rock."

"Aaah, deceit!" the Highpriest of Shuruk's angry helpless cry echoed.

The Lady of Algiras was unmoved. "Your brethren of the Left Path in the Fûna Mountains are next."

By now, the children and the two Dwendis had reached the doorway into the mountain. They were unaware of what was happening behind them when they heard the eerie screams ringing off the mountains.

"Hurry! Quick!" Katherine screeched in a panic, her face flushed all pink from running so fast. "They will get us!"

"Not, if we use the protection spell Zeruana taught us," Trevor panted. "I am putting myself into an armour of light." They said it together, even the Dwendis.

Trevor searched for the latch of the outer mechanism. In his hurry he couldn't find the stone with the carved lion and a stern Lubbo helped him.

"It's usually a different colour. Try this one." Lubbo pointed to a newer-looking stone. It was the one with the lion. Trevor pushed the stone into its groove. It gave way and the door opened.

"Get inside!" Trevor yelled and pushed everyone roughly through the opening.

"Ouch, be careful friend Trevór!" Gwendola snarled at him.

"My apologies, athenai." Trevor withdrew his arm just in time as the doorway slammed shut. They stood safely inside the dark mountain at the bottom of the stairs.

"Let's sit down for a moment, until we can see something." They groped for the stairs and sat down on the stone steps.

"I can't believe we fell for it again," Chryséis said angrily. "I just can't believe it." She was still clutching her backpack with the Speaking Stone.

"Who was that giant in the boat?" Lubbo demanded to know. "Where did he come from? And where are Prince Artû and Amadis?"

"Oh brother, you are so slow sometimes," Gwendola said. Katherine explained what it was they had seen mirrored in the water.

"The 'Evil Ones' you say, friend Kathín, are you sure?" Lubbo snorted scornfully. "Giants are nothing but trouble. Nothing but trouble, I say."

"To be sure. We saw the sorcerer in the boat before," Chryséis said. "In the dungeons of Shuruk. He had imprisoned our Gabari friend Túvar."

Lubbo grumbled. "A Gabari friend, giants are all the same…"

Trevor ignored him. "What happened to the 'Speaking Stone'? The false prince must have stolen it."

"Oh Earthmother. Whatever shall we do?" Lubbo threw his arms up in the air.

"No, Lubbo. The false prince doesn't have the stone. I have it," Chryséis piped up. She told them how the real prince had given her the têrakhon sphere with the stone and asked her to take care of it.

"Why did Prince Artû give the 'Speaking Stone' to a child for safekeeping?" Lubbo sulked. "In all fairness I am the most senior of the five of us."

"But brother, the Lady of Anaá must have consulted the 'Speaking Stone'," Gwendola said in a soothing tone. "Prince Artû surely just followed its advice."

"Perhaps we should speak to the stone ourselves. If there was ever a time…" Chryséis took out the sphere. In the near-dark, the moonstone gleamed softly.

"The false Amadis and Artû didn't know where the stone was, no doubt. That's why they didn't kill us straight away," Trevor said, wiping his forehead.

"If the prince and Amadis are still alive. They might need our help," Gwendola said.

"You think they may have killed them?" Lubbo's heart sank.

"Let's ask the stone, then. It should know the answer." Chryséis held the sphere up. "Hello stone, can you hear me?" Nothing happened.

Tepi barked and sat down, wagging her tail with her tongue hanging out. There was a noise and they stared at the stairs above them, then turned around and jumped to their feet, half expecting some dreadful Firbolg sneaking up on them. A light flashed and they looked straight at Artû and Amadis, on the first landing. They were surrounded by D'Ånu warriors and Dwendis.

"You…you are alive." Chryséis nearly dropped the sphere with the stone with relief. "Are you the real Prince Artû and Amadis?"

"Yes it is us, athenai. Do not be afraid," Amadis greeted them. "And glad to be alive. Thanks to the Speaking Stone."

"What happened?" Lubbo asked.

So Artû told them how the Lady of Anaá had summoned the help of the Council of Civilised Nations in Algiras after learning of the sorcerers' intentions.

A plan was decided on and she had sent D'Ånu troops to

the citadel in the Gogmagog Mountains. They both had been rescued and the Firbolg, who were lying in wait in the mine had been stunned and bound.

The Ioannu had done their bit before the Ladies immobilised and banned the sorcerers into the mountains. And that in the form of mirages.

"The Lady of Anaá didn't trust the peace. Not after the Prydhanian Gabari sympathetic to the 'cause' had begun to attack Anaá."

"She knew what was going on and let us go with the fake Prince Artû and Amadis into the mine? We were used as decoys?" Katherine couldn't believe it.

"We needed to catch the evil ones red-handed. D'Ånu warriors and Dwendis were inside the mine keeping watch," Amadis explained.

"But something could have gone wrong. And what about the Speaking Stone? Prince Artû gave it to me in Anaá."

"No, he didn't. You were given a regular egg made of selenite, which looks very similar. We couldn't take the risk of losing the real stone."

"You lied to me. And you risked our lives!" Chryséis complained.

"We apologise. The Speaking Stone was certain that you'd be safe."

"Oh, that's very reassuring."

"I am very sorry that you feel angry, friend Chryséis. Perhaps you come to understand in time that it was for the good of all."

"I don't think so," Chryséis grumbled. "Using us like that..."

"Oh Chris, everything went well, right?" Trevor said.

"But only just." She folded her arms.

"Ding dong, the witch is dead…" Trevor began to sing the melody from the movie 'The Wizard of Oz' to their companions' and the guards' great surprise.

"Really, you have to sing that now?" Chryséis grumbled.

"I feel like singing 'Ding dong the witch is dead, which old witch, the wicked witch, ding dong the wicked witch is dead...'"

"That's so cheesy, Trevor." Katherine had to laugh.

"So? I feel like singing." But then he just hummed the melody and everybody began to hum the upbeat melody with him.

Preparations were quickly made and at last they were on their way to Caradoc with the 'Speaking Stone'.

Not by boat, but inside a comfortable vimaan that floated alongside the shore of the Mor Maalbec lake.

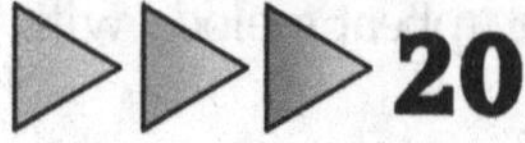 **20**   # THE STONE SPEAKS

Soon after their arrival in Caradoc, the children were summoned by the Lady to the citadel. They climbed the stairs to her quarters and stood in front of the door to the reception room.

"The dog must stay behind, athenai," the citadel guard, who had come to escort them, announced.

"But she won't be a problem," Chryséis protested.

The guard was adamant. "The Lady said only the children."

"You go on, friends; I will stay behind with Tepi," Gwendola offered.

"Shukri, friend Gwendola. Tepi stay," Katherine said. They heard Tepi whimper a little when the door was closed, but the young dog obediently stayed with the familiar Dwendi woman.

Up and down they followed the citadel guard and a maiden this staircase and that, until they faced a wall covered in the mosaic of a lioness with a deer lying between her paws.

A door next to the mosaic opened. They entered and now found themselves in the audience room. The Lady of Caradoc was a dark, petite woman, who seemed to possess a great deal of authority. After the customary welcome and official thanks on behalf of the people of Caradoc that they had participated in returning the Speaking Stone, the Lady bade the guard and the maiden to leave the room.

"Dear children from the future," she said without much ado. "Please follow me." The time travellers were by now used to such remarks and didn't ask any questions. They followed her through a flight of smaller private rooms. At last, the Lady of Caradoc opened butterfly-wing doors and lead them into a windowless room. The dark blue walls were decorated with glittering stars and the ceiling was a pyramid-shaped têrakhon roof in an iridescent green sheen, letting in a soft light from above. Right underneath the apex of the roof stood a table, inlaid with mother of pearl, and a similarly decorated chair.

"Woah, what's all of this?" Trevor was impressed.

"This is the home of the 'Speaking Stone'," the Lady of Caradoc answered. On the table, the large pearly-white egg, the children had come to know so well during their journey, was propped up inside a bejeweled silver box, lined with dark blue silk. The stone began to glow and the Lady prodded them forward. "Go on children. The stone wants to speak to you."

"The stone wants to speak to…us?" Katherine asked.

"Yes, I will leave you alone now. You may ask whatever is on your mind." The Lady of Caradoc withdrew and they walked cautiously up to the table. The children stared at the glowing egg. "How does she know that the stone wants to speak to us?'

"The glowing must be some sort of a sign."

"Okay." Chryséis sat down on the chair a distance away, while Katherine and Trevor stood behind her. They stared at the egg that just kept glowing.

"What are we supposed to do now?" Trevor wanted to know.

"I don't know," Chryséis answered.

"What if it sends out a stun-ray or something?"

Chryséis rolled her eyes. "Don't be silly, Trev."

"You never know."

The 'Speaking Stone' did nothing of the sort. Instead, the face of a kindly man with white hair and beard appeared on the surface of the shining egg. Now that was amazing!

"You can come closer now then I don't have to speak quite so loud."

The man had a twinkle in his eyes, as if he knew what they were thinking. The children gasped. Was that a mirage of some sort? At first, it didn't occur to them that the stone spoke perfect English.

"Who are you? What are you?" Trevor stammered. "What is your name?"

The old man beckoned them to come closer. Then the stone began to speak again. "Ah, Trevor my friend. I am not any old moonstone, you know. I am real and then I am not. A very sophisticated program, if one can call it that. My name is of no consequence."

"You are a program? Like a computer program?" Chryséis moved the chair a little closer.

"How do you know my name?" Trevor was confused.

"But, I know all of you well." The image's eyes darted around the room as if it was looking for something or someone. "Where is…oh never mind."

Obviously, the stone had been mistaken.

"Oh yes, of course, you told the Lady of Algiras that you wanted us to come with you to Caradoc. So she told you our names," Chryséis said.

"If you say so."

"And you can actually speak?" Trevor asked naively.

"Why else would they call me the 'Speaking Stone'?"

"We thought it was more like a trick. To get people here to behave properly."

"Well, you are not too far off the mark. Like all other 'Speaking Stones', I am charged with the knowledge and wisdom of the At-tee'kah D'At-tee-keen. That means the 'Ancient of Ancients'. A gift of guidance to mankind, before they chose to depart 'Rokana', as this heavenly body was called a long time ago."

"Rokana? You mean planet Earth?"

"Yes, planet Earth, that's what Rokana will be called in your own time."

The image was too responsive to be a hologram – more

interactive like a type of Artificial Intelligence.

"So it is true then that some 'gods' have left the 'Speaking Stones' behind. We've heard quite a bit about that," Chryséis asked shyly. "Where did they go?"

"Not really 'gods' as such, my dear. But a very - shall I say - highly-developed group of people. That is all I am prepared to reveal for now."

"Oh." The time travellers were disappointed.

"You must be running on an endless power source." Katherine didn't quite know what to think of such a programmed stone, but a scientific approach was always a safe bet.

"In a manner of speaking. But nothing so elaborate is needed. My 'power source' is 'fohar'. Pure energy. Much more advanced than a vacuum battery and rather hard to explain. Let's leave it at that."

Trevor was intrigued. He'd heard that word before. "What is pure energy? Is it like electricity?"

"It is far simpler and yet more powerful than electricity or any device made by earthlings."

Katherine noticed something. "How come you can speak our language?"

The man in the stone smiled and scratched his beard. "I understand the languages of those who come near me. You might say that it is part of my 'programming', stored inside this stone."

"But when did all of that happen?" Trevor asked.

"I've been here for a good long while," the man in the stone said.

"For a long while?"

"A very long while indeed. I was also programmed as a sort of ... record keeper."

"Don't you ever get bored?" Chryséis wanted to know.

"The idea of boredom is unfamiliar to Speaking Stones."

"But how could people be so smart such a long time ago?"

The stone actually laughed. "That's not a paradox. After

the 'First Time' when life in peace and bliss had come to an irrevocable end, the 'Ancient Ones' decided to leave mankind to its own devices. At least for a while. Other tasks were waiting in far-off realms and evil had set off a tragic chain of natural disasters on Rokana.

The noble D'Ånu, who already existed back then, and persons of high moral standing, the most promising of all humans, were entrusted with the 'Speaking Stones'. Twelve worthy rulers were given each in secret a 'Speaking Stone' to use for the greater good. A safetycatch, so to speak."

"Like the Ladies of citadels…" Trevor said eagerly.

"Like the Ladies of citadels, indeed. We could be used to communicate with the At-tee'kah D'At-tee-keen in the 'heavens' – until their return. To this day, 'Speaking Stones' are consulted in times of need, to find the best approach in keeping and restoring peace and safety for the people of the land," the 'Speaking Stone' continued.

"When word got out, the prospect of possessing a speaking stone from the 'gods' appealed to the dark nature of many, who had not been chosen. A number of us speaking stones were stolen by those who are driven by an absurd desire for power over others. Senseless wars were fought. I suppose you are familiar with the concept?"

The 'Speaking Stone' sighed faintly, if that was at all possible for a stone. The children nodded.

"They ended up on the bottom of the vast seas – the 'Speaking Stones' that is. Thrust there in hot rage, when it was discovered that the unprepared could not speak to the 'gods' at all. No evil ruler was to have the benefit of 'godly' advice, but they still try to this day."

The stone paused for a moment.

"Only three of us are left. An amethyst on the continent of Patâla, which once harboured a civilisation of the highest order, an emerald in Kharsag and naturally - yours truly." He made a little bow.

The children remembered Gwendola telling them about D'Ånu missionaries working at a plantation in the mountains of Rusicada.

They wondered where exactly Rusicada was, but that was not so important right now.

"So it's not true then that a Speaking Stone must give advice and share its wisdom with anyone, who has it in his possession?" Trevor asked.

"No. The At-tee'kah D'At-tee-keen would not have been so foolish as to allow such abuse of their knowledge and wisdom. At least not where Speaking Stones are concerned. Greed is a bad advisor, always short-sighted and concerned with personal gain."

"But then the sorcerers and the Edfunians didn't know that. This whole journey was for nothing!" Chryséis jumped up from the chair.

"No, Chryséis " came the prompt answer. "The journey you undertook to return me was not in vain. I wouldn't be of much use to mankind at the bottom of the sea. Earthlings learn very slowly."

The man in the stone sighed again.

"Alas, the desire for power is persistent and the truth is not so sweet as honey in everyone's ear."

"All the Ladies, who spoke to you knew this all along...and let us go anyway?" Chryséis was shocked. "Why?" She sat down again.

"No, Chryséis they didn't know the exact reasons. Just that your presence was essential to the success of the mission."

"How so? Why were we so important?"

"You had already proven your courage by travelling through time and space. What's more, you two girls knew the Highpriest of Shuruk. None of your travel companions would have recognised him. It is thanks to you, that I am still able to give advice. And that all of you survived."

So the 'Speaking Stone' had known this all along?

"Speaking Stone, sir. Could you please tell us, if we are

doing the right thing by still being here. Are we still safe in prehistory?" Trevor asked him.

"Hmm, let's see Trevor. How about this answer:
'Not yet at the end of your journey,
You have gone where few have treaded before.
Your innermost desire…prickly and burny,
will lead you safely to the shore.' Hmm, that should do…"

The man in the stone seemed satisfied with his effort.

"I guess this an oracle-type answer?" Chryséis asked frowning and thought, what's up with all this rhyming?

"As good as they come. Common sense and basic knowledge are part of our program," the Speaking Stone answered. "And a little rhyming."

"Can't you be more specific?" Trevor wanted to know more. Then he apologised for being so forward. "Just asking…"

"Continue to be pure at heart and strong of mind and you shall conquer every challenge, young friends. You shall conquer many challenges, indeed. What you learn now you must remember when you return to your own time."

"Why?"

"You already know why. Why else would you be keeping a journal, take pictures and ask so many questions? There is much to be learnt."

The children were surprised that he knew such things, but apparently, the stone knew just about everything.

"Please, Mr. Stone," Chryséis was keen to get something off her chest. "If you can see into the future, please tell me, if my family is alright?"

"Dear child, although it is true that I can see into the future, along with my fellow 'colleagues', I am unable to tell you such things. As you know full well, you will return at precisely the same moment you have left your own time. So, the desired information will be accessible to you, as soon as you return home. Nothing will have changed by your presence here."

"So we will return home safely then?" Chryséis asked eagerly. "We didn't change anything then?"

"Ah," the Speaking Stone said in a fatherly tone. "But not everything is predictable. Be careful. The records I hold may change due to the future actions of those involved. I can see a safe if adventurous journey. As long as you remember your purpose and don't get yourself into sticky situations."

"It's too late for that," Trevor sighed.

"Oh, but you must be careful. Use your invisibility cloaks when necessary and take decisions for the right reasons. You are smart enough."

"What do you mean?"

"Don't get carried away. Always remember where you came from and that you must take this journey to the end. No butting out. Your presence here has importance."

"Thank you, Mr. Speaking Stone. We will remember that."

"Yes, of course you will. I shall retreat now, to recharge and to leave you to walk your chosen path. It was a pleasure to personally meet such young explorers."

"Thank you…Stone," Trevor called out, before the glow grew fainter and soon disappeared altogether. The man in the stone was gone.

"And this Ladies and Gentlemen was the Speaking Stone." Trevor couldn't help a bit of sarcasm. In Kamûk they had not believed that it was possible, and now the stone had practically given them an interview.

"I wonder why Queen Elfinûr gave it up. It's awesome." Katherine still stared at the now blank moonstone.

"What a random question," Chryséis scolded. "Maybe she's not one of the people the 'Speaking Stone' wants to talk to, and she was really quite mad anyway."

"Why didn't he say anything more specific? Like 'I can see that you'll have a great journey back to Cydonia and then through the timeportal to Carter Valley'."

"Oh Trevor didn't you listen to anything he said? Things can change, depending on what choices we make,"

Chryséis rebuked him.

"I know, things can still change." Trevor sounded annoyed. "But I expected more than a poem."

"He said we'll be okay, if we stick to our original plan."

"Our original plan?"

"Yes, dodo! Exploring time travel like scientists. Collecting information for the quantum physics project and so on." Now it was Chryséis' turn to be annoyed.

"Yes alright, 'always remember where you came from'…'"

"I think what he meant was that we shouldn't get too comfortable in prehistory," Katherine nodded.

"Fat chance of that happening."

They were now walking alone through all those chambers and up and down the stairs back to the audience room.

"Yes, fat chance. I wonder why he was looking for somebody else in the room… and why is there a vimaan waiting outside?" Chryséis looked down through one of the large windows.

"It's too late to ask the stone about that now. And it's time for our sightseeing tour, remember?" Katherine replied.

"Of course… I nearly forgot."

"Maybe he thought that Artû would be here or Amadis and the Dwendis," Trevor pondered. "Where is the Lady?"

"It's probably not important for her to be here when we leave." Chryséis was already halfway out the door. "Handy, a speaking stone like that. It's like having a clever friend around."

"Gee thanks, so we're not good enough anymore?"

"You know what I mean. There're things you guys don't know."

"Do you think there are still 'Speaking Stones' somewhere in the future? Like hidden in caves or dug into the ground in a box."

"Just imagine that. He mentioned two other stones, so who knows."

But of course, none of them knew the answer to that question.

 **21**   **THE STORM**

"Lyonesse is such a great place," Chryséis sighed and shut down the palmtop computer. She looked out the window. "I never thought I'd see Europe that way. We must definitely take some pics today."

The time travellers were relieved that their journey had come to an end, althought the meeting with the Speaking Stone had been awesome.

Their tower room had windows on three sides and a balcony all around. They couldn't use the balcony when a wind rose, which happened often. But the view of Caradoc and the surrounding countryside was breath-taking.

"Pity it's so windy up here," Katherine said with her mouth full of food. The tower was just above a jumble of balconies with washing hung up to dry in the warm morning sun.

Fountains and mosaics were reserved for backyards and rooftop gardens and there were also a few ancient buildings with pillars that spoilt the medieval feel.

Green banners with a red stalking lion, the blazon of Lyonesse, fluttered from nearly every rooftop in Caradoc. Chryséis took a couple of pictures with the little digital camera.

"It's so different here. Where else do you find stone steps that lead from the road up and into the fields?"

"Yes, people here have an obsession with staircases. Up and down and up and down." For some reason, the Lyonessals loved to build lots of stairs in between their houses with terraces and roofed-in bridges that stood cheek to jowl. But that didn't seem to bother the inhabitants.

It was pleasant to have some shade in the heat of day. The cobbled streets were a confusing maze with many squares. They dared not go out without one of the citadel guides for fear of losing their way.

"Not as steep as Poseidonis on Atala, right? Why are those pictures so blurred?" Chryséis deleted the pictures and tried again.

"Can you give me some of the salchi?" Katherine was still busy with breakfast.

Salchi was a Caradocal specialty. Strings of peppers, onions and the thin long salami called 'salchi' were hanging from rafters of nearly every home in the country.

"Katie you are eating as if you were starving," Chryséis scolded her.

Katherine took a big bite of the salchi Chryséis had handed her. "I'm hungry. As long as it's not fried cockroaches again. Yuck."

She gave Tepi a few morsels. The dog lifted her head off the floor and whimpered with pleasure. "Mmh, this is just too good. I wonder what that yellow cheese tastes like."

Lyonesse was the breadbasket of the region, farmers grew everything in the rich volcanic soil, from grains to vegetables to fruits and grapes for wine. In fact, the west-facing flanks of the Ushantil Mountains appeared striped black and green with all those vineyards.

The Ushantil Mountains extended almost along the entire length of eastern Lyonesse. The lowlands were stippled with red-roofed villages in rectangular fields. One could see everything from up here.

"I'll miss the view when we leave. It's a shame how all of that will disappear in a few hundred years. You can even see a blue line on the southern horizon."

"That's the Atlantic," Katherine said while she ate a piece of cheese.

"I know that."

Vimaans flew leisurely above the busy streets. An

artificial waterway, the Usk canal, connected Mor Llyn Llion to the seaport of Haithabu down south, on foot about a day's trip away.

Tall cypress trees lined the paved avenues to the left and right of the canal. The only boat they saw so early in the morning was a painted craft, decked in flowers and just returning from a bridal celebration.

"Maybe we should go out now. The best time for boating's early in the morning when the traffic isn't that heavy."

"That cheese is not bad at all," Katherine said and took another bite of the salami she was so fond of. "Do you want to go on another tour?"

"Why not? It's not like we'll come back anytime soon."

They had been on a boat tour around the lake only yesterday. The boat had anchored by a small island and they had explored the ruins of an ancient town, drowned long ago by the waters of an overflowing Mor Llyn Llion.

Tangled roots of trees and shrubs had wedged themselves between the carved ashlars. The ruins that were still above water were inhabited only by bats and scorpions. It had been unbelievable how old the ruins must be.

"Come on Trevor, I'm growing a beard here," Chryséis called. "Hurry up." They had found fine clothes hanging over chairs this morning. Long white dresses for the girls and flowers to wear in their hair.

A shirt and short pleated skirt in the same colour for Trevor. There were also embroidered velvet waistcoats and belts with leather pouches to complete the look. They were expected in these clothes at the citadel later for the festivities in honour of Gradlon, an ancient D'Ånu ruler and bringer of civilisation.

"I'm coming!" Trevor's muffled voice came from behind a heavy curtain.

It separated a nicely appointed bathroom from the sleeping section in the tower room. As ramshackle as the houses of Caradoc might be looking on the outside, they were spacious and comfortable on the inside.

"What's wrong, Trev? Are you too shy to show yourself?" Chryséis laughed and Trevor stuck his head through the curtains.

"I look stupid in this," he declared. "A mini skirt! That's what they expect me to wear! What happened to good old trousers?"

"Come on, nobody at Pemberton will ever see you in this." Katherine couldn't help smiling. "All the men here wear clothes like that. The Lady of Caradoc just wants us to fit in," Katherine tried to placate him.

Trevor wasn't convinced, but what choice did he have? Perhaps he should leave behind the black cap, decorated with small wings above the ears. "I feel like Asterix. Who invents something stupid like that?"

"Well, better you than me," Katherine said and finished the salchi.

Trevor's face crinkled in despair. "See what I mean?! I look stupid. No photographs, understood?"

"Oh, just a teeny weenie little one Trevor…" Chryséis couldn't help but tease him and held up the camera.

"Don't you dare!" He chased after Chryséis, who took off jumping on the beds, waving the tiny digital camera, which had served its purpose so well until now. It had captured images of monsters, elves, centaurs, cities and mermaids, but Trevor was not in the mood.

"Trevor…I'm just joking." Chryséis 's pleasure at winding up Trevor ebbed away. He was sitting on top of her, holding her playfully down, when one of the citadel maidens called them to get ready. "Athenai, make haste. It is getting late."

"Is it time already?" Katherine asked. No time for a boat excursion, then.

"You must leave soon, please get dressed."

Chryséis struggled to her feet. "Geez, Trev, do you have to be so violent?"

"No pictures, I'm serious."

"Okay, okay."

Below in the narrow cobblestone streets, the Caradocals were already on their way to the citadel of Caer Llion by the canal.

"No time to go more sight-seeing then. Pity." Katherine put one last piece of the aromatic apple into her mouth. "That's really too bad. What was the festival called again?"

"Festival of Gradlon. Remember, the D'Ånu ruler from Ker-is…"

"Ker-is, the city that was submerged?"

"Yes that's right, Trev, you listened."

"Sure I did. Let's go." They were dressed and ready in no time and Trevor even decided to wear the winged hat that was part of his outfit.

Tepi bounded ahead of her human friends, excited by all the commotion. She had been bathed and brushed yesterday. Her fur shone like spun gold in the morning sun and Katherine had tied a blue ribbon around her neck.

Their feet were crushing rose petals as they walked down the pier behind the citadel guard.

A boatman steered his decorated gondola under a bridge and into a narrow side canal, lined with sober houses leaning into each other.

"You can look at that later, come catch up, Chris."

Friendly smiles and hushed voices followed the foreign children down the road. "Maybe that's what it feels like to be a pop star," Chryséis said. The companions had been welcomed like celebrities in Caradoc, but they hadn't seen much of Prince Artû and the others since the lavish dinner on the first evening.

There were sales booths in the street and Katherine and Chryséis wanted to buy little souvenirs with the mother of pearl tender they had left in their saurian leather purse.

"We can't drag around backpacks full of prehistoric curios. We have enough stuff already," Trevor objected. What was it with girls and shopping anyway? They were magically drawn to shopping malls everywhere, it seemed.

"Don't worry, I think all the shops are closed for the holiday."

"Yes!" Trevor airpunched.

A gaggle of tittering girls in their festive finery milled around in front of a closed corner shop. A white and pink cloud with ribbons and flowers. Noses went up in the air when they saw Chryséis and Katherine in the company of such an attractive boy. The noses went up a bit higher, eyes hooded with envy as the foreigners walked past.

"Guess there are Natashas and Hollys everywhere," Chryséis whispered. "Even here in prehistory!"

"I had totally forgotten about them," Katherine admitted. "Even what they look like. But I still remember their nasty little remarks."

"I had to sweep the back veranda for a week, because of Natasha." Trevor gave a playful moan. "When she saw me in the school garden at night."

"Oh yes, that's right. When you tested the timeportal finder by the golf course," Katherine said.

"That's ages ago."

They reached the festooned square in front of the citadel. Rows of standing stones escorted them to an open space by the bank of the canal. A choir had just finished a glorious rendition of 'The Speaking Stone Returns', a hastily composed song and a traditional play about Prince Gradlon was planned after the speeches.

High poles decorated with broad ribbons of red and green had been mounted to the left and right of the stage. Katherine stared in fascination at young men flying in circles around the poles with their arms outstretched. They were hanging from ropes tied around their waists,

"That looks odd. Like carousels at a carnival."

"I wonder what that's all about. Some kind of a tradition?" Trevor asked. "Don't they get sick from all that circling? What if they have to vomit?"

"Oh, that's disgusting!" Chryséis felt dizzy just from watching the flyers. "You have a sick mind Katherine

MacDougal. I'm sure they have plenty of practice."

"I hope they don't ask me to do something like that." Trevor stared mutinously at the spectacle.

He didn't have to worry. The citadel guard led the three children to an elevated platform right in front of the citadel building. Their Dwendi friends, Artû and Amadis were already seated on benches and greeted them with friendly smiles. They hadn't seen much of them here in Caradoc.

From the platform one had a good view of the stage and the canal behind it.

Somebody yelled a command and the circling youths slowed down. They loosened the knots and jumped to the ground. Here they were lying down for a few moments before getting up and staggering away to receive goblets with diluted wine from smiling young women.

"Pathetic. They just try to get the girls' attention," Chryséis snorted.

The orchestra blew deftly into deep-voiced conch horns. It sounded much like the blaring of Australian didgeridoos. The signal prompted the crowd to grow silent and the Lady of Caradoc walked onto the stage.

"My fellow Caradocals," she said. "Before we continue with our celebrations, I would like to pay homage to our brave friends, who heroically protected and brought home the 'Speaking Stone' that we all revere. Safely back to our shores."

Approving murmur rose in the crowd. The time travellers felt the gaze of the audience on them and were a little embarrassed by the attention.

"Only three of these priceless stones are still left of the original 'Brothers' of twelve. Back then, Hanôk was put in charge, helped by the faithful D'Ånu tribe. Hanôk, the one who lived five times the length of a human life." At this point, the Caradocals applauded.

"Only three of the wise stone counsellors remained to aid humankind after the gods were driven from the Mother planet before the Dark Age. Then Hanôk pronounced his successor among the D'Ånu and departed among the clouds, joining his brethren in the heavens."

She gave the citizens a little history lesson and the time travellers listened up. "How did he do that? What's his name again?"

"Chryséis you're supposed to understand Akkadian best," Trevor whispered, but Chryséis just shrugged. "I think he was one of the gods. Hanuk or something."

"...'Stones of the Righteous'," the Lady of Caradoc continued, "guiding mankind in their struggle to justice and civilised conduct. Gradlon was Hanôk's successor..."

Katherine yawned a little behind her hand.

"How much longer is she going to speak?" she whispered in Trevor's ear only to jump at calls of the Caradocal audience, bursting into 'Halloos' and 'Huzzahs'. She had missed the part where the companions were honoured for bringing the Speaking Stone back to Caradoc.

Little girls climbed up on the platform and handed them badges for bravery, made of gold, rose quartz and brilliant green feathers.

"You shall henceforth be known as 'Heroes of the People of Caradoc'. Hazana ó jana ó Caradoc!"

"Hazana ó jana ó Caradoc!"

Their moment of glory didn't last very long, this was Gradlon Day after all. "Let us now remember how 'Gradlon the Great' 'Gradlon Meur', introduced the vine and civilised ways to Lyonesse. How the city of Ker-is, first outpost of civilisation in Lyonesse, was sunk by treachery.

Let us remember, so it will not happen to our beautiful city. Wealthy in commerce and the arts and ruled by the wise Gradlon with the help of a Speaking Stone Ker-is enjoyed peace and prosperity. Ker-is, in the Bay of Lavana, lay opposite Ker-enac, the 'hidden corner'...," the Lady carried on and the crowd listened to the well-known legend.

"Gradlon protected Ker-is from the approach of the sea by constructing a large basin to receive the water at high tide. This basin had a secret outlet, of which Prince Gradlon alone possessed the key. But his evil daughter Dahut stole the key and opened the sluice gate on a whim.

As the tide rushed in, it flooded the city. Beneath the watery plain now lies the palace of Gradlon with its marble pillars, fragrant cedar walls and golden roofs, the houses and streets of Ker-is, forever hidden from human eyes. Dahut drowned with all the other citizens, but Gradlon was on his way to Ker-enac where the Speaking Stone was first kept. He turned in his saddle and saw his life's work disappear. Despite his premonition, it was too late. As we all know, he still had the strength to found Caradoc and urged us never to forget vigilance against evil. So be ever vigilant, people of Caradoc!"

The speech ended abruptly with hymns of high praise for the civilizer Gradlon. As if on cue, a trading ship from Amelút passed the citadel on its way to the sluice gate of the Usk canal.

"Look mommy, pretty lambswool clouds in the sky." A little girl pointed up at rows of small rose-coloured clouds. A slight breeze picked up. But nobody paid much attention.

*

The following morning, as the three time travellers boarded a ship bound for Aztlan in the seaport of Haithabu, the sky was overcast.

"I can't believe we are going home now. How long has it been, since wie started out. Three months?" Trevor asked.

"Almost four," Chryséis corrected him.

"Wow. I just hope that we were right with our calculations. I mean that we go back to the same moment in time we left Carter Valley."

"I'm sure of it," Chryséis insisted. "Remember, the Speaking Stone said so." They walked onto the pier. Each of them had received a packet filled with sweet and savory oggies and marzipan squares.

Katherine was especially fond of the sweets that were

made from finely ground almonds, rosewater and honey.

Two young boys walked in front of them, throwing dark red flower petals into the air. Three older boys proudly carried the backpacks. It was an honour to carry the bags of such great heroes.

"We'll easily find the timeportal again in Vallé Cydonia and then it's a short vortex trip home through the space-time continuum. Back to the 21st century," Trevor said softly. "It must still be spring there…"

"Yes, of course. We'll be back in Carter Valley in spring. And Dr. Wilkins will be there and Holly Benson and Cook Hadley with her iced tea."

"And Sport's Day and then our quantum physics presentation."

"And there is also the rose garden," Katherine sighed. After all they'd been through Pemberton Academy suddenly seemed like such a nice place to return to.

"We'll take our time in Cydonia to change into modern clothes, cut our hair and say goodbye. Nobody at Carter Valley will notice that we were gone at all. Weird that." Chryséis shook her head.

They marched farther down the pier and became aware of cheering and the deep hooting of conch shells. Looking around they saw hundreds of people gathering on the wharf, waving red handkerchiefs.

The Lady of Caradoc, Prince Artû, Amadis, Gwendola and Lubbo were waiting by the ship with a choir of maidens to see them off properly.

Their friends had plans of their own. Gwendola and Lubbo were going to stay in Anaá, Artû was going home to Avallûn and Amadis had spoken of visiting the plantation of Kharsag.

The captain was in his cabin, still battling the effects of too much wine and celebration. He smiled bravely and waved at the crowd.

"I wish they wouldn't make such a fuss!" Katherine

swallowed back a tear.

"Oh well, just don't look back." Katherine walked on, bravely looking ahead. She didn't look back again until the 'Navis Terumal' lifted anchor to sail down the Usk canal and into the Gulf of Morbihan. In the 'Strait of Caldera', the 'Wheel' would take them back west, past the Atlandian islands.

"Phew that was something," Chryséis said.

"Nobody is going to believe us," Katherine moaned.

"We have pictures of Caradoc as proof."

"I don't just mean Caradoc, I mean the whole trip."

"We can always demonstrate the vortex," Trevor suggested.

"Yeah, I guess we could."

As the bell on the landing tolled softly, the ship cast off, leaving behind a country that would disappear just like the city of Ker-is had so long ago. The scenic mountain ranges, the farmland with its villages and the city of Caradoc couldn't have looked more idyllic right now. *How sad*, Katherine thought.

Two odd-looking Zeuglodon whales followed the ship past the harbour of Haithabu. Trevor saw them and grinned.

"Feel like taking a last swim here, Katie?"

"Not the same as swimming with cute dolphins," Katherine answered and marvelled at the shimmering sea beyond the harbour buildings.

Shelanti Alun, we are on our way to Atala. See you soon. Trevor thought of their first friend in Cydonia.

'Shelanti, it is good to hear from you. I will be seeing you in Aztlan. I will come to greet you when you arrive.'

'That's nice of you.'

'Have a good journey.' The thought transfer ended and Trevor was proud of his telepathic abilities that had improved tremendously in the past few weeks.

The 'Navis Terumal' had just passed the island of Braisal, when dark cumulus clouds began to pile into cauliflower shapes in a darkening sky.

"Just look at that sky!"

They were sitting on the deck as before. Trevor looked up

from studying the hero's badge he had received the day before.

"It's going to rain. Just like when we arrived in Algiras," he said.

Massive thunderheads formed and faint lightening trembled behind the clouds. Seabirds were flying low and soon disappeared altogether.

"This is different. It's happening so quickly. Let's go down to the panorama room, before we all get wet."

The peaceful Gadiric Sea soon showed itself from its dangerous side. A side the captain should have foreseen. Clouds began to blot out the sun and a surprisingly chill breeze turned into a gale-force wind.

The ship lifted off the chopping waves, but any hope of outrunning the storm soon disappeared as quickly as the seabirds. A gale hit with full force, pushing and pulling the 'Navis Terumal' into troughs of water and back on top of mounting waves. The ship turned and twisted helplessly, drifting ever closer to the 'Seven Daughters of Atlas' and the coast of Berberia.

Lightning flashes hit all around them. Then the mast of the ship caught fire and cracked. The fire was soon extinguished by the waves, but that didn't help the ship back on even keel. The passengers sat huddled together below deck, while the seamen struggled above.

"This is worse than the sea monster attack!" Katherine cried. She could hardly think for fear. Everything was happening so quickly! There was a stomping sound. The mate of the ship came swaggering downstairs and yelled, "Everybody on deck!"

"Where are the Ioannu? Shouldn't they be here to help us?"

"The storm must be dangerous for merpeople. I wish we still had a guardian with us."

"Oh, all of a sudden!" Chryséis yelled.

Trevor took charge. "We must hurry up. Take the extra plastic bags and blow them up like balloons. Make a tight knot. Stuff them back inside the backpacks No time for questions!" he yelled when Katherine opened her mouth.

The time-travel devices were still carefully wrapped in plastic bags as always. "Leave them. Now the water bottles. Empty them."

The mate called down from above again. "Come on deck NOW!"

"We're coming!" Chryséis yelled. But they weren't quite finished yet.

"If we empty the water bottles, we'll be out of drinking water," Katherine cried.

"We can't worry about that now. Hurry up, we need them to float! Don't blow the plastic bag up too much or it might pop. Let's put on the backpacks… no on the front, close the buckle."

"We should take out some stuff to make them lighter," Chryséis screamed over the growing noise of the waves and splashing and thunder. the TPFs are more important than anything else."

"Yeah, like what?" Another gale hit the ship.

"Here, we don't need all those presents." Chryséis threw the badges they had received in Caradoc onto the sofa next to her. The others did the same. Water began to seep in and rose slowly around their feet.

"Aah, we' going to drown!"

"Stop it Katherine. Pull yourself together!"

Another thunderclap. Tepi winced and whimpered, trying to get away from the rising water. Trevor took out a dragon egg he had found in the Fûna Mountains on the way to the nuraghi. He deposited the egg on the sofa. "Okay, here, that should do…whoops!"

The 'Navis Terumal' had swung to the side and righted itself up again with a creak. Katherine was thrown on top of Chryséis . "Ouch, that hurt!"

"Come on guys, get up!" Trevor grew impatient.

"Don't be so damn bossy!" Chryséis struggled to get up. "What, is that your job?"

"Don't fight now!" Katherine walked toward the stairs.

"We must get up onto the deck. If we stay here, we'll be dragged down." Water was seeping in through a crack.

"Damn, what are we doing here?" Katherine cried. "We could all die!"

"Can we talk about this later?" Trevor shouted over the noise and picked up the whimpering dog. "Come!" The children pushed upstairs through the frothing water. "Where are all the sailors?"

The battered mast could take no more. It creaked and spun and splintered, crashing into the water. The ship bobbed helplessly in front of coastal rocks, breaking the waves. Then the 'Navis Terumal' began to sink.

"Hold onto the mast!" Chryséis screamed and grabbed hold of the wooden pole with both arms. She wasn't sure, if the others had heard. Blood was pumping in her ears. Another squall drove the mast toward the land, but Chryséis clung to it fiercely.

Rain pounded her face and shoulders and she began to swim with desperate strokes toward the beach. When Chryséis felt sandy ground she started to run, lost her balance avoiding the shifting mast and fell.

The others were washed up by the surf behind her and stumbled to their feet. Two sailors, who had managed to hold onto an empty vat, were also pushed against the beach by a foaming breaker. They let go of their vat and sat down catching their breath.

"Just run!" someone screamed. Chryséis was so cold and wet and she had lost one sandal, but she got onto her feet and ran, clutching the backpack, water running down her face and neck.

She couldn't see much for rain, but what she could see may as well have been a scene from another planet.

The yellowish sky and long dark curtains of pouring rain and then…cliffs, gleaming bright in the flashes of cracking lightening. There were nests on the cliff. large nests, like huge baskets!

Growling thunder spurred them on and the time travellers ran for the cliff as fast as their legs would carry them. Determined to survive and to go back home.

Soon.

End of Book 2

Discover the next book in the series:

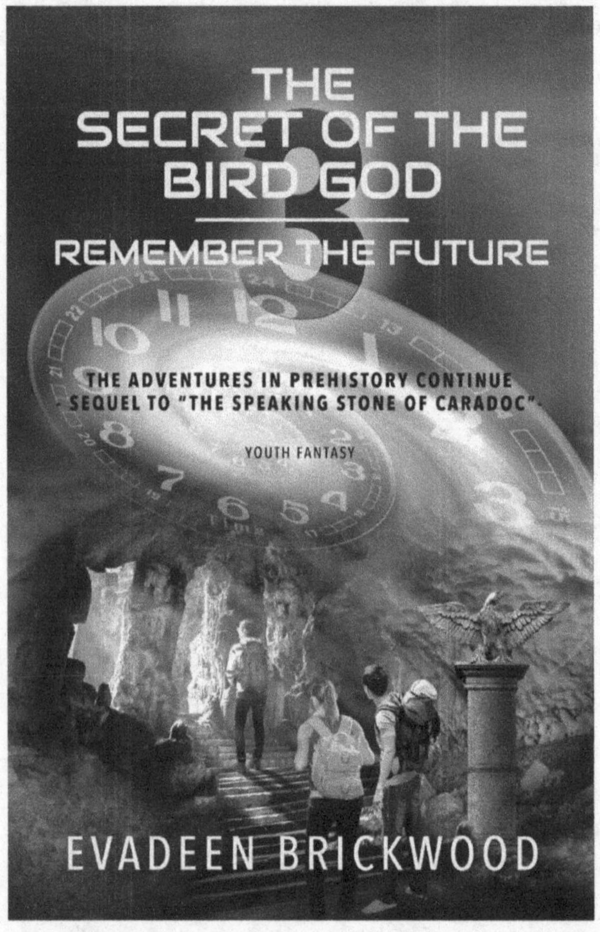

Finding their way back to Alesia and their home in the future, turns out to be more difficult than the time travellers thought. War breaks out in the Mediterranean Sea and forces Katherine, Trevor and Chryséis to flee inland. Nothing here is the way they thought it would be, and who has ever heard of Egypt without pyramids?

ABOUT THE AUTHOR

Evadeen Brickwood grew up with two sisters in Germany and studied cultural sciences and languages. As a young woman, she travelled extensively and many of her books are inspired by her experiences abroad.

Feeling adventurous, the newly qualified translator moved to Africa in 1988 and worked for two years as a secretary and language teacher in Botswana. The author eventually settled in South Africa, where she got married and raised two daughters.

In Johannesburg, Evadeen Brickwood studied computers and management of training and worked as a corporate software trainer, professional translator and lecturer at WITS University.

In 2003, she began her writing career with youth novels in the 'Remember the Future' series, about adventures in prehistory. The award-winning Book 1, 'Children of the Moon', has been published twice in South Africa and was translated into German.

The author now self-publishes and other books in the series are released on a regular basis. She has also published Adventure Mysteries and a new series 'Charlie Proudfoot Murder Mysteries".

About Writing This Book

When the first book in the series was published, my youngest reader was 8 years old. According to his mom, he carried 'Children of the Moon' around with him wherever he went. Cameron landed up in hospital having his tonsils taken out and clamoured for the second book. 'The Speaking Stone of Caradoc' wasn't finished yet and to my regret I couldn't comply. Maybe he hears about "The Speaking Stone" now and hasn't lost his love for fantasy books.

'The Speaking Stone of Caradoc' takes the reader further on an exploration of an ancient world sometime after the last ice age and before the great flooding that would change the face of the earth. Around this time, humankind recovered from the Dark Age and has not quite rekindled its former glory. The children travel on a sea we now call the Atlantic Ocean and many of their adventures are inspired by old legends.

I borrowed heavily from stories in the Odyssey and the Mabinogion. Speaking stones and large moving stones have their place in the legends of the British Isles.

One particular rock fascinated me, as it was held down by metal embrasures and - despite guards being posted - regularly found its way across the sea to another land from where it had to be recovered. I reconstructed possible locations of former landmasses in the Atlantic Ocean according to ancient and modern maps and gave them a different climate. Hi-Bresil is one such landmass mentioned in Gaelic legends.

Atlantis, Avalon and Lyonesse, make their appearance, as well as lesser known islands, such as Maligasima of Asian lore. Fabled creatures are supposed to have lived then as well. The Bermuda Triangle receives a special mention. In such an ancient world, even the languages must have been very different and Akkadian is a mixture of ancient Irish, Greek, Latin and Sanskrit, I also borrowed from other languages as the time travellers move eastward. Whether monsters still existed is not known, but I couldn't pass up the opportunity to include dragons and giants, which are mentioned in very old and reputable literature.

Evadeen Brickwood

This book is available from all good bookstores and the e-book can be purchased at most online stores.

The author's websites:

http://www.evadeen.wixsite.com/novels
http://www.evadeen.wixsite.com/youngbooks
http://www.evadeen.wixsite.com/charlieproudfoot

She is also on social media, incl. Facebook, Twitter, Instagram, google+ and Goodreads.